Built to Last

Built for Love, Volume 1

Chelle Pimblott

Published by Chelle Pimblott, 2019.

BUILT TO LAST

First edition. February 2, 2019.

Written by Chelle Pimblott.

Thank you to my 'Book Bitches'. You know who you are, and you mean the world to me xx

Thank you to my editor extraordinaire. Without our brainstorming sessions and many, many discussions this book wouldn't be what they are xx

Thank you to my proofreader who worked her tail off to get the last proofread done in what I think was record time xx

I want to dedicate this book to my high school friend, Kristy Lee. You put up a massive fight, but cancer sucks babe. I will forever use you as inspiration to live my life and to work hard at making this writing dream become a reality.

Love you always beautiful xx

Chapter One

KAMI

At 6 foot 3, with a mischievous twinkle in his light blue eyes, a week of scruff on his handsome tanned face, and a body built from hard work not lifting weights in a gym, James Harvey is most girls fantasy, myself included. If I talk to him for longer than a few minutes, my mind starts to wander to the dirty things I want to do to his body.

I try to not let my mind wander too often to the place where I think about what *he* could do to *my* body! I don't think I would get anything done if I went down that dirty track on a regular basis. I only go down that very dirty track when I'm alone, after a long day and I feel the need to relax.

Shoot! He's talking to me and I haven't heard a darn word! Too busy with my dirty thoughts and daydreaming. By the smirk on his gorgeous face, I think he can read my mind, maybe it's written all over my face? Obviously, he can't read minds .... can he?

"Did you hear a word I just said to you, Kami?"

"I'm sorry James, what were you saying?" I shake my head trying to clear it.

"Are you OK, Kami? You look a little flustered. What were you thinking about just now?" He looks at me, concern all over his handsome face.

"Me? I'm fine. I just have a lot on my mind. Sorry, I just kind of lost focus there for a few minutes."

"Did you have a few too many last night, sweetheart?"

"What?" What the dickens is he talking about? A few too many what!?

"Did you go out and have a few too many drinks last night?"

"What the devil are you talking about James Harvey?"

"Well, I'm kinda assuming you're hungover, and that's why your brain just isn't functioning properly. My brain takes some time to recover after I've had a drinking session with the boys."

Is he asking me if I'm hungover? I don't think I've ever *been* hangover before. Mainly because I never let myself get drunk enough to feel it the next day. I don't like that feeling of being out of control when I have too much alcohol. It rarely ends up any place good that's for sure! Yes, I've been drunk, it's never resulted in a hangover, per se.

"No, James. I don't have a hangover but thanks for asking. I think." I shake my head, he makes my brain go all fuzzy. I need to ask him something, but for the life of me, now that I'm looking at him, I can't remember what it was.

"Are you coming down with something then? Cause you're still a little flushed, but kind of pale all at the same time sweetheart." He *looks* concerned, worried almost, but that can't be right. I'm not even a blip on the man's radar, trust me, I know. I'm not stupid, we run in totally different circles, we always have, and my group of friends don't even come close to talking to his. "Do you need me to drive you to see Doc Roberts? It's not far but I don't think you should walk. Come on sweetheart, my cars just here ..." He wraps an arm around my shoulders and steers me towards his car and my body lets him! What the heck does my body think it's doing?!

I stop dead in my tracks. James isn't expecting me to stop, so he stumbles a little before he manages to stop and look at me in surprise.

"I don't need to see the doctor James, I'm fine, I'm not feeling unwell." I shake his arm from my shoulders and continue, "So, you can stop right there and take your hands off me please."

He holds his hands up in surrender and says, "Sorry Kami, I didn't mean to upset you." He runs a hand through his messy dirty blonde hair and then across the scruff on his chin. He looks at me and says, "I'm just concerned Kami, this isn't like you at all."

"And how the devil, would you know what I'm like, James?" I ask, and I realise that I honestly want his answer. He's barely even noticed me in the past, rarely spoken to me in the present!

"I know you Kami, I know what kind of girl you are and you're normally so quick and witty. The fact that you're red and burning up but pale, I'm worried that you're coming down with something. I don't want to see you sick, sweetheart."

How on earth can this guy know what kind of person I am? We barely acknowledged each other's existence in high school. "Look, James, I'm fine, I just got up from the bench too fast!" I shake my head, finally managing to clear the fog talking to him always seems to create. "I need to ask you about a job, actually."

"You can ask me about anything you want sweetheart." He says with a grin that I assume is meant to be sexy and I mean it is, but I need it not to be. My underwear could be easily convinced to drop to the floor, along with the rest of the clothes I'm wearing!

Geez, hold it together woman, he's just another guy, no-one special and you just need to ask him to do a job for you. Yeah right! *Just* any old guy, not one you've had a crush on for what would seem like forever.

<u>JAMES</u>

Huh, this girl, well she's a woman now and boy is she *all* fucking woman, thinks that I don't know her! That I never noticed her in high school, she couldn't be more wrong! Just because we ran in different circles and school rules said we couldn't meet, doesn't mean I didn't notice her. It doesn't mean I don't know who she is, then or now. I sound like a creeper, but I've watched her from almost every angle for years. Taking every opportunity to see her smile, laugh and sometimes even cry. Every emotion I've seen her display, I've wanted to be there for her, but I wasn't because it wasn't acceptable to others. I know it's stupid, especially now that we're adults, which is why I'm trying to do something about it and if she needs something from me, I'm going to give it to her. Specially if it means I get to spend time with her, even better and I'll give her whatever she wants.

Yes, ANYTHING she wants!

"Are you sure you're OK Kami?"

"Oh, for the love of all that is holy, James Harvey, I am *perfectly* fine."

"Well, if you say so, OK."

"I know how to look after myself James, I've been doing it for quite a long time now. I don't require your assistance but if and when I do, you'll be the first to know about it, I assure you."

"I look forward to that call Kami."

She shakes her head at me and says, "So, about that job?" I nod for her to continue. "I need some help to move a few things around for a display in my bookstore and some extra shelving built in. I was told you were the man to see about building of those shelves and I was hoping that you would do me the favour of helping me move stuff out of the way as well, please?" She asks with this amazingly cute smile. So sweet and innocent, I wonder if she's that sweet to taste? Or in bed? She's all sweet and innocent in public and I can't help but wonder if she's wild and adventurous in the bedroom. I hear her clear her throat and realise I've drifted off and haven't answered her about the job she has for me. I would love to hear her ask me so nicely to lick her .... everywhere. Fuck! Now my jeans are starting to feel a little tight and uncomfortable.

"James? Are you sure *you* don't need to go see Doc Roberts?" She sounds concerned but I can see a twinkle of mischief in her eyes. Fuck. I wonder what she'd do if I just pulled her in for a kiss? No preamble, just desire ruling my decisions. I can't do it, it's not what I do and it sure as fuck isn't what Kami would do, but damn, it's all I'm thinking about it while I stare at her lips.

"Hmm? Yeah sure Kami. My crew can do all that, it's what we do." I wink at her.

"Fantastic, thanks James." Her smile spreads across her face.

"I haven't done anything yet, sweetheart." I smile at her because how can simply *agreeing* to help her make her so damn happy?

"I know that," she smiles and says, "Now, if you want to send one of your guys over to work out a quote for me, I'll let you know if we can afford you."

"You can afford me, Kami Parker," I mumble.

"What was that?" She asks, leaning in a little closer to me. All I can smell is vanilla, sunshine and I think it's cinnamon. Not quite sure what that other thing is, maybe it's just her. I'm determined to find out what that other part of her is.

"Pass me your phone," I say and flash her a smirk. Normally it gets me what I want, and I *want* Kami Parker, even more than I did in school.

"Why.... why would I give you my phone?" She stammers out and I'm glad I'm not the only one feeling off kilter here.

"So that you can contact me about the quote and book in a time that's convenient for all of us?" I answer her with my hand held out, waiting for her to pass her phone over to me.

"Oh yes of course! Silly me, how else are we going to get in touch?"

"Thanks." I simply say as I grab her phone out of her hand. I tap through to her contacts and add my name and number to the list. Then I message myself so that I have her number. I'm hoping I won't be using it just for business purposes, "Call me any time you like Kami."

"When did you want to send someone to see what I have in mind?"

"I can come around this afternoon if you like? We finished a job earlier than expected and the guys have the afternoon off, but I can come any time you want me to."

As I watch the blush creep into her cheeks, I realise what I just said and how it must have sounded. I grin, because the fact that it made her blush, means she's been standing there thinking dirty thoughts about me, just as much as I have about her. That's reassuring.

She clears her throat and says, "Well, I was just walking to the café to get some lunch and then heading back to the bookstore, you can come ....." She blushes some more and it's just so sexy. I wonder if she blushes like that as *she* comes.

Before she can finish her thoughts, I say, "I'm grabbing lunch too, let's do it together and then head back to the bookstore?" Yes, that *was* meant to sound suggestive.

"Sure." She manages to squeak out and then coughs to clear her throat before speaking again, I'm thinking I hit the mark. "Sure, we can do that. Why not?"

"Are you asking me, yourself or for a public vote?"

"It was rhetorical, definitely rhetorical." She mumbles as she starts to walk towards the café. This is going to be *so* much fun. More fun than I've had in a very long time!

<u>KAMI</u>

What the devil did I just agree to? I can't have lunch with this man AND then employ him to work in my store. When I asked around to see who I should get to build me some extra shelving, I was inundated with people telling me to get Harvey Carpentry to do the job.

I hadn't put two and two together until I saw James standing beside his truck. I know, I know, it's not like we live in a huge town or anything, but I live in my own quiet world and even though I see him around, I never considered that it would *his* Harvey name that was connected to the carpentry business. It's been up and running for quite a few years and given the number of people who raved about them, I didn't think that it would be James' business.

Don't get me wrong, I know the guy is smart. A lot smarter than he ever let on at school, but it still never occurred to me that he'd had enough time to build, no pun intended, a business in the years since we'd left school. I don't know how he did it, but he's been very successful. I shouldn't judge though to be honest because I have my shop and that had all happened in the same timeframe.

When we reached the café, James opens the door and steps aside and waves me in. I can feel my cheeks flush again. Is he always a gentleman or is it just a show for me? "Thank you." I say and walk in the door.

"Anytime sweetheart, anytime." He mumbles from behind me and when I look back, I think I catch him staring at my butt!

I order an iced chocolate and a chicken salad sandwich, as I reach over with my card to pay, James places his order and pays for both orders.

"You didn't need to do that James, but thank you."

"I asked you to lunch Kami, therefore I'm paying." He replies, like it's a no-brainer. I can't let myself think of this as a date. He paid because he's being a nice guy.

"This isn't a date, James."

"Are you sure sweetheart? I wouldn't complain if I was having a lunch date with you." I shake my head no, but he continues. "OK, let's call it a business lunch then."

"Well, in that case the next one is on me then. If there's a next time that is." I stumbled over my words. Geez this guy turns me into a bumbling idiot. I *want* to be on a date with him and even a lunch date would make me deliriously happy. Wow, now I sound pathetic.

"The next one, hey?" He asks with a smirk and I'm about to start to backtrack when he leans in close to my ear and says, "I can't wait, sweetheart." I feel a shiver run down my neck, down through my spine and into my ......

"Here's your lunch Kami, are you sitting at a table today?" Josie the waitress asks me, but before I can answer a deep voice right behind me says, "Thanks Josie, we'll be eating in today, enjoying some lunch while we talk business. Isn't that right, Kami?"

"You're having lunch with *Kami* today?" Josie asks James. She sounds like she can't quite believe what she's hearing, not to mention seeing.

"Sure am Josie. Would you mind bringing our order over for us, please? Thanks." He says, looking at her only briefly to make sure she's heard what he's said. Otherwise, those light blue eyes are holding mine in a very steady gaze.

I swallow, take a deep breath, break his stare and look over to Josie and say, "Yes thank you, I'll be eating in today." We walk over to a vacant table for two and James pulls my chair out for me. I'm feeling more and more like I'm on a date and I have to make him stop. I can see why he has the reputation he does, especially if he treats all his dates like this!

This is *not* a date. I have to keep reminding myself of that fact. He isn't trying to date me, seduce me or anything else. He just doesn't know when to turn the charm off and he's used to using it to get what he wants and what he wants is a job, *not* me!

"Thank you, James."

"The pleasure is all mine, sweetheart."

He sits down and grins at me from across the table, but I have to get a few things clear and my mind is definitely one of them if we were going to be working together for the next few weeks.

"Do you call everyone that?"

JAMES

I'm too busy thinking about how I want to be closer to her, to get this table to disappear from between us so that I can smell her sweetness again. Fucking hell, I think I'm going insane! No woman has ever had me in a spin like this before. Not even this one back when we were kids, and I knew even then she was someone special.

"Hmmm, what now? Do I call everyone what?" I ask, genuinely curious.

"You keep calling me sweetheart and I'm just wondering if that's something you call everyone?"

What she meant to ask was, 'is it something that you call me, just me?' She doesn't want to ask that though, because this isn't a date and she's trying to convince herself, and me, that she can't feel this thing zapping between us every time we get close.

"I call everyone that, I mean the guys on my crews just love being called sweetheart, makes them move a little faster, with a spring in their step."

She looks at me shocked for a second and then bursts out laughing. It's the best sound I've heard in days, weeks, hell probably months. I want to keep making her laugh like that. While she tries to catch her breath, she's also trying to spit some words out, "I. can.. just ... hear... you calling.... out... hey ... sweetheart... on. the. job ... site!" Then, she breaks out into another fit of laughter, just as Josie brings us our lunch.

"Is she alright James, did you break this one? She's the sweetest thing in town, you better watch out this time or the town will lynch you."

There was the reminder that no matter what I did with my life, no matter how successful my business becomes, I'm always going to be the son of the town heartbreaker and no matter how hard I try to convince people I'm not my father, no-one ever believes me.

I look out the café window and stare at the trees blankly. I feel a hand rest on mine, and I look at our hands joined on the table, then up to meet her beautiful golden brown eyes, just as she says, "You're not your father James. No matter what anyone else believes, *you* have to believe that. Don't let others dictate how you think of yourself, you're your own man. You have a successful business that you've built from the ground up and if you're good enough to build for the people of this town, then you're good enough to walk out from your father's shadow."

"Do *you* believe that? That I'm *not* my father's son? That I shouldn't be tarred with the same brush as him, just because we share DNA?" I understand what she just said to me and most of the time I couldn't give a shit what anyone else in this town thinks of me. I know I'm 'that' kid, but I also know that I'm not *him* and I've made a success of myself without his help or anyone else's for that matter. I've worked hard for everything I have, but in this moment, the only thing that matters to me was what Kami thinks of me. She's lived in this town just as long as I have, and she knows what my father has gotten up to and she knows the reputation I've been given as a result. "Or do you think the same as everyone else? That I'm worthless, just like *him?*" I'm desperate to know what she's thinking. If she thinks the same as most of the town, then I'm out. I'd take her business and then I'd be done. I don't want to believe that she's that kind of person though, I want to believe that she believes in me enough for the entire town.

"No James. I don't believe that just because you share DNA with that man that you *are him*. You are your own man and you've made a life for yourself that doesn't include him." She pulls her hand away from mine and I feel the loss immediately. "Let's eat lunch and then we can go talk building business."

We eat our lunch in relative silence after that. It was pretty much only, 'pass me the salt' or 'how's your lunch' before we finish, and it's not far to her bookshop, but I don't want to leave my truck behind, and I'm not letting her walk while I drive. I'm keeping her with me for as long as I can.

I feel terrible, but talking about my father always brings down my mood. Our lunch was eaten in comfortable silence, it wasn't even slightly awkward but it sure wasn't how I'd had planned it to be when I asked her to join me though.

Chapter Two

KAMI

What am I going to do if his quote fits within my budget and he takes this job? I can't be this close to him for weeks on end as he works for me. I'm going to have to find reasons to stay away and hide in my office or just work on the other side of the store. It was hard enough sitting opposite him at a table in the café. He was so close that I could feel the heat emanating from him and his body wasn't even touching mine. Not that I think his body will be touching mine as he works in the store, but still, just the idea that his knee could have slightly touched mine under that table had me so frazzled that I couldn't speak. Well, nothing beyond asking him for the salt and if his lunch was ok. That's just insane.

As we drive from the café to the bookstore, I can't look at him. I feel him look my way a few times, but I can't bring myself to even look at his face. I feel like everything I'm feeling, and thinking is written all over my face and I'm too embarrassed to let him see all those emotions. Nor do I want him to know what I'll be doing once I get in the privacy of my own home tonight.

"You OK Kami? You've gone very quiet." James asks as he pulls up out the front of my bookstore. It isn't a long drive from the café, I always walk to get my lunch. So, it wasn't really necessary to catch a lift, but I wasn't up for arguing with him about it.

"I'm sorry James, I was just thinking about what I want you to give me a quote on and I was lost in my thoughts." He gives me a look that makes me think he doesn't quite believe me but instead of calling me out, he jumps out of the truck.

I open my door to do the same when I feel hands on my hips and suddenly I'm on my feet and the door to the truck is slammed shut. "Ummm thanks but I can get myself out of a car, James."

He smiles and says, "I know, but I like helping you." Gosh, if he keeps smiling at me like that, I think my clothes might just combust!

I start to walk into the bookstore and he's right there, opening the door for me and motioning for me to enter first. Seriously, who *is* this guy? If he behaves like this towards all women, it's no wonder he has the reputation he does, and he gets lucky so dang often. When we get inside, Ed is at the counter and without looking up says, "Hey Kami, what took you so long? Did you get lost along the way?"

"Funny Ed, no I found a possible lead on someone who can do the renovations that I want to do. We had a lunch meeting and now he's here to check out what I expect him to do. I expect *you* to do *your* job while I show him around." Sometimes Ed thinks he's the boss around here.

He finally looks up from the paperwork he's doing, "So when are we meeting this guy then?" He looks up and sees James standing there and I don't really know what happens but they *both* start behaving strangely. "*Him*? Really Kami, are you *sure*?"

"What the hell is *that* supposed to mean, Eddie?" growls James.

"The name is Ed, not *Eddie* and you know *exactly* what I mean."

"No *Eddie*, I'm not sure I do. Why don't you explain it for the whole class?"

"I don't think I really need to, you know what I mean." Ed turns to me and says, "I'm not sure this is your smartest move boss."

"Well, I *am* the boss here Ed and I think James will be a great fit. I'm not sure what you two have against each other, but I suggest you both get over it." I don't give either of them the chance to speak anymore and keep walking. I hope that James follows me and doesn't continue whatever that was out there.

"Does he always talk to you like that Kami? You're the boss around here right? It's your store, and he's the employee, right?" James asks.

"All correct assumptions there James. Ed and I, well, we go way back and he's just looking out for me. He likes to think he's protecting me, from myself mostly, and I let him think he can. Mostly, I smile and nod and then go about my business. I do whatever it is I wanted and then he gets over it."

"He thinks he can *control* you?"

I look back at James and realise he doesn't understand. "Look, this is the shelving I want replaced. It's been here since I opened and it's starting to fall apart. I need it removed and replaced as well as a few others around here." I look over to see if James is listening, and he's nodding, so I continue. "I want some built-ins added along the wall under the windows and the side wall over here." I turn and look towards him again. "Do you think your crew could handle that?"

"Yes, Kami, my crew and I can more than handle all that. Nothing to it sweetheart, nothing at all. Is there anything else that needs to be done?"

"Well, I did want to put some new shelves up in my office, but either I can do them, or Ed can help me out ......"

"You don't need to ask Eddie, I can get some built and put them up for you."

"You don't need to do that, I can do it myself. Like I said earlier, I've been looking after myself for a long time James."

"So, I can build you some new shelving, but I can't put up some shelves in your office for you and Eddie can? Got it." I roll my eyes at him, but he doesn't even look up from the notepad I didn't even know he had. "I understand. I'll have a quote for you by the end of the week."

"You haven't even taken any measurements or noted down any details."

"I can do you a quote Ms Parker, I have plenty of experience with these things. I can build shelves and put them together for you. If you choose not to use our services, no hard feelings." He closes his eyes and lets out a big sigh.

"What do you mean, 'if I choose not to use your services'? I thought you'd agreed to build them and help me out?"

"You obviously don't think I'm capable, but I will send you a quote, just like you've asked and then you can make your decision. Have a nice day Ms Parker."

"Miss," I say.

"What?"

"It's *Miss* Parker, not Ms, I hate being called Ms, it annoys me." I frown at him, "And what happened to calling me Kami?"

"Well, we've gone to a professional relationship obviously, so it wouldn't be appropriate to call you something as familiar as Kami, don't you agree?"

"James, I don't understand ....."

"Mr Harvey to you, thanks."

"... I don't understand what just happened. All I said was I didn't need help to put up some shelves in my office and if I did, I'd ask Ed. He always helps me out, I don't want you to feel like I'm getting you to do every little thing around here while you're here working on the other stuff." I explain, I really don't want him to think I'm a useless female and I'm using him for smaller stuff while he's here. I'm paying him to do a job, not every little thing around here.

"I'll send you the quote and if you choose Harvey Carpentry, we'll sort out a quick start date. Don't leave it too long though *Miss* Parker, we have other jobs on the books."

JAMES

I say my goodbyes to Kami and get out of there. I need to leave before I say something stupid because I know that my reaction to her 'friend' and employee Ed is beyond fucking ridiculous. Seriously, what kind of an idiot am I? How does she not know that Ed isn't working at that store because he likes books or reading? He's staying there because he wants Kami.

"I'll just get Ed to help me with the shelves, it's OK I don't want you to think I'm getting you to help me with every little thing." I didn't even realise I was talking out loud until I hear a deep voice behind me say, "Really Harvey, talking to yourself again? Are you getting all the answers you need or has some hot thing got your knickers all twisted up?"

I close my eyes and count to ten because I know who that voice belongs to and I'm in for a world of pain if he realises who I'm muttering to myself about. "Fuck off dickhead, I was just thinking about a new job and I was sorting out a few things in my head so that I can get the quote right."

"Yeah sure, I've never heard you talk out loud about a possible contract before, man, but whatever." Joe laughs.

"Whatever arsehole." I shake my head to get Kami and *Ed* out of my head so that I can get the quote done. Maybe I can get Joe to take it into the shop, so I don't have to see either one of them again before we start the job. I can't, because if I ask him to take it in, he'll know why, and Kami will be hurt and want to know why I didn't take it and she might think I don't want the job and boy do I *want* this job. Then again, if I sit out here in the truck and work out the quote and then take it right back into her, won't I look desperate for the job? I don't want her to think that I *need* the job because I sure as fuck don't need it. I sure as fuck *want* it though.

"You know you're still mumbling to yourself bro and frowning. I've never seen you concentrating so hard on a quote before that you're *frowning* at it! Who the hell is this quote for anyway?" he looks up at the store and I know he can see Kami still standing there, her fingers on her lips and watching me through the window. "Oh no. Fuck no, you didn't, did you?" When I don't look up from the paperwork or answer him, he continues, "You're not, I mean *we're* not taking a job for 'Kamo Kami' are we? *Are we James?* You've got to be shitting me." Joe almost yells at me.

"A job is a job arsehole." Is the only reply I can form to give him. If I get stuck into him about the old shitty nickname he gave Kami in high school, I'll never hear the fucking end of his bullshit. Kamo Kami, because she blended in with her surroundings and didn't want to be noticed. He's the only person that knows how I felt about her back then and he still gave me shit about it as often as he could.

"It's not like we *need* the work though man, you could have said no to her. It's not like it's going to be some huge project that we'll be working on it for months, it's just a bookshop man."

"It's not just a bookshop, *man*. Its *Kami's* bookshop and it's *my* business and if I want to take on a smaller job, then I fucking will. I'm not asking you to work in the crew with me, you don't actually work for me at all." I ground out.

"You're right, but I think I might need to be working on this crew in Ms Parker's shop. If for no other reason than to keep a really close eye on you." I think he's joking, but I'm not sure.

"Miss Parker." I say, and he raises an eyebrow at me, "She doesn't like being called Ms Parker, she prefers Miss Parker."

"*Miss* Parker it is then. Is that what she asked you to call her, *Miss Parker*?"

"No, arsehole, she expects me to call her Kami, but I got a little pissed at her earlier and called her Ms Parker, she hates it and so I think I'm gonna keep calling her that for a while." I can't help the smirk that spreads across my face.

"Argggh fuck! You just need to remember your rule, no dicking around with a client. I haven't forgotten how you felt about Miss Parker in high school and by the looks of that stupid grin on your face, things haven't changed too much."

"Ohh things have changed my man, things have changed a hell of a lot since then," I mumble, and Joe shakes his head and walks away, back to his real job.

"I'll meet you at your place in the workshop to discuss this new project of yours in about half an hour OK? Don't be late arsehole and don't make our labour cheap so that you can see Kamo either." I throw him a one-finger salute and I can hear his laughter as he walks away. I want to get this quote done so that I can hand it over to Kami and leave the rest up to her.

KAMI

I'm not sure what I did or said to annoy James, but I know I did something. He went from being relaxed, funny and dare I say, sexy, to being distant and calling me *Ms Parker*. All within seconds and I'm left standing here wondering what the dickens happened!

"Kami are you OK?" Ed asks from behind me, "Did that jerk do or say something to upset you? Because I can go out there and tell him that the job offer is off the table and he can get lost."

"What? Why would you do that? He didn't do anything wrong Ed, and the job is his. If he wants it that is." Ed shakes his head and walks back to the counter to serve a customer.

I watch out the window as James talks to himself and writes out some notes in the cab of his truck. I'm assuming he's working out my quote and might be back in with it soon. Then I see someone walk up to him and start talking when I realise who it is, my stomach churns. Joe was James' best buddy when we were all at school and the guy gave me a really hard time. I'm sure it was him who coined the term, 'Kamo Kami' and that was just the start of his tormenting. I have no idea whatsoever what the guy has against me, but he sure doesn't like me, and he doesn't even know me. He's never had a conversation with me, the only words he's ever spoken to me were of the tormenting variety. I wonder if he's trying to convince James not to take the job, maybe it's just not a big enough project for them. That's when I realise that maybe this wasn't my smartest idea, if Joe works with James, I could be in for a world of pain if he's on the crew that works here. That is if James takes my little project on that is.

I watch as James and Joe have a conversation that James doesn't really look very happy to be having, and Joe looks towards the shop. I've been standing there since James walked out the door and he can see me, staring at the truck with my fingers touching my lips. He looks back at James and shakes his head, obviously I can't hear them, but James looks up, then back down to his notes. When Joe walks away laughing, I notice that James flips him the bird, but doesn't look up from what he's doing.

"You know, staring at him won't make you his type Kami." I hear Ed say from behind me. I don't understand what his problem is, but he'll have to get over it, because unless that quote he's writing out is so far out of my reach that I couldn't justify using him, he's building my shelving for me, dang it!

"I know that Ed, but you can't blame a girl for looking." I turn to walk towards the counter where he's standing and continue, "I've been looking at that man since I was a 14-year-old girl and he's just gotten better with age." I can't help the sigh that escapes my lips.

"One would have thought your tastes would have matured by now then, boss." He growls out and I can't help but laugh, just as the door opens and I hear the deep voice that stars in all my dirty dreams.

"Sweetheart, can we have a word, in private, please?" he looks pointedly at Ed and I sigh *again*.

"Sure James, come into my office."

"My dreams have come to life!" he laughs with a wicked grin on his face and I hear Ed growl behind me.

I turn and leave them both standing there. I can't believe their behaviour and I shake my head as I walk to my office, not caring if James is following or not, if he wants to talk to me I'm not waiting for him or issuing another invitation. When I reach my office, I walk in and sit behind my desk, I look up to see James closing the door behind him. "I'm not sure that closing the door is necessary, is it? Nothing we have to talk about is that private, James."

"Ohhh if I can get you to do private things, that door needs to be closed tight." He mumbles.

"Can you please stop mumbling? Nothing annoys me more than mumbling and you've been doing that a lot today. If you have something to say, just say it!"

"Business first, then I'll repeat what I just said, sweetheart. Here's the quote you asked me for, I think you'll find it competitive and reasonable."

"I wasn't expecting you to bring me a quote right away James. I thought you would have to go and work out the costs of materials and such before you could give me an accurate cost."

"Well, admittedly there could be a few variables within that final cost, but it won't be too much. I didn't need to go away and cost things out specifically Kami, I've been doing this for a long time, and I know how much my materials cost, generally speaking, and I know how much labour is, for obvious reasons, and how many men I'm going to need on the crew to help me. Like I said, there will always be variables, but I'll check in with you before we do anything that changes the bottom line, especially if it's going to cost you more than what is in that quote."

"You're going to be here every day?"

He looks directly into my eyes, steely determination pouring off him, "Yes sweetheart, I'll be here every day working on your renovation. Will that be a problem, Kami?"

I stutter over my words, something I haven't done in decades, "Umm, err, no, that's perfectly fine. I... I just assumed." I take a deep breath, "I just assumed that my renovation would be too small for you to be here and working on it daily, that a small crew would be able to do it without the boss' supervision, so to speak."

"Make no mistake, sweetheart, my crews don't need too much supervision, that's why they get hired, but this project isn't too small for the 'boss' to take on, believe me."

He hasn't touched me, nor have his words come close to being sexual and yet I'm feeling that draw to him, just like always. It's the intensity of him, his look and jeepers those eyes of his, they're just so, expressive. Even at the age of 14 he drew me in, and I knew then that it was never going to happen, there's no way he's going to want anything but business from me now either, but that won't stop me from dreaming!

"OK then, if you say so. When can you start? I mean when can you be here? Ohhh gosh I mean when can your crew be here to start my renovations?"

"My crew and I can be here whenever you're ready to start but you haven't even looked at the quote I wrote out for you Kami. You can't agree to a contract without at least looking at the details sweetheart, you might miss a very important detail."

"I trust you, James, if you and your crew can start as soon as possible, you're hired." He looks at me surprised, "I glanced over the contract James, the bottom line cost is acceptable to me and I know you won't let me down with the quality of the work, so like I said, you're hired. Just give me your start date and I'll have stuff around here sorted out to make it easier to move around."

A slow grin spreads across his face as he realises he has the job, he didn't even have to negotiate, I guess that makes me easy? He rises from his chair and holds out his hand to seal the deal. I reach out my hand, he takes it in his, and I can't help but notice how small my hand looks in his. I also notice the tingle that starts at my fingertips and runs right through my body to my damn toes. I am in *so* much trouble, at least with him busy doing the renovations he won't have time to touch me while he's here, hopefully.

<u>JAMES</u>

She's right. Her 'little' job doesn't require me to be on site at all but lucky for her, and even luckier for me, I've just finished a larger project a little earlier than expected and now I have a couple of weeks where I have nothing scheduled in. I hadn't decided whether to look for a few smaller projects to fill in the gaps or take some time off. Guess I got my answer this morning when I ran into Kami Parker.

I take a deep breath and sigh, then I drive off towards my place where I have my workshop and office setup. I have a meeting with Joe and I really don't want to go. He's going to give me so much shit for taking on Kami's reno and when he sees what I'm charging, he's gonna give it to me even more. This is my business, but he's a partner, silent for the most part because he couldn't build for shit, even with me helping him. The problem is, he's my accountant and money man. He tells me what we've got in the bank and keeps me from going bankrupt. Still, I take on the projects I want to, he has no say in it. I just don't want to deal with his bullshit today. After all the intensity with Kami, I'd rather just head on up to my house and relax for the night.

When I don't see his car in the driveway, I feel like I might be in for a chance of that quiet night at home *alone*, that I'm craving but nope, he greets me as I open the door of the truck.

"Hey Jimmy, did you get that quote to Kamo and did she baulk at the idea of paying your arse so much money for a small project like hers?"

"Don't call me *JIMMY*, *JOEY* and her name is Kami, can't you just call her that? We're not in high school anymore Joe, just let it go would ya?"

"What's up your arse man? I was just joking around, I know you've always had a thing for her but surely you've grown out of that by now?"

"Yeah, just like you've grown out of calling people stupid names. Are you really that hard up for some fun you have to continue picking on a woman? Grow the fuck up man, it's truly embarrassing."

We've reached my office and I'm sitting behind my desk, looking across at him and I'm pissed. He's the one telling me to grow up, but he's still pulling girls pigtails and calling them names!

"I meant it all in fun James, don't get your knickers in a bunch."

"It's not funny anymore Joe, in fact, it wasn't even funny back then. She was shy, unlike you or even me, but in reality, neither of us know what she was going through at home. It's not like either one of us had perfect homes man, we just took it the other way and got loud and obnoxious. She took the other route and didn't come out of her shell, she's a strong woman these days and I want you to stop calling her that."

"You've always had a soft spot for this girl, James, are you sure that you want to take on this job?" Suddenly he looks concerned, but is his concern for the business or me? Guess I'll have to wait and see.

"Yes Joe, I'm very sure I'm taking on her project. She agreed to my terms on the contract and I just have to sort out when I can get a small crew together to get started and give her a start date. Luckily we finished off the Benton project earlier than we were expecting, so I can have some guys from that crew." I can't help the grin that spreads across my face and I decide I don't really want to. I'm happy to be doing this for Kami and I can't wait until she reads that contract properly. I'll give her a day, maybe two, to get around to reading it properly and if I haven't heard from her, I'm going to call her and cash in.

"What have you written into that contract, you idiot?"

"Just a little bit of fun." I can't help the smirk that spreads across my face.

He knows me too well and shakes his head, "Let's get down to business so you can enjoy your new project."

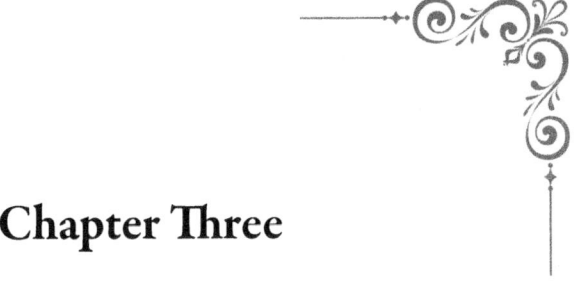

Chapter Three

KAMI

I've been sitting at my desk since James left, just staring off into space and that's exactly how Ed finds me when he comes in to let me know it's closing time. Holy smokes, I've been sitting here doing nothing for way too long. I've still got the contract in my hands, so I drop it down onto my desk and walk out to the shop to help Ed close up and get ready to leave for the day.

When Ed asks me to come out for drinks with him and some friends, I decline because honestly, I don't want to. I can't keep my mind off James long enough to concentrate on anything or anyone else. That and I know Ed wants something more and I've told him that it's not going to happen. It's not that he's not an attractive guy, it's just that he's more like a brother to me and no matter how many times I try to explain that to him, he doesn't seem to get it. He says he does but then he gets all weird and protective of me if I have a date, which isn't often.

Something James said earlier is playing on my mind as well. Am I letting Ed walk all over me at work? I think I'm just letting stuff go but am I, really? Does it send mixed signals to him? I like to think I'm an easy-going boss, but maybe it's just the opposite and I'm just a pushover?

Jeepers, I've had James back in my space for all of a few hours and already he's got me questioning myself! I'm not going to change how I run my business, my very successful business in fact, just because he can't deal with another man being around me. What the devil does that mean, anyway? I knew they were both trying to lay down a claim on me but neither of them have one, so they can shove it.

Ed's gone home now, even though he didn't want to leave me alone at the shop. He'd have a flipping heart attack if he knew just how often I was here alone at night! I sit back down at my desk, determined to get some of the paperwork done that I didn't manage to do this afternoon because I was too busy daydreaming. When I see the quote with the Harvey Carpentry name on it, I can't help the smile that creeps across my face! His handwriting is bold and decisive, like he knew exactly what everything was going to cost him, and I smile because I remember him telling me how he didn't need to wait to write up my quote, because 'he knew what he was doing because he'd been doing this for a long time' and then I see a note down the bottom of the page that I hadn't noticed earlier. To be honest, I was only looking at how much it would cost me and nothing else earlier.

"WHAT ON EARTH!? James Harvey, what the devil have you done?" I'd already agreed to this contract, and he knew I hadn't read that little condition of his. No wonder he was smiling like he knew a secret, he darn well did! He walked out of here knowing that he'd written a condition or two into our contract and that I wasn't going to be happy about it. I was just about to grab my phone and call him, but then I decided that two could play his little game. He still wants to think I'm 'Kamo Kami', well he's in for a rude shock!

<u>JAMES</u>

I was bitterly disappointed when I didn't get a call or message off Kami after yesterday. I thought for sure that she'd go over the contract with a fine tooth comb after I left the building. I have a strong feeling I'd know about it by now if she'd read it *all*.

I let a huge grin spread across my face as I walk into the café where we had lunch the day before. Yes, I am hoping she'll be in here again, especially after she said this is where she usually goes for lunch and *yes* I know that's fucking ridiculous. I just want to see her reaction to the contract that's all. It has nothing to do with the fact that I just want to see her, I've always had this pull towards her.

Josie looks up at me, smiles and tells me to grab a seat anywhere. I sit down facing the entrance but still I miss seeing Kami walk in until I hear Josie speak to her.

"Hey there Kami, did you want your usual for lunch today? Or maybe you're looking for something different?" Then she looks my way and smiles.

"You know what Josie, I'm thinking I might eat in today. I could do with the break from my paperwork." Kami says in reply to Josie, but she's staring right at me. Again, I can't help the grin that spreads across my face. I'm not gonna hide how happy I am to see her gorgeous face.

"Good afternoon sweetheart how are you today?" I ask, still smiling.

"Ohhh I'm back to sweetheart am I, Mr Harvey? You do like to run hot and cold don't you?" she says with a little more snark in her voice than I'm used to hearing.

"Well, we're not talking business here Kami, so I thought we could be a little less formal," I say. "Would you like to take a seat and have lunch with me again, *sweetheart*?"

Before she can answer me, Josie interrupts, "So, is the foreplay over yet or do you two need some more time to decide what to have for lunch? Other than each other that is." I start to laugh until I see the blush slowly creep up Kami's neck and face.

Instead, I say, "Kami please take a seat. I'm ready to order, are you?" She nods her head slightly and I turn to Josie, "Do you talk to all your customers like that Josie?" before she can answer I continue, "Cause I know we've known each other for a long time but I don't think that's great customer service on your part. Embarrassing a customer isn't on the top of any list as far as I'm concerned." She has the decency to look embarrassed.

"You're right and I'm sorry Kami. I shouldn't have said it like that," I shoot her a scowl. "I shouldn't have said anything, it's none of my damned business what either one of you does."

"Thank you, Josie." Kami mumbles, then we order our lunch and Josie leaves us in peace.

"That wasn't necessary James. You embarrassed Josie as much as she embarrassed me, you know. You didn't need to say anything to her, she was joking around."

"Well, no matter how she meant it, she shouldn't have said it. We may have grown up around each other but that doesn't mean she can treat us any differently to any other customer. I found her joke to be insulting, to be honest." I watch as her face falls and I realise how what I just said would have sounded to her. "That's not how I meant it Kami.."

"No, it's ok I understand James. I'm not insulted, I understand exactly what you meant."

"I don't think you did sweetheart what I meant was, it was an insult to think that if I wanted to seduce you, that I would do it for the world to see. If, *when*, I seduce you Kami Parker and we get to foreplay, it won't be in public for the world to see .... it will be for *my* eyes only." I look her dead in her beautiful multi-coloured eyes and don't look away until I see her swallow and nod her head. "You'll be all mine, only mine. Do you understand, Kami?"

She takes another swallow and replied, "I understand." Josie picks that moment to arrive with our lunch, we thank her and then Kami clears her throat and says, "You and I both know that's never going to happen, James, I'm not your type and you're not mine."

Now it's my turn to look hurt, mainly because I am fucking hurt. "What the fuck is that supposed to mean? You're not my type. How the fuck do you know *what* my *type* is?" I shake my head. "And I thought you weren't the judging type, I've seen them all my damned life, and I never saw that in you. Not you of all people, but I guess I was wrong. Enjoy your damned lunch sweetheart, it's on me."

I nod to Josie on my way out and say, "Put it all on my tab please darlin'?" She nods, and that means I don't have to stop on my way out.

When I get to my truck and slide into the driver's seat, I slam the door shut. I'm so angry, not just with Kami but with myself as well. I thought she was different that she didn't judge me like everyone else but apparently I was wrong. Not to mention she obviously hadn't read my quote properly, otherwise, she would have known that what I said was no fucking joke.

I wonder what will happen when she *does* read the fucking thing now?

KAMI

What did I just do? Why did I say that? I've ruined everything! My lunch sits in front of me, untouched and I don't think I'll be eating it today. Not now anyway. I'm still trying to work out what the heck I did when Josie walks over and says, "Hey hun, I really am sorry about what I said before. James was right, it really wasn't appropriate, no matter how long we've known each other."

"Thank you, Josie, but honestly, I embarrassed myself more than you did." I smile at her, at least I hope I am.

"I don't think so Kami, I saw how that man was looking at you and he wasn't pissed because of anything I said. If I'm honest, I was jealous of the way he was looking at you, I've always had a thing for James Harvey and he's never looked at me the way he looks at you." She smiles at me, "Don't give up on him, he's one of the good ones. Did you want me to wrap up your sandwich, so you can take it with you today?"

"Thank you, Josie, that would be great." I can't even acknowledge what she said about James or how she might have gained that knowledge.

I reach for my wallet to give her some money, but she stops me and says, "James already paid honey." She gives me a sad smile and then walks away to serve her other customers.

I sigh and walk back to the bookshop with my lunch all wrapped up in a nice parcel, paid for by James. Even after I basically told him he wasn't good enough for me.

If only he knew how many times he starred in my fantasies. I might use my vibrator to give me an orgasm, but I'm picturing James Harvey giving me all the pleasure. How many times I've *pictured* his fingers playing with my clit and my pussy, wringing every ounce of pleasure out of my body because doing it myself, it's never quite enough. If only he knew that those words, the ones he spoke to me in the café, were all of my dreams, my fantasies, come true.

"Hey Kami, darlin', are you OK?"

I look up to see Ed giving me a weird look and I'm wondering how the heck I got back to the shop! "Yes Ed, I'm fine why do you ask?"

"I'm asking because I've been talking to you for 5 minutes and you've been staring into space the entire time and haven't even realised I'm standing here." He rubs his hand up and down my arm and says, "What happened, Kami? You went out for lunch almost an hour ago, you're normally back here within half an hour and I was starting to worry about you."

"I'm going to have my lunch in my office today Ed. If you need me, just come get me but I'd really rather you didn't."

"Okayyyy Kami. You go and sit down, I'll come and check on you a little later." I nod at him, but I would really rather he just left me the heck alone. I've done enough damage this afternoon without having to deal with Ed's 'feelings' as well.

So, instead of behaving like a functioning adult, I shut myself in my office and don't answer the phone for the rest of the day. Ed sticks his head in the door once, later that afternoon, but he left pretty quickly. He didn't need me out on the shop floor, I have a casual that comes in during the week for a few hours so that he can have lunch and so that I don't need to cover the floor. If we're busy today, then she can stay on a few more hours, I can't deal with customers today. Ed only comes back to let me know that he's closed up the shop and is heading out.

"Hey, Ed." I said just as he turned away, "I'm sorry about today. My mind just wasn't in it after lunch. I'm really sorry."

He turns back to look at me and says, "No worries Kami but I'm really worried about you. This isn't like you and well, can I speak honestly?" When I nod at him, he continues, "It's only been since James showed up that you've been acting all weird. I don't know what it is about him, but I don't like him. I think it might be a good idea to get some other quotes and go with someone else. Don't you think?"

He's not wrong about the changes in me since yesterday but I'm not going to change my mind about Harvey Carpentry if only to prove to James that I think he's more than capable of doing an amazing job with my renovations. "Thanks, Ed, I'll think about it."

He nods and starts to leave, then he turns back and says, "Don't stay here by yourself for too long OK? I worry about leaving you here alone."

I snort and reply, "It's OK Ed, I've lived in this town all my life, I think I can get to my car and then home without incident. I've been doing it for years now but thank you for your concern. I do appreciate you looking out for me. Now go, get out of here and go have some fun."

Ed smiles, but he still looks kind of sad. I hear him lock the front door as I start to pack up some papers to take home and look through after dinner. That's when I spot the Harvey Carpentry letterhead and read his handwritten note again.

*Special notes

1. For the duration of this renovation the owner of the bookstore, Miss Kami Parker, will have lunch with Mr Harvey every day ... to discuss progress, of course.

2. Miss Kami Parker will agree to have at least one date a week with Mr Harvey until the project is complete. Away from the job site and café after work hours.

3. Mr Harvey will always be on his best behaviour around Miss Parker, but he can't promise that he'll keep his hands to himself.

4. Last but not least, Miss Parker agrees to let Mr Harvey put up those damned shelves in her god damn office for her.

5. You already signed my crew on to start this project, it's not my fault you didn't read the fine print!

I can't help but laugh. He knew I wouldn't read it all. He knew I wouldn't see his 'fine print' until after I agreed to employ him to do the project. These 'special notes' of his, they're one of the reasons I like him so dang much. His sense of humour and adventure is what attracts me to him. I mean, I'm not going to lie, he's a gorgeous man. More than easy to look at and very, very edible but that sense of humour of his is the real killer. He knows how to have a good time and he knows how to make me laugh. He always has, without trying.

I pick up my phone and send him a text;

Kami: *I've read your 'special notes' and I agree to every one of your terms .... as long as you're on your best behaviour* ☺

I sit there at my desk, waiting for a reply but when I don't get one within a few minutes, I pack everything up and head out to my car to head on home. There's nothing else I can do, if he wants to reply and continue with the contract, then he will. If not, well then I guess he won't, and I'll have to move on, in every sense of the word.

And so, I wait.

JAMES

I'm sitting at home, on my couch watching the football when my phone buzzes with a message. When I look at it, I see Kami's name. My hands itch to read her message, but I keep telling myself I don't need to see it. I may not need to see but I really want to read it. I give in and reach for my phone, then there's a knock on my door and my heart leaps into my throat. She wouldn't message me and then come over would she? I'm not even sure she knows where the hell I live. It wouldn't be hard for her to find out, but I wonder who she would ask.

My heart drops to my feet when I open the door and apparently I don't hide my disappointment too fucking well.

"Well, fuck man, don't look so happy to see me. I'm going to take a guess and say I'm not the face you were hoping to see on the other side of your door tonight? A hot date or were you hoping for a certain bookshop owner to be here, begging for your cock?"

"Fuck Joe, do you always have to be so?.."

"Honest? To the point?"

"I was going to say brutal or crass even but OK, I guess you could call it being honest to the point of brutal."

"You're not denying that you wish it was Miss Parker and not me. I'm really feeling the love the last couple of days man."

"Shut the fuck up and get your arse inside so that I can shut the god damn door."

We sit on my couch, drinking beer and watching the football. I don't forget about the message that Kami sent but I'm not reading it while Joe's here. He'll give me shit just for getting the message, if I answer it while he's here, he'll bust my balls.

A couple of hours later, when I've put Joe in a taxi and sent him on his way, I read the text that Kami sent;

Kami: *I've read your 'special notes' and I agree to every one of your terms .... as long as you're on your best behaviour* 😊

It's too late now to text her back, but it does bring a smile to my face. That and I don't think drinking lots of beer and texting Kami are a good mix. I might say things that I have no intention of speaking out loud yet if ever. She does things to me this woman and I don't know what I'll say to her without my filter switched on. After what happened at lunch today, I think I would be better off letting certain things go unsaid.

I place my phone on the bedside table and fall asleep, smiling and dreaming of brown wavy hair and eyes that sparkle in the sunlight.

WHEN I WAKE UP THE next morning, I feel like my head has been hit with a sledgehammer. Now, I've been hit in the head with many, *many* things and a regular hammer is one of them unfortunately, and I can only imagine how much worse a sledgehammer would feel, but this morning I'm feeling it. I can't remember the last time I got so drunk drinking beer that I felt this bad the next morning. I don't usually drink to get drunk, my old man was drunk a lot and I don't ever want to be like him. He always blamed his poor decisions on the drinking, but it was really just an excuse to behave badly.

I'm glad we've had a few days off, but it's time to get back to work and get some plans drawn up for Kami to have a look over and see which one she likes the best. Then we can get started moving stuff out of the way and building her new shelving.

I'm thinking about Kami as I soap up and wash my body. My hand reaches down to wash my cock, I'm hard as a fucking rock, I close my eyes and all I can see is Kami looking back at me happy and smiling, telling me to be on my 'best behaviour'. Little does she know that what I can do best is make her come! My thumb runs over the slit at the top of my cock and I can feel the beginnings of my orgasm building there. With one hand stroking up and down my cock and the other one resting on the wall of the shower, I let out a loud groan. In my head, I hear her say, 'come for me James, you know you want to' and without another thought, her name comes out as a whisper and I blow my load into my hand.

It's been a while since I've rubbed one out in the shower, but I can't say it wasn't worth it. I went to sleep thinking about Kami, I woke up thinking about Kami, I'm pretty sure I dreamt about Kami, and I just needed the release before I could get down to work and then go and see Kami in the flesh.

I turn off the shower, rub a towel over my hair and then wrap it around my waist as I walk into my bedroom. When I get closer to my bed, I see that my phone is flashing with a message. I didn't even check it for the time before I went and had a shower, I just knew it was time to get up and get moving. I needed that shower to shake off the remnants beer from last night.

I get a little nervous when I see in the notification window that there's a message from Kami waiting for me, then I pull my head out of my arse because why the fuck am I nervous? I didn't reply to her yesterday and ... ohhh what the *fuck*?!

Kami: *What do you mean, what kinds of things do I do to you, James?*

Kami: *James? You can't just say something like that and then not answer me*

Kami: *James?*

Kami: *James?*

Kami: *Well, ok then I guess I'll talk to you tomorrow? That's if you still want the job?*

Shit! Fuck! Shit! Fuck it! Five messages from her and I have to scroll back to find what it is she wants an answer to. I get to where her messages start, only to see my message that started them all.

Ohhh, fuck what did I do?

KAMI

I got James' text last night, well early this morning and normally I would have been asleep, but I was too busy reading. I got to a good part in my romance novel and when I saw who the message was from, my imagination just went wild.

I had to put the book down and take matters into my hands! With thoughts of James doing to me what the characters were doing in that book, let me just say that it didn't take me long to get out my favourite vibrator to help me along. With one hand squeezing my nipples and the other one working the vibrator in and out of me, I came apart hoarsely whispering James' name.

After that text if he means that I do the same things to him that he does to me... I guess it should make for an interesting few weeks as he completes my renovations. Being that he hasn't answered my text though, I'm wondering if he sent it to the wrong person and now he just doesn't know how to tell me that it was meant for another woman. I can feel my chest tighten just at the thought of him speaking to another woman who isn't me, like that and I don't like that feeling. I've always been drawn to him but I've never and I mean never, let a man have that much control over me, my thoughts or my actions.

When I still haven't heard from him by mid-morning the next day, I start to think that he meant to send that text to someone else and I should just forget about it. If I stop thinking about it, it can't hurt. Right? Heck, I'm a grown woman, I don't need a man to make me happy, I've got my trusty B.O.B (battery operated boyfriend) in my bedside drawer, not to mention a few other little toys that join him in there.

I sigh, because I *know* none of them are going to be as good as the real thing. James is the most attractive man I've ever met and let's not forget, he's a warm-blooded male. Let's face it *nothing* and I mean nothing, is *ever* as good as having an attractive, warm-blooded male in your bed. Or your couch, armchair, dining or kitchen bench, for that matter

Chapter Four

JAMES

After my 'relaxing' shower and then absolute freak out over my text to Kami, I went to the café for some breakfast. Well OK, it was more like lunch really but still, I wasn't in the mood to cook anything for myself and I really needed some food. When I wander in Josie is here, I'm not sure what her hours are, but she seems to be there all the damned time. I'm starting to think there might be two or more of her but in my hazy state, there could be more of everyone in here.

"Morning Josie how are you this fine morning?" I ask as I sit myself at a table for two.

"It's no longer morning James, so I'm guessing I don't have to ask you how you're doing today?" she smiles at me and I'm waiting for the smart arse comment, but it never comes. "What can I get for ya today James? Some hangover food by the looks of those eyes." There she is, I knew the smart arse wasn't lurking too far away.

"You know what Josie...." I don't get to finish because she cuts me off.

"Look, James, if I was out of line yesterday, I'm sorry. Let me rephrase that, I *was* out of line yesterday and I'm really sorry. I apologised to Kami after you left, and she looked like she was about to cry. I didn't mean to embarrass or upset anyone, it's just... never mind, I shouldn't have said anything. Let me get you a big breakfast and a coffee that should help the hangover."

I don't have a chance to respond to her apology before she walks off to put in my food order. Instead, I'm left to sit at my table staring out the window and trying not to think about why Kami looked like she was going to cry yesterday. I don't think it was all due to Josie's poor taste in jokes, if at all. When Josie comes back with my coffee, I say, "Thanks for the coffee

Josie, but what did you mean when you said that Kami looked like she was close to tears before?"

"Ummm exactly that James. I'm not sure what happened between the two of you after my, ummm comment, but you left in a hurry and she looked really upset. It's one of the reasons I apologised, she looked so upset and I honestly didn't mean to embarrass anyone."

"I don't think it was what you said." She gives me a pretty disbelieving look, so I try to explain, "We had some words.... the other day and while it was kind of about what you said, it was more about, perceptions than anything else. I was ... upset when I left, and I didn't stop to think that I might have upset Kami as well."

"If anything I said made you two have words, I'm sorry James. It wasn't my intention." Josie starts to walk away but stops and turns back to me, "If it makes any difference, she wouldn't have been that upset if she didn't care. Girls don't get upset about what a guy thinks of her unless she actually *cares* what he thinks."

Josie may be right, but I just can't get past the fact that Kami dumped me in with the jerks like my father by saying that she's not my type. She wouldn't know my type, we haven't said more than a few words to each other in years. Lost in my thoughts, I don't hear the door to the café open or notice the new customer walk in until I hear her voice.

"I'll take my usual to go please Josie." I hear Kami's voice before I see her, I look up and she's not looking my way. I can't help but wonder if she saw me sitting here before she came in and she's not looking this way on purpose.

"Are you sure you don't have time to eat in today, Kami?" I hear Josie ask her. I can see Josie bobbing her head in my direction, trying to let Kami know I'm here.

"No time today Josie, I have a contractor coming into the store soon to look at a few things for me, so I have to get back just in case he's early."

She's got another contractor coming in today? Is she looking for someone other than me to do her renovations? I thought we'd agreed that I would draw up some plans and we would see if she liked them? I *thought* we had a fucking agreement!

Another waitress already dropped off my breakfast, but I didn't get the chance to take a bite before I realised Kami had walked in. Then she dropped the bombshell that she was looking at another contractor! I can't believe she'd go behind my back like this, I mean I know it's just business but ... I bet fucking Eddie has something to do with this. That fucking arsehole, he's had it in for me since we met yesterday.

I slam my hand down on the table and it makes one hell of a noise, everyone turns to look at me, including Kami. She looks surprised to see me there, so maybe she didn't spot me earlier but I'm still furious. She starts to walk towards me until she sees the anger on my face and her footsteps falter. "Are you Ok James?"

"Am I OK? Is that what you just asked me, am I OK?"

"Y-yes, you look and sound p-pretty angry." Kami stammers. I haven't heard her stammer for years. I know it's my anger that's causing her to stutter, but I can't reel my anger in.

"You got another contractor? I thought we had a deal, Kami. I thought I was your contractor, but I guess I was wrong, huh? I guess you're just like all the others, hmmmm? Can't trust me, I'm just like my old fucking man."

"Now James, I think you need to calm the hell down," Josie says to me.

"No Josie, I don't think I do. I *think* I need to get the hell out of here before I say anything else but no, I think I'm allowed to be pissed off when I thought I had a contract, only to find out I really fucking don't." I throw twenty dollars down on the table and stalk passed everyone and out the door. I can hear mumbled words, but I don't give a fuck what any of them are saying. She stabbed me in the back, the last person I ever thought would do it and I don't know what to do now. I can hear someone calling my name, but I don't stop walking until I get to my truck. I stop because I can't find my keys to open the door and that's when I feel the light touch on my shoulder. I know who it is before I turn around, but I don't want it to be her. I don't want to talk to her. I don't want to hear her say she doesn't want me in her store and that I'm not good enough for her. It's gonna hurt like a bitch and I just don't want to hear it. So, instead of turning around, I drop my chin to my chest and wait, just wait for her to speak so that I can move on.

KAMI

After yesterday and then his text last night, I have no clue what the heck just happened, but I can't let him believe that I got a different contractor and just dumped his company without even telling him. Does he think so little of me that he believes I could or would do that? When I reach him at his truck, I reach out and rest my hand on his shoulder. He actually flinches at my touch and shrinks away from me a little. I take a deep breath and speak to him;

"J-james, what's the matter? What did I do?" I ask.

"Nothing Kami, you did nothing. It's all business right?" he grinds out and I can tell it's hard for him to even speak to me.

"James, I'm not looking for another carpenter, we already have a contract and if you think that I would back out on you, with anyone, well that kind of hurts. I would never do that, not without talking to you first. Look, I don't know what happened back there in the café, but I was talking about an electrical contractor because I need some lights repaired and new ones fitted, as well as the electricals checked out so that it can handle the new additions I want to make. If you want me to look into getting a new carpenter, because you don't want to work with me, I can but I honestly don't want to." I take another deep breath and take a step back. "I'm sorry that I upset you, but I really have to go, or I'll be late to see the electrician and Ed won't be able to tell him what I want because he has no clue."

"You don't discuss this stuff with him? You don't tell Eddie all your plans?"

"No, not really. He knows basically what I want to do, I've bounced a few ideas off him but no, he doesn't know what I have planned or pictured in my head. Why would he have any say? It's my store so I get the final say in what I do to it."

James nods and I can see his shoulders relax slightly. "I've drawn up some plans, a few different options for the renovations if you want to have a look at them?"

He still hasn't turned to look at me but at least he's speaking to me normally now. "Of course I want to see what you've come up with, I can't wait. How about I come to your office after I close up the shop tonight? Unless that's too late for you to be at the office, then I can organise to come over tomorrow?"

"No, it's not too late. Do you know where my office is, Kami?" he asks, still not looking at me.

Now that I think about, I have no clue where his office is, I only ever see the trucks rolling around town with the business details on them. "No, to be honest, I have no clue, James."

"Send me a text when you're about to leave the shop and I'll send you the address."

"OK, I can do that. It should be around 5pm if I can get Ed moving fast enough." I say with a smile that he never sees because he still hasn't turned around to face me. "Talking of text messages James, let's talk about the one you sent me last night ...."

He finally spins to face me and cuts me off, "How about we don't talk about that text until later. After we've talked about the plans I drew up for your renovations."

"I'm going to hold you to that Mr Harvey." I say with a grin that I hope is bordering on slightly sexy. I don't know if I come close to succeeding but it gets me a small smile from James, so I'll consider it a success.

I turn and walk back to the shop, which isn't that far. It's not until I get there and see the electrician talking to Ed, that I realise I never actually managed to get my lunch. Now I'm going to be hungry all afternoon and probably pretty grumpy! I shake that off so that I can walk around with the electrician and explain to him what I want done.

An hour later, I have another quote in my hands. The biggest differences between this one and the one from Harvey Carpentry is, there are no 'special notes' and it's not a done deal, yet. I have another electrician coming in, in half an hour and with any luck, after he's gone, it'll be time to close up shop for the day and I can go and see James. About the drawings he's done, of course, it's business, not pleasure today.

Mmmmmm, pleasure. With James. And on that note, I have to stop daydreaming and get myself brain back to business, because the new electrician is a little early and I have to say, that's a tick next to his name.

About forty-five minutes later, I find myself standing at the register with yet another quote in my hands. Another contract without, 'special notes' but I do think this one might get the go ahead. I felt a little more at ease with this man than I did the last one, he asked some weird questions and made me uncomfortable. This man, Sam, he was professional, to the point and knowledgeable, so Sam it is!

I look up at the clock and realise all my thinking has lead me to closing time!

"Have you decided which electrician you're going with boss?" Ed asks me. He thinks he's funny when he calls me boss, but I kind of like the reminder that I am, in fact, his boss!

"Yes, I think I have. I'm going to go with Sam, what you think Ed?" I ask because I wouldn't mind a second opinion.

"Is that the guy that just left?" he asks and when I nod my head he says, "Yeah, he seems like the better fit. The first guy was a bit strange, I can't put my finger on it, but something wasn't quite right about him."

"I'm glad I wasn't the only one who felt that way. I'll give them both a call in the morning and let Sam know he got the job."

"How do you think the other guy will take not getting the job?"

"I'm not sure Ed, but it doesn't matter because it won't make me change my mind." Ed nods his head in agreement and then grabs his stuff to leave.

"You OK if I head out now boss?"

"Yes, go on. I'm not staying back tonight, I just have to grab a little bit of paperwork then I'm heading out as well. Have a great night Ed, see you tomorrow."

"See you tomorrow Kami, have a great night." With that, Ed's out the door and I lock it behind him while he watches. Sometimes, it's annoying just how protective he can be but then I remember he's doing it to make sure I'm safe and I'm happy to have someone around me that cares enough to make sure that I *am* safe! I walk back to my office and send a text to James. While I'm waiting for his reply, I pack up the papers that I need and grab my bag to start the search for my car keys. I find them just as a notification comes through that I have a message. I read it and it can't be right. That's not an office, it's a house address. Instead of texting back and forth for the next ten minutes, I decide to call James and ask him about it.

He picks up on the first ring, "Good evening Miss Parker, do you need some help to find your way here?"

"Good evening Mr Harvey," I reply in kind to his greeting. "No, I know where the address is, I'm just wondering if *you* got it right. That's a residential area, not a business area, you know that, right?"

"Yes, I am well aware that it's a residential address Kami, it's where I live."

"But I thought we were meeting at your office?"

"Yes, we are but my office just happens to be at my home. I have a workshop attached to the house, and that's where I keep all my plans and drawings, that way the two things are separate but I'm not too far away from home." He explains, and I know it makes perfect sense, but I wasn't prepared to go walking into his *home*! "Why Miss Parker, are you worried about coming to my *home*? Are you worried about being *seen* coming into my *home* after hours?" his voice has this deep, husky tone to it and it's as sexy as all get out and I can feel my body reacting to him.

"No." I squeak out and then I cough to clear my throat so that I can speak normally again. "No Mr Harvey, I just wasn't expecting it that's all, I was unaware that your office was next to your home. I'll be there in ten, fifteen minutes max."

"OK, Miss Parker." He replies with a voice that still sounds a little too gravelly to be his normal tone. "Do you have dinner plans this evening?" he asks, and I shake my head, then I realise I'm an idiot because he can't see me through the phone!

So, I say, "No, no plans, why do you ask?"

"Good, I'm cooking and there's more than enough for the two of us to share."

"Oh um OK thanks, James." Is all I can manage to get out.

"See you soon... Kami." Ohhh that gravelly voice sends shivers through my entire body that time. That conversation will be fuelling some vibrator sessions for weeks to come!

"See you soon, James." I hang up before he can say anything else because if I hear him speak another word right now, I'm going to have to take care of business before I leave for his house.

His *house*!! This was *not* part of the plan and I don't know how I'm going to deal with it. I want to see his plans and yes, sure I could have just gotten him to bring them into the shop one day but then Ed would want to stick his nose in, and I didn't want to share with him.

As I register my thought, I come to the realisation that I simply don't want to share my time with James or his drawings with Ed. Ed will get to see the plans soon enough, he doesn't get to decide which one I go with.

I get in my car, lock the doors and head over to James' house. When I get to his street, I slow down and look for the number he gave me. I'm not sure what I was expecting, but this wasn't it!

JAMES

I can't believe I got Kami Parker to agree to meet me at my house! I guess I did kind of trick her into believing that it was an office, but the truth is, my office is here. I could have disclosed that a little earlier in our communications, but I didn't want to give her the chance to say no. She would have had me bring my plans into the shop and for some reason, I can't explain, I don't feel like sharing them with *Eddie*. These are *my* plans and I want to see what Kami thinks of them, not what Kami and *Eddie* think of them.

Yeah, yeah I know I'm being a possessive bastard, it's not like the woman or the shop are mine, but I still don't want to share my drawings with anyone but Kami. At least for now anyway, hers is the only opinion I want to hear, I haven't even shared them with Joe yet.

I'm putting dinner in the oven when I hear a knock on my front door. "Hang on, I'll be there in a minute," I yell out. I thought she would actually go to the office first, there's a path that leads away from the house towards my office and I had a feeling that's where she would head, but I have to say I'm glad she came to the house.

I open the door and find Kami standing there looking a little nervous but with a cute smile on her face. "I hope this is OK? I wasn't sure whether to come here or go down the path to the office, I figured I'd try here first because you said you were cooking."

I'm not sure what she means by that, but I choose to ignore it. "I did say I was cooking dinner, so I guess the house was the logical choice, wouldn't you say?" I ask.

Her smile gets larger, and she says, "Yes. So, can I come in, please?"

Ohh shit! I've been standing here just watching her and forgotten my manners. I step aside, open the door a little wider and grandly gesture for her to come in. "Please, come in Miss Parker and allow me to give you the grand tour." Kami lets out a chuckle and I want to make her laugh more often just so that I can hear it again and again. As she walks past me and into my house, all I can smell is her.

I never share my house, my home, with anyone. My friends come over, like Joe and some of the guys from my crews, but women are never invited, not unless they come with one of the guys. I never invite any woman here, ever. I can imagine the fit Joe would be having if he was here now, I can't help the chuckle that escapes my lips. Kami looks over her shoulder at me and I say, "Sorry, I was just thinking about something Joe said earlier." She shrugs her shoulders and continues to walk further into my home. My sanctuary. I've worked hard for my business and my home and I can't help but wonder what she's seeing when she looks around my space.

"This is beautiful James. It's so you, I can see why you love living and working out here." She says as she looks out the floor to ceiling windows, leading out to my back deck, off the living and kitchen areas. "The view out of these windows is worth it if nothing else."

"Yeah, it's gorgeous." But I'm not looking at or talking about what lies outside my windows, I'm talking about the woman who is staring out them. I cough to clear my throat and say, "Come on, let me give you the guided tour so you know where everything is." Namely my bedroom but of course she'll likely be needing the bathroom at some point.

We've finished all the 'public' areas and then we head to the main bathroom where I tell her she can 'powder her nose' if that's what she needs to do. Which draws another loud laugh from her, and I can't explain how much I enjoy hearing it and knowing that I'm the one who made her laugh. Not at me but with me.

"Of course, last but by no means least, this is my bedroom." I can hear the gravel in my voice, and when Kami takes in a deep breathe, she makes this hoarse little 'oh' noise that travels straight down to my cock. Fucking hell, she's going to kill me if she sees that! "You never know, one day soon you might even make it over the threshold." I shoot her a wink and walk away. I can't stay at the doorway to my bedroom for one more second with Kami fucking Parker! I have her in my home but there's no fucking way I'm getting her in my bed tonight, not even if she throws that gorgeous body at me. I won't do it, not yet.

I walk into the kitchen and start setting the table before Kami walks out into the main area of the house. She leans over the kitchen bench as I open the oven door to check on dinner. I know she's there, but when she speaks I still jump, like I said I'm not used to sharing my space with others. "Something smells good, what's for dinner?" she asks, her voice is still a little husky.

"Lasagne," I reply as I head to the fridge and get out the salad I made earlier. "And salad." I finish as I put it on the dining table and then go back to get the lasagne out of the oven.

"Wow! Did you *make* the lasagne?" I understand *why* she's surprised, but I still find it offensive, cause no guy could ever just enjoy cooking a meal for himself? I've lived alone for a very long time, I had to learn to cook or starve!

"I made it Kami. From scratch, I can show you the leftover sauces if you need the proof?" I look at her with a raised eyebrow, silently questioning her.

"Ahh no, I believe you, James. I guess I'm just surprised, there aren't too many guys out there that like to cook a meal."

"Well, I've lived alone a long time Kami, I needed to learn to cook or I would have starved." At her look of shock, I decide to hedge closer to the truth. "OK, so not *starve* so much as getting very overweight by eating out a lot." I shrug a shoulder and continue, "I actually find it relaxing at the end of the day to come home and cook myself a meal. It's kind of boring only cooking for myself most nights though."

"You don't cook for other people often?" She's looking at her hands, and not at me. I know exactly what she's asking but I'm going to pretend I don't understand. She needs to learn to be honest with me and ask for what she wants. In every fucking way!

"What do you mean, other people?" I ask as I gesture for her to join me at the table.

"I mean other people, you know, people who aren't you." I can hear the frustration in her voice, but I'm still not going to give her the answer she's desperately looking for.

"I cook for Joe and the guys sometimes, is that what you mean?" I ask, innocently, as I dish up a slice of lasagne on a plate and hand it to her.

She mumbles what sounds like, 'not quite what I meant, no', but then looks up with a smile and says, "Thanks for dinner, it looks and smells delicious." Then we start eating.

Chapter Five

KAMI

What a freaking frustrating man! He knows what the heck I'm *trying* so very unsuccessfully, to ask him. I want to know how many other women he's cooked a meal for. In this house, his home and then invited into his room. I can't be that direct though. Can I? I know he knows what I'm trying to ask him, what I don't understand is, why he can't just answer me dang it! So, instead of asking and finding out what I want to know about his cooking habits, I ask a different question and see if he'll answer that one.

I take a bite of his lasagne and holy smokes its tasty. Really dang delicious actually. "Dang James, this is the best lasagne I've had in, well I want to say forever, but I don't know, I don't want to give you a fat head. It sure is freaking delicious though." I watch as a huge grin spreads across his face, even his eyes are sparkling at my compliment. If this man tells me it's some joke, and he *didn't* actually make it, I think I might just kill him!

"Thanks, Kami. That means a lot coming from you. Joe seems to enjoy it and he's from a large Italian family, so I figured it couldn't be too bad." He says as he starts eating his own dinner. "I made some dessert too, so eat up, we've got more to go."

For a few minutes, we sit there just enjoying the meal that James has put in front of us. I have to say, it's nice having someone else cook for me for a change. I haven't let his culinary skills side-track me though.

"I have a question for you James."

He nods his head and says, "Shoot, I'll answer anything you want sweetheart."

"Really?" he nods his reply and so I go straight for the question I want answered tonight. "What did you mean by your that text last night?" he starts choking on the food he has in his mouth, I guess he didn't really mean *anything*, huh? I smile at him, waiting for him to reply.

"What text that I sent last night sweetheart? I can't remember sending out any texts last night." This is the way he's going to play it is he? Does he think that I haven't kept the message that I wouldn't have proof of the words he sent me?

"So, you don't remember texting me then?"

"Nope, sorry. What time was it?" he asks to avoid answering my question.

"Oh, it was pretty late. I was lying in bed reading and I have to say I was pretty surprised to see a message that late, especially from you after our conversation at the café." I smile, hopefully, I look like I'm happy! "You see, I read on my phone, books that is, and normally I'm asleep by 1am, but I had just gotten to the part where, oh you don't want to hear about my romance novel do you?" I smile innocently, "then in comes this message from you and well, let's just say, I didn't go to sleep right away."

I see his Adam's apple bob up and down as he takes a large swallow of food.

"Let me read it out to you and see if it sounds familiar." I get up from the table and head to the kitchen bench where I left my bag and pull out my phone. I've finished my dinner, at least what I plan on eating of it anyway and I lean up against the bench as I scroll through my messages. "There you are," I announce as I find James name in amongst the messages list. "Did you need me to read it out to you or is your memory starting to come back to you?"

I can see the panic on his face. I can't believe he's worried about what he said, surely he's already seen it himself. Maybe that's the problem, he's seen it and he doesn't want to discuss it at all.

"Kami, I don't think we need to go over what I said when I was drunk..." he says in a deep voice. "Let me get the plans I've drawn up and we can go over those. You are here for business after all."

"No. I'd really like to read this message out to you, I'm dying to know what you meant by it."

"Nope, I'm good ..." he starts but I start reading at the same time.

James: *"Arghh holy shit Kami what do you do to me woman? ... I've just spent the night getting drunk with my best friend and I can't stop thinking about you. I'm about to get into my bed and all I can think about is you."** *

I try to imitate his deep voice, but I just can't get deep enough. I guess I'm trying to play it off with a bit of humour but all I really want is an answer.

Just when I think he's going to answer, I hear his front door open and someone walks into the house. I move back over to my side of the table and sit down. I need to be sitting to deal with the one person who hates me the most. If only I knew why he hated me so much, not that it would make hurt any less.

JAMES

Fuck! I knew she wouldn't just let that message be, but a man could hope ... right? It didn't even occur to me that she would bring that up tonight when I invited her here. We're here to talk business but I had to cook her dinner first, and that's taken it to a personal level, not professional. Which is what I wanted, but fuck!

Then I hear the front door open and I can't for the life of me remember if I invited anyone else over, but I'm sure, positive actually, that I locked the front door when I let Kami in. Then I hear his voice and I can't believe that tonight can get any worse than it is right this second and I haven't even gotten around to showing Kami my plans for her renovations.

"Hey cocksucker, I came by to pick up my car after last night, thanks for not letting me drive my stupid self home." Joe yells from the living room, "Hey where are you man and who's car is that out there in the driveway? I know you don't bring chicks here, so it's not your latest conquest."

Kami looks at me and I can see the panic written all over her face. Joe has always been mean to her and I don't think he'll ever change. I don't know why he does it, but he seems to take a real joy in making Kami feel as uncomfortable as he possibly can. She looks like she wants to hide before he gets into the kitchen. "Kami, it's OK, it's just Joe."

"Just Joe. *Just Joe!* Joe is the guy who gave me the hardest time at school. He's the one who started the whole Kamo Kami saying and so many others."

"I know but he's a grown man now and we're here talking business." She nods, but I can still see the terror in her eyes. I yell out, "In the kitchen Joe."

"Of course you're in the kitchen, cooking up some masterpiece for dinner hey?" he stops dead in his tracks when he sees the woman sitting at the table with me. "Oh, I'm sorry I didn't mean to interrupt, you just never have ... anyway, let me just grab my keys and I'll get out of your way. Can I talk to you for a minute before I leave, James?" he smiles at both of us and Kami hasn't looked up yet, but I know he knows who's sitting at my dining table.

I reach my hand over and rest it on top of Kami's, "I'll be back in a couple of minutes, OK sweetheart?" I say as low as I can, hoping that Joe doesn't hear me. She nods slightly and then I follow Joe out to the other room.

"What the fuck James? What are you doing here with Kamo Kami? She's a client isn't she?" he asks in a loud, too loud, whisper.

"Yes, she's a client. She came over to look at the plans I've drawn up for her shop, OK?"

"You've got plans drawn up and you haven't shown me yet? You want to show her first don't you? You want to impress her and then she signs off on your design and I can't veto any of the things you want to do for her without looking like a douche bag!"

"You already look like a douche bag where Kami's concerned, and I told you already, stop with the Kamo Kami. Her name's Kami, Kami Parker. Call her Kami or Miss Parker but don't ever say Kamo Kami again. Not around me and not around her, I won't have it Joe. We're not in high school anymore, fucking grow up!"

I didn't realise that my voice was getting louder and louder until Kami walks into the room and says, "It's OK Joe, I understand. This is a business meeting even if it doesn't look like one. I couldn't get away from the shop and James was busy earlier, we agreed for me to meet at the office, and well it's here. I hadn't eaten yet, so James offered me dinner." She's rambling, and I don't want her making excuses to this idiot, we were having dinner together before getting to the business.

"Kami, you don't have to explain anything to Joe, he walked in here cursing up a treat without knowing who I had in here. Yes, you're a client and I get that you don't need to hear that either." I turn to Joe and say,

"How dare you walk in here and start shooting off at the mouth when you have no clue who I have here. It could have been another, less forgiving client, it could have been my fucking mother, for all you knew."

"You're right, Mrs Harvey would have kicked my arse ..." Joe starts to say, just as Kami speaks as well.

"Look, James, thanks for dinner but I'm going to get going. I think perhaps you should bring the plans you've drawn up to the shop and we can go over them there."

"NO!" I shout and both of them stop moving. "No! Kami stay right where you are, we're not finished yet." I look at her, I'm not trying to scare her, but she shrinks back a little. "You," I point at Joe, "Get ya fucking keys and get out of here, we'll talk tomorrow, but the next time you see a car you don't recognise in my driveway, assume it's a client and behave appropriately. No matter the time of day *or night*. Understand?"

Joe nods and looks at Kami, I can feel the warning in my look at him, but he says, "I'm sorry for barging in and my language Kami, it won't happen again." I nod and watch him as he walks out the front door.

I take a deep breath and look over to Kami's beautiful face. She's shocked and a little scared, I can see her body shaking. I walk closer to her, but she flinches when I reach my hand out to hold her, so I drop my hand back down to my side.

"I'm sorry sweetheart, I didn't mean to scare you." I drop my chin to my chest and pull in a deep breath to calm myself. I look up, connect to her beautiful eyes and say, "I would never hurt you, sweetheart. Ever. I know you think you know about my childhood, but you don't know all of it and I would never, ever raise a hand to you, at all."

"I ... I don't think you would hurt me, James, it's just ... you don't understand my childhood either." She says with a shake of her head. "I think it's time for me to leave James. Thank you for dinner, it was delicious."

"Please, Kami, don't leave yet. At least finish dinner with me and then have the dessert I made. I made it just for you, the least you can do is stay and taste it for me, please?" I give her what I can only hope are my best puppy dog eyes!

"OK James, I'll stay for dessert. Maybe you can get your plans out too and show me?" I nod but don't step any closer to her. "I'll be back in a minute, I need to go to the bathroom." Without another word she turns and walks away.

The only reason I know she's going to come back and actually eat dessert is because I can see her handbag still sitting on my kitchen bench.

KAMI

I can't believe I let him talk me into staying for dessert. After he raised his voice, I didn't want to be here anymore. I can't stand it when people yell, I know he wasn't yelling at me, but it still brings up old wounds. People like Joe think they know me, think they know why I was so quiet and studied so hard at school, but they have no damned idea. None at all. I should have walked out the door behind Joe, but the honest truth is, I didn't want to. I didn't want to be near him, and I didn't want to leave James.

Admittedly, the temptation of something sweet, that he made just for me, I can't resist that! Holy crap, that look he gave me! I'm pretty sure the man could sell ice to the Eskimos with that dang look!

I message my best friend, Katy, just to let her know that I'm ok. She knew where I was coming tonight, and she was worried that I would get hurt somehow, but she doesn't understand that I truly believe that James would never hurt me on purpose. When she replies asking me to let her know when I get home safely, I finish up in the bathroom and walk slowly back to the kitchen where James has his back to the door, and I take a few minutes to study him while he can't see me.

The man is built, you can tell he does physical labour for a living. He's not weights, and gym built, but you can tell his muscles work every day. He's definitely not the boy he was back in high school. Even then, he wasn't built quite like the other boys, you could tell even then, he did physical labour to keep in shape.

I'm staring at the muscles in his back work as he moves around the table doing, whatever it is he's doing when I hear him clearing his throat. I look up at him and suddenly I'm embarrassed that I got caught looking, I can feel the blush heating up my cheeks.

"So, what's for dessert then Mr Harvey? You said you made something special, what is it?" if he says he's for dessert, I think I'd take him up on the offer, and that thought makes my mouth go dry and my cheeks heat up even more.

"What I wouldn't give to know what thought you just had that made you blush even hotter than being caught checking me out did, Miss Parker." He chuckles, and it's this deep throaty sound that I feel vibrate right down to my pussy.

"I don't think you want to know, Mr Harvey." He raises an eyebrow at me but doesn't say anything else. "A girls got to have some secrets you know. If I tell you everything now, you wouldn't be interested in hanging around for more."

"I doubt that very much sweetheart. I think if you told me what you were just thinking, we'd be having a very different conversation to the one I'm going to start because we need to talk about the shop." He rumbles off all the words in a rush, like he's trying to get everything out all at once, so that he can move along faster.

"Business it is then Mr Harvey. Show me what you've got." I say with a grin. I meant it to sound like an invitation to things that aren't business and by the heat suddenly in his eyes, he picked up on the double meaning. If he keeps looking at me like I'm dessert, I might just be in a bit of trouble.

"Why don't you come a little closer and I'll show you exactly what I've got 'going on' over here." Ohh wow! His voice is deep and rumbly, just the kind that brings me to my knees. Yes literally. I blush even more because if he could read my thoughts right now, there wouldn't be room for the plans he's drawn up, dessert or anything else. My tongue licks my bottom lip without me thinking about it and the movement draws his eyes to my lips. I swear I just heard a groan escape from his lips and that causes me to bite my bottom lip and draw it into my mouth. The air surrounding us is electric, we stare at each other's lips and then all of a sudden there's a noise that isn't me and isn't him, but it draws us both out the haze that surrounds us.

I hear James curse, "Motherfucker!" That's when I realise it's a timer's buzzer that's gone off. I guess I have dessert to thank for breaking the tension.

Don't get me wrong, I desperately want to kiss James Harvey, I have wanted to kiss him since we were 14 years old, but to start something here, in his home. That would be a huge mistake. If we start here, things could just keep moving along and I won't be able to say no to him. I'm not saying I would regret sleeping with him either, I highly doubt that it would be a regrettable experience, and I'm no virgin, so it's not like he'd be my first. I just think it would be moving too fast for me, we only reconnected yesterday. I have no desire to tie him down, but I'm not really interested in a one-night stand either. Maybe after my renovation is done because then I won't have to see him every day and wonder who he's with after this all ends.

"Kami ... Kami, I said dessert is ready. Do you want some cream?"

Well, it would seem that no matter what we talk about now, it's going to have some sexual connotation to it.

JAMES

I close my eyes because, after the tension and electricity that was just zapping around us not 5 minutes ago, everything I say seems to have a sexual undertone to it. I'm not even trying, for the first time in a long time, but it sure does seem to be coming out that way. I clear my throat and go to speak again but Kami beats me to it.

"Did you *make* an apple pie ... for me?" She asks. Here I was thinking that she'd gotten past my cooking skills, apparently not.

"Yes Kami, I made an apple pie, from scratch, for dessert. For you, well yeah cause you're here but I also felt like eating an apple pie, so I made one."

"From scratch?" I slowly nod my head in answer to her question because I can't be bothered voicing the same answer, again. "Wow! Umm yes, please, can I have some cream on top?"

I groan at the double meaning and dish us both up a slice of pie with cream on top. I can't even look at her, the thoughts that are rolling around my head, if I look at her I'm sure she'll be able to read my mind and go running out my door. Then I'll have lost the only chance I have with this beautiful woman. I've waited so long to have this chance, an opportunity to prove to her that I'm not as bad as everyone thinks, I can't get ahead of myself. It may have been a mistake to cook dinner for her and bring her out to my home, but even if it is, I wouldn't change it for anything. Well, except maybe an overnight stay with her, which included me getting to do all the things I want to with her.

Her groan snaps me out of my head and makes my cock instantly hard. When I look across the table at her, she's got her eyes closed, and she's licking her lips. My spoon is hovering somewhere between my bowl and my mouth, while I watch Kami take another mouthful of my apple pie to her mouth, open wide and moan again as she closes her mouth around the spoon. Fuck me, she's killing me, but what a way to die.

Her eyes open as she tells me, "Holy heck James, this is delicious. I swear it's the best thing I've had in my mouth in, forever." Then she realises what she's said as my jaw drops to the table and the cream starts to drip off my spoon. I should have changed out of my jeans, there isn't enough fucking room in them to eat dinner with this woman. "I, ummm, didn't mean that the way it came out. It's ... you're a really good cook James."

"Thank you Kami, coming from you, that means a lot." I say.

"Why? You don't even know if I can cook, I could be really bad for all you know, I mean I *do* go to the café every day for lunch." She laughs, and it's become my favourite sound in the last couple of days. "Maybe next time, you can come to my house and I'll cook for you?" Her whole body freezes as she realises what she's just said, and her spoon clangs back into her bowl.

"That's a deal Kami. Next time it's at your place and you're cooking for me." Without another word about it, I pick up my bowl and hers and take them to the sink. "Let's look at the plans I drew up for the renovations shall we?" It seems like it might be a safer subject right now and it should, with any luck, help my hard on become less hard!

Chapter Six

<u>KAMI</u>

That apple pie was to *freaking die for*! I can't believe he took it away from me before I could eat it all. I was hellbent on protesting until I saw the storm clouds in his eyes, and I realise that perhaps going over the plans for the renovation might be for the best. Especially when I notice the large bulge in the front of his jeans.

"Stop looking at my cock Kami, otherwise I'm going to do something neither of us is ready for." In a voice that is so tight, so deep and *so* full of lust that I have to squeeze my thighs together. He groans loudly, and my head snaps up, our eyes lock, steady and unforgiving. "Don't do that either Kami, if I know you want me even half as much as I want you right now... fuck!" he runs a hand over his face, trying to calm himself down.

"I'm sorry," I croak out and then cough to clear my throat and start again. "I'm sorry James, I didn't mean to stare, it's just that, well ..." He looks at me and his eyes are still dark with lust, "You're right, it's too much, too soon. Show me the plans you've drawn up."

"Just ... give me a minute, OK? I'll be back." He leaves me standing in the living room while he goes to the bathroom ... maybe?

Then we spend the next 30 minutes or so, looking over the different plans he's drawn up and deciding which parts will work better and what areas fit with what I already had planned in my mind.

"Could you grab me some paper and a pen please?" James nods, walks to his office and when he gets back, he hands me a sketchpad and a pencil. "That's a bit fancier than I'm used to, but I guess I shouldn't have expected anything less." I say with a smile.

James shrugs his shoulder and says, "Tools of the trade and well I highly doubt you're going to do any damage to them. It's just paper and a pencil sweetheart."

"No you're right of course, I was just expecting a notepad and pen, that's all. I'm not an artist like you, but I'll give it a try."

"I'm no artist and you don't need the exact measurements Kami, that's my job."

So, I sit there, sketching out my thoughts, working in a lot of the ideas from his drawings as well. Most of them are pretty close to what I want, I'm just making small adjustments here and there. I'm not sure how long we sit there, concentrating on the plans and making sure James understands what all my little squiggles mean. We've got drawings everywhere, when James draws out a final sketch and asks me if that's the one I want.

We're grinning at each other like lunatics, we've got the design and plans all decided on, now all James has to do is draw up what he calls, 'a proper copy' so that his crew understand what the plan is. That's when I realise how close we've been sitting for I don't even know how long. I look at the clock on the wall and see it's close to midnight. Even though it's late and I have to go to work tomorrow, I don't want to move. I'm almost sitting in James' lap and I can feel his heart beating behind me because I'm leaning back into his chest. His hands were leaning on the floor, now they're resting on my thighs and my hands are holding onto his forearms. I can feel his muscles working to hold on to me and now that we're both aware of where I'm sitting, he's flexing those muscles even more!

I'm not sure how long we sit there, not moving a muscle, not willing to burst the bubble we've created. I think both of us are so aware of the other person but neither one of us wants to move or make the first move. Our breathing is laboured, and I close my eyes to try to, I don't know, I think I'm trying to decide what to do. Do I turn my head and kiss him like it's the last time I'll ever do it, do I turn around and kiss him like he's the air I breathe or do move myself off his lap and pretend it didn't happen? I don't want to pretend it didn't happen, and I think he's waiting for me to make the next move. I turn slightly to look at his face, I need to see what his eyes are saying but I don't get too far.

"If you're turning around to tell me, this isn't happening you better leave now." He says in a raspy voice, "but if you're turning so that I can kiss those lips, you better be ready for me, sweetheart." His raspy voice turns into a growl when I turn my head and reach a hand up to his cheek.

"Kiss me James. God, please kiss me." My own voice is so raspy and breathy I barely recognise it, but I don't even get a second to think about it before his lips land on mine. The rest of my body turns, meaning that I'm straddling the sexiest man I've ever known.

His tongue runs along the seam of my lips, begging for entry and I gasp, allowing him complete access to my mouth. Our tongues tangle, he's got one hand twisted in my hair, holding the back of head, and pressing my lips closer to his. His other hand is resting on my lower back, holding my body close to his. My hands were resting on his shoulders, but now one is twisted in his hair and the other one is scratching up and down his back, well the parts I can reach, anyway. I can't get close enough and I move my body closer to his and he lets out a groan that rattles through my insides because he hasn't taken his mouth off mine! I can feel his cock nestled between my thighs and I'm rubbing myself over him, I need to feel *him*.

James pulls away from my lips, his eyes are closed, and he rests his forehead on mine, in a voice that is sexily breathless and deep he says quietly, "Unless you want me to make a mess or you plan on staying here, with me tonight, I think this is where we'd better stop." For a second I don't understand, I'm still in a lust haze. Then he continues, "I want you so much right now Kami, but I don't think you're ready for that and I don't want you to run away from me."

I know he's right, but I also know I don't really want to stop. I like how I feel when I'm in his arms. "I should go." It's all I say, all I can say but neither of us moves for at least another ten minutes. My head is resting on his shoulder and he's resting his cheek on the side of my head. His hands are running up and down my back, my arms are wrapped around his neck, hanging on like I don't want to let go. I *don't* want to let go, it feels like, if we move the spell is broken and we go back to before. I don't want to move, and I don't want to leave his house, but I know I have to go, and I have to go now, *before* I can change my mind and stay.

JAMES

I can see the emotions of her decisions playing across her face and I know when she's decided it's time to leave. I don't want her to go, but I know I have to give her the space she needs to get to where I am now. I've wanted this woman for what feels like forever and I'm willing to wait. I'm not talking about having one night with her either, even though I think that's where her mind is, this won't be a one off for me. For that to happen between us, I need Kami to be ready, I need for her to be on the same page, and right now, she isn't even close.

I can see her mentally leave me before she moves physically, and I know I've lost the fight tonight. I let my hands fall down to her waist and pick her up to set her on her feet. I'm not pushing her away, I just know that's what she needs tonight. I get to my feet and reach out for her hand, thankfully she doesn't pull away, in fact, she seems to need to touch me. Thank fucking god!

"I'm sorry James, I'm just not ...." she starts, and I can't let her finish, she doesn't need to explain herself to me. Or anyone else for that matter.

"Don't Kami. You don't have to explain anything to me." I reply, taking a deep breath. "Can I tell you something, without freaking you out?" I wait for her to nod before I keep going, "I want you sweetheart, I think that's pretty obvious, and I'm pretty sure you want me too. No, don't say a thing. What I'm trying to say is, I'm OK with waiting, I don't want you to feel pressured into doing anything you're not comfortable with. Just know that, I'm not going anywhere unless you tell me to, OK? We take this as slow as you need to."

I need to know that she hears me and understands what I have to say. She nods her head, but that's just not enough for me tonight. She seems to be able to see that and finally speaks, her voice is quiet, but not nervous. "You're right. I want you too and I need you to know that, but I just." She takes a deep breath and continues, "it's just moving so quickly. Can we work on this renovation together and see what happens? I mean I already agreed to all of your special conditions in our contract, and you can add cooking meals for each other to the list as well."

"Oh sweet Kami Parker, you better believe I'm cooking for you again, and you already promised me a meal, I'm not letting you out of that one." I say with a smirk, I can't wait to eat what she offers me. "How about, I come by tomorrow to show you the plans after I've drawn them up properly again and then I can take you to lunch?"

"You've got a date Mr Harvey." She says then blushes when she realises what she's implied.

"Yes, yes I do have a date Miss Parker." I say with a grin that I'm sure is wider than my face, making me look like an absolute idiot, but I couldn't be happier about calling our lunch an actual date. I walk her out of my house and to her car.

"So, I guess I'll see you tomorrow then?" She says as we stand beside her car, not letting go of each other's hand just yet. I'm really not ready for her to leave but I know it's time to let her go. For now anyway.

"I guess you will." I reply. I can't help myself, I curl my other hand behind her neck and pull her mouth to mine. The kiss is sweet, but too long to be had in a fucking driveway! I pull back first and drop my forehead to hers, "Get in your car Kami and leave, before I take that decision away from you. Please?"

She releases my hand and I feel the loss of her touch. "Good night James." She starts to drive away, and I tap on her bonnet until she stops.

"Text me when you get home, OK?" She rolls her eyes at me and I say, "Please, I need to know you got there safely."

"You know it's maybe a five minute drive right, and I've done it a million times?" I nod my head agreeing with every point she makes, but I still want to know she's gotten there in one piece. "Sure James, I'll text you when I get to my house if it will help you sleep better."

"It will help me to relax and sleep, so yes I want that text." She smiles at me sweetly and nods again.

I stand in my driveway like an idiot watching until I can no longer see her tail lights and then head back inside. I look at the kitchen and decide that it can all wait until the morning. We packed most of the dishes into the dishwasher earlier, anyway. Then I look in my lounge room, seeing all those papers all over the floor, makes me remember where we ended up tonight and how it could have ended differently.

I'm not gonna lie, I've got a serious fucking case of blue balls, but Kami is worth the pain. Worth the wait, and hell, I've waited all these years, I can wait a few more weeks or maybe months, right? Fuck I hope it's not months! I pick up all of our papers and put the final design on the top of the rest. I'll make up a couple of copies in the morning that the crew and I can work off that has all the right measurements, but that copy we drew up together, that one I'm keeping. That's a piece of Kami and me that I'm not willing to throw away.

I switch all the lights off and walk into my bedroom. I stand in the doorway and try to see it through Kami's eye but it's just a room to me. When I reach the side of my bed, I'm already half undressed, and I place my phone on the side table to wait for Kami's text. I'm just taking off my boxer briefs, when my phones chimes with a message.

Kami: *Goodnight handsome. Thanks again for dinner*

I smile, because I know she didn't want to message me, but she still did it. For me.

James: *That's not a I'm home safely thank you for a great night handsome*

Kami: *You know you shouldn't look for compliments or assume you'll get them*

Kami: *I'm home safely and getting ready for bed. Thank you for an exceptional night, handsome*

I get one seconds after the first one comes through and I can't help the laugh that escapes me. With that last one, I can't help myself I have to send her one back;

James: *Getting ready for bed .... what does that entail sweetheart?*

I wait for what feels like ten minutes but I'm sure is only a minute, maybe two, before she answers me.

Kami: *well, it includes me getting naked*

My breathing stops for half a minute, and I can't believe I got her to admit that she sleeps naked! Then another text rolls in before I can get my scrambled brain to respond;

Kami: *Then getting into my pyjamas and getting all comfy in bed sweet dreams James x*

Holy fucking shit! My mind wanders to what she could be wearing as pyjamas, and I want to ask but I don't.

James: *Sweet dreams Sweetheart, I'll see you tomorrow*

I wait to see if she's going to text be back, but when the phone stays silent, I put it back on the side table. My cock is hard, and my hand is wrapped tightly around it. Then I start to pump my cock up and down, imaging all the different things Kami could be sleeping in and then there's nothing. Just her, no lace or silk or anything else covering that amazing body of hers. I felt all those luscious curves tonight when I had my hands on her and I can imagine what they look like without those layers covering them. With that thought and a wicked imagination giving me the perfect visual, I come all over my stomach. It's late and I'm completely wiped out now, so I grab a couple of tissues, clean myself up and throw them in the bin next to my bed.

I check my phone one more time before I set the alarm and drift off to sleep, dreaming about curly brown hair, mesmerising multi coloured eyes, depending on her mood and the smiling face of the most beautiful woman, looking only at me. She looks happy, and I feel happy just looking at her.

I have the best night's sleep I can remember having in months. Even Joe's grumpy face greeting me in my kitchen the next morning can't dull the crazy happy I'm feeling.

KAMI

I wanted to ask James what he wore to bed, but I wasn't sure how to. 'What are you wearing', seemed like a really idiotic thing to say, so I didn't. 'What do you wear to bed', seemed even more ridiculous, so again I didn't ask him. I really wanted to know but I let my imagination run free and it came up with the best answer imaginable. Nothing, he sleeps naked.

I picture every other possibility in my mind too though and boy, my mind doesn't let me down! First off were the traditional pyjama pants with a plain white t-shirt. Then there was the no t-shirt version, just those blue striped pyjama pants slung dangerously low on his hips. Whoa, talk about getting a girl all hot and bothered. Then I thought that perhaps he just stripped out of his clothes but left his black boxer briefs on. Oh yeah, I glimpsed those babies tonight, and I have to say, yum!

Then, my favourite version of all comes along and I decide that's how he's sleeping, even if he isn't in reality, he is in my mind. I feel like a pervert but dreaming about a real man is surely better than drooling over a celebrity like a star struck fool ... right?

I can't get the thought of him being naked, in bed and ready for action, out of my head. After feeling what he's packing in those jeans, I think I can imagine what he's offering. My hand slides down my stomach as I imagine just how much he could fill me and make me scream. When my finger reaches my clit, I can feel sparks lighting up my whole body, James' name escapes my lips on a moan and just like that, I'm coming. I didn't even need to push a finger inside myself, I was that worked up from his kisses and thoughts of him naked and pounding into me!

I check my phone to see if James has sent me another message, when I don't see one, I put the phone on my side table, turn off the light and fall into blissful sleep. Wishing that I'd taken a chance and stayed the night, even while knowing I'm glad I didn't.

I can't just jump into bed with him, no matter how long we've known each other. Or how long I've wanted him for. It's not me, that's not what I do. The fact that he's not pushing for more, and he's willing to wait until I'm ready to have sex with him, that makes him even more perfect in my eyes.

Chapter Seven

"Good morning Joseph, to what do I owe the pleasure of your company this fine morning?" God, I sound stupid happy even to my own ears! No wonder Joe's looking at me like I belong in the psych ward of the local hospital, but I can't help the grin that spreads across my face this morning. I'm happy.

"Why the fuck are you so happy? It's too early in the morning for that kind of shit man!" Joe shakes his head and hands me a coffee. "It can't be because you got laid *'Miss Parker's'* car isn't here anymore." He looks at me and I just smirk and drink my coffee. "Did she leave already? I didn't pick her for a pump and dump kind of chick, I figured she'd be a stay all night cuddling and then she's here for life, deal. I would never have guessed it!"

He turns away from me to put some more milk in his coffee and I hit him on the back of the head, then I walk over to sit at the table. "She's not a 'hump and dump kinda chick', as you so eloquently put it. Which is a disgusting phrase by the way. Kami left a little after midnight after we finalised the plans for her project."

"And that's it? Just plans happened?" Joe asks.

"I didn't say that, I said she left when we finished her plans."

"So you fucked her, then finished the plans, hey? Are you sure this project is a good idea, Jimmy?"

"Don't call me *Jimmy!*" I grind out, "You know how much and why I fucking hate it, arsehole!" This makes him laugh and that pisses me off even more. "Don't be so fucking crass, we didn't *fuck* ....."

"Oh man, don't tell me you made lurrrve? You're really in deep with this one aren't you, huh?"

"We didn't make love either. Just shut up OK? It's none of your fucking business what we did or didn't do, anyway."

There's not a lot that Joe and I haven't shared over the course of our friendship if I'm honest, so I guess he has a reason to be surprised that I'm not sharing details, but Kami wouldn't like me telling Joe and that's what stops me from talking. When I look up to see why he's gone so quiet, I see the hurt written all over his face.

"I'm just worried James. Worried about you and the business. You've worked your arse off to get to where you are, and I'd hate for this one job to cause you any trouble." I go to speak but he doesn't give me the chance. "I know how you feel about Kami, you've always had a thing for her, but you've always managed to keep your distance. I'm just worried about how you'll react later if she doesn't feel the same, that's all."

"That's all, huh? So, now I'm not good enough for her, is that what you're saying? You're right, I've worked my arse off to get away from my family history and prove myself. Yet I'm still not good enough? Before, when we barely spoke to one another I was good, but now, now that I'm my own man and I can give her everything, I'm not good enough, huh?"

"That's not what I meant ...." Joe starts but I don't want to hear it.

"Get the fuck out Joe. I've got plans to draw up and a crew to round up." He goes to speak again, but I don't wanna hear it. I get up, put my coffee cup in the sink and storm towards my bedroom. "Just get out Joe and remember what I said last night. Don't come in if you see her car here. EVER!"

I don't think I've ever been this pissed off with Joe, not in all the years we've been friends. He's always been my biggest supporter, but even knowing how I've always felt about Kami, he's the one telling me I'm not good enough. Well, he can get fucked.

KAMI

I don't want to wake up when my alarm sounds the next morning. I want to stay cocooned in my warm, snuggly bed and keep dreaming. My dreams were filled with James. His body, his smile, his intelligence and my word, his kisses.

James doesn't come close to being my first, not that I have a long list of lovers or anything, but I've been kissed before, multiple times. I can tell you now though, not one of those previous kisses even come close to what James' kisses are like. He kisses me like he needs it to live, breathe and survive. I'm becoming addicted to his kisses, and it hasn't been that long since I've been on the receiving end of one. I know I can't get too lost in James, I've always felt this draw to him, but I also know that it can't last. If I decide to have sex with James, I have been aware that's all it is, and it has an end date. The end of the contract and the project.

At the end, I can walk away. Can't I? I can agree to this, 'let's see what happens over the course of your project' and still walk away with my heart intact if I walk into it with my eyes open. Wide open. Sure I can. With that decision made, I get my body out of bed, shower and dress for the shop. I grab myself a coffee and a breakfast bar, get in my car and drive to my bookstore.

I open every morning and Ed comes in at 11am, sometimes earlier if I need him to, but I'm always the first and only one here early in the mornings. I like the quiet. The time for me to get back to selling people books, it's why I opened the shop to begin with, obviously. But I find myself sitting in the office more often than not these days, doing paperwork, ordering stock, following up on products, special orders for customers and just stuff. My favourite thing though is to be out on the floor, helping people find the books they're looking for and some that they're not. I enjoy the peaceful mornings when it's just me, the books and a few customers.

Well, usually I do anyway. Today I just want the morning to disappear. That way lunch time can get here faster. I want Ed to be here now so that I can hide away in my office and think about James. Daydreaming about James sounds so much more inviting than any kind of work I could distract myself with and that's where the real danger lies!

I work all morning, serving customers, shelving new books and organising the space where James and his crew will need to start work. I start clearing books from the shelves and finding new homes for them. I'm in my own world getting stuff done and I've forgotten all about watching the clock. This is why I love my job, my business because everything else just fades away and I get lost. Lost in getting things just right and lost in the worlds created by the authors. I find myself reading the backs of some of the books I'm supposed to just be moving and finding homes for, but you know what? You can't find their new spot if you don't know what they're about now can you? That's my theory and I'm sticking to it!

I've had quite a few customers this morning as well and they're always happy to have a quick, sometimes not so quick, conversation about their reading choices as well. So you see, I'm actually doing research to make my customer service so much better! That's exactly what I'm doing when Ed arrives for his shift, talking to a lovely older woman about her favourite romance novels and getting her recommendations for some new ones for myself. Whether I read them or not, is not the point, she's happy to chat and I'm more than happy to hear that she's a happy returning customer.

When Ed walks in she loudly whispers to me, "This one, he's not a romantic, he doesn't like talking to me about my book boyfriends. I think he thinks I should be dead at my age, but I'm still allowed to have the hots for these gorgeous men. Gets the blood pumping after all my years, and then I don't need to walk so far to make sure I'm still alive!"

"Now Olive, I've told you before, I don't think you should be dead, you know that. I just don't need to know the intimate details of how much you love your book boyfriends, not from you or anyone else for that matter." Ed says with a pained smile on his face.

"You would if the gorgeous Kami here was telling you all about those details, but I'm an old woman now and you, you handsome devil, just like to keep me coming in here. You know I come to buy my books because of you. Oh and you too Kami, of course!" Olive says, with a wicked glint in her eyes. Ed walks passed her to put his stuff away and leans over to set a light kiss on her cheek, she giggles like a school girl and heads towards the door. "Now *that's* customer service, my boy!" She lets out a loud laugh and then she's gone!

I look at Ed and burst out laughing. "Well, I didn't know you were 'handsome Ed' and giving out kisses to our customers." I laugh. "No wonder she asked me where you were today!"

"Jealous? You know, if you want a kiss from me Kami, all you have to do is ask." He says with a smirk and I'm about to answer when I hear a cough from the entrance. I didn't even hear the bell chime when the door opened, I was laughing too hard, but I have a funny feeling Ed knew exactly what he was doing because when I look up to see who's standing in the doorway, there's James looking handsome as ever and a little pissed off. Well OK, he looks like he could drill a hole into the back of Ed's head and then he swings his look towards me and while his face softens a little, he's still mad!

I don't even look towards Ed when I say, "I know, that's why I've never asked Ed you for one and you know it." I don't hear his response either.

All I can hear is the blood thrumming through my veins because James glances towards Ed for a heartbeat and then back to me. "Can we go talk in your office please Kami?"

"Sure." I start and have to cough to clear my throat, "Sure James, follow me." I finish. "You're right out here for now aren't you Ed?"

"I sure am K, call out if you need me." He says and looks at James, I get his meaning, but I don't need to be rescued from James. I nod his way and lead James to my office. When we get there, I move to sit behind my desk, but as I hear the door close, my hand is held tightly in James' and he spins me around to face him. We're close but not touching.

"Am I the only one you're asking for kisses right now Kami?" I stand there looking at him, I'm dumbfounded that he would even feel the need to ask that question. Things are happening pretty quickly between us, but I would never have two guys on the go. Geez, I can barely keep up with the one I think I've got! "Sweetheart answer the question." He growls at me.

JAMES

She looks surprised that I have to ask, but seriously after walking in to what *Eddie* just said, I need confirmation that I'm the only one. She's the only one for me. I may have a 'player' reputation, but that's not my doing. Any woman who comes home with me knows from the beginning what the deal is, I don't make promises I can't keep.

"Please Kami." Her silence is killing me.

"Yes." At least that's what I think she says. Then she coughs, straightens up her body and says, "Yes James, you're the only one that I'm asking to kiss me. I can't believe you even need to ask that question, honestly! You know Ed was saying it to get a reaction out of you and you walked right into it! He knew you were standing there, I would have too except I was too busy laughing at his behaviour towards an older customer who had just left."

Is she pissed at me for asking? Is she for fucking real right now? "You're angry ... with me for asking?"

"Yessss!" She rolls her eyes at me, "The fact that you had to ask me is ridiculous! Whatever issues you two have, you better get over them and fast. I'm not losing a valued employee because you guys have to get into a peeing contest every time you see each other. He's been here for years and knows this place almost as well as I do." She pulls her hand from mine and stomps around the desk to sit in her chair.

"So, what you're telling me is, you'll get rid of me before you will *Eddie*?" I ask, I can feel the anger building up in me, because even though I realise he's an employee and I'm just a contractor, I want her to choose *me*!

"That's not what I'm saying James, I'm saying you'll both be working here for the next few weeks, so you *both* need to get over it. Don't worry, I'll be telling Ed the same thing. I need everybody to be on the same page here." She says. She's all business and here I was thinking we were about more than just business.

"All business, hey? Nothing else going on here?" I wave my hand between the two of, indicating the two of us. I don't even know how this conversation went downhill so fucking fast! I came in here, happy to see Kami again and then that arsehole was talking about kissing her and I saw red.

When I see the look on her face soften, I relax for the first time since I heard that idiot talking about kissing her. "No, not all business James, but yes, here it has to be about business. This is how I make a living you know and you're making your living here for the next few weeks too. Do you really want to give your crew the opportunity to talk about why you got this job or why you took it?"

"I have a question. Did you hire me because you thought I might fuck you?" I know I'm being crude, and I know I could have worded it better, but I just can't find those words right now. I realise I should have made the effort though when I see Kami blush from her lickable neck all the way up to the tips of her ears.

"I didn't, and you know it. Do you have to be so dang crass about it? Really, James!" she shakes her head at me, and I can't say I blame her, but I won't be apologising any time soon for it.

"So what does it matter what anyone else fucking thinks? My guys know better than to question me about business or my private life, for that matter. Do we talk about stuff, yeah of course we do," I shrug a shoulder, "but they would never assume that I slept my way into or out of a job for that matter? I've never slept with a client in the past, in fact even up to this point, I still haven't, have I Kami?"

"No, you haven't."

"Yet." It's a statement, and it's filled with a promise. "It's not something I make a habit of Kami, just so you know." I can see her swallow from here and I take another step closer to her desk and lean over, close to her face. "Not yet anyway, Miss Parker."

"Your point has been made Mr Harvey." She responds in a husky voice that sends my cock hard.

I step back from the desk, "I'm glad to hear it. Now, are we looking over these plans now or after lunch?" I ask.

"You. You still want to have lunch with me?" She stammers out.

"Why wouldn't I want to have lunch with you Kami? We made plans last night didn't we?" I'm looking at the plans rolled up in my hand, but I bring my eyes up to look into hers and ask, "Unless you don't want to, of course. I won't *make* you have lunch with me, but I haven't changed my mind, sweetheart." I really hope she hasn't changed her damned mind, I've been looking forward to having lunch with her all day.

"No, I haven't changed my mind. I just thought." She takes a steadying breath. "Well, never mind what I thought. Let's look at these revised plans and then we can go grab some lunch." I decide not to push her on what she means by that and roll out the new plans I drew up this morning after Joe left me in peace. First him and now *Eddie*. What is it with everyone? What do they think I'm going to do her? She's not as sweet as they all want to believe, I've tasted those lips. Maybe it's just the thought of her with me, the town 'bad boy', having any kind of chance with her that gets them all riled up? I didn't earn that title, I was labelled with it thanks to my rat bastard father and the company he's kept, and I've been tarred with the same fucking brush. No matter how hard I work, or how successful my business becomes, when it comes to women, I'm only good for one thing.

FUCKING.

I just hope I can prove to Kami that's not all I'm worthy of.

We spend the next half an hour going over the new draft of the plans we sketched up together last night. Once Kami has agreed and signed off on everything, I'm a happy man. Especially when I see the smile on her face, it makes me smile too. I want to make this beautiful woman happy. I want to be the reason she smiles. Moans and screams my name too, but for now, I'm good with the smiling.

It's only when we're done that I realise we didn't have any interruptions, not even one from Eddie. Either Kami told him not to interrupt us before I got here or he's actually using his brain for a change. When we open the door to head out for lunch, I realise it could have been because he was busy!

"Ed! Why the dickens didn't you come and get me when you were so busy?" Kami whisper yells at him.

"Well, I knew you were in a meeting with him," he nods his head my way, "so I called Mel in. I didn't want to interrupt you guys, I know how much you want these changes done and well, Mel was available."

"Thanks, we got a lot of work done, we've finalised the plans and the Harvey crew will be starting on the work within the next couple of days. Right James?" She turns to look at me as she asks the question.

"We can start whenever you're ready Kami. I spoke to the crew today and I've got a couple of guys ready to start at your go ahead." I reply.

Kami looks back over at Eddie and says, "Would you be able to stay back for a while tonight and help me get some more stock packed up and stuff moved around so that James and his crew can get started sooner rather than later? You too Mel if you don't have other plans?"

"You don't need to move anything, the guys and I can do that."

"No, we need to pack up the books and get them moved out of your way. Then we need to move the current shelving out of the way ..."

I don't let her finish. I reach out for her hand but change my mind when I see Eddie give me a look and reach for her arm instead to turn her to face me. "Kami, you don't need to move the fixtures sweetheart, I already told you that's what we're doing."

"You don't have to do that James. Ed, Mel and I are more than capable of getting these things done tonight so that your guys can start with construction straight away in the morning."

"Kami, it's in the contract. We do the heavy lifting, you guys just have to move the stock out of the way so that nothing gets damaged."

"Oh, OK. Well, I guess I'll go get some boxes so that we can get started on packing up the books."

"No!" Eddie and I say at the same time and it makes us look at each other. I can see the question written all over his face and I wonder if my face looks the same.

"You go and get some lunch Kami. Mel and I have things covered here, when it gets a bit quieter, I'll grab some lunch and then Mel can go get something. I'm sure James would love to talk about more details over lunch."

What the hell is this fucker up to? He's been on my case since I walked in here to work out a quote for this job and now he's suddenly on my side? What the fuck?

"We do have a lunch date today Kami," I say to her while making sure Ed knows it's a date, pre-arranged at that.

"We did but I have so much work to do now." She starts.

"You still need lunch Kami and the rest can wait. The guys and I can help with anything left to do in the morning."

"The customers have died down. You're right, we did have a lunch date. OK, let's go grab something quickly."

Has she learnt nothing? I don't do anything quickly, and yes I do mean I take my time with details. ALL the details. I can't help the smirk that crosses my face.

"What's that smile all about Mr Harvey?" Kami asks me with her own smile, as we walk towards the café.

"I get to have lunch with you Miss Parker, what could possibly upset me?"

Why? Why did I have to ask that question? It's like I was setting the world a challenge or something.

Chapter Eight

KAMI

Josie brings our lunch over, and we have a quick chat before she moves off to another table with a smile. James and I fall into an easy conversation about everything and nothing. I thought it might be a bit awkward after what happened at the shop, but everything is good. Great even, while we chat and laugh. Then the time and our lunch is gone, and I have to get back to work.

"Thanks for lunch James," I say with a smile. I genuinely enjoyed the time we spent together.

"Any time Kami. That was one of the best lunches I've had in a long time and I couldn't even tell you what I ate." He sends me the biggest smile my way and I couldn't be happier. Nothing and no one else matters in this moment, we're both just happy.

I hear someone clear their throat and look up to see Josie smiling at us. It's not until I look at her that I realise that I've been standing next to the table and James has my hand in his. I try to pull my hand back, but he won't let me. It's a very public display of affection that makes my heart pound in my chest. "Hey Josie, can you put our lunch on my tab again please?" he *speaks* to Josie, but his eyes never leave mine.

"I sure can, but you do know you have to pay that sooner rather than later right Harvey?" her voice is serious, but her smile takes away any real heat out of her words.

"You know where to find me, Josie."

"Yeah, I sure do," Josie mumbles as she walks away with our empty plates.

"James, I have to get back," I say quietly and try to take my hand back again.

"I know you do sweetheart, but I need to ask you a question." I nod for him to continue, "Will you have dinner with me tonight?" He looks so hopeful, but I need to get these books boxed up and get the shop ready for his crew to come in.

"I would love to James," it just about kills me when his smile gets broader because I have to say no, "but I can't. I have to get all the stock boxed up, and the area cleaned up for you and your guys to be able to start work tomorrow. You were there when I asked Ed and Mel to stay back after we close today. I can't ask them to stay and then head out to dinner myself. That hardly seems fair to me."

The way his face drops breaks my heart. "I know you're right sweetheart, but I was looking forward to sharing another meal with you. Don't get me wrong, I completely understand why you can't, but that doesn't take the sting away." He flashes me another smile but when he drops my hand, I feel the loss of his touch immediately. I realise that I'm becoming way too attached to this man, way too quickly. I've always felt that connection with him, but I can't let this get out of control, because whatever 'it' is, has barely even started.

"I want that too but, if you want to start this project tomorrow, then I need to get this stuff moved." I know he understands that, but he looks so unhappy about it. "We can take a raincheck though. We can see how we go tomorrow and then maybe I can cook for you this time?"

I'm granted another grin that makes his blue eyes sparkle when he replies, "That sounds better than me taking you out for dinner. I can't wait for you to cook for me, sweetheart."

I can't help the blush that creeps up my neck and floods my cheeks, as I remember what happened when he cooked for me. Josie's laughter breaks the tension and brings me back down to earth with a thud. She's not laughing at me or us for that matter, but with the customer she's serving, it's enough to break the spell and make me move away from the table. I still don't want to leave, but I know I have to in order to get things ready for an early start tomorrow morning.

"I'll see you later James." I smile back at him as I leave the café.

"See ya later, sweetheart." If it's at all possible, I think his smile is bigger than mine!

I walk back to the shop with a bounce in my step and a smile on my face. When I walk into the shop, I see Ed and Mel huddled together at the counter, whispering to each other and smiling like fools. How the hell did I miss this? No wonder he calls Mel in for his back up. I'm happy for the two of them. I cough as I get closer, I know they think they've hidden themselves from view at the front door pretty well, but this is *my* shop. I know all the nooks and crannies because I need to know where people can hide to pocket a book without paying for it. I also know that from that vantage point, Ed can still see most of the store and the front door, he's just not really looking at it right now and I can't say I blame him. The shops empty anyway, so no harm done.

"Good afternoon you two, any problems while I was at lunch? It seems to have gone pretty quiet." I watch from the corner of my eye as they jump apart, and I can't help but chuckle. "Why don't you two go grab some lunch? I'm pretty sure I can deal with the shop for a little while." When I look over at them I see that Mel has dashed behind the counter and Ed is just standing there, like a deer in headlights. "Ed, why don't you take Mel out for lunch? It appears that the rush is over, for now at least."

"Did you want me to come back in after lunch Kami?" Mel asks me, her voice is a little husky, and I have to hold back yet another laugh.

I stand there and think for a minute, we could probably do without her customer wise this afternoon, but if she comes back after their lunch, then we can get stuck into moving these books and maybe we won't have to stay so late tonight. "You know what Mel? If you come back after your lunch, we can start on packing up these books and hopefully not be here too late tonight." I smile at her, and I realise she was holding her breath. Did she think I was going to tell her not to come back because I caught her and Ed doing what? Nothing much of anything, to be honest, it's not like they were neglecting customers or doing anything else inappropriate. I will, however, have a word with them later and tell them to try to keep their hands to themselves on my time.

I grab some boxes out from my small storage area, along with some tape and scissors, then I get to the business of sorting out these books. I serve a couple of customers in between but mostly I'm just sorting and packing, which is what Ed and Mel find me doing when they get back from lunch.

They're looking a little more dishevelled than when they left for lunch, but I don't care what they get up to in their own time. When the store closes tonight though, I'll mention what I saw earlier and lay out some rules.

The next couple of hours fly by. I'm sorting and re-shelving stock, while the other two are boxing stock up and serving customers. We're a well-oiled machine, and we've got most of it completed by the time we close up for the day. We decide to work through dinner so that we can just get it all done. A couple of hours later, I've got just a few piles left to sort through and then put away, so I tell Ed and Mel to go home. Ed argues with me, as usual, about leaving me here alone, but I brush him off.

"I'll be fine Ed, but as usual, I do appreciate your concern." He returns my smile as they both collect their coats and bags to leave. "Just one thing before the pair of you go." Now they're both looking at me worried and while I know I have to be the boss right now, I'm not mad at them at all. "I'd like a word about what I walked in on this afternoon. No," I raise my hand as Ed starts to speak and Mel starts to blush, "let me finish, please. I know what I saw when I walked in, and I know you were out of the view of any customers walking into the shop, but the fact is, I can't have you guys bringing that part of your relationship in here. This is a place of business and if you can't work together and keep your hands to yourselves, you're going to have to work different shifts."

"You mean you're not going to fire me, or Ed?" Mel's voice is barely a whisper, I've never known her to be a reserved girl, she must be worried about what I'd say.

I look between the two of them and say, "Heck no! I'm not letting anyone go. I just want you to both know that you can't be cuddling and canoodling in the shop when you're supposed to be working, that's all." Mel takes a deep breath, "I think you make an adorable couple and I can't believe I didn't realise it earlier."

"We didn't see it sooner ourselves. It just kind of snuck up on us, and well, we'll try not to bring it into the shop Kami." Ed says, but I'm standing there looking at him and he quickly says, "We won't bring it in here, I promise. It's just all so new and well, thanks for understanding K." He's got his arm firmly around Mel's waist and they look so happy, how could I possibly be mad at them?

"Did you really think I'd fire you because you've found love together? Seriously?" I ask.

"Honestly? No, I didn't but Mel was worried, especially after what we thought you saw earlier this afternoon." He says with a guilty look on his face.

"Well, just for the record, I'm not firing anyone, least of all because you're together. Just like I say, keep it out of the shop and I'll be happy." I smile at both of them and they return it. "Now get out of here and take her out for dinner, Ed. I'll see you in the morning."

When they leave I lock the door behind them and walk back to finish off the few things I have left so that the Harvey crew can get to work first thing in the morning. I'm off on another planet thinking and singing to the music I've got playing quietly in the background. I've just returned to the shop floor from putting a box out in the storage room when I hear a knock on the front floor, and I hold a hand over my heart! When I look at the door, James is standing there with a sheepish look on his face. I unlock the door and wave at him to come in.

"Geez James you just scared the life out of me!" I say, my hand over my heart!

"I'm sorry Kami, I didn't mean to scare you." He says. I'm not mad at him, it's not his fault I wasn't taking in my surroundings.

"I know you didn't mean to, but it's still a fact!" I say with a smile. I notice he's carrying something in his hand, so I ask, "What's in the bag, James?"

JAMES

"I bought you some dinner. I hope you don't mind? I figured you wouldn't have eaten yet and then I saw Ed grabbing some food and I thought if he's just getting dinner then you wouldn't have eaten either. Then he spotted me and told me that he and Mel hadn't long left you here to finish off a few things and confirmed my suspicions." I cough and start to get slightly uncomfortable because Kami hasn't said a word and I'm thinking that maybe I've overstepped, and I should have just left well enough alone and gone home, but I couldn't. Not when Ed told me she hadn't eaten yet. I just want to spend some more time with her, alone. Without the eyes of the whole fucking town watching our every move. "I'll just leave this here and let you get back to what you were doing. I'll see you in the morning I guess. We'll be here at 7.30 to get things sorted before you open the shop and we can work around the shop being open after that." Kami still hasn't said a word, she's just standing there, looking at me like I've grown another head. Well, a head is *growing*, but she doesn't need to know that, because it happens just about every time we're in the same room. When she still doesn't say a word, I nod and move towards the door I came in.

"Ahhhhh," Kami coughs and then says, "Where are you going, James? I thought you bought us dinner? You did buy *us* dinner, right? It's not all for me, is it? Because I have to tell you, I don't eat that amount of food in a week, and especially not in one night!" she says with a giggle. I stop walking, but I don't turn around. I don't know what it is about this woman, but she sends me completely off my game every time we talk to each other, even more so when we're not talking at all and it's about our physical attraction. I can't seem to find my footing around her. "Please, stay. Join me for dinner, you did bring it by after all." There's a short pause then she says, "Unless of course, you've already eaten, in which case, thank you for thinking of me and bringing me food."

I didn't eat already, something kept telling me not to because I wanted to eat with Kami, and I know her well enough already to know that she wouldn't have stopped for dinner when there were just a few more things to get done. "Ummmm no. No, I haven't eaten yet, I thought we could eat together?" I turn to look at her and all I can see is the broad grin spread across her face that's making her beautiful eyes sparkle.

"So, you'll stay and share this with me then? I just have to put this box out the back and then this pile of books on a shelf and I'm done." She looks back at the area we're starting in on tomorrow and then frowns, "but I haven't moved those old shelves out of your way. I meant to get Ed to help, but I sent him and Mel off to get dinner." She looks so adorable when she frowns, thinking. Fucking hell, who am I? I never think anyone's adorable, not even little kids!

"How about I go put the box away while you shelve your books where you want them? Then we can sit down and eat. The old shelving can be taken out tomorrow Kami that was included in the quote." My voice comes out gruff, making me sound annoyed and I guess I am, just not with Kami, more with myself.

"If you're sure James, that would be great. Thank you." She sounds a little unsure, but I've already lifted the box and started walking towards the storage room. I feel like an arsehole for how I spoke to her, but I can't explain to her why my mood has changed.

When I walk back out to the shop floor, I can't see Kami, so I call out to her. Either she didn't hear me, or she decides not to answer me. She wouldn't have left with me walking around her store would she? Then I start to panic and wonder if something happened to her in the two minutes I left her alone. Did she lock the front door after I came in? Did someone come in after me and now she's gone? I get back to where we were standing and notice that the food I bought in, is now gone. Where the hell did she go? Then I hear it, just a faint voice singing to the quiet music playing and I follow the sound. That's how I find her, in her office, singing along to the music, shaking her arse a little and setting the containers of Chinese take away down on her desk.

She squeaks and holds her hand on her chest again when she turns to find me leaning against the doorframe, just watching her. "Oh, James, you scared the heck out of me again!" she says with a laugh. When I don't move, just stand there and watch her, she starts to become nervous. "What's the matter, James? Why don't you come on in here and we'll eat the food you bought in?" She makes a move to sit behind her desk, but as she walks past me, I reach out and take her hand in mine. The overwhelming desire to touch this woman has had me in knots for most of the day. Now that we're alone, I can't resist the urge to hold her, so I don't. I slip my fingers between hers and pull her closer to me. I can see her breathing change, her chest suddenly rising and falling harder and her mouth is slightly open, her eyes, fucking hell, her eyes are half closed and yet so dark with desire.

They're my fucking downfall. Her eyes. I pull her body flush with mine, our lips barely millimetres apart. "I'm going to kiss you now Kami Parker," I tell her, I'm not asking for permission, but I am giving her the chance to back away, say no to me, but I'm fucked if she does because I want her! When she doesn't move, I lean the rest of the way in so that my lips touch hers. Finally. I start off slow, I don't want to spook her again but when she sighs, causing her lips to open a little more, I take full advantage. My tongue runs along her bottom lip and then pushes passed her lips and tangles with her tongue. I groan and kiss her harder, her taste is intoxicating, and I can't stop. I don't want to stop. Kissing Kami is like nothing I've ever done before, it's heaven and hell, all at the same time. It's so damned fucking good and I just can't get enough of her, and it drives me fucking insane.

The hand that isn't holding tightly onto hers, dives into the hair at the base of her head and tangles itself in there, making it easier to pull her even closer to my own mouth. Our teeth clash and still, I want to be closer to her. I need her more than I've ever needed anyone before. Her free hand is running up and down my back, but it stills, resting at the base of my neck, just resting there. I can feel her skin on my skin there and heats us both up more. I use our hands that are twisted together to pull her hips closer to mine, I need to feel her closer to me. When her hips slam into mine, she gasps, and I smile against her lips. I know she can feel my hard-on pressing against her hip. My cock is trying to get out of the confines of my jeans because there isn't much room left and there sure as fuck isn't any give in the fuckers, but I'm not having sex with Kami in her office. Well, not the first time we have sex, anyway.

I pull my hand from hers and squeeze her butt cheek as she brings her knee up to my hip and grinds harder against my cock. We're both just grunts, groans and moans now, but when her hand reaches out to feel my cock through my jeans, I pull away, my breathing is ragged and heavy. With my hands resting on her shoulders and my forehead on hers, my hips angled away from hers I say, "We have to stop Kami, if we don't I won't be able to and I don't want to do this here."

Her hands are running up and down my chest, so I grab her wrists and bring them both to my lips, kissing her palms. If she keeps touching me, I'm going to do something that I won't so much as regret but wish I hadn't done. Here, yet. Kami's not ready yet and I don't want to push her too fast. "You don't want me? That felt like you wanted me, James." She says with a pout. Holy fucking hell! There she goes again, being all adorable. With any other woman, I'd walk away right now, but I know she's not doing it to get me to do what she wants.

I take her hand run it over my cock so she can feel how much I want this, want *here*. I watch the blush creep up her cheeks. "Does this *feel* like I don't want you sweetheart?" she shakes her head no, "I guess you've got your answer then. The fact is, I don't want to have sex with you in here, in your office, even after hours."

She looks down at the floor and says, "Oh, well OK, I understand." But I really don't think she does.

I place a finger under her chin and gently raise her face until her eyes meet mine and then I say, "The first time we have sex will not be in an office, or lounge room. It will be in a bedroom, in a bed where we have privacy and I can take as much time as I want, as I need, to take all of you in. To savour every part of your body. Do you understand me, Kami Parker? I will kiss every inch of your skin and then go back and lick it all. Yes I mean *all* of it, sweetheart." I leave light kisses along her collarbone, neck and jaw as I speak. I feel her shiver and she rolls her head to the side to giving me easy access to her neck, and I take full advantage. "I want to get to know your body. Map it so that in my mind I can wring every last drop of pleasure from you. Every. Single. Time. We're. Together." I say between kisses on her neck, collarbone and shoulder.

I plant one more light kiss on her lips, then I take two steps back until we're not touching at all. Her eyes shoot open and she looks at me in frustration and need. I have to leave her wanting more and if she needs me even half as much as I need her, then we're going to explode when we finally get together.

Chapter Nine

KAMI

We settle in at my desk to eat dinner and even though we're chatting amicably, I can't say I'll remember anything of what we've said. My head is a mess of physical want and need. I can't help it, I keep thinking about all those promises he made. What he's going to do to me when he gets me into his bed. Or my bed for that matter. To say I can't wait is a freaking understatement! He makes me feel like I've come apart at the seams and only he can put me back together. Excited isn't a strong enough word to describe how I'm feeling, it's more like hot, needy and desperate for his touch. Any touch to be honest even if his hand brushes my arm or leg my whole body reacts.

"Kami. Sweetheart are you OK?" I hear James ask. I'm not sure how to answer him, am I OK? What was he saying? I got lost in my daydream of *finally* having James after all of these years. I can't believe it's even a small possibility! "Kami?"

"Hmmmm. Sorry James, what did you say?" I look at him, and realise I was staring blankly at the wall behind him, seeing nothing but a haze of lust!

"Kami are you sure you're OK?" he sounds worried, but I'm not going to explain to him that I was daydreaming about him taking me to bed, because even though I'm sure he'd take it as a compliment, I'm not ready to share those thoughts. Not yet anyway.

"Yes of course. I'm sorry, I was lost in my thoughts." I smile at him, hoping to smooth things over.

"What thoughts would they be Miss Parker?" he asks. He's got his sexy smirk on his kissable lips, there's a twinkle in his beautiful light blue eyes.

It's almost like he knows what I was thinking about, but he couldn't, possibly.

"Just thinking about the work that you and your crew are going to start for me tomorrow. I actually can't wait, I'm so excited to finally make some of the changes I've had planned for so long." Now it's my turn to smile like an idiot.

"You've got plans for more changes? I didn't know that, I thought this was it. What other things do you have in mind?" he asks, and he really does seem interested but still, I'm not used to guys wanting to know anything at all about my 'little shop' so I deflect.

"I have some more ideas, yes but I'm not ready to move on them yet."

"Do these plans include a superbly talented carpenter to help you with the work, by any chance?" he says with a laugh but I'm looking into his eyes and he's deadly serious. I decide to try to keep it light though because I'm not making any promises and I'm definitely not accepting any, right now either.

"I don't know when I find one I might just ask them to help me out," I reply with a chuckle and look down into the bowl of what's left of my dinner. Suddenly the bowl is out of my hands, on the desk and James is kneeling in front of me. I didn't even hear him move for goodness sake! "What the heck James? How on earth did you manage to move so fast?" I can't help the squeak of my voice, he's surprised again.

"Are you serious? You don't want to use my business or my crew again to help you finish your renovations?" he asks, and I can see it in his eyes, he's seriously hurt.

"I haven't even seen how you guys work yet James, maybe you won't fit my business as well as we think," I say, looking deep into his eyes, he doesn't even blink. So I look down at my hands, "I haven't shared any of my other thoughts and ideas with anyone, James. No one. I just want to go one step at a time and well, who knows what will happen when this project is done. I may not even do any others."

"You haven't even told Eddie about your other plans?"

"I haven't told anyone James. I only recently told Ed about the ones you're starting tomorrow." I stop speaking and then look back up him. "Why you do care if I tell Ed or not, and why are you suddenly calling him

Eddie again? I thought you'd gotten over whatever it was between the two of you? I won't have you two doing that stupid 'I'm a bigger man than you' dance again. Not while you're working in *my* shop. It's my business and *my* employee, not yours." I push him off me and stand up. I brush past him and walk out of the open office door.

As I walk out of my office, I hear the front door rattle. "Argghhhhhh!" I scream!

James comes running out of the office, "Kami, what's wrong, what happened?" he yells then follows my stare and see's exactly what's wrong. There, at the front door stands Ed, looking rather embarrassed now, but still motioning for me to unlock the door. I unlock the door, and usher Ed in.

"Holy crap on a cracker Ed!!!!! What were you thinking?" I say just as James says, "Fucking hell Ed, you just about gave us both a fucking heart attack! What were you thinking?"

"I'm sorry Kami, James. I was just checking up on you K because I saw the lights were still on as I walked passed on my way home. I *thought* you were still here alone. I didn't know you would walk out of the office at the same time as I was about to knock on the door. Talk about surprising a guy!"

"I surprised *you*? Holy crap Ed, at least you knew I was *here*." At least he has the decency to look a little flustered about the situation.

"Yeah, I'm sorry. I guess I really didn't think it through properly, but I didn't want you to be here by yourself this late. I would have thought you'd have finished up those last couple of things ages ago." He looks at James and then back to me.

"I did finish them a while ago Ed, James bought me some dinner and we were eating in my office."

Ed nods looks to James and says, "OK, well I'm sorry to interrupt, I'll let you get back to your dinner." He looks back at me and says, "I'll see you in the morning then. The usual time or did you want me to come in a bit earlier seeing that the Harvey crew will be here?"

"We'll see you tomorrow at the usual time Ed, I'll give you a call if I need you to come in any earlier. If that's alright or did you have plans?"

"Nope, I'm free to come in early over the next few weeks, whenever you want me to."

"Thanks Ed," I say and walk him back to the door.

Which he opens and says, "See you tomorrow guys, enjoy the rest of your night."

"On that note, I think it's time for me to go home. We both have an early start tomorrow and I need some sleep." I walk back into my office, expecting to have to clean up our mess, only to discover that James managed to do that before Ed scared the life out of me. So, instead of cleaning up, I grab my bag and my jacket and meet James at the front door.

He watches as I lock the front door, "You know I've done this on my own for a number of years now James. I don't need, nor do I want, a bodyguard or someone looking over my shoulder to make sure I'm doing everything right. I was doing it before you came along, and I'll be doing it long after you're gone." I didn't mean to sound harsh, but it's the damn truth! I've been looking after myself for years, and even though it feels nice to have someone who gives a toss looking out for me, I don't *need* someone to do it. He needs to understand that.

"I know that sweetheart, but while I'm here, I want to take care of you."

While he's here. He didn't argue that whatever this is has a time limit. Even though I've already told myself that, to hear him all but confirm it, well it kind of hurt. I wouldn't call James a manwhore like a lot of people in town do, he's not his father, but I can't remember the last long term relationship he was in. That's none of my business anyway, he's here to do a job, that job isn't me, but if I can get some of my fantasies ticked off, then I'll be a very happy woman. I just have to remember, it's not forever.

JAMES

When I'm gone? I wasn't planning on going anywhere. Apparently, Kami doesn't think I'm hanging around. I have to admit, I'm hurt by her assumption that this thing between us has an expiration date, it's been brewing since we met in high school. Although it's been a very slow burn, it's still been a burn. I'm going to have to convince her that she's it. There is no one else for me that's when it suddenly hits me. Kami Parker is it for me, my forever. Now I just have to convince her that I'm not going anywhere.

I walk Kami to her car. This isn't how I was hoping tonight would end, but it is what it is. "Good night Kami," I lean into her and place a light kiss on her cheek. "Sleep well sweetheart, I'll see you bright and early in the morning." Without another word or a backwards glance, I leave her at her car and walk myself over to my truck, get in and drive home.

Definitely not how I saw tonight ending.

I pull the truck into my garage and slowly move myself into the house. I have some work I could, *should* be doing but I don't have the inclination, nor the desire to do any of it. Instead, I grab a beer from the fridge, park my arse on the couch and turn on a replay of the latest football match. I'm not really that interested in the game, so in the end, I start channel surfing to see what the hell else is on, but there's nothing so I turn the TV off. I've already finished my beer, so I chuck the empty into the recycling and walk into my bedroom.

I'm almost naked when I notice my phone vibrating across the side table and grab it. I forgot that I'd put it on silent while I was eating dinner with Kami because I didn't want us to be interrupted, that went well for me. I unlock the phone, open the messages and start reading them.

Kami: *Hey James, thanks for dinner. I can't remember if I said that already*

When I don't answer in a few minutes, there's another one and then a few more that quickly follow.

Kami: *Did I do something to annoy you?*

Kami: *Goodnight James, I'll see you in the morning*

Kami: *That's if you're still working for me*

Kami: *Dang! I meant doing the work I want you to do*

I can't help but chuckle. She's flustered and wondering what the fuck just happened. Good! So am I and I'm still trying to work it out.

James: *Kami, you did say thanks for dinner and you're still welcome*

I'm taking a few minutes to work out exactly how to word my next text when my phone vibrates in my hand.

Kami: *So you ARE still talking to me then? I thought the radio silence was because I'd annoyed you somehow*

James: *Radio silence was because I was having dinner with a beautiful woman and I didn't want to be interrupted so I put my phone on silent. I hadn't change it back yet. I probably wouldn't have until the morning either because I'm getting into bed*

Kami: *So, how come you answered me then? ..... did you say you're getting into bed?*

James: *I noticed because it skittered across my side table. Yes Kami, I'm stripping down to nothing to go to bed*

Did I do that on purpose? You bet your fucking arse I did. I want her to imagine me naked, in bed, doing whatever her imagination wants me to be doing.

Kami's turn for radio silence!

James: *Goodnight Kami, I have an early start and my new client is a ball-buster, so I need some sleep.*

I can't resist getting in a last dig at her! Then I turn off all the noises and vibrations, go to the bathroom and get into my bed. Alone and naked, thinking of a certain woman and her beautiful eyes that reflect the sunlight. I drift off to sleep, seeing her beautiful face and thinking about all the things I want to do to her luscious lips and that curvy body of hers.

KAMI

I don't know what to say to answer that text! He just told me he's naked and getting into bed and I can't help but imagine just what that would look like! Does he snuggle into the covers, or is he an arms out sleeper? Maybe he's one of those guys who gets too hot and the covers are lying sexily along his hips, showing off that body that works hard and showing just enough happy trail to make you wish you could see to where it leads?

If I'm going to get any sleep, I have to stop thinking about James being naked and his happy trail leading down to what I know he's packing. I know because I felt it when he pressed up against me at his house the other night and then again tonight. Don't think for a second that I've stopped thinking about it either. With the way the man kisses, I'm going to assume he knows what he's doing when it comes to sex. I just don't want to think about all the 'experience' he's had to get that knowledge.

Geez, I just burst my own bubble with that thought. I send James a good night text, wait a few minutes for him to return it and when he doesn't, I decide it's time to get some sleep. Tomorrow and the next few weeks are going to be flat out and I can't allow myself to get distracted by James.

IN MY DREAMS THAT NIGHT, James and I have no reservations about getting into bed together and letting the hot and heavy chemistry between them flow.

James kisses the skin he reveals as he removes every piece of clothing except my underwear, then he picks me up, wraps my legs around his waist and walks me over to the bed, where he lowers me down to sit on the edge of the mattress and then gently pushes my shoulder, making me fall back on the bed, my feet on the floor. His eyes are a molten dark blue, staring down at me, holding promises of making all of my dirty thoughts come true. Then I shiver as he falls to his knees, never once breaking eye contact and kissing up my right thigh, moving over my pussy where all I can feel his hot breath, then kissing down my left thigh. His teasing is almost killing me, and I reach out to grab his head to drag him to where I *need* him. He dodges my movements easily and chuckles, as he grabs both of my wrists in one hand and rests them on my stomach, making his head just out of my reach and impossible for me to move my hands. My frustration builds, making my hips wiggle around and my legs to wrap around his shoulders, trying to drag his mouth to where I need him.

He chuckles, "What's the matter, sweetheart? Do you need something from me?"

"Argghhhh James!!" I ground out. "Pleaseeee!"

"Please what, sweetheart? What do you need?"

"Just, please James!" I just need him to touch me, I don't care if it's with his finger, his tongue or his cock, I just need *him*. "I need you."

"You need me to what, Kami? Come on sweetheart, tell me. Use your words." He chuckles.

"Touch me! I *need* you to touch me. Crap! Please, just touch me." I beg, while my whole body trembles with need.

"Like this Kami?" He runs a hand up and down my thigh and while his touch his amazing that's *not* where I need him to touch and he damn well knows it!

I growl and lift my hips up off the bed, trying my hardest to get closer to him and I can feel his hot breath on my pussy again, but he still doesn't touch. "James, please. I need you, I need you to touch me." I pant out between frustrated breaths.

"I *am* touching you Kami."

"No James, you're not!" I yell at him, this time he doesn't just chuckle, he throws his head back and roars with laughter. I free my hands from the one he's been holding them captive in and start to sit up. If he's not going to touch me, then I'm going to start touching him and making him crazy. Screw this shit! "Oh. My. GOD!" I scream at the top of my lungs and fall back to the bed as his mouth lands on my lace covered pussy, as he rubs his tongue across my lips and clit. Before I know what's going on, he's moving the lace aside and has plunged a finger deep into my hot, throbbing pussy .....

"Hallelujah, Hallelujahhhhhh." Rings out and wakes me from the *best* dream I've had, well since the last time I dreamt about James touching me! I hit the off button on the radio and lay back into my pillows.

Perfect song, crappy timing. I'll be screaming hallelujah once I finally get my hands on the body of the real James Harvey, not this damn dream version.

Chapter Ten

JAMES

When my alarm goes off the next morning, my cock is in my hand and my thoughts are on Kami. I've got business to tend to and there's no way I'm mixing it with pleasure, not today. So, I roll out of bed and head for the shower. A cold fucking shower! I need to prove to Kami that she can trust me to do all the renovations and any changes she has in mind for the shop in the future and not just for the continued business either. After 5 minutes of the cold shower not working, I give in and turn up the heat. In more ways than one! The woman drives me crazy, in every fucking way and all I have to do is picture her beautiful face and my cock twitches in my hand and starts leaking precum on my fingers, making sliding my hand up and down it even easier. I close my eyes, lean a hand on the shower wall and just let myself go. It's better than walking into her bookshop with an erection as hard as steel! It wouldn't be very professional of me to walk around a work site with a hard cock all fucking day!

At least that's what I'm letting myself believe as my hand rubs up and down my cock, my eyes closed tight and think only of sweet Kami. When I imagine hearing her say, "Fuck me James, fuck me hard," that's breaks my restraint. Those words coming out of her sweet and unswearing mouth, is all I need to unload all over my shower wall. Jesus. She's killing me, seriously killing me. I need to get laid, but I'm waiting until she's ready for me. I'm hoping she doesn't make me wait too long, I'm burning with the need to feel the warmth of her pussy wrapped tightly around my cock... but she's more than worth the wait.

I take a deep, shaky breath and clean down the shower, then myself. As I get dressed, I can't help but wonder what the day ahead holds. Kami hasn't seen me working, or as a boss and I can't help wondering if she'll like this version of me. Not that it matters, she's employed me to do a job and that job will be completed to her satisfaction. No matter what happens between the two of us away from the job.

I shake my head as I grab my keys and wallet, ready to head out the door. I have to leave those thoughts behind and get to work. Business James has to rule this morning, otherwise, nothing is going to get done!

I'm relieved to see my crew waiting for me when I arrive at Kami's bookshop. By the looks of it, they haven't been there for too long and Jeff offers up a coffee to me. "Morning boss."

"Thanks for the coffee, Jeffrey." He nods, he's stopped trying to get me to call him Jeff, he knows I call him Jeffrey to stir him up and the more he protests, the more joy I get out of it.

"You're the last person I expected to see here this morning, Joe, especially first thing in the morning. It's an early start for you." I don't even look at him, I'm pissed off he thinks he needs to be here. It's not like he knows how to handle tools, powered or not. He's a hazard to everyone and himself, around any kind of tool. He *never* gets up this early for anything.

"Just thought I'd swing by and check on the new project. Is there a problem with that?" He asks, with a little bit too much attitude for my liking! This is *my* business, he handles my finances, my contracts.

"There's no problem, Joe, I just don't know why you've got such an interest in *my business* all of a sudden." I glare at him and then turn to my guys. "OK guys, first thing this morning I want the rest of the demo and removal done *before* the shop opens for business. Once that's done we can look at the plans and set up the beginnings of the build." There's a few mumblings of yup, no worries and OK boss. I made sure to tell the guys to park out the back of the shop so that we didn't take up any customer parking and Kami's car is already parked there, so I know she's inside waiting for us.

I start to walk towards the door, and it opens suddenly and then Kami's standing there, right in front of me, looking like an angel in the morning sunlight that's rising in the sky, making her hair look like it's made of copper.

"I was wondering if you guys were going to stand out here talking all day, or if you planned on getting some work done today." She says it with a bright smile on her face and laughter in her voice.

The guys all chuckle, drawn in by her just like I am. Well, all except Joe, he goes to speak but before either one of us can say a word, Billy, the youngest and newest crew member speaks up, "Well Miss Kami, if you open that door and show us where we're working, we'll be happy to stop chatting with the boss man and get to work."

Kami giggles, fucking giggles at the little fucking charmer and replies, "Come on in Billy, Jeff, Frank, I've got some coffee ready to go and there's even some cake with your names on it!" The guys all groan and rush into the back of the shop, which gets another laugh out of her, before she looks back at me and smiles. "Good morning Joe, can I get you some coffee too? Will you be staying? I wasn't aware that you worked for James." She may have been speaking to Joe, but her eyes never left mine.

"No, you're right I don't work for James. I just thought I'd swing by this morning to check out the new project he's been so busy with. You must have him making a few changes in there Kami, he can't seem to concentrate on anything else." Joe says.

"Well, aren't you a good friend checking in to make sure he's not working too hard this early in the morning, on the first day of said project?" She answers him, again without breaking eye contact with me. "I'm sure it's nothing he can't handle, so unless you're supervising today or are in some desperate need of a coffee, I need to get back to work. I'm sure you can understand being that you're so busy with *your job* these days." She smiles at me, "I'll see you inside James," then turns around and walks inside without once looking at Joe.

"What the fuck was *that*?!" Joe says with indignation.

"What was what Joe? I think what you mean to say is, 'I need to get to my own job, so see ya later James.'" I say with a chuckle. "Kami only said what I was about to dude and she said it a lot nicer than I was going to." I shake my head at his look of surprise, "I don't know why you have such an issue with Kami, me working for her or spending time with her, but you need to get over it. It's happening whether you like it or not and you don't get a say in how I run my business either. If I was doing something that would kill it financially, yeah sure speak up but I'm not, so let it go."

"I'm not worried about your business, man, that's on solid ground." He says without hesitation.

"So, what's your problem then?" I ask, wanting an honest answer.

"Honestly?" He asks, and I nod my head. "I don't want to see you get hurt, man. This girl, woman, she could hurt you, and it would affect your entire life. I know how long you've liked her, remember?"

"Yeah I remember, and I also remember, that we're both adults and we know what we're doing. No one's rushing into anything here, so I need you to get off my case. You can get off Kami's while you're at it too, she's never been who you assumed she was, not in school and not now. So back the fuck off."

"You're right, you're a grown man, who knows his own mind, but that doesn't mean I can't have your back. Don't get me wrong, I don't think she's going to hurt you on purpose, I just know she has the potential to hurt you like no one else could."

I nod my head, "I understand that, but if that's the case, then I think I've got the same kind of potential to do the same to her and I have no intention of doing that to her or myself for that matter."

Joe looks at me for another long few minutes, then nods and says, "OK, I guess I'll talk to you later."

"Talk to you later Joe." I agree. He gets in his car and leaves, but I don't wait to see if he leaves, I walk in the back door to the shop. What do I find when I get in there? All three of my guys, eating cupcakes, drinking coffee and staring at Kami like she hung the moon, the stars and sun for them! "Unbelievable!" I mutter.

Kami who heard me come in looks over at me with a huge grin on her face that I can't help returning. None of the guys have noticed that I'm standing there yet, and I can't say I blame them. The woman is truly captivating, but I can't have her distracting them all day. We haven't even started working for her yet and they're drooling all over their work boots!

"All right guys, come on, cupcake time is over. We've got work to do and so does Kami, so let's all get to it!" The guys look at me like I'm intruding on their time, that is until they see the look on my face and realise that

I mean business. This is after all *my* business and I'm their boss, not Kami. "We need to dismantle some shelving and get all the rubbish cleared out of here before the doors open." There's a chorus of yes boss and thanks for the cupcakes, as the guys wander off.

"I'm sorry James, I didn't know how long you were going to be talking to Joe and I wasn't quite sure where you wanted them to start, so I gave them coffee and cake." She looks adorable as she apologises but I can't let her get to me. This is still a job even if it is for the sexiest woman I know.

"They knew where they were starting Kami, Jeff should have known better, he's worked for me long enough and has led more than enough projects to know what he's supposed to be doing." She looks at me like I've wounded her. I'm wondering if my tone was too harsh, but after last night's change in her tone, I can't help it. "We're here to do a job Miss Parker and we'll get it done for you. We'll be professional while we do it, all of us." I walk over to the guys to get to work without giving her the chance to comment. I know I'm behaving like a jerk, but I can't help it. After her not-so-subtle hint that I'll be gone in a few weeks, I'm not really feeling too generous.

KAMI

I watch James walk over to his crew and start dealing out the workload. I'm not sure what changed last night but something did. He's not being nasty, just, professional I guess would be the word I'd use. I can't help but wonder if it's because I didn't give him the go-ahead for any other changes I'm thinking about or whether he's just being this way because the guys are here. It could be whatever Joe said to him outside too. I know Joe isn't my biggest fan, honestly I'm not his either, but I know they're as close as brothers and I can't help but wonder if Joe said something to make James change his mind about us.

I'm standing at the counter 'working', entering stock into the computer system and pricing books, instead I'm watching James work. He's working with the guys taking all the shelving apart, getting it out of the shop and into the back of a truck. There's a relaxed camaraderie between them all, but the guys listen when James speaks. It's amazing to watch as the guys seem to be willing to follow James' lead. Even Billy, who told me before James joined us this morning that he's only been working for James a few months, seems to be ready and willing to do whatever job needs to be done.

It's a different side of James and I can't help watching him do his thing. I'm so busy watching the guys, and James, that I don't hear Ed come in the back door or realise that the shop has to be ready to open in ten minutes until Ed speaks!

"Morning boss." Ed stops at the counter and stares at me. "Ummm boss, you OK? You're staring off into ... ohhhh OK. I get it now!" He grins and puts his belongings away in the back room.

"What do you get?" I ask him.

"I see your man working away and you staring at his flexing his muscles." He laughs at my shocked gasp.

"I am *not*! I'm entering stock into the computer, Ed I've been pretty busy this morning, actually. Thank you very much!" I sat with as much innocence and shock as I can muster. How dare he insinuate that I haven't been doing any work. I've been working hard this morning, I think to myself as I look down at the pile of books I've finished off to find there isn't as many as I thought there would be! "Well, I'll let you open the shop and I'm going to my office to get some paperwork done."

Ed smiles at me and shakes his head, "Sure boss, you go get some work done."

When I get to my office, I sit down and stare off into space. Thinking, dreaming about all of those muscles James was using this morning and how he could use them with me any day. I can hear James and crew out on the shop floor, laughing, joking with Ed, and getting the job done, but it's James' voice that rumbles through my body and makes me shiver. I shake my head to clear it and look down at the papers on my desk. I need to get Mr Harvey out of my thoughts so that I can clear up my desk. I pick up my pen with renewed determination, I can't let my business slide while James is here working. So, I push the man's body out of my mind and start working through the pile of papers sitting in front of me.

I don't know how long I've been working when there's a light knock on the office door and I look up as I call out, "it's open." Only to see the face of the man that's starring in all my dreams right now, day and night. Let's face it, he's had a recurring guest role for a number of years now. "Hey James, what can I do for you?" I say with what I hope is a smile and not a frown. A frown simply because the man is distracting, and it'll take me some time to get my concentration back once he leaves the office, and get more work done.

"Hey Kami, I'm just coming to remind you of your contractual obligations." He says it with a smile on his face that looks like he's just won the lottery.

"OK, which obligation would that be Mr Harvey?" I say, hoping that I look as serious as I'm trying to be but really, I'm just happy to see his face.

"The one where you have lunch with me every day while I'm working here." He raises his eyebrow at me in question, almost daring me to deny it, to back out.

"Ohh yes, OK, well you can come back and get me at lunchtime then Mr Harvey ..." I start but he interrupts me.

"Miss Parker, it's almost one in the afternoon. You've been in here for a few hours now and I think you could use the break."

"Ohh no, that means Ed needs his break first, so you can go on ahead.." I don't get to finish what I'm saying when I'm interrupted, again.

"Kami, Ed's had his lunch, Mel came in and he took off but he's back now and there's the two of them manning the shop floor. Let's go grab lunch." How on earth does this man know more about my business today than I do? I can't believe I let all of that slide while I was locked away in my office. Avoiding watching James work is bad for business but great for the paperwork I've always hated doing.

"Let me just grab my bag and we can get going then." He nods as he opens the door a bit more, waiting for me, "I just need to speak to Ed before we leave."

JAMES

I take hold of Kami's hand and pull her towards the door, so we can get out of here, "James, hang on a minute, I need to talk to Ed." She says.

"Eddie and Mel are fine, aren't you guys?" I ask barely taking the time to look their way. I hear Ed chuckle and say, "Kami, we're fine, enjoy lunch."

When I finally get the woman out of the shop and headed towards the café, I turn to look at her and she's beautiful. She's looking slightly confused like she's just woken up and it's fucking adorable! "Kami, sweetheart, are you OK?"

"Hmmmm?" She says as she turns to look at me and when her eyes connect with mine, I'm done for. The gold flecks in her gorgeous eyes are glimmering in the sunlight, fuck listen to me getting all poetic. "I'm sorry James, but you kind of startled me and dragged me out of the shop. I was actually working, and it's taking me a few minutes to catch up, that's all." She answers with a bit annoyance in her voice.

"Well, it's not like I wasn't working too sweetheart, but you promised me lunch every day of this build and I plan on cashing in on each and every one of them."

Her face softens, and she says, "I didn't mean to imply you weren't working James, I just meant that I need a minute to take a breath, a minute ago I was drowning in paperwork, now I'm outside, the sun's shining and I'm going to lunch with a handsome man.."

I stop us right there in the middle of the footpath and an older guy almost walks into Kami's back. "Sorry," he mumbles as he walks around us.

"You're right, I'm sorry, but you needed a break, and you promised me lunch." I smile, hopefully with the full-on charm assault I've been told I have. "Did you just call me handsome?" I ask, and I'm rewarded with watching a blush creep up Kami's throat and into her cheeks. Fuck, she's adorable. I can't help but wonder if she'll blush like that when I whisper dirty things in her ear as I push my cock into her body. Yeah, shouldn't have had that thought while standing in a public. It's getting uncomfortable in my jeans again, then she looks down because I try to adjust myself and my cock jumps towards her. When I see her throat move as she swallows, hard, I grab her hand, turn around and walk even faster to the café, "Sweetheart, you're gonna have to stop looking at me like that or we're both going to get arrested for indecent acts in a public place." My voice is hoarse and low, full of desire.

Kami doesn't speak until we've found a table to sit at and we order lunch. She hasn't even looked me in the eye since we sat down. "Are you OK Kami?"

"Yes. I'm sorry James, I didn't, I don't..." She hesitates, and I can see she's struggling to find the right words to express her feelings. I completely understand her struggle. Although, I *can* put my feelings into words, I don't want to freak her out, it's too soon. "Why are we here James?"

I don't understand. "We're here for lunch Kami," I reply with complete confusion.

"No, not here in the café, I mean why are you here? I don't mean for lunch, I mean why are you here with *me*?"

Is she fucking crazy? Why wouldn't I be here with her? "I'm here because I want to have lunch Kami, with you. I want to get to know you, the grown-up Kami. The gorgeous woman who has her own business and I just, I want to know you." I don't know how to explain to her *why* I'm here because I've always just wanted to know her, be with her and grown-up Kami is every man's wet dream but that's not why I'm here. I'm here because I've always felt this pull towards this woman, even when we were kids. "I'm here because I want to spend time with *you*. I want to get to know you, Kami." She looks at me like she doesn't believe me, how can she be confused about someone wanting to get to know her? I reach across the table and take both of her hands in mine, gently rubbing my thumbs over the backs of them. "Kami, I'm not going to lie to you, I'm attracted to you and the thought of getting you into my bed does things to me that I'm not going to get into right now, and while you may think that's the end game here, it's not just about sex to me." I hope my face is showing her the honesty in my words because I know what the rumourmongers say about me and my sex drive. While I'm not going to deny the sex drive and stamina rumours, what man in his right mind would? I am trying to let her know that I'm not the man-whore the gossips like to portray me as either.

"You sure about that Mr Harvey?" she says with a cheeky grin. Fuck, she's killing me.

"I am 100% sure Miss Parker." I send her back my sexiest smirk, at least I hope I do! "Look, Kami, I know we didn't really know each other at school." She cuts me off with a loud laugh that attracts glances from almost everyone in the café.

"That's how you saw high school? We '*didn't really know each other*'?" she says in a deep voice that I'm guessing her trying to imitate my voice, which is fucking adorable. "James, we didn't even come close to knowing each other. You were in a completely different league to me, you still are and we both know it. Joe sure knew it then, and he knows it now too." She says, still laughing.

"I'll give you the fact that we hung out in different circles, but I was never out of your league if anything it was the other way around. I was just the guy from the wrong side of the tracks, getting through school so that he could make a life for himself. Away from the prejudices of others, especially teachers. You were the smart, cute, reserved girl that was always too good for a guy like me." She looks at me in surprise. "Maybe you're still too good for a guy like me, but I still want to find out, if you'll give us a chance."

"High school wasn't like that for me James, I always just wanted to fade into the background. My family were all about the limelight and I never wanted any of that. Most of the other kids gave me a hard time for being quiet. Once Joe gave me that horrid nickname, I wished I was camouflaged every day."

Josie coughs as she reaches our table, "I have your lunch guys, I'll just put it here and leave you guys to it." She puts the plates on the edge of the table, there's no other space because I haven't let go of Kami's hands yet, and when she goes to pull away, I hold on tighter.

"Kami." I wait until she's looking up into my eyes, hopefully, she can see the honesty there and will believe the words I'm about to say. "I don't give a flying fuck what Joe thinks, OK?" she gives me a slight nod. "In fact, I couldn't care less what anyone else thinks about you, me or us together. All I care about is you, what you believe and what you want." I search her eyes and I think I can see the spark in them that I want to see. "I want this Kami. Us. Whatever that means, and I don't care about anyone else's opinion about it, it's our business."

"OK James." She says, barely above a whisper but I'll take it for now because I need it.

I release her hands and pass over her lunch. Before she can take a bite though I say, "I would never lie to you Kami, can you trust me?"

"Yes." Again, it's barely above a whisper but she's got a beaming smile on her face, so I'll take it. For now.

Chapter Eleven

KAMI

James' words stick with me for the rest of the week. We spend the first week of the renovations getting into a routine. I open up the shop for the Harvey Carpentry crew to get started on work early, while I potter around the shop floor getting things done and by getting things done, I mean making it *look* like I'm doing stuff. In reality, what I'm doing is watching James get stuff done. He's so sexy, watching him discuss and direct his guys around. Watching him work, well watching his muscles work as he builds and moves stuff around. I'm not sure if he realises what I'm doing, he's not once mentioned it, he just gets on with business as usual. In order for me to get anything useful done, I need to be in my office or without James in my direct vision. Even then, sometimes I find myself staring off into space while sitting at my desk and I can see his body working and moving. If I try to shelve books or check stock, I find myself gravitating to wherever James is, whether he's working or not. Even if the man is just standing there discussing a change or particulars of a job, I find myself looking at him.

James may not be noticing but Ed is, and he's very amused. He tends to ask James to lift or move something any time I'm nearby and then all I can hear is his chuckle as I watch in rapt attention. When Mel is in the shop, she tells him off for hassling me but to be honest, I quite enjoy the beauty of James' moving body so I'm not complaining.

As for James, he's been a man of his word. We've been going to lunch every day, and he holds my hand or touches me any chance he gets. Josie is a lot friendlier towards us when we talk to her. Well, she's much friendlier towards me since she first saw me with James, before my lunches with James, we were cordial with each other, but now, we're almost friends. Don't get me wrong, I'm not going to the movies with the woman any time soon, but we're on a level playing field now. I'm sure that's got more to do with me being with James than just being myself but I'm OK with that.

Every night, after his crew and my guys have all gone home, he walks me to my car and kisses me until I can't breathe and am left barely standing upright. Then he puts me in my car and sends me home. He hasn't asked me out to dinner, over to his place or invited himself to my house since our talk on Monday and I'm starting to wonder if I did something wrong. Maybe I sent him the wrong signals? Either way, every night I get home, eat, have a bath and then give myself an orgasm by my trusty vibrator, wishing it was James between my legs. Every night he sends me a message;

James: *Goodnight sweetheart, sweet dreams*

If only he knew just how sweet my dreams aren't, he might change his mind about sending me home alone! If only he knew how he starred in each and every one of my dreams and how freaking horny I am when I wake up! Wet, willing and wanting. That's me every morning this week! I'm sure if I called him and asked to come over, and I mean *come over*, he'd be here in a flash, but I want him to want me. I'm pretty sure he does, but he's obviously not ready to go there yet. If I'm being honest with myself, I'm not sure I'm ready to go that far yet either, but watching him work, muscles straining and getting to know him over our lunches, getting those smouldering, sexy glances of his sure are making me hot and bothered. I'm wound up tighter than a jack in a box ready to spring free!

As it is, I'm sitting in my office 'doing paperwork', but what I'm really doing is daydreaming about all the dirty things I want to do to James and hell, what kinds of dirty things I'd let that man do to me! I'm startled out of my sex dreams by a knock on my office door. When I look up, there stands the man in my dreams, looking even more sinful in reality than any version my brain can come up with. When reality beats the made-up version, there's something right with the world, don't you agree?

I smile because I'm happy to see him and ask, "What can I do for you, James?" Dang if I don't want him to say that I can lick him all over, several times I hope!

Instead, I'm greeted with a chuckle and the sexiest smile known to womankind. "It's lunchtime sweetheart, are you ready to go?" He's got this knowing glint in his beautiful blue eyes that I can't look away from. Does he know what he caught me thinking, by the look on his face, I feel like it might have been written all over *my* face, but he can't read my mind and I'm just going to go have lunch.

"Yup, I'm ready when you are." Talk about a double meaning! If only he knew that the statement *had* two meanings for me!

"Let's get out of here then, let me wine and dine you, at the café." He winks, and I can't help the tingle that runs up my spine. His smile gets wider as if he knows what he just did to me and the tingles start to flow to other parts of my body before I can stand up from my desk I squeeze my thighs together and take a deep breath, bracing myself for another lunch filled with sexual tension.

Every day this week we've gone to the café for lunch and I've enjoyed each and every one of them. The food is good but the company that's the highlight. He's been charming, genuine and funny. I've enjoyed getting to know the man he's become, not that I knew the boy that well, but getting to know the man he's become is amazing.

"Kami, did you hear me?" I smile across the table at James, I'm trying to think, *did* I hear him speak. Nope, I was too busy daydreaming about him.

"I'm sorry James, I was thinking about work," I say, hoping he can't see the lie written all over my face.

"Are you sure about that sweetheart, because it looked like the most amazing and tasty work thoughts I've ever seen. I know you love your work and the shop, but surely books can't bring that blissful smile to your face?" He smirks at me and continues with, "I'm sure it's the books and paperwork that bring you so much joy you have to press your thighs together."

Oh. My. GOD! He did see that! I can feel the blush heating up my cheeks as he chuckles from the other side of the table. I should have known better than to think this man would miss that! "Well, I was just..." dang it! What's the point, he knows so why hide anything? Maybe I can work this to my advantage and get him all hot and bothered for a change! "You know what James? You're right, I wasn't thinking about work, books or paperwork. I was distracted by other thoughts, thoughts that cause my body to heat up, tingle and throb .... in certain areas."

I can see the minute my words hit just the right spot, he shifts in his seat and his eyes darken with lust. When I see the storm brewing in his eyes, I realise what I've done, and I swallow hard. I've never been big on the dirty, sexy talk, I always feel like an idiot, but I can see what my words do to James and I want to keep going. Sort of. Then he speaks, and his voice is thick, deep and husky, full of desire. It's the sexiest thing I've heard in forever, and it makes me want him, right here, right now on the table in the café where everyone can see us. Not that I'm noticing who is or isn't in around us.

<u>JAMES</u>

Fucking hell! Did she really just admit she was thinking about sex in her office? She did, didn't she? God fucking damn it those thoughts better have been filled with me, me filling her.. I cough before I can speak to clear both my throat and my thoughts!

"Kami Parker!" I can feel my voice rumbling through my chest, "Were you getting a little dirty in that office of yours while the rest of us were sweating away on the shop floor?" I can't tear my eyes from hers, even when Josie brings our lunch to the table and speaks.

"Ahhh here's your lunch guys, just let me know if you want that in take-away packaging."

"Ahuh, sure Josie." Kami murmurs to her.

"You sure you don't want me to just do that for you two now?"

"Go right ahead, Josie." Neither of us has broken eye contact with the other, "I think we may just need to leave sooner than we were expecting." I reply.

"Yeah, just so you know, this isn't the place for public displays of, well indecent exposure, if you know what I mean?"

Kami's blush deepens, but she says, "You're right Josie, this isn't the place for this conversation. Are you ready to leave, James?"

I smile and say, "We haven't even touched our lunch yet sweetheart. You sure you wanna leave already?"

"You haven't even looked at your lunch more like it." I hear Josie mumble as she walks away to wrap up our lunch.

"I have never been more sure of anything in my life, James. I'm not hungry, not for my lunch anyway." Her eyes drop to my mouth and I can feel the blood in my veins starting to heat up. If I don't get this woman alone soon, we're both going to get into some deep trouble with the law!

We both stand up from the table at the same time, both thinking the same thoughts without speaking them. We get to the door, her hand in mine, our fingers tangled together and neither one of us seeing anyone else in the café until Josie catches up to us and says, "Hey you two lovebirds, you forgot your lunch."

"We're not hungry Josie, give them to someone else who needs them," Kami says without looking away from my eyes. How the fuck are we going to make it anywhere safely if we can't look away from each other?

"Yeah, right you're not hungry, not for food anyway!" Josie mumbles as we walk out the door. I can help the laugh that rumbles out of me.

"Do you think she knows where we're going?" Kami asks me, with a hint of embarrassment.

"She has no idea *where* we're going sweetheart but I'm pretty sure she knows what's going to happen when we get there." She giggles and finally breaks eye contact with me, "But we're all adults here right? Who cares what anyone else thinks?" I hope she's not embarrassed about others knowing that we're together, or whatever this thing is right now?

"I've just never been this openly affectionate before. It's a bit overwhelming to know that other people can tell what we're thinking, that's all. Not that I think anyone else is very interested in what we are or are not doing but still."

I let that sink in. She's not used to public displays of affection, hey? Well, she's going to have to get used to them because I won't be able to keep my hands off her for long. I've never been an overly affectionate, touchy-feely kinda guy either, but I just can't seem to help myself with Kami. I just want to be as close to her as I can be. She doesn't seem to be complaining either.

"I like touching you Kami, I like knowing you're right here, next to me," I say.

"I'm not complaining James," she says as I help her into my truck. I stand in the open door with my hands resting on her thighs. The same thighs she had to rub together not thirty minutes ago. "It's just not something I'm used to, but I sure don't want you to stop either."

I stand there, looking into her eyes for a few more minutes in silence. Looking to see if I can see any hesitation. Looking for the truth and all I can see is a woman who is happy with her decision right now. I nod my head slightly, the decision made for me, and I take a step back, causing my hands to run down her thighs and drop off her knees. Then, I close the door and hurry around to the driver's seat. I don't know where we're going or what will happen, but I do know I want this woman and she wants me. Nothing else matters right in this moment.

KAMI

I can't believe this is happening, but I think I'll die if anything stops us at this point. Dramatic I know, I'm not a dramatic girl generally speaking, but I can't help myself right now. I've been waiting for him to touch me again for what feels like so long, that I would kill anyone or anything that stopped us today!

Which reminds me, I better send a message to Ed and let him know I've got business to attend to and won't be returning to the shop this afternoon. I grab my phone out of my bag and quickly type out a brief message;

Kami: *hey Ed, are you able to close up the shop for me today, please? Something came up that I have to tend to*

Within a minute I get a reply, I have to wonder why his phone was close by and why he answered so quickly but I don't care about the why today, so I'm not going to ask.

Ed: *Sure boss, you tend to your urgent business. I'll see you tomorrow*

He doesn't know, does he? Ohhh who cares? Not me, not today.

"Everything Ok Kami? Who are you firing a text off to with those speedy fingers of yours?"

"Oh, I was just asking Ed to close up the shop for me today, I told him I had other business to tend to this afternoon," I say with a shy smile, but James' smile is anything but shy!

"Other business, hey? Urgent business?" he asks with a wicked grin.

"Very urgent business," I reply.

He groans and reaches out for me, "Move over here closer to me, sweetheart, I need to touch you." I slide over the bench seat and snuggle into his side as he wraps his arm around my shoulders. "So where are going, sweetheart? Your place or mine?"

"Mine's closer, if you want to come over?" I ask like I'm inviting him over for dinner!

"Closer is better, especially if you keep touching me like that sweetheart."

I didn't even realise what I'd been doing but now he's mentioned it, I am *very* aware of where my hand is touching. I've been absently running my hand up and down his thigh, his jeans are stretched tight over the muscle and I can't help running my hand along that hard muscle. I can feel it twitch under my touch and it feels amazing! I notice that his breathing raspy and deep, and there's a noticeable bulge in the front of his jeans. I look up into his eyes and I'm not sure what I see there. Pain, pleasure or frustration. "I'm sorry, I can stop. You look like you're in pain."

"Ohhhhhhh make no mistake Kami, I'm getting uncomfortable because there's not enough room left in my jeans. My cock is trying to push its way out of the zipper, but do I want you to stop touching me? Fuck no. It feels so fucking good to have you touching me like this Kami. I've wanted you for so long, but I think perhaps you should *try* to keep your hands to yourself just for a few minutes more, if you want to get to your place without having an accident, that is."

I can't believe that I have this effect on James. *James Harvey* is hard for me! I don't know if I can make it to my house without self-combusting either. I'm so hot and he's the star of so many of my hottest dreams and fantasies.

A minute later, we've pulled into my driveway, James has his door open and he pulls me out of the car by my hand. "Where are your keys Kami?" Crap! I hope I didn't leave them at the shop! I have a bad habit of throwing them down on my desk when I get inside rather than into my bag. I'm searching through my bag, hoping for some luck when I finally locate them. Before I can celebrate my good fortune, James takes them out of my hand and has my front door unlocked and slammed shut with me shoved up against it before I can even think. The next thing I know, his lips are on mine. Not soft or gentle like previous kisses, oh no, this time his kiss is full of need, want and desire.

Then, just as suddenly as he pushed me against the door he pulls away and takes two steps back, leaving me struggling to find my feet and my breath. "James?" I breathe out his name, I can't manage anything else. I open my eyes that I only just realised were closed and look at him, "James, is everything OK?" He looks unsure, uncertain. Does he not want this? Me? I don't move, I can't move closer to him while I'm feeling so vulnerable, "James, if you don't want to do this, it's OK, I understand." I don't, but I have to make this easier on myself.

He growls but doesn't move, the only muscle that moves is the one in his throat showing that he swallows deeply. "Oh sweetheart, you have no idea. No fucking idea how much I want this, you, us, but I don't want to be rough and quick. I want to take my time and savour every millimetre of you, but when I'm touching you, I can't control myself." He closes his eyes in frustration.

I take a step towards him and his eyes fly open, "Then don't control yourself. Take me how you want to. We can do slow and controlled later. Much later." I take another step towards him and he groans. I can see his cock straining at the front of his jeans, and he keeps making fists with his hands and then releasing them like he's trying so hard not to touch me. "I'm not fragile James, you don't have to be gentle with me, well not all the time." I say as I take another step closer to him, I'm almost in reach of him when I say, "I want you James, so bad right now that I'm throbbing all over. My clit is pounding and I'm so damned wet there's not much point in me wearing underwear anymore." I reach my hand out to touch his cheek and he leans into my touch.

"Kami, you deserve.." he starts.

"I deserve you, James. I *want* you, James. I want your cock buried deep inside my body, now, fucking me hard."

His eyes fly to meet mine, he's never heard me swear before and I very rarely do, except for when I'm hot and full of desire. He's not the only one who can do the dirty talk.

"What did you just say?" He asks, his eyes wide open and searching mine.

I smile and lean in close to him and whisper in his ear, "I want your cock buried deep in my pussy, fucking me hard."

His whole body stiffens and then, with renewed energy he's lips are on mine, "Fuck me Kami." He mumbles on my lips. Now we're on the same page and I can't wait!

Chapter Twelve

JAMES

I can't believe what I just heard! I've never heard Kami utter a swear word even when they were kind of warranted, but hearing her say the words, 'I want your cock buried deep in my pussy, fucking me hard', with such confidence and desire? Well, *fuck me*. I can't really say no to that. Without another word, I pull her body into mine and kiss her like there is nothing I want more in the world right now. Let me tell you, there's *nothing* in the world that could make me leave Kami's house in the next few hours, except a fire that we could possibly start.

"Fuck me, Kami!" I mumble into her lips.

I feel the smile pull at her lips, rather than see it, as she whispers, "That's the plan James, if that's what you want."

"I want nothing more, sweetheart," I whisper against her lips.

She sighs into my kiss, her body relaxes into mine and I can't hold back anymore. I pull her hips tight against mine and I can feel the heat between her legs on my hard cock, through her jeans and mine. Fuck! She's so hot and so ready!

"What are you doing to me, sweetheart?" I murmur against her neck as my cock gets even harder and I drag my lips down to where her neck meets her shoulder. I stop there to suck and nibble on her, hopefully, I leave a mark, making sure everyone knows she's taken, she's mine. Kami stretches her neck to the side to give me better access and moans softly, her lips right at my ear and her noises send shivers down my spine, making my entire body shake with need. My hands leave her hips and run up her sides, causing her body to ripple and I love how responsive she is to my touch. With my hands under her top and on her skin, I'm finding it hard to control myself. I lift her top up and she raises her arms above her head making it so much easier for me to get rid of her clothing.

Her lips graze my ear and she whispers, "Fair is fair you know James." Again, I feel her smile against my skin, then her hands are under my work shirt and this time it's my turn to react to the skin on skin contact with a shiver that runs all the way down my spine, as she draws her nails across my nipples and down my chest to my abs. I'm lost to the sensation of her touch, I can't concentrate on anything but her hands. My own hands have stopped moving, they're resting on her rib cage, my thumbs gently rubbing the soft skin under her breasts. Before I know what's happening, my shirt is hanging open off my shoulders, waiting for me to shrug it off. So, that's what I do and before it even hits the floor, my hands are back on her body. My hands rest on her back and pull her chest to mine, so close nothing can come between us. Except for her fucking bra, my fingers make light work of the clasp and the straps drop off her shoulders and rest at her elbows. I don't want to let go but I want nothing between us, so I lean back just enough for her to drop her arms and allow her bra to hit the floor with a soft thud.

I look up from the white lace crumpled on the floor and my breath catches in my throat when I take in her beautiful, plump rose-tipped breasts. I've imagined what those nipples would look like while I've been in the middle of a jacking off session and I'm not disappointed at all. In fact, my imagination didn't do them justice. My hands move of their own accord and start to knead her breasts and skim the outer edges of her nipples, making them stand even more erect and their surrounds to pebble. Kami rests her hands on my forearms as her head rolls back and a loud moan escapes her mouth. "Yes, James. Yes!"

"Do you like having your nipples played with sweetheart?" I don't need her to answer, it's written all over her face and the only answer I get is another soft moan. My hands move to her gorgeous arse and I lift her up, her legs wrap around my waist and her eyes open, and look deep into mine. My legs won't hold me up much longer if she keeps making all these noises, so I carry her over to the couch and sit down so she's straddling my hips.

When we're settled, I knead her breasts again, squeezing them together and pushing them up towards my mouth, teasing her with the warmth of my breath. She stares into my eyes and says, "Please James, please."

"Please what, Kami?" I ask, even though I know what she wants. Before she can answer me, I lean down and draw a stiff nipple into my mouth. I bite, lick and suck one breast while still playing with her other one. Then I swap, I mean it's only fair that they both get the same attention, right? The noises coming from Kami, are driving me insane with lust and need. The way she's moving back and forth in my lap, while her hands twist in my hair and give a slight tug with every gentle bite on her nipple, I may just make a mess in my jeans for the first time, ever. I'm pretty sure I didn't even make that kind of mess as a teenager, something I'm pretty fucking proud of, but this woman makes me lose control. I put my hands on her hips to still her, "Stop Kami!" I growl into her chest, my eyes closed tight.

"Did I do something wrong?" Her whole body stops and stiffens. Fuck! If only she knew that she could never do anything to make me not want her!

I force my eyes to open and look into her eyes that are flaming with her own desire. "No Kami." I grab her face and pull it towards mine so that I can look deep into her eyes so that I can see that she understands me. "Sweetheart you couldn't be more perfect, but that's the problem." She looks at me, confusion written all over her beautiful face. "If you keep moving in my lap like that, I'm gonna come in my pants baby and neither of us wants that, do we?"

"Really?" she asks with a sly grin. Cheeky woman, she's fucking happy she's got me this worked up! She wants proof, I'll fucking give her proof.

"Yes, really!" I grab her hand and guide it down to feel my cock. At the touch of her hand, I'm pulsing and trying to get to her. Any part of her will do, he just wants to feel flesh on flesh. "God, I want you so much Kami, even my cock is trying to get to you, anyway it can."

She giggles, the woman *giggles*, while she's cupping my cock through my jeans, for fuck's sake. I growl, and she stops, that's when I realise while I was growling, and she was giggling, she managed to open my jeans! I lift my hips up to help her pull them down and my boxer briefs go with them. My cock, free of his confines bounces against my stomach and then stretches up in search of her touch. Kami's sitting in my lap with way too many clothes on, but I can't move, because she's staring at my cock like she's never seen one before. I never considered that perhaps she wasn't very experienced, I mean at our age you expect people to have a history, but maybe she doesn't.

I open my mouth to ask when she speaks, her voice is low and husky, "Holy fuck James." She licks her lips like she's just found the tastiest ice cream and she needs to lick it. I mean I know I'm not a small guy, but I've never had a woman look at me like Kami is, like she wants to devour me and it's the hottest thing I've ever seen!

"Kami ..." I've never heard my voice sound like that before. It's husky like I'm out of breath but it's so deep that I can feel it rumbling in my chest. Kami's fist is moving up and down my hard cock and it's taking everything in me to breathe *and* not come in her hand. I feel like a teenage boy who can't fucking control himself. "You need to stop sweetheart, I can't.." she rolls her thumb of the slit in the top of my cock and I can't breathe.

<u>KAMI</u>

I'm not a virgin, I've slept with my fair share of guys. Ok, it's a handful, but I've never seen a cock like James'. I'm not saying he's the biggest I've seen, and I'm not going to say he's the prettiest either, that's insane. What I'm trying to say is that I've never met a cock I've actually *wanted* to have in my mouth as much as I want to lick his, like he's my favourite lollipop. I've never been big on giving a guy a blow job. I don't ever want them to come in my mouth, and I still don't, if I'm honest. What I *do* want is to suck James' cock to the point where he can't breathe, control himself or think about anything except getting inside my pussy and fucking me.

"James, I want your cock in my mouth. I need it to happen." I start to slide my body down his, but he stops me.

"No Kami, please don't. Not now, not this time please?" I pout at him, I never beg, especially to *give* a blow job, but I'm close to it right now. "I swear you can suck my cock later, but I need to be inside your warm, wet pussy first. Right now, preferably before I explode, which means you need to move your hand off my cock, sweetheart."

Instead of moving just my hand, I move my whole body off him, as he starts to protest I move hands down to the button on my jeans, then pull down my zip. His entire body goes stiff and his cock is bobbing up and down, throbbing. I kick off my shoes, toe off my socks, all while slowly pushing my jeans down my legs.

"Holy fuck, sweetheart!" James toes off his shoes and socks as well but before he rips off his jeans and boxers, he reaches into his wallet and pulls out a condom and throws it on the couch next to him. "Keep going sweetheart, I'm enjoying the show."

I take a couple of steps closer to him, kick his clothes out of the way and then kick mine the rest of the way off. I stand between his legs, lean down to rest my hands on his shoulders, bringing my lips to his ear, I nibble on his lobe then lick it. "Fuck me James, please." He hasn't touched me yet and I'm already dripping wet. I hear the crinkle of foil and look down to watch him roll the condom onto his hard cock. I move to straddle him again, but he stops me from lining myself up to his cock, his hands on my hips. He's ready, what's he waiting for? Ohhh ... ohhh wow!

"You're so wet Kami, is that all for me, sweetheart? Are you ready for my cock?" His finger moves in and out of my pussy, then he spreads my juices through my lips and up to my clit.

"Yes, James. Yes, yes, fuck yes!" I almost scream, he's still holding me right above him and I need him to be inside me.

"You want my cock in this hot, wet pussy do you sweetheart?" he asks as he pushes two fingers into me. Oh god! My hips jump at his touch and I start to move my body to get some relief from all the need that's coiled up tight in my body, but this other hand stops me from moving.

"Yes James, I want your cock in my pussy, I am so ready for you." My voice is strangled with need. I cry out as he removes his fingers from me but I'm groaning with relief when he pushes my hips down as he brings his up to meet me, and in one push he's deep inside my body. "Argghhhhhh! Yes!" I cry out.

"Fuck, you feel so good." He grounds out between clenched teeth. "So hot and tight." I try to move my hips but again, he holds me still with his hands. "Don't move, you have to give me a minute."

"But I need to move James. Let me move please?" I say with a whine.

Slowly he releases his tight grip on my hips, and I start to move. So slowly at first that it's barely noticeable. With my hands resting on his pecs for balance, I start to move faster, James grunts and pulls my lips to his for a deep, all-consuming kiss. Then it feels like his hands are everywhere all at once and I'm moving faster and faster above him.

"James, I'm going to come," I whisper.

"Sit back a bit sweetheart." He grounds out and then he has one hand squeezing a nipple and his other thumb on my clit and I throw my head back, hair spread out over his muscular thighs. With one hand on his chest and the other massaging my other breast I come so hard I swear I black out for a second, and all I can see are stars. "That's it baby, come for me." James voice is husky and full of restrained need. "Arghhh Kami!"

I lean down to kiss him and then whisper on his lips, "Come for me James, come for me now."

He roars his release, pumping up into me a few more times before he comes. His spent body relaxes back into the cushions of the couch and my spent body relaxes on to his. My head is resting in the crook of his neck, the only sound in the room is our heavy breathing while we both take our time to come back down to earth.

I think I drifted off to sleep because I suddenly become conscious of my body moving but I'm not moving it. "Shhhhhh baby, I'm going to take us to your bed."

"Second door on the left." I murmur into the side of his neck, I feel his chuckle rumble through my hair. I don't know why I bothered telling him, it's not the first time he's been here. It is the first time he's been in my bedroom though and suddenly I'm hoping I left it reasonably clean this morning, but then he lays me down on the bed and I don't care what state my room is in. He untangles our bodies and stands up, "Where are you going?" I can hear the panic in my voice, the fear that now that's he's gotten what he wanted, he's going to leave me.

"I'm just going to the bathroom to clean up, Kami."

"You don't need to clean up, we just got messy together."

He chuckles again and says, "I know sweetheart, but I need to get rid of the condom. Don't worry I'm not leaving, believe me. I'll be right back."

He covers me with my blankets and takes care of business. Before I know it, the covers lift behind me and I feel him lay down, bringing the blankets back down with him. He snuggles up behind me, wiggling one arm under my neck and draping the other one over my waist and dragging my body back, closer into his.

"Are we spooning now?" I ask

"Well, I forked you so it's only right that you get a good spooning," he replies, and I can't help laughing. What an idiot! He's right, he did fork me well, the best I've ever had.

"You're the best fork and spoon I've ever had, James Harvey," I say on a sigh, my eyes are already closed, and I'm drifting off to sleep.

"That's nice to know sweetheart," he says with a chuckle. "Just for the record, you're the best fork I've ever spooned Kami Parker. Now get some sleep, you're gonna need some rest for what I have planned!"

We both drift off to the kind of sleep only the truly satisfied can enjoy!

JAMES

I'm not sure how long we sat naked and tangled together on her couch before I carried her to bed, but I do know that we both need to lay down for a while and rest. I don't know what time it was when we fell into bed and I have no idea what the time is now as my eyes start to open again. I don't care what time it is, but it *is* starting to get darker, so I have to assume it's later afternoon, or early evening.

No matter what time it is, I've woken up with my body still wrapped around the sweetest body I've ever known and I'm about to drag myself away from her when I feel Kami's arse move against my groin. Now, I find myself giving even less of a fuck as to what the time is. If she's awake, she's a teasing vixen. If she's still asleep, she's a tease she just doesn't realise it. Yet!

The arm I have wrapped around her waist reaches up and moulds to her breast, causing a low moan to escape her barely open lips. I slowly pull my other arm out from under her head and lightly trace my fingers down her spine starting at her neck. My lips follow my fingers, sucking and kissing along the way. Kami's whole body is moving now and I'm going to assume that even though she hasn't made it obvious that she's awake, she is. I find out just how awake she is when I reach the perfect round globes of her arse cheeks, and I take a little nibble of them!

"Oh. My. GOD! James!" I don't give her any time to catch her breath because I run my tongue down her arse crack, over her puckered hole, dip lightly past her pussy lips and then land on her clit. She spreads her legs open for me to get better access and I push my head and shoulders in to hold her wide open for me.

I flatten my tongue and run it from the bottom of her pussy all the way up to her clit, suck on her for a few seconds and then run down and back up again. "Fuck me you taste like heaven sweetheart," I mumble on her pussy lips, she shivers from the vibrations my words cause. I flatten my tongue and run it up and down, up and down, with each up I nibble gently on her clit. She's moving so much now that I have to push a hand into her hip and the other one into her back, to keep her where I want her to be. Now that I've restricted her movements, her hands reach down and twist into my hair, her nails scraping along my scalp, causing me to growl sending more vibration through her pussy and Kami loses all control.

"James. Oh god, James!" she sounds hoarse like she can't get enough air. "I'm gonna come. Fuck me stop, don't stop! Fuck!" the sound of her cursing does weird things to me. I can feel her body starting to get tighter, ready to explode. I push two fingers into her pussy, curling them up and hitting her g-spot, while my tongue continues to lap at her. It's the fingers to the g-spot that do it and she's coming loudly. "FUCKKKK JAMES!" she screams, and my tongue is lapping up her juices.

I pull myself out from between Kami's legs and watch as she flops onto her back and tries to catch her breath. I'm still sitting between her legs, and I slap her on a thigh. Her eyes open quickly and if looks could kill, I'd be fucking dead, until I put the fingers that were just in her pussy in my mouth and suck them clean. Her eyes are full of dark desire then and apparently, seeing me lick her off my fingers gives her a renewed energy, because the next thing I know I'm flat on my back with the most beautiful woman I know straddling me.

<u>KAMI</u>

I thought I was dreaming when I first woke up. Then I remembered that James is here and that we finally had sex! Boy oh, boy did we *have* sex! I've been with a few (not a LOT but a *few*) guys, but never have I felt anything like that before. Holy shit!

Then, *then* I woke up to the feeling of lips running kisses down my back. It felt like a dream and I didn't want to wake up properly, but *then* he ran his tongue along my butt crack, and I knew I wasn't dreaming! I can't say I've ever had an orgasm while a guy has gone to town with his tongue and fingers on me before. Have I come like before that? Hell yes, but I've never orgasmed that hard before. That was mind blowing, earth shattering and extreme. He left me boneless, and then he slapped me on the leg, only to put on a show of sucking my orgasm off his fingers! Holy shit, I've never seen anything that hot before and I couldn't resist jumping on him and kissing the ever-loving shit out of him! The taste of me and him on his tongue!

Before he can catch his breath, I've shimmied down his body and I take the tip of his cock into my mouth. I run my tongue through the slit at his tip and then suck the head, he lets out the longest groan I think I've ever heard in my life! "Fuck Kami! What are you doing?"

I let his cock fall out of my mouth, look up him through my eyelashes and say, "If I have to explain that babe, I'm doing it all fucking wrong!"

"Oh, sweetheart that was a rhetorical question." He replies.

I let his cock fall against his stomach again and say, "Babe, if you can still say 'rhetorical', I'm definitely not doing it right!"

I grip the base of his cock in one hand, and slowly stroke him up and down, then I suck him into my mouth again. I look up at him just in time to see his eyes roll back into his head and close tight. His head is thrown back, pressing hard into the mattress, his hands are twisted in my hair and his body is starting to shake. I move up and down his hard cock faster and faster, my hand keeping pace with my mouth.

"Fuck Kami, I'm gonna come!" I pull my lips up to his head and suck hard once, twice, a third time and then pull away. My hand still pumping him as he bites the corner of his mouth, trying to control himself.

"Come for me babe, come on my boobs." My words break him, and he roars and comes all over his stomach and my boobs! I fall back onto my bed, I've never felt so ..... fulfilled!

I feel James move off the bed, but I can't move, and I don't know how he can muster the energy either. Then again I have no idea how long we were laying there before he moved. I hear him in the bathroom, opening and closing cupboards, but I don't care what he's doing! Then he's back and wiping my boobs with a warm, wet washcloth.

My eyes open at the gentle touch and I look up into his eyes. "I went to the bathroom to clean myself up and well, I figured you'd be feeling a little chilly with my come all over you by now and you didn't seem to have the energy to move."

I smile at him, "Thanks, babe."

"Anytime sweetheart, any time at all." He smirks. Cheeky bugger! He drops the washcloth on my bedside drawers, drops down beside me and pulls the covers back up to cover us.

Chapter Thirteen

KAMI

We're lying in my bed, lazily running our fingers over each other's bodies. Our legs are tangled together, we're facing each other, leaving light kisses here and there as we explore. The house is quiet, nothing but our quiet moans and kissing noises filling the air, when we hear a knock on the door we ignore it, but then I hear the handle turning and a voice yelling out ... "Hellooooooo. Are you ready to go out to dinner and drinks yet Kamibear?" There's only one person in this world other than me with a key to this house!

I curse up a storm. My version of swearing anyway. "Arghh holy crap on a cracker!"

"What's wrong sweetheart?" James asks, his arms are still wrapped around me like he doesn't have a care in the world. I guess he doesn't really, he didn't forget that he had plans tonight!

"I forgot I was supposed to go out with Katy tonight and I'm nowhere near ready!"

James reaches for me as I tumble out of bed in a rush, "You're not really going to leave me here and go out tonight, are you?"

"We organised this night out weeks ago, I can't cancel on her now it wouldn't be right!" I whine without looking James in the eyes.

James stares at me like I'm crazy! 'I think she'll understand why you can't go now, Kami.' He says as he pulls me back to his chest and kisses me until I can't breathe, again!

"Hey, Kam are you in your room? I hope you're decent cause I'm coming in."

"NO!" I yell out, "I'll come out there!! Just give me more than a couple of minutes, geez woman, I'm coming!"

He kisses my shoulder as I scramble to get off the bed again. Just as I stand up he says, "We both know you can do that now, don't we, sweetheart? At least a couple of times!"

I can't help blushing furiously and throw on some pants and a shirt, then walk out of the bedroom door looking completely ... fucked. Much to James' satisfaction.

I know he can hear us talking but I don't think he'll be able to make out exactly what we're saying.

"What are you doing, Kam? Are you ok? It's not like you to have a nap. Not to mention we have plans and you never flake out on anyone!"

"I'm fine. Perfectly fine." I smile at my best friend and repeat, "Absolutely, perfectly fine."

Katy starts to call me out, but we hear the bedroom door open and then the shock shows all over Katy's face, as James freaking Harvey walks into the room looking sexy as sin with just his butt hugging jeans on. Thank fuck he's done them up properly, but they're still barely hanging onto his hips. What is it about a man in jeans and nothing else that makes him look so damn sexy? Bare feet, bare chest, messed up hair and a grin on his face about a mile wide. Now that I know what he's hiding behind that zipper I can't help but drool as I watch him walk past us to grab a drink from the kitchen.

"WOW!" Katy sighs. "Well, now I understand the 'afternoon nap' Kam, you had a boy in your room and not just any boy either! James freaking Harvey!" She thinks she's whispering, but I can tell by the smirk that spreads across James' face that he heard every goddamn word!.

Before I can stop myself, I reply, "Oh that's not a boy Katy, he's all man!" Now I'm sighing like a lovesick fool too!

James leans against the kitchen counter, one ankle crossed over the other, one hand in his jeans pocket and the other holding a bottle of water to his lips. Lips that are lifted up in a sexy smirk and eyes that twinkle with mischief and satisfaction. He knows what he did to me, he knows that I'm pretty freaking satisfied after our session this afternoon. His ego isn't going to deflate anytime soon now that she's swooned over him being *all man* either.

Katy coughs and breaks the tension that's settled in the room as James eye fucks me from across the room. He's so sure of himself, he has every freaking reason to be and I know it too.

"Well, I'm going to go and let you guys .... get back to it. I'll show myself out." Katy says.

I look at my friend and say, "No Katy, come on, give me 10 minutes and I can be ready to go to dinner." I look towards James and say, "*We* can be ready to go, can't we James?"

Katy doesn't give James the chance to respond, "No Kam, dinner can wait for another day." I start to protest but Katy shakes her head. "Just shut up. I'm leaving now, you two just make sure you get some sustenance and come up for air once in a while, OK? Good."

JAMES

Katy grins like a Cheshire cat at Kami, "Take care of our girl Harvey."

"I'll look after Kami, don't you worry about that Katy."

"I don't think I need to worry about that at all!" She says out loud but mumbles, "Lucky bitch!" as she reaches for the door.

I can't help but laugh at her, Katy has always been the more outgoing and outspoken of the two of them, even in school. "Bye Katy, good to see you again."

"Yeah, nice to see you again too Harvey." She slings a look at Kami, and they have a silent conversation that I don't understand, then with a wave of her hand, she's gone.

I can't decide if the silence between us is uncomfortable or not. Neither of us has moved and Kami won't look at me, but I can see the blush that's worked its way up from her chest to her cheeks.

I put the water down, push off the bench, and slowly stalk towards her, giving her time to move away. When I reach her, I grab her chin gently between my thumb and finger, which allows me to pull her eyes up to meet mine. "What's the blush for sweetheart?" When she doesn't answer me, I keep talking. "Are you embarrassed you were caught 'napping'?" She shakes her head slightly because I still have her chin in a loose grip. "No? Embarrassed because Katy knows what we were doing, maybe?"

"A little," is her whispered response.

"Did I embarrass you by walking out here, half naked?"

"Not really, no," she whispers again, her eyes meeting mine. Searching.

"Are you embarrassed that you were caught with your pants down with me? Do you think Katy will think less of you?"

"What?" Her eyes go wide and they're searching mine to see if I believe what I just asked her. She searches a little longer to see if I believe her answer. "Never James. I would never be embarrassed to be 'caught' with you, ever. Honestly, it's just ..."

"It's just what Kami?" I need to hear her explanation, I need to know that she's not embarrassed to be seen with me. It will kill me if that's how she feels and whatever this is, will end right here, right now.

"I can't believe you're going to make me say it out loud!"

"I'm confused now sweetheart, what could you possibly find so difficult to say to me? After everything we just did to each other, how could you possibly find it hard to *speak* to me?" I can't believe what I'm hearing. "We've spent the better part of the last few weeks getting to know each other, properly."

"One has nothing to do with the other James," she says

"Well, I have to disagree with you there, sweetheart. If I can have my head between your legs, licking at that sweet pussy of yours and you can wrap those luscious lips around my cock, I don't think there are too many things that we shouldn't be able to talk about." I know it's crude, but I can't help the way I feel. Sure, I could have found a better way to say it, but then I wouldn't be watching another blush creep along her soft skin.

"Oh James, you can't tell me you have no idea. Seriously!" I stand there, not moving, looking into her eyes waiting for her answer. I'm holding my breath, I feel like this could be a defining moment for us both. She sighs, "You're really going to make me say it?" When I still don't make a move she says, "Fine! You're a walking sex machine James. One every girl and yes I do mean *every* girl dreamed and drooled over in school. No-one was immune."

I don't release her face or make a move to step away from her, "OK, so what does that have to do with this Kami? With us being here, together and Katy seeing it? Why would that make you embarrassed?"

"Because *no-one* was immune to you James." I look at her, I'm still pretty confused. "Not even me!" Yeah, still not getting it.

"I must be stupid Kami because I still don't understand what the problem is. We're adults, not teenagers and that was a long time ago, sweetheart."

"Yes, it was a long time ago and we are adults now, but Katy knows, well she knows what I was like back then."

My thumb is gently rubbing along her jawline and cheek and I'm still pretty confused. Call me dumb but I've no clue what high school has to do with anything today.

"James! Do you *really* not understand? You're not just trying to get me to admit that I had the biggest crush of my life on you back then?" I shake my head, I can't find my voice to answer her, I don't know what to say. I always watched her, wanted to talk to her, but I never thought she would ever want to talk to me, never lone have a crush on me! "Katy heard me get all dreamy over you for years and just now she walked in here and saw us. Together. Well, you like that," she waves her hands up and down to indicate my body. "And I'm 'I just had fun' messy and she can make a pretty educated guess as to what happened between us this afternoon. She knows that I dreamed about this and now it's reality. She also knows how easily you could hurt me." Kami closes her eyes and takes a deep breathe, "Look, it's simple, she thinks I'm a lucky bitch because we *all* wanted you back then and even now, I'm sure there are plenty of women who would trade places with me in a heartbeat. But the fact is she's also worried about me and thinks that I need to be careful. She also now has the capacity to compare our thoughts back then to the reality of what you look like now under your clothes, and you are far better than we could have ever dreamed up. It's not like you're an unattractive guy you know James." I don't know what to say, I can't form words, I don't even know what words to speak and Kami takes my silence for what? Me being insensitive, unfeeling? It's none of those things I just don't know what the hell to say. "Shit! This is mortifying!"

Kami pushes against my chest and turns to move away from me, I let her go because I'm stunned!

"You thought about what I might look like under my clothes in high school?"

"Is *that* what you take away from what I just said James, *really*?" She sighs. Obviously, that wasn't the answer she wanted and I'm trying to think of what I can say to save this. Today, this afternoon, was the best day and sex of my life. "Maybe you should go home. I think I need to get some rest."

"What?! No! I'm not leaving you now." I sigh and run my hand over my face in frustration and to give myself some time to think. "Kami, please don't make me leave, I want to talk about this. I want to understand what just happened." I walk to her and touch her arm gently, trying to get her to turn and look at me. "Please, sweetheart?"

KAMI

Why can't he understand what just happened? I'm not embarrassed or regret what we've done. I could never regret being with James freaking Harvey, but that's the dang point. Never in my wildest dreams did I think that this could be my reality! He was and still is, the sexiest guy I've ever freaking met. I can't believe that he's here, with me.

"James, why are you here?" I ask because I really I need to know his answer.

"What do you mean, Kami? What kind of question is that?" he asks, he looks adorably confused but I want to know why he's here, why we just had sex. If I'm just another conquest, I need to know now, so that I can walk away with my heart intact.

"You can't answer a simple question?" I look into his eyes, trying to get a read on what he's thinking but I just can't see the answers. Maybe they're not there, or maybe he's not feeling anything. "I really think you should leave. I'm going to have a shower and then go to bed."

I turn away from him and start to walk towards my bathroom when I feel his hand on mine. I hesitate but then decide to keep on walking away. I can't do this, him and me, if he won't be honest with me.

"Kami," my name comes out as a whisper, I want to stop walking but I don't. "Sweetheart, I'm here because I want to be here. I want to be with you, I don't want to be anywhere else. Running into you that day, all those weeks ago was the best thing that's happened to me in a long time."

"Yeah, so you get another contract and the girl?" It's a statement I guess, but I'm asking him a question. "I get it, once the contract is done, we're done. I really need to get some sleep tonight though, so I'd really appreciate it if you'd let yourself out."

"No," he says.

"No. What do you mean, no?"

"I'm not going anywhere."

"Well, I guess that's your choice, isn't it? I'm having a shower though and I do *not* want any company. In fact, I'd rather you be gone by the time I get out of the bathroom."

He lets my hand go and doesn't say another word as I walk into the bathroom, lock the door and start the shower. I let my clothes fall to the floor and step into the water. Steaming hot water rolls down my body and I let myself fall apart. I knew it was too good to be true. We've spent weeks together, getting to know one another, and it left me thinking that maybe he was different. That I was different, but he was just a schoolgirls fantasy. Even Joe tried to warn me, and I didn't listen. He warned me back in school and he tried to warn me this time too, but I knew better. I don't realise I'm crying until a sob breaks out of me and I lean my head against the wall and let it all out. I'm an idiot and Katy was right to be worried. I thought I could separate school from the present and my feelings from business. Now I've got hurt feelings and I have to see him every day at the shop! I screwed myself over and I feel like the biggest idiot on the planet!

I don't know how long I've been in here but once the water starts getting colder, I realise it's time to get out. Surely I've been in here long enough for him to get out of my house, he wouldn't have hung around this long. I wrap a towel around my body, then one around my hair. I unlock the door and peak out to see if he's still there, but he's not. I'm not sure if I'm relieved or annoyed. I take a shaky breath and sigh. Oh well, it is what it is. He just did what I asked him to. I guess I was hoping he'd fight for us a little bit, at least now I know the truth.

I'm looking at the floor, calling myself some nasty names for asking him to leave when I walk into my bedroom, so I don't see him at first. Not until I get a few steps from the bed, then I see movement and I let out a small squeal of surprise.

"You didn't think you'd get rid of me that easily did you, sweetheart?" he asks, without even looking up from his phone. He's stretched out on my bed, back resting on a couple of pillows up against the bedhead, dressed only in his jeans still and looking sexier than any one person has the right to.

"What? What are you still doing here? I asked you to leave." I stammer out. I can't think, I wasn't expecting him to still be here, and I sure as hell wasn't expecting him to be half naked still! Seeing him like this, relaxing in my bed like he belongs there, it's too much.

"Well, sweetheart, you had your chance to speak, but I never got mine." He looks up at me as he puts his phone on the bedside table. His eyes connect with mine and I stop breathing for a second.

I shake my head to clear it, "Fine, have your say and then leave."

"I'm not going anywhere, sweetheart."

Why do I feel like I did something wrong? I asked him a simple question and he couldn't answer it. I poured my heart out, and he said nothing, just stood there, in stunned silence.

JAMES

I almost left. When she asked me to be gone by the time she got out of the bathroom, I really considered it for a minute. Then I heard her sobbing come floating out of the bathroom and I couldn't. I realised I'd been an idiot and decided then and there that she would know, understand that this isn't a 'just for now' deal for me. So, instead of doing what she asked me to, I got comfortable on her bed and waited. I mean, her hot water has to run out eventually, right?

It took everything in me not to look up and drink her in when I heard her footsteps quietly padding into the room. I could see her out of the corner of my eye, and with her skin tinged red from the warmth of the water, still slightly damp and almost glowing, my hands were shaking with the effort it took to stay where I was. I've never had such a physical reaction to anyone in my life. I know when she's close by, I can sense her and just like the need to protect her, its instinctual, primitive even.

I'm sure she'd just love me going all caveman on her right now, I'm trying to pull her closer, not drive her further away. So instead of doing what I want to, I put my phone down and lay my hands in my lap, hoping I look casual, even though it's so far from what I'm feeling it's not funny.

"Can you at least put something other than a towel on your body, please? You're distracting me." I know I sound like a prick, but I really do need her to cover up just a little bit right now.

She rolls her eyes but reaches for a t-shirt and her underwear, anyway. When she's done, I pat the mattress beside me, inviting her to sit down. She does, but far enough away that I can't reach her without making the effort and her noticing.

Guess I can live with that, for now.

"Kami, what you told me earlier, about your feelings in school, I was surprised."

"You're surprised that all the girls had crushes on you, really James?" she snorts a laugh, it's a cute sound and that's when I know I'm fucked when it comes to this woman.

"Well no. You're right, I knew that girls thought I was cute, and I'm trying to not sound like a complete arsehole right now Kami. They were attracted to my looks and to the perceived 'bad boy' persona that my father's actions created. I'm not my father, I've never been like him, not even in school. You might think you know what I was like then, but I can assure you, you're wrong. I didn't sleep with almost every girl there, nor did I sleep with any of the teachers. Male or female." She blushes and at least has the decency to look uncomfortable with those particular rumours. Whether she believed it then or now, isn't the point. "Yeah, I heard all the rumours, trust me. Joe and I used to laugh about them, but believe me when I say, nothing hurt me more than hearing the lies that people spread about me just because they could." I sigh and take a deep breathe, steeling myself to continue. Only Joe and I know the truth and soon, Kami will too.

"So, you didn't sleep with half the school then?" Kami asks with a shy smirk.

"No, no, I did not Kami. In fact, I didn't have sex with anyone at that school. Before you even ask, no not even Samantha. Sammi and I were together for over a year and while in public we were all over each other, it was for show."

"What do you mean, for show?" she asks.

"I guess seeing as Sammi doesn't live anywhere near here and she's happy, I can tell you her secret. She'd kick me in the balls if I didn't, especially if it means I get to have a relationship with you." I cough to clear my throat, Kami lets out a quiet giggle, I guess me getting kicked in the balls is hilarious. "She's gay Kami, and she knew even back then. She didn't want to admit it to anyone back then, but we got drunk one night and she spilled it to me. We agreed to a mutually beneficial relationship, and that's what we had. Nothing more, nothing less. She was and still is, one of my best friends. She lives in the city with her wife and they have a couple of kids now, she's happy and I'm happy for her. We never even explored having sex with each other and believe it or not, I was 17 when I lost my virginity to a random chick that Joe set me up with."

"So, what did you get out of the fake relationship with Samantha then? You said it was mutually beneficial, so how did you benefit from it?"

"You know my dad's reputation. You know it followed me then and it still fucking follows me, even now. I'm a grown man Kami, with a business I built from the ground up, with my own hands, quite literally. And yet, men warn me to keep my hands off their women and women seem to think 'good with my hands' means something completely different to my carpentry skills." I shake my head, I still can't get passed my father's indiscretions, "Most of them say it all as a joke but there's always a hint of a threat or even hope behind it." I take another deep breath and figure I might as well just get it all out there now.

"So Samantha helped you by making the girls or ladies flirt with you less? You know that sounds ridiculous, right?"

"Yeah, I know what it sounds like Kami, and no, women still flirted but while I was with Sammi, it was OK for me to say thanks but no thanks. That wasn't the only thing she helped me with though. There was a girl that I had a massive crush on, and I knew she wouldn't give me the time of day. We were like night and day and I was wayyyyyy too nervous to make a move on her. I feared rejection just like anyone else, but I was also well aware of our differences on the social ladder at school and as a teenager, that kind of shit mattered. I knew what everyone thought of me and I knew they'd all think I wasn't good enough for her. I probably wasn't back then, but I'm hoping I am now." I look into her eyes, my eyes darting between hers, trying to see if she understands yet. I'm hoping for just the slightest spark of understanding in them.

"What are you saying, James?"

I reach out and gently take her hand in mine, my thumb lightly caressing the back of her hand. At least she hasn't pulled away from me yet.

"I'm saying that Joe is just as protective of me as Katy is of you. Joe doesn't dislike you Kami, he's just worried about me." This is it, this is where I put my heart in her hands, which I guess is only fair seeing as she's already done that to me. "He behaves like a jerk towards you because he knows just how long I've liked you, and how long I've wished I could ask you out. He knows how often I would watch you at school and wish things were different and now that things are different, he's worried that you'll break my heart."

Chapter Fourteen

KAMI

"Joe's worried about *me* breaking *your* heart?" I ask James. I can't wrap my head around that statement. I mean I understand it, it's exactly what Katy was trying to communicate silently before with that last look as she left us alone, but she knows how long I've been lusting after James. What does that mean? Is James saying that he's wanted me for ages as well? Is that why Joe has always been so horrible to me?

"Yes, Kami, is that so hard to believe?" I look up into his eyes, trying to see what he's feeling, is he being truthful? All I can see in his eyes is hurt and my hand starts to drop to my side because he's letting it go, I reach out for it, not wanting to lose that connection. I can see how much this is hurting him, he's used to people taking him only at face value and now, it appears like I've done it too.

"I'm sorry James. No, it's not hard to believe that you can get hurt, I know that you have feelings." I take a breath and bring our hands up to rest on his pec, over his heart. "It's just hard for me to believe that I can have that kind of power over you. Over anyone in fact. You've always appeared to be unbreakable and I know that appearances aren't everything James, but you always *seemed* to have your shit together."

"None of us had our shit together in high school Kami, no matter what it appeared like." He closes his eyes and sighs, but he doesn't disconnect our hands nor does remove them from his chest.

I can't help but laugh and say, "I don't know about that, Joe always seems to have his shit together, then and now!"

"Again, appearances can be deceiving Kami, but yes, Joe is definitely more put together than most people I know." He says with a chuckle, "he's always looked out for me, he's more like a brother than a friend, but that doesn't mean I won't tell him to fuck off. Especially when it comes to you."

"I can understand that, Katy's not just my best friend, she's more like a pain in the butt older sister who thinks she knows me better than I know myself or what's best for me."

"Exactly, except less girly." He says with a smirk that earns him a slap to the chest. "Oomph, I want to say that you hit like a girl, but that actually hurt a little and I don't want to encourage you to hit me any harder." He says with a wince, but he's still got that smirk on his lips.

"I'll give you hit like a girl! I'll have you know that I can hold my own in a fight, thank you very much!" I smack him on the chest again but this time we're laughing.

"Seriously Kami, Joe knows me better than anyone and he's just worried. Don't take what he says to you personally." James sighs.

"How can I not take it personally James, he says stuff that's pretty hurtful and he's trying to keep me away from you." I shake my head, "and I still don't understand why."

"He's trying to keep us apart because he's worried about me." he says quietly. "I've always liked you Kami. I've always been drawn to you and you've always been unattainable to me. You're the perfect girl." He holds up his hand that isn't in mine, and continues, "You may not see it that way, but you were. You were this perfect girl, smart, pretty, caring and what you thought was quiet, to me was just reserved and shy. I was used to girls being in my face all the damn time and throwing themselves at me, and yes I know what I sound like but you and I both know it's the damned truth. It's also why Sammi and I worked out well for each other. But, I've gone off track," he says as his thumb gently rubs across the back of my hand. "You were gorgeous without trying and I just felt drawn to you, but I also knew we couldn't be together. You were too good for me, I was just the guy with the sleazy dad and a bad reputation. You were the sweet girl that everyone adored even if you didn't think so thanks to Joe."

"I wasn't that girl James, far from it, to be honest. I had my own issues, I was quiet and reserved because I didn't want to draw attention to myself. I didn't want the attention, my sister caught enough of that herself and she didn't want to share it with anyone, especially me! If she had ever picked up that I liked you and if there had been *any* chance of you feeling the same way, she never would have given up on trying to get to you, even though she's a couple of years younger than you. If for no other reason than to make me feel even worse, but also because every girl at school wanted you and she'd be better than them too."

"There was only ever one Parker sister I wanted, and it was always you. You're the reason that no one else made a dent in me and the reason Sammi and I worked perfectly." He strokes his thumb along my cheek and jawline. "Joe's worried because it's always been you that's had all of me. He knows it, just like Katy knows it about you, I always watched you and hoped. I hoped like hell that you would one day see me for *me*."

I drop his hand but only so that I can place mine on either side of his face and hold him still while I look into his beautiful light blue eyes. "James Harvey, I see *you*! You are not your father! You are a gorgeous, caring, funny, sarcastic, hard-working man with his own business that has a reputation for great service and attention to detail. Your employees like working for you and work hard to earn your respect." I kiss him lightly on the left corner of his mouth, then say, "That boy you once were? He was a fighter, he was surviving the best way he knew how." I kiss him lightly on the right corner of his mouth, "The *man* that boy became, is even more attractive to me in every way."

"Really? Are you sure about that Miss Parker? I feel like I'm still chasing my tail, that people still think of my dad when they see me."

"Of course they do James, but now they're wondering how such a strong, confident man made it through the rubble that jerk left in his wake as he destroyed lives. I take a breath and lay my lips on his, kissing him gently. I want him to understand that he isn't his father, that Kevin Harvey was a sperm donor and nothing more. James made himself into the man he is today, and he should be damned proud of that man. I lean back from his lips so that I can look straight into his eyes and say, "You are *James* Harvey, not Kevin and no one, and I mean no one mistakes one for the other, ever." I kiss him until we're both breathless and hopefully, he understands that the only one whose thoughts matter are his. He has to understand that he's a better man than the man that he calls a father.

<u>JAMES</u>

I rest my forehead on Kami's, my eyes are closed, and I say, "Some days I still wonder Kami. If they see *him* when they look at *me*. Do men who hire me to work in their homes, then wonder if I'm sleeping with their wives. Do women who hire me to work in their homes *assume* I'm up for sleeping with them because of him?" The questions, they're almost a whisper, because I've never spoken those thoughts out loud to anyone before, not even Joe, not really. We've joked around about it but never really had a proper conversation.

"Have you ever slept with a client James?"

My eyes spring open, I can't believe she needs to ask me that question. I already told her that's not what I do, but then I see the look on her face. She asking me not because she thinks it's what I do, but because she wants me to realise, it's *not* what I do. "No Kami. I never have, and I will never sleep with a client. Ever. I might get a little flirty, but it never goes anywhere."

"What about me then James? I'm your client and didn't we just sleep together?" There's mischief in her eyes, but she's still seeking an answer from me.

"You're more than a client to me, you always have been Kami. If anything, I took the job with you so that I could be around you and to get to know the adult you."

"Ohhh really Mr Harvey? I'm not sure you gave me any other option than to hire your business, but just so you know, I didn't even get a second quote for the job." A smile spreads across her face, making her eyes sparkle. "In fact, I hired you so that I could get to know the adult you as well, and to watch you work. I mean I *am* a woman after all, and I wanted to watch you flex your muscles and perv on your butt all day." She laughs until she sees that I'm not. "I was only joking James, well kind of. I really didn't think it would go any further than business with us, even when you did show an interest in me, but I'm glad it has."

"Are you sure Kami? I want you like I've never wanted anyone else in my life. I can't do this with you if it's not a forever deal, sweetheart. I just." I take a deep shuddering breath, "I wasn't going to jump in with all of this now, it's too early for this kind of talk, I don't want to rush you, don't want to spook you. I don't even know if we're dating to be honest, but here we are. This conversation has lead us here and while we're talking I need you to know, I'm in this sweetheart. Heart, body and soul, I am in this with you and only you." I close my eyes, I don't think I can watch her face to see how she feels. I've just laid it all on the line to her, opened my heart without saying those three little words that are dying to be said.

"I wouldn't change anything that's happened with you for the world. You mean a lot to me, James, I know we've taken it pretty slow, until today, but if you want a label for us, we can say we're dating." She says it with a shy smile that makes me love her more than ever. Yup, I'm head over fucking tail in love with this woman, but I can't tell her that yet. Those words though, they're sitting right there on the tip of my tongue, but even I know it's way too early for that shit just yet! So, to stop the words from falling out of my mouth, I kiss her. I kiss her until I'm seeing stars. My hands have her face in a light grip so that I can take her mouth the way I want to and when she sighs into my mouth, I can't hold back. My hands leave her cheeks and tangle in her hair, my grip helping me to pull her in even closer to me.

Kami pulls back, but only slightly, just enough so that she can take a breath. Her eyes are closed, and her lips are bright pink and swollen from my kisses. Our foreheads rest against each other's, and we're trying to pull some oxygen into our lungs. I've never been more turned on or wanted any woman more than I want this one in my arms right now.

"James." She whispers, not opening her eyes.

"Yes, Kami?"

"Make love to me. Please?"

She doesn't have to ask me twice! From my position sitting on the edge of her bed, I reach out my hands and run them down her back and continue down to the back of her thighs, pulling her into my body, so that I can kiss her waiting lips. My lips only leave hers for a second to pull her t-shirt up over her head and drop it the floor. I don't give a shit where it lands, only that it's not covering her body anymore. Then slowly, I fall to my knees, dragging her underwear with me and when they get to her ankles, I lift her feet, one at a time and throw them as well. The whole time I've been looking up into her beautiful, almost golden brown eyes. I stand up, my hands on her hips and turn us around so that her back is to the bed, then I gently push her down onto the covers. I stand in front of her, letting her watch me slowly undo the button and zip on my jeans, but I don't let them fall to the floor, I only wanted to give my cock some room to breathe, because this woman, naked and ready for me makes me so fucking hard that it's painful to be in jeans.

Kami's hands reach up, but I grab her wrists, "What do you think you're doing sweetheart?" my voice is deep and raspy.

"I thought I'd help relieve you of those sexy jeans of yours, you seem to be running out of breathing room in them." Her voice is breathy, and it's sexy as fuck!

"I can take care of myself sweetheart." I fall down on top of her, one hand around her wrists, the other one stopping me from falling onto her body. When I let go of her wrists, she reaches up and runs them along my spine and I shiver. It's the lightest of touches and yet I can feel it sizzling through my veins and I need more. When she reaches the waistband of my jeans, I move my body down hers, she lets out a moan of disapproval and I chuckle against the skin between her breasts.

"Not funny James, I need you naked, now." Her hips are pushing up trying to touch mine, her hands are reaching out for my jeans and her back is arching into me.

"You will baby, you just have to wait until I'm done first." Her head rolls from side to side, letting me know all about her disapproval. "If you can't behave yourself, I will tie your hands together and you won't be able to touch me at all, sweetheart." Her eyes are suddenly wide open in surprise and looking into mine, searching to see if my threat is real. Oh, she can fucking trust me, I'll tie her up if she doesn't behave! She obviously sees the truth in my face because her hands move up my body and hold on to my shoulders. Far away from temptation! "Good girl," I say with a smile.

I grab a breast in each hand and bring her pink nipples together so that I can tease, nibble, torture and please them together. My hands massage her mounds and my lips play with her nipples until Kami's lost all control over her body and she's a wiggling temptation below me. Just when I think she might come just from me playing with her breasts, I let them go and kiss down her body, slowly sucking on her flesh every now and then.

"Ohhhh, James! Please, James. Please!" Her body is moving underneath me and it's the sexiest thing I've ever seen. She's not thinking, not controlling it, her body is just feeling *me*.

"What do you want Kami? What do you want me to do baby?"

"Arghh! James, please I need more."

"More what baby?"

"More James. Just more. More of you."

"More of me? More of me, like this baby?" I ask as I run my thumb through her wet pussy lips but only just touching her. Her body freezes, hoping that if it can stay still, I might keep going.

"James! Fuck me!" it's a scream, all be a quiet and hoarse one!

"Soon baby, soon but first I want to taste you. Do you want me to taste you Kami?"

"NO!"

"You don't want me to lick and tongue fuck your sweet pussy? You don't want me to suck and pull on your swollen clit? Really baby?" I ask, lightly running a finger through her wet and swollen pussy. "Look at that sweet pussy baby, it's all swollen and puffy, just waiting for my tongue to reach down and lick it from bottom to the perfect clit at the top."

Her body is moving everywhere, trying to get me to touch her just the way she wants me to. She's so worked up, so ready that when I plunge one finger into her pussy, she lets out a low, guttural moan that makes my cock twitch. My hand reaches down to wrap around my cock, I need to relieve some of the pressure before I fucking explode everywhere. My jeans fall to my knees, they were only just hanging on as it was, so my movement makes them fall. My eyes shut, taking in and enjoying the pleasure of having her pussy milk my finger and my hand running up and down my cock.

I open my eyes and make to let go of my cock to reach for a condom on her nightstand, only to see Kami watching me pleasure her and me at the same time. She's reaching for the condom, so I keep doing what I'm doing. "If you want me inside you Kami, you better make quick work of that condom baby," I say between gritted teeth. "I won't last much longer if you keep looking at me like that."

My words take a few seconds to reach her but when they do, they do what they were intended to do, and she moves fast. Tearing open the foil packet and reaching over to roll the condom over my cock. "Shit Kami," I say through gritted teeth and a groan, as she holds onto my cock for a few seconds too long.

"What? What did I do?" She asks, concerned.

"Take your hand away baby or I'll be coming before I can make love to you." Her hand makes light work of the job at hand and moves away.

I stand up and flick the jeans off my feet and in seconds I'm laying my body down on Kami's.

"James, please I need you inside me now!" I know how she fucking feels. So, I grab the base of my cock and guide it towards her pussy, just as the head slides past her swollen lips, we both let out low groans of pleasure. "Yes, James more."

I take my weight off her, leaning up on my elbows, with one hand I grab her thigh and hook her leg around my hip, then without waiting I plunge balls deep into her wet and waiting pussy. When I bottom out, I stop and we both take a minute to catch our breaths. "You feel so good, sweetheart."

KAMI

I can barely breathe and all I can feel, is this man. This gorgeous man inside me, hitting all the right places. The way he treats my body, I could almost orgasm right now, and he hasn't even moved inside me yet. I need him to move, but I feel like he might need a minute or two to collect himself, so I don't move. My hands grip tightly onto his biceps, my hands can't wrap around them, they're just too big!

When he starts to move, slowly, too slowly, I move my hands around to his chest and play with his pecs. When my fingers brush over his nipples, he gasps and moves harder, faster. He lets out the most guttural, feral noise I've ever heard from a man. "Do you like it when I play with your nipples, babe?"

He growls out a response to me that sounds something along the lines of, "You better fucking believe it baby, but I like you touching me anywhere."

He's slowly pumping in and out of my body and I want more, but it feels so damned good all at the same time. He pulls out slowly, and then pushes in with force, bottoming out and hitting just the right spot for me to see stars. "Ohh James, babe, I'm gonna come! Fuck me, fuck me harder James."

My words are just enough to send him bucking wildly into my body and we're both lost in the bliss. I scream out his name and he leans down, buries his face in my shoulder and growls out my name. He collapses on me and I wrap my body around him, I don't want to let him go, ever. We lie like that for, well I don't know how long for, until he moves off me to the edge of the bed and takes care of the condom. I can't move, my body is too limp. When he's done, he pulls the covers over us, tucks my body into his, holding me close. He kisses my shoulder and says, "Sleep now Kami. I have plans for later."

I chuckle quietly but I'm asleep within seconds. I feel so safe, protected and loved. Yes loved, in this man's arms and I sleep better than I have in years.

Chapter Fifteen

I wake up tangled in the most beautiful female body I've ever known. I was awake for about twenty minutes last night after Kami fell asleep. I just watched her sleep, listening to her breathing and revelling in the fact that I actually have her in my arms. When I finally fell asleep myself, I had the best dreams of my life, Kami is finally mine!

I gently untangle our limbs and climb out of her bed. I need to go to the bathroom, otherwise, I wouldn't have left her warm body for anything. I look at myself in the mirror and all I see is a smug, satisfied bastard reflected back at me! I pop my head out of the doorway and notice Kami's still fast asleep, so I decide to have a shower.

I lean my forehead against the wall of the shower, my hands resting just above my head for balance, enjoying the warm water pounding on my back. I don't know how long the hot water will last, but I'm going to make the most of it while it does.

I don't hear her come into the bathroom, but I'm not complaining when her hands curl around to rest on my chest. Her chest pressed into my back and my cock gets hard just feeling all that skin on skin contact.

"Good morning sweetheart," I say, my voice is still rough from sleep.

"Good morning sexy." She replies and I'm not going to argue with her new nickname for me. "I woke up, and you were gone, I thought for a second you'd gone home. Then I heard the shower and I couldn't resist coming in to help you get clean." I can feel her smile spreading across my back and it makes me happy. I can feel it, the happiness low in my stomach and spreading up to my chest. This woman means everything to me, and I can't let her get away. Not now that I've finally got her, and she wants me too.

"You know we better be quiet, my girlfriend might get jealous if I have another woman giving me a wash in her shower." I hear her gasp behind me, I know she said we're 'dating,' but that's just not enough for me. I want to be able to introduce her as, 'Kami, my girlfriend', not this is Kami, 'we're dating'. "There is the possibility she might enjoy having another woman in here though, she surprises me all the time with what she's got swimming around in that dirty mind of hers!"

"Is that what I am James? Am I your girlfriend?" her voice is just above a whisper and I almost don't want to break the spell, but I need her to know where I stand. What I want from her, from us.

"That's what I want Kami. I want you, just you and I want to be able to tell the world that we're together. That we're an *us*." I've turned myself around to face her and my hands are holding her face so that she's looking right into my eyes. She can't mistake that I'm telling the truth when she's looking right into my soul.

"Really? Are you sure James? Me? You want me, you want us to be a couple?"

"A couple, yeah sure. A couple of what, I don't really know yet, but yes, I want to tell the world that you're mine sweetheart."

"So, we're exclusive now?" she says with a small frown. I don't know what she thought we were before, but I haven't seen anyone else since we ran into each other in town and had that first lunch together. Honestly, it's been a while since I was seeing anyone at all.

"I don't quite know what you mean by now sweetheart, but yes, exclusive," I say, then I realise what she's just said. "Hang on a fucking minute, does that mean you've been seeing someone else while we've been dancing around our attraction to one another? You were seeing some other guy as well as me?" I can't help the anger that seeps into my voice.

"No, James, no I haven't been out with anyone else. I just, I guess I just thought you might be seeing someone else, not just me. I mean, I didn't know if you were seeing someone when we had that first lunch and I didn't know if you were seeing someone when we started.."

I can't let her finish what she's saying, I just can't! I turn off the water, the actual cleaning can wait for now. I step us out of the shower and wrap both of us up in her super soft towels. I sit down on the edge of the bathtub and pull her down to sit across my lap. It couldn't have taken me more than a couple of minutes, but neither of us has spoken and I can feel the tension rolling off her body.

"You listen to me Kami Parker, I have never cheated on anyone in my entire life. Ever. And I don't plan on starting now but that being said, I want to set some things straight with you. I wasn't seeing anyone before that first lunch, and I haven't been on a date with anyone but you since. I haven't slept, had sex, with anyone but my hand and you in the last few months." She blushes at the hint that I've taken my pleasure into my own hands! "We are exclusive now yes, but I want you to know that in my mind, we've been exclusive since that very first lunch."

"I haven't been with anyone except you, my hands and B.O. B in months. Six months if not more, probably more like closer to a year. In the last few months, you've taken all the space in my mind that I don't use for the shop."

I pull her lips down to meet mine, but just as her lips are within millimetres of mine, I stop and ask, "Who the hell is Bob?" I watch, mesmerised as her head falls back and she lets out this huge belly laugh. I didn't think my question was that amusing, she just told me she hasn't been with another guy in close to a year, but it suddenly registered that she mentioned this Bob dude and I think I have the right to know who the hell he is! Is that too much to ask?

<u>KAMI</u>

I lean my head against James' forehead and calm my laugher. He looks confused and kind of angry right now and I find it hard to keep the laughter contained. I stand up and reach for his hand when he doesn't offer it up, I grab it and twist our fingers together, then I pull him up from the bathtub and drag him back into my bedroom.

When we get there, I push him to sit on the edge of the bed. He looks damned sexy with just one of my pale blue fluffy towels wrapped around his waist. Nothing else, just him and one of my new favourite towels.

"What are you doing Kami? If you're going to show me a photo of some guy you use to get yourself off when you're alone, I don't want to see it." I look at him and he's actually got this pained look on his face. Does he really think that I'd show him a photo of another guy, one that I use to get myself off, seriously? If he showed me a photo of his fantasy girl that got him off on lonely nights, I'd be hurt beyond belief.

"It's not a photo of some guy James, in fact, it's not a photo at all," I say with a smile as I pull open my bedside drawer. I hear him groan beside me and I'm reminded of what he sounds like when I do something in bed that he enjoys, and I have to clench my thighs together, the things this man does to me! My hand stills as it lands on B.O.B, I can't help but want to tease James for just a little while longer. "You know, I'm not sure if you're ready to meet Bob. He's not used to meeting new people, he's generally for my eyes only." I say, trying with everything in me to keep a straight face.

"Now look here Kami, I know you don't have a *real* guy hidden there in your drawer, but if you don't explain yourself real soon, I'm just gonna have to leave. I can't share you, sweetheart, with anyone."

I don't want him to walk out on me so, I pull out my vibrator and introduce the two men in my life that have made me come in the last year .... or more. I may have omitted a few months when I told James how long it's been between a real man and a silicone trip to coming!

"James, meet B.O.B!" I hold my vibrator up between us, with a huge grin on my face!

"What the..! Bob is a fucking vibrator? Are you fucking kidding me Kami?" His face is, I'm not sure whether he's angry or surprised, maybe? I'm hoping he can see the funny side, I know I'm finding it pretty damn funny. "You can't tell me you've never seen one before James and I'd be even more surprised if you said you've never used one before." Before he can reply, I say, "I mean on a woman, not yourself!"

"I can't believe you call the damn thing Bob! I know what a vibrator is, I'm not an idiot sweetheart. I just wasn't expecting you to have one or to give it a name!"

"Ummm well, I *didn't* give it a name, that's just what they're universally called James. B.O.B, it means 'battery operated boyfriend.'" Then everything else he says hits me, "What do you mean, 'you didn't think I'd have one'? What I'm not that kind of woman, huh? Can't I take my pleasure into my hands? Too innocent for that kind of thing, huh? Well, let me tell you, Mr Harvey, you're not the only one around here with needs and when I feel the need, then I take matters into my hands. It's not like I have revolving doors of guys wanting to help me out when I need them to!" I can't believe he thinks I'm so bloody virginal and innocent! What did he think that I was just sitting around waiting for him to decide that the timing was right?

I'm not saying I wouldn't get upset with him if he told me he was using the image of some other girl to get off. Especially since we've been doing, whatever the hell it is we've been doing these last few weeks, but I never would have joked about B.O.B if I'd thought for one minute he'd get this upset over it. Who would have thought that a vibrator would cause so much freaking drama! I step away from him and put the vibrator back in the drawer and pull on some underwear, drop a t-shirt over my head and then let the towel drop to the floor. I don't want to show him any skin, I don't want him to see me naked right now.

JAMES

Honestly? I feel like such a fucking idiot. It never actually occurred to me that my sweet Kami would have a drawer with any kind of sex toy in it and I've never heard a vibrator given a man's name before either! Am I surprised? Fuck yeah but I can't say I'm disappointed. I have to say, even with all the drama it's caused, I'm relieved that's what she has in her drawer and not a picture of some naked stud that she uses to get herself off when I'm not around! Now I just have to find the right words to get out of the hole I just dug for myself.

"Kami, sweetheart, I'm not suggesting that you had a string of guys in the house, I'm not saying you can't have a vibrator or a million other sex toys. No, please, let me finish OK?" I ask as she opens her mouth to speak. "It's just that, I didn't want to hear about or see for that matter, a picture of some naked dude that you've been using to get yourself off. Call me a douchebag if you want, but I don't like the idea. I was kinda hoping that in the last few weeks at the very least, you've been getting yourself off with *me* in mind. Not to mention, I didn't really *think* about what you were *doing* to get yourself off, if I had of, my cock would be red raw. Trust me, because every time I've gotten myself off in the last few weeks, months and if I'm honest, probably years, you're the only image I have in my head! I was kinda hoping it was the same for you, thinking of me not you, obviously."

By the time I've started talking and trying to explain myself, Kami has put on some underwear and a t-shirt, covering up her delicious curves and making me realise just how far wrong I went here. I'm rubbing my hands up and down the towel covering my legs and wondering how the fuck I can salvage this. It started out as one of my favourite mornings ever and I wanted to take her out for breakfast. Well OK, maybe brunch, cause I'd planned on enjoying her body again before we left the house.

"I can't believe you, James. I thought you were different, that you knew me, but you're just like every other guy that thinks he knows me. Why is it OK for guys to 'take matters into their own hands', but the minute a female does, oh no, oh my god, she's a sexual being! She doesn't need a man to satisfy her, so she must be abnormal! Every guy wants a nympho until they're actually face to face with a woman who enjoys sex!"

She's really on a roll now and I can't help but chuckle at her rant. I know it's the complete wrong thing to do in this situation, but I can't help myself, she looks so fucking adorable. The minute her face turns red, and she stomps out into the kitchen, I know without a doubt, I've fucked up big time. I get up from the bed and pull on my jeans and shirt. I highly doubt we're having the morning I had planned now, so I might as well get my stupid self dressed.

When I get out to the kitchen, Kami is rattling around looking busy, but I don't think she really is. "Can I help you with something sweetheart?" I ask because it's the only thing I can think of doing.

"Nope." She says, and the 'p' comes out as a pop! So instead of speaking, I walk up behind her and wrap my arms around her waist. She stiffens in my embrace and I feel like I'm back to square one. I know it's partly my own idiotic fault, but it's a small misunderstanding, we can fix this ...right?

"Sweetheart listen to me, please?" I say softly in her ear. When one shoulder lifts slightly and then drops back down again, I take that as my cue to continue. Speaking softly still, I say, "Sweetheart, I didn't mean to make you feel ... I don't know, less than? I didn't mean to make you think that I thought less of you because you had Bob in your drawer. I just ... it was me. I didn't want to think of you getting yourself off to anyone else but *me*. I lost my mind thinking there was another guy. If that makes you mad, then I guess there's nothing else for me to say." I drop my arms to fall at my sides and walk towards the door.

"You were being stupid." She says as I grab my shoes and start putting them on.

"Yeah, I was, but that's what you do to me. You make me crazy." I say without looking up at her. I can't believe I fucked it up so soon and over a fucking vibrator! "I'll leave you to your day and see you at the shop later."

"No!" She says it so forcefully that I can't help but look up at her face. "No actually, you won't see me at the shop today James. Ed and Mel are working at the shop today. I took the day off because I have plans."

"OK, well then I'll let you get on with those plans and get to work." I don't need to go to her bookshop, the guys know exactly what they're doing. I made sure they did before we left for lunch yesterday. No, I didn't think this was where we were going to end up, the sex or the argument honestly, but I *was* hoping to spend the day with the girl of my dreams and win her over. Guess I totally screwed up that idea without even trying.

I find my jacket and start to put it on when I feel her hand on my arm and I freeze. I'm guessing this is where she lets me down gently and we say our heartfelt goodbyes. Yeah OK so I'm being an overdramatic dickhead but that's me.

"James, I had plans ..."

"Yeah, so you said. I'll get going so that you can get ready for them, I won't take up any more of your time."

"What the hell are you talking about James?" I look at her, hands on her hips, which just happen to be pulling the edge of her t-shirt up those soft, sexy thighs and I'm lost again. "James." She clicks her fingers, "I'm up here, baby!" When I finally look at her face, she's got a grin a mile wide on her face, but then she frowns. "Are you really going to leave me? You're not going to stay and spend the day with me?"

Is she for real? "What are you talking about Kami? You can barely talk to me because of a fucking vibrator and you think I want to stay here with you? You just said you had other plans for the day, plans that don't appear to include me! So, I'll go to the bookshop and get as much done as I possibly can so that the guys and I can be out of your hair as soon as possible."

"Are you for real right now? You're giving up on us because of a god damn sex toy?" she shakes her head and paces in front of the door, my exit and mumbles to herself, "B.O.B! of all the things that I thought might destroy us, I never in my wildest dreams thought it would come down to a god damn sex toy!" When she stops pacing and stares out the window, I try to escape but I'm not that lucky. "Now you're going to just sneak out of here?"

"I already told you I'm leaving Kami, no sneaking happening here."

"Is this because I *have* a vibrator?" she asks.

"God no Kami. The visuals of you using B.O.B to pleasure yourself will keep me aroused for months if not years to come." I drag my hand over my face, "I'm not even sure what the hell this is anymore, I'm not even sure I knew what it was when it began if I'm being honest!"

"What do you mean by this? Us?"

"Fuck no. My feelings for you, those I'm not even close to being unsure about. I've been sure about those for years, sweetheart. I'm not sure what this argument is about, why or how it even happened, but I feel like I need to give you some space."

"What if I don't want you to give me space James?" she asks me, and I don't know how to answer her and when I don't, she continues, "I was upset that you thought I would show you another *guy* in the first place, especially since the guy that has been in my fantasies for at least the last few months, and if I'm being honest years, is you. Then you made me feel ashamed, like I shouldn't have a vibrator to bring me some relief from the frustration of not having sex in, oh god, in sooo long James. You have no idea how long it's been for me." Kami comes and stands close to me and places her hand on my chest. I'm guessing she can feel the beat of my heart, it's going pretty fast at the moment. "Last night, and this morning," she says with a blush, "is the only sex with an actual man in the room for over a year and it's not just that the last time is a distant memory, but it was the best I've *ever* had. I've never felt that connection with anyone else. Especially not Bob, he's not re-al! Only with you." She says with a pleading in her eyes, she wants me to understand.

I laugh but not because what she said was funny, but because I feel like a fucking idiot. "I feel the same way Kami. I haven't been with anyone for months either. You've haunted my dreams and fantasies for so long and no one else has ever made me feel like I did last night. And this morning."

"Does that mean you'll stay? Here with me, spend the day with me, like I had planned?"

"Your plans for your day off were with me?"

"Who else were they going to be with you idiot? Bob? He's not much of a talker but he's definitely got good vibrations!" she laughs.

Kami stretches up on her tiptoes and lightly kisses my lips, I can't resist taking it deeper until we're both breathless and panting. I want more but she pulls away and says, "Breakfast first, then showers, not together otherwise we'll never leave the house. Then we can go out and see how the rest of the world has moved on in the last 24 hours."

With swinging hips, she walks back into the kitchen and starts up the coffee again. When she reaches up for the mugs and the curve of her luscious butt cheek flashes at me I groan and have to adjust myself in my jeans.

What this woman does to me! I'm still not sure what just happened, but I don't care anymore. Bob might get a new name I think, but it'll come in handy very soon!

Chapter Sixteen

KAMI

Something changed between us that day. The day B.O.B became the person we never spoke about. OK, so it wasn't like that at all, but things definitely changed for the better that day. In the weeks that followed, we spent our days at the bookshop, me working in my office, mostly anyway and James working on the renovations with his crew. It was like everyone else on the planet just disappeared. I don't know if Joe kept his distance because of me, or because James told him to, but either way, I barely saw him.

I kept in contact with Katy via text every day. She claims she had to check in on me to make sure 'sex god Harvey', hasn't broken me yet! I can't say it would be a bad way to go, that's for sure. I haven't told James about his new nickname, his ego doesn't need that kind of boost!

We see Ed every day, so at least he can verify to other inquiring minds, that we are definitely still alive and functioning. James' crew are almost done at my shop and I'm going to miss seeing them every day, but they have a new project to move on to, and as much as I'd like to try, I can't keep them around forever. It's not just James I'm going to miss seeing all day either, those guys are awesome.

We have lunch a few times and seeing Josie at the café on those days means that she can also attest to the fact that we do actually come up for air every now and then. Not that I'm sure there are too many people that are interested in our movements. These days when we sit down at a table, we sit on the same side, rather than opposite each other. The first day James sat down next to me, Josie seemed to revert back to being the snarky girl, like she was jealous, but when she came back with our order, it was like nothing had even happened. She was all smiles and even told us she was happy we'd worked it all out.

We didn't have lunch together every day because James had to go meet with Joe about a few things. He had to go and check out new jobs and write up more quotes as well. It didn't seem to matter though because we were having dinner together every night. Either at his house or mine, we didn't really care where, as long as we were together.

The nights, oh boy the nights together were unforgettable! Katy's nickname for James wasn't unfounded, let me tell you but I'll never tell her that. He's everything I ever dreamed about, everything I could have ever hoped he'd be.

One night, he did something so unpredictable, I never thought he would even think to do it and yet, he did, and it wasn't his worst idea. Not at all. Although, I honestly thought Bob had been retired for the immediate future, that night, he came out of the drawer and bought many, many orgasms with him.

JAMES

Knowing that Bob was sitting in that drawer of hers and not being used now, on the one hand, made me exceptionally happy, but I also kinda felt sorry for the guy. So instead of hiding him away, I decided to use him to my advantage and see just how Kami used to get off without me around. She never saw it coming, every pun intended, and I loved every fucking minute of it.

It started out like every other night, but even I didn't know where the night was going to end!

I knock on Kami's office door to announce my entrance because if I don't the woman jumps claiming that I've scared her, and she didn't hear me coming. I think it's a load of crap myself, I'm not sure how much actual work she gets done in here, especially since we put a window into her wall so that she can look out into the shop floor and get some sunlight into what used to be a dark and dingy office of hers.

"Hey sweetheart, you just about ready to go home?" I ask her.

"Hey babe, yup I just have to do one last thing and we can go." She hits a key on her laptop and then shuts it down. While she's waiting for it to do its thing, she looks over at me with a beautiful smile on her face.

"Your place or mine tonight sweetheart?" Personally, I don't care which house we go to, as long as we go together. Yeah, I've become one of those sappy bastards, but I don't care, this woman means the world to me and no-one, not even Joseph French can take that away from me.

"Do you mind if we go to my place tonight?" she asks, and I can't say no to her.

"Of course not. Let me just clean up my tools and chuck them in the truck. The guys have already gone for the day, and Ed is closing up the shop as we speak." I say, letting her know what's going on outside her office door. My guys went home a while ago, I was just finishing up a few last minute touches. We've got one more day of work here and I can admit. I'm going to miss seeing her face all day every day. I keep trying to find more things that need to be repaired or replaced but I just can't do it anymore. I was going to make today our last day here, but the guys wanted one more day too. My girl, she's got every guy in the nearby radius sucked into her orbit and none of us wants to leave her. Luckily for me though, she's *my* girl and those other fuckers can't have her!

When I walk back into the shop, I see Kami standing there talking to Ed about something, they're both laughing and even though I still feel like I want to punch him in the nose because of how close he is to her, I'm mostly over it now. I only call him Eddie for a bit of fun now. He's with Mel and I understand now that he was just protecting a friend he thought might get hurt. Funny how none of these bastards ever thought this woman could be *my* downfall though. Apparently, I don't have a heart to break! I walk up to the two of them and wrap my arms around Kami's waist from behind and ask, "So, can we get out of here yet or is there still important book business to attend?"

"This is my business James, it's all important book business..." she tries to break free of my arms, but I won't let her, she's so easy to rile up some days!

Ed laughs and says, "Go on, get out of here you two. I'm just closing up and then meeting Mel for dinner."

"Just in case you two forgot, this is *my* business and I know how to close up, I was doing this long before you two came along to boss me around," Kami says, her voice full of indignation and she's fucking adorable!

"I know this is your business K, but you're also allowed to head out early. You don't have to live here you know, isn't that what you employed me for in the first place? So that you *didn't* have to do everything around here by yourself?" Ed says before I can say anything.

I feel Kami's body relax before she speaks, and I know that Ed said the right thing, I probably would have just gotten her all worked up again. "If you're sure Ed, I mean James and I can stay and close so that you can get out of here earlier and meet Mel, because you can do that too you know?"

Ed laughs, "I know I can boss, but the fact is, Mel can't meet me until later, so I don't mind hanging around to finish up a few things I didn't finish today and then locking up. That is if you can trust me to do it?" he says with a smirk like he knows exactly what button he just pushed. I don't, so I'm interested in Kami's response.

"I thought we'd already discussed this Ed. Of course, I trust you, this isn't a matter of trust, it's a matter of you two assuming I can't look after myself or my own damned business!"

"We both know you can run your business sweetheart, that's not what we mean. I just want to get you out of here, I want *both* of us to get out of here and Ed volunteered to close up tonight. That's all, no ulterior motives OK? I just want to have dinner with you and Ed has time to kill before he can see Mel." I say.

"He's right Kami and I'm sorry if I made you feel like it was anything else. You're my boss but I also count you as a good friend and I just want to see you happy. You're normally pretty happy when this knucklehead is around, so I thought I'd close up, that way you guys could get going early." Ed says.

I feel her whole body relax in my arms and I sigh in relief. I don't want to argue with Kami, I want to take her home, feed her and then do all kinds of naughty things to her. Ohhh the naughty things I want to do to this woman's body! It's almost like Ed can read my mind, the filthy bastard because he pipes up and says, "Get your man out of here before I see things I don't want to see Kami. He looks like you're on the menu tonight and he's a man who's starving!" I can hear him chuckling as I walk Kami out the door without another word. He's right, he might just see something I don't want him to see if we hang around here too much longer.

When we get to my truck, I open the passenger door and lift her up into the seat. She should be used to it by now, but she still squeals every time, and that's why I keep doing it. I don't do it every time we get in the truck, just often enough and getting that little squeal out of her makes my fucking day.

I settle into the driver's seat and start up the truck, "So, what do you feel like for dinner tonight sweetheart?" I ask, even though I know what I want for dinner and it has nothing to do with food. Well, not unless I can spread it all over her luscious body and lick it all off, *then* I might be interested.

"I was thinking we could go to the supermarket and get something, what do you think?"

"Whatever you want, sweetheart." I grin over at her and point the truck towards the supermarket.

KAMI

James has been strange tonight since he asked me if I was done for the day at the bookstore. He seems a bit on edge but every time I ask if everything's OK, he says it great. Not fine or good, it's great! I don't get him at all sometimes, and they say women are hard to understand. He drives me insane some days.

When we get home from the supermarket, we get to work making dinner. Well, I should say, I get to work making dinner and James does his best to distract me under the guise of saying he's 'helping' me in the kitchen! As tempting as the man is, I need some sustenance *before* he gets me into the bedroom, otherwise, I'm going to pass out before he can get me to an orgasm.

"Babe, you need to stop trying to distract me, I need food," I say giggling as he spreads light kisses along my neck. "No, seriously James, I forgot to eat lunch today and now I need to eat something *before* you get to have your way with me."

He stops what he's doing and says, "What the hell do you mean you forgot to eat lunch sweetheart? Who the hell forgets to fucking eat lunch?" he asks a little too harshly. Before I can pull him up on it he says, "I'm sorry sweetheart, I just want you to look after yourself. I need to know you're OK when I'm not there, and I have to move onto other jobs this week and I don't want to, I want to be with you every day." He shakes head, "I can't stay with you every day, that wouldn't be good for us or our businesses, but

I have the overwhelming desire to just stay cocooned with you and tell the rest of the world to go fuck itself."

Wow! I can't stay annoyed with him after that speech now can I? He's such a passionate man, whether he's talking about his work, my shop, friends or us.

"I want to stay in our safe little bubble too James, but that's just not going to happen. We both knew eventually you would have to move on to other jobs and we would have to get used to being a normal couple and not be living in each other's pockets day in and day out." I say on a sigh. I don't want him to move onto another job either, especially one that might take him out of town for a day or two.

"Do you think we're spending too much time together? Are you trying to tell me we need to slow down cause I have to be honest Kami, I don't know if I can." His hands are resting on my waist and his eyes are darting between mine, trying to find my answer there. To see if that's what I'm thinking, but the truth is, I don't think I could spend less time with him either.

"No James, I don't think we spend too much time together, I just think we've been spending more time together since we got together than most couples do, that's all. It's about time for the 'real world' to step in and pull us back into reality is what I guess I'm saying. Most couples don't spend all day, every day together and then go home together every night as well. They go to work in different places and then see each other again at the end of the day. We've been lucky, and that's all about to change." I rest my hands on his strong shoulders and look in his eyes, "I'm not looking forward to those changes but they're inevitable I guess. I wish we could stay the way we are, but things change all the time James, and we just have to accept."

His face wrinkles up like he smells something rotten, and I can't say I blame him. I don't want real life breaking in just yet either, but it is inevitable. I'm just about to tell him that again when he says, "What's that smell? It smells like something's burning."

"Arghh holy crap on a cracker!" I let him go and turn around to see the dinner that was once cooking on the stove top, now burnt beyond being edible! Damn it, I guess he wins the dinner versus sex discussion then.

"Ohhh shit! Don't worry about it sweetheart, we'll order some pizza for dinner. Why don't you go get the menu and I'll get rid of this mess?" I nod and walk away. He's too distracting for my own good, I can't even cook a damn meal with him around!

I don't need the takeaway menu to decide what I want, so I give it to James and tell him what I want and tell him to order when he's ready. He's already cleaned up the mess in the kitchen, so I head to my room to get out of the clothes I wore to the shop and into something more comfortable. I know what you're thinking, and I didn't mean that kind of 'something more comfortable' but with James around, it always turns into that kind of situation.

JAMES

After I've ordered our dinner, I'm feeling a little guilty about distracting her so much that dinner was burnt beyond recognition, but when I find her to apologise, I almost swallow my tongue. I find her in the bedroom, stripping off her work clothes and getting into something more comfy, but I can't let her cover up her delectable body without tasting her. I decide there on the spot that we've got more than enough time before dinner arrives, but before I make my move, I stand in the doorway just watching her move around the room. She doesn't know I'm standing here yet and I don't want to scare her by speaking, I'm enjoying watching her too much.

I've always been physically attracted to Kami, even when we were teenagers, but the more time we spend together and the more we get to know each other, the more beautiful she becomes to me. The more I want everything, forever, with her.

"Argghhh jeepers, James, I didn't even hear you walk to the door, how long have you been standing there?" Kami's voice pulls me out of my daydream, and I smile at her.

"Oh, I've been here long enough sweetheart."

She stands up straighter, hands on hips, "Long enough for *what* James?"

"Long enough to watch your cute arse bend over." I start to stalk towards her, closing the distance between us as fast as I possibly can without making her too nervous. "Long enough to get uncomfortable in my jeans and hard as a fucking rock." I reach my hands up to cup her cheeks in my hands, staring deep into her eyes. I hope she can see all the revelations I just had before I take her mouth with mine. There's nothing else in this world like kissing Kami fucking Parker! Our tongues tangle and our teeth clash, but her lips are soft and there's a need there that can't be faked. We're both almost breathless when Kami pulls away from my lips, but I don't let her move too far away from me, we're still breathing in the same oxygen as each other when she says, "Don't start something we can't finish Harvey," her voice is just above a whisper. Like she can't get enough air to make the sound any louder.

"Oh we can finish Parker, don't you worry about that." I lean in to take her mouth again, but she stops me, and I can't help the growl that escapes me. I'm frustrated as fuck!

"What about the pizza guy? I wouldn't want him to walk in on something he doesn't want to see."

I close my eyes, trying to gain a semblance of control, "For one, who the hell is the delivery guy if he can just walk on into your house? For two, I'm not sharing you with *anyone*." I growl even louder as my lips rest lightly on hers. "For three, get that gorgeous butt over here, they're busy and won't be delivering for at least another hour."

Kami moans and I feel it vibrate across my lips, I can't hold back anymore. I take her mouth with mine once again, and she squeaks in surprise but the moan that follows the squeak, signals her surrender. As does her tongue, tangling with mine once again and I know I've got her full attention this time.

"Are you sure babe? I wouldn't want to get interrupted while I'm in the middle of ...." her words fade, as she slides down my body to land on her knees. I'm not sure how, but on the way down, she managed to undo my jeans and slide them down my legs.

"Ohh we've got more than enough time sweetheart," I say on a moan as she reaches into my boxer briefs and pulls out my hard cock and runs her hand from the base all the way to the head. She runs her thumb over the slit, there's already pre-cum oozing out and she uses that to lubricate the movement of her hand. When she wraps her lips around the head of my cock, I swear my eyes roll into the back of my head. My hands land in her hair, scratching at her scalp, just hard enough to make her moan, sending vibrations through my cock, into my balls and down my legs, making me unsteady. Then her lips are resting at the base of my cock and the head is in the back of her throat and my hips are moving without any conscious thought. Our moans and noises are mingled together until I can't breathe anymore and I'm not sure how much longer my legs can hold me up. I hook my hands under her arms and drag her body back up mine until she's back on her feet.

"But babe, I was ..." Before she can finish, I've taken her mouth again, it's an assault and I only stop it when we're both struggling to breathe anymore. Then I rest my forehead on hers, dragging in oxygen like I've run a marathon. "Why did you make me stop? Did I suck?" I can just see the smirk on her beautiful face.

"Yes, actually, you did suck sweetheart. A little too well, my legs were going to give out on me if I let you keep going." I say as I walk her backwards until the backs of her knees hit the edge of her bed and she's forced to sit down. "My turn now," I say with a smirk while ripping my shirt off over my head and watching her eyes darken further with undeniable lust!

Chapter Seventeen

<u>Kami</u>

I lay back, resting on my elbows on the bed, watching as James strips off the rest of his clothes. I could watch him undress for me forever, honestly. While I'm off in fantasy land, James has somehow managed to strip me naked without me noticing. *How* does he *do that!?* I have no clue but it's sexy as freaking hell!

I don't get the chance to catch my breath, before he's on his knees beside the bed, hooking my ankles over his shoulders and bought his lips within a breath of my pussy lips. He's looking up my stomach, his normally pale blue eyes are dark and stormy. Full of lust and desire. He's making me squirm with just a look! This man is something else. He quirks an eyebrow in question, but I can't be sure, my brain is struggling to keep up. "James, please!" I don't even recognise my own voice, it's so raspy and sexy.

"Please what sweetheart? What do you want me to do?" I can feel every word he speaks, his breath puffs out against my pussy and it adds to my desire.

"You know what I want, James."

"I do but I want to hear you say it." I want to, but I can't, he knows it too. "Eyes open sweetheart and looking at me," when I find his eyes, I melt a little more and he continues in a deep, husky voice that I can't resist, "Tell me, sweetheart. What do you need me to do?"

"Nugh, I want.." I mumble out. "Damn it you know what I want babe." Glad that my voice is full of the frustration I'm feeling.

"Ohhh I *know* what you want Kami, but I *need* to hear you say it." He growls out.

"But whyyyy?" I whine.

"Because, Kami, it's the sexiest thing I think I can ever hear when you ask, *beg* me to do dirty things to you. You normally hold all that back, but when we're in the bedroom, your dirty side comes out, and it's only for me and I love it!"

I can't resist him anymore. The words, mixed with his breath on me I can't take anymore. My pussy clenches, searching for relief, so I give in. "Fuck me James. Fuck me with your mouth. Fuck me with your tongue. Fuck me with your fingers."

He doesn't need any further invitation, without hesitation he drags his tongue through my pussy lips, starting at the bottom working his way up to just below my clit. My throbbing fucking clit that wants all of his attention right now. My hips jerk, trying to get him to go where I want him, but he just goes back and starts the torture all over again! His flat tongue spreading my lips open each and every time, but he stops short of touching my clit and my entire body is buzzing, shaking in anticipation.

"Jamessssss," I growl out in a voice that I didn't even know I had!

He pulls his mouth away from me and looks directly into my eyes, "Yes sweetheart. Is there something I can do for you? I'm a little busy right now, but I'll see if I can accommodate any requests."

"Ohhh holy fuck!" How can he be so flippant right now? "James. I need you to," he runs a finger along my lips, spreading my juices up and down, up and down.

"What was that, sweetheart? What did you need from me?" His voice is so, fuck! I can feel it rumbling through his chest, the vibrations are running up my thighs and into my pussy. My pussy that is already tingling with need and clenching around nothing, searching for something, anything to grip onto for relief.

Just when I think I'm going to pass out, I feel a finger slide into my pulsing pussy. Before I can feel any release though, it's gone again. "What the fuck, James!"

He plunges two fingers back into my pussy and then he takes them out again. In hard and out slow and tortuous until I'm about ready to kick his butt and make him let me come. As if he senses my need, he curls his two fingers up and his thumb hits my clit, causing my hips to lift up higher into the air. My hands grip on tightly to my boobs and I scream out my release.

"Is that what you wanted sweetheart? Did you finally get what you wanted, your orgasm?"

The bastard has crawled up my body, and he's kissing the sensitive skin on my neck just below my ear. I can feel the grin on his face, the satisfaction is coming off of him in waves. His hips are resting on mine, my legs have dropped to rest around his waist. We're chest to chest and he's resting on his forearms, his hands twisted in my hair, as his hips start to move against mine. I've barely come down from my orgasm when he groans in my ear, "Fuck Kami, my cock needs to be inside you. Now."

"Well, what are you waiting for? Fuck me James, I want your hard cock pounding into my pussy. Bring us both to climax this time."

"Fuck me if that potty mouth of yours when you're turned on doesn't do the craziest of things to me. When you let go and this foul mouth starts, it makes my cock even harder." I scratch my fingernails up and down his back, grabbing hold and squeezing his butt cheeks, before I starting the scratching all over again. "I can't wait, sweetheart, I need you now."

"You have me babe. Fuck me. Now James." He reaches over near the lamp on the bedside table and grabs the condom I didn't even know was there. He rolls it onto his cock and before I can take another breath, he slams his cock into me in one smooth move. He takes a few seconds to gather himself and then he starts to move. Slowly at first, taking his time. Making sure we're both climbing up to the brink again before he starts moving faster, harder. I can feel my body reacting again. Tingles start in my toes, making their way up my legs. Just when I think I can't take anymore, James pushes himself up and off my upper body, just enough that he can bring his mouth down to my nipple. He sucks it into his mouth, runs his tongue around it and then nips at it, before sucking and licking it again.

My breathing is rough, and I don't know how much longer I can hold out. When he swaps over to my other nipple, I'm done within seconds. "Ohh fuckkk! James, I'm gonna.. I'm gonna come babe. God, please don't fucking stop!"

"Come for me, sweetheart. I won't last much longer."

It only takes one more hard thrust and I'm seeing stars. Screaming his name as he kisses me with more passion than I've ever known. Then his mouth leaves mine to rest just on the shell of my ear as he roars out his orgasm.

James collapses on top me, his face resting in the crook of my neck, leaving tiny kisses in his wake. I'm falling in love with this man. I already had a kind of love for the younger version of him and the more time we spend together, not just in the bedroom, but getting to know one another as well, I fall a little deeper. I watch as he walks to the bathroom to get rid of the condom, I do love to watch the man walk away. When he comes back with a warm washcloth and cleans me up, I fall even further.

Who the hell am I kidding? I'm not *falling* in love with James Harvey, I'm already in too deep. I'm in love with James Harvey, not the boy he used to be but the man he is now. I'm in deep, deep trouble!

JAMES

When I've finished, I drop the washcloth onto the bedside table. Kami watches me intently, not saying anything the whole time, and I can't help wondering what's going on in the head of hers. What is she thinking? I just can't tell what it is that's got her wheels turning. I lean down and gently kiss her lips, her soft hands come up and cradle my face as she gently returns the kiss. This kiss means something, it's intimate and loving. I feel like something has changed, there's a charge in the air that I can't describe, and I don't understand it. I'm about to ask what's going on when there's a knock on the door.

I reach for my jeans, pulling them on as I start to walk out of the room, when I get to the door I turn around and look at her, "Keep that thought, I'll be back in a second after I've dealt with the pizza guy."

"You're going to greet the pizza guy like that?" She looks me up and down, her gaze heated. "Shirtless, with your jeans barely done up and your cock still a kinda hard?"

"It might be a pizza girl," I say trying to get a rise out of her, but she just rolls her eyes. "Anyway, I'm sure the pizza guy has seen way more interesting things than my half-naked body sweetheart."

"There's not much that's more interesting than your half-naked body babe. Unless we're talking about you being completely naked!" she says on a breathy sigh as I leave the room.

I hear another knock and yell out, "Keep your shirt on, I'm coming."

Which earns a loud laugh from the bedroom because, yes I see the irony, me being shirtless and all.

"Hey man, sorry I didn't know if you heard the first knock. If I don't deliver the pizza, I get my arse handed to me .... "his voice peters off as he looks at something behind me. "But if I had that waiting for me, I wouldn't be answering the door for pizza either. I'd say have a good night man, but you're already living the dream," he says as he hands over our pizza.

I look over my shoulder to see what caught his attention, I see Kami and my breath gets caught in my throat. No wonder the poor kid was choking on his tongue! "Yeah, thanks man, have a great night," and I close the door in the kid's face. I'm not trying to be rude or cut off his view, well not on purpose anyway. I'm a little distracted by the vision standing in front of me, to the point where I almost drop our dinner. Wouldn't that be great, two ruined dinners in one fucking night, both my fault!

"Are you OK James?" Kami asks like she doesn't know that she's every guy's wet dream standing there in nothing but my work shirt and her underwear. Messy, just fucked hair and eyes that have that satisfied kind of twinkle in them.

After a few minutes, I find my voice and manage to reply. "Sweetheart, you almost made that poor kid swallow his damned tongue when you came walking out here looking like that." I wave my empty hand up and down in the air between us, indicating her!

"Oh OK, so you mean you can walk out here shirtless, but I can't walk out here pantless? I mean I'm more covered up than I would be if we went to the beach. Your shirt is pretty long on me, it almost hits my knees, that's longer than some of the skirts I wear."

I hear her talking, but I don't really comprehend what she's saying. The sight of her standing there in front of me in just my shirt and her lace underwear is breathtaking. "Kami, sweetheart, you can walk around your house or mine for that matter, in not a stitch of clothing if that's what you choose to do, but you took that kids breath away. He pretty much called me a lucky sonofabitch, and he's right. Abso-fucking-lutely right. You look like sin walking around in only my shirt and your underwear. Your face is glowing and so are your eyes, your hair is a mess and you *look* like a just fucked sexy hot." I watch as the blush creeps up her neck and into her cheeks. I place the pizza box on the coffee table and reach out to hold her face in my hands, "You are everything Kami. That kid just saw what he hopes he can have in his future. I sure hope he finds his Kami, everyone should find their version of my Kami." Then, I kiss her. Gentle, loving and I hope it tells her everything I wish I could say to her.

<u>KAMI</u>

I have never felt more loved, or more wanted. No man has ever made me feel the way James freaking Harvey does. Even when we were kids there was something about him that drew me to him and to find out that he felt a similar pull towards that's just mind-blowing!

"What about dinner? The pizza will be getting cold babe." I mumble against his delectably soft lips. I don't want to pull away, which is why I'm trying to make him do it, because I'm hungry. I feel the huff of his breath against my lips and I hear the low sigh of a man resigned to not getting his way. "You know you need to feed me every now and then, right? I mean a girl needs food every once and awhile to keep up with your demands."

James' hands drop to my shoulders and he pulls all the way back from my body. I'm already missing his touch and that drives me crazy. His pale blue eyes are staring into mine, I don't know what he's trying to find in them, but I smile, and he nods his head slightly. Obviously, he found whatever it was he was looking for and he smiles tenderly back at me.

"Alright, sweetheart let's eat. Give you that energy boost so you can keep up with what I've got planned for later." With that, he turns to the pizza, but I don't think he missed the shudder that passed through my body at his promise for later.

We sit on the couch, eat pizza and watch a movie. What movie? I have no clue, because the only thing I can concentrate on is the gorgeous man sitting next to me, the promises he made for later and how I'm in deep, deep trouble.

This man, us, this relationship, if it ends, it has the potential to shatter me into tiny pieces that will never be able to be glued back together. Perhaps it's inevitable, maybe this relationship was never meant to be forever, and I've set myself up for this heartache, but I can't regret it. I've never felt more loved, accepted and at peace with myself. Ever.

Even if I'm not his forever, he's mine! No one else will ever measure up to James Harvey.

JAMES

Sitting here on Kami's couch, relaxing and just enjoying her company, is like a dream come true. It's just so easy. No airs and graces are needed, it's just us and we're comfortable. I couldn't tell you the name of the movie we're watching. I picked an action flick that I'd already seen with the express purpose of just being able to sit here, stare at the screen and enjoy just being. I can count on one hand the amount of times I've done this with a woman ever in my life. My mother doesn't count and well I don't know if I would count Sammi either because we were just friends, never lovers in any way and Joe was always with us, anyway.

When the pizza is finished, and Kami curls herself into my side. Her head is resting on my shoulder, my arm is slung around her shoulders and we're just staring at the TV. I'm pretty sure neither one of us is watching the movie, but it's nice to be just sitting here, relaxing together.

I realise just how relaxed Kami is when there's an explosion on the TV and she doesn't jump. Her breathing has slowed down and when I look down at her face, I see that she's fallen asleep. I pull the blanket she's got thrown over the back of her couch, down and cover her up and sit back to watch the rest of the movie. I'll move us both to the bedroom when the movie's over.

I rest my head on the back of the couch and close my eyes for a second. I'm tired, Joe might think that the work we're doing in Kami's store isn't much, but he's wrong. It's still physical labour, something I can assure you Joe tries his hardest to avoid.

When I open my eyes again, the movie is long over, and Kami is still asleep on my shoulder. She can't be comfortable laying like that, so I decide it's time for us to move. I gently slide myself out from under Kami while trying to keep her head from falling down onto the couch cushion. When I get to my feet, I slide one arm under her knees and the other around her shoulders and lift her up. She startles at being moved, so I whisper in her ear, "Shhhhhh I'm just taking you to bed sweetheart."

"Mmmmm take me to bed James, I've always wanted you in my bed James Harvey. This can't be real, Katy is going to pee her pants!"

I chuckle because I realise she's not even awake. "You dreaming sweet or sexy things about me Miss Parker?" I whisper in her ear.

"Sexy dreams, they're always sexy dreams when James Harvey is involved, but you know that, right? Cause they've been happening for years." She murmurs to me, and just like that, I'm hard, again!

"Fuck Kami what you do to me!" I groan under my breath.

She's still in just my shirt and her underwear, so I pull back the covers and put her down on the mattress and just take her in. I can't believe I have this woman in my bed, well her bed technically, wanting *me*. I shake my head and walk around to the other side of the bed, drop my jeans to the floor, crawl in and curl my body around hers. She sighs and relaxes into me. I'm in heaven but if she wiggles that cute butt of hers against my cock one more time, she's gonna be awake and moaning, cause a man can only show so much restraint!

If I didn't know better, I'd think that she heard my thoughts because she finally stops moving and I can relax. I can relax with the woman I love, sleeping in my arms and knowing that in the morning, when I wake up, she'll still be in my arms.

Yup, I'm in love with Kami Parker. I'm in so deep I *should* be scared, but I'm not.

Chapter Eighteen

JAMES

I wake up the next morning when I feel movement next to me. I'm not used to having anyone else in the bed with me, even after all these weeks of staying with Kami. I'm not complaining, it's nice waking up to her warm, sexy body in my arms. Except she's not in my arms right now, well not properly, she's trying to untangle herself from my arms.

"Where the fuck do you think you're going, sweetheart?" I grumble without even opening my eyes. She lets out a squeak as her body jumps slightly in my arms, and I chuckle against her shoulder. "Well, you gonna answer me or do I have to tickle it out of you?"

"No! No tickling!" She squeals and tries to get away again. "You scared the crap of me, James, I thought you were asleep!"

"I picked up on that sweetheart, but you still haven't answered my question." I still haven't opened my eyes or let my grip on her hips loosen either. "Well?"

"Why do you need to know? I was awake, and I thought I'd let you sleep for a while longer. No big deal." She answers me, but she can't look me in the eye. I know because I've cracked one eye to open to watch her face, and she's looking at the mattress. She's hiding something, but I don't know what.

"What's wrong Kami?" I ask, my eyes completely open now and looking right into her beautiful face, not letting her get away from me.

"Nothing is wrong James." She blushes, seriously blushes! What the hell is she up to and why doesn't she want to tell me? "Do you *really* need to know?"

I nod my head, "I'm not letting you go until you tell me where you're off to in such a rush."

"Geeeeez James I need to pee, that's why no tickling and why I need to go ...now!" she says as she wiggles out of my hands.

I let her go because I can't keep my grip on her hip, I'm laughing too fucking hard!

"I'm so glad you find this funny!" I hear her mumble as she runs for the bathroom. "You're lucky you're cute otherwise being an arsehole wouldn't be so great for you!" She says as she slams the door shut!

That parting shot just makes me laugh harder and I can hear her growl from the other side of the door! I lie back on the pillows, my arm across my eyes, trying to catch my breath from laughing so hard when I feel the bed move. Before I can react I've got a sexy body straddling me and I can't say that I mind too much. My arm is pulled from my face and slammed down onto the mattress and I'm looking up into the most beautiful eyes I've ever seen, they change colour with her mood and right now, I can't decide if they're a storming brown with green or a stormy green with brown. Yes, there is a difference and one means she's thinking sexy thoughts. The other one doesn't! She thinks she's tough, holding me down but in fact, I'm letting her hold me down, if I wanted to I could have our roles reversed in a second, but I don't, I'm enjoying her being on top!

"So, you think I'm cute, huh? I'd really rather be considered sexy, manly or even studly. Cute is for puppies, kittens and you!" I say because I'm really enjoying getting under her skin. She's fucking adorable when she gets all worked up.

"I'm not *cute*. I'm annoyed with you right now and I don't want to be cute!" she growls, actually growls when she's finished speaking. It takes everything in me to not burst out laughing again but I know she can feel the laughter building in my stomach by the way she scrunches up her face. Instead of laughing, I use my free hand to pull her face close so that I can kiss her.

When her lips are millimetres from mine I say, "Sweetheart, you are the cutest, most adorable woman I have ever met, and that also makes you the sexiest." Before she can speak I take her lips with mine, gently biting her bottom lip, making her gasp and in turn, granting me access to her mouth and allowing me to tangle my tongue with hers. She stiffens for a second and I know she's trying to decide whether to give in to the passion we both feel or to pull away, still annoyed with me. When she gives in to my touch, her entire body relaxes into mine and her lips soften. I can't help the smile that creeps across my face, it spreads even further when she hits me in the shoulder and mumbles, "Jerk," against my lips but doesn't stop kissing me!

KAMI

I cannot believe the jerkface laughed at me needing to go to the bathroom. I tried to sneak out from under his very tight embrace, without success, obviously. I thought he was still sleeping soundly, I mean I laid there for a while just listening to his breathing to make sure he *was* sleeping. Just when I thought I'd made my escape, his strong arms banded around my waist and I couldn't move. The pressure of his forearm pressing into my stomach just made the situation a lot more painful for me, not that he knew. Where the hell did he think I was escaping to, anyway? I mean we're at my house, it's not like I could escape him even if that's what I actually wanted to do.

Instead, once I've done my business, I sneak back into the bedroom and my breath catches in my throat. There's the man of my dreams, literally, lying in my bed, naked with the covers just covering his hips. He's got his arm resting over his eyes and a smile is spread across his luscious lips. I take a few seconds just to take him in before I launch my sneak attack. I might be annoyed, but that doesn't mean I'm going to give up an opportunity to kiss him. Ever! When I feel his lips spread into a grin, I take a gentle bite out of his bottom lip. He sucks in a breath and his eyes go a deeper shade of blue. Yeah, that's right buddy, I'm still pissed at you!

"Jerk," I say when I hit his shoulder, but I don't give him the chance to think about what I'm doing. While I'm kissing him, hopefully to the point where he can't think, I reach over to grab the condom on the bedside table, rip it open and then slide down his body.

"What the ...?" he groans as I fist him and then roll the condom down his hard cock, and when he twitches in my hand, I meet his dark, lust filled eyes and I grin.

I move my hands back up his chest and lean down, not quite within reach of his lips. "Surely you should be able to work that out by now babe?." On my last whispered word, I slide my pussy onto his hard cock. Never giving him the chance to speak, he gasps instead of using words. I take a few seconds to adjust to the sudden intrusion in my body, then I start rocking my hips. James' hands have moved to grip my hips, but his eyes haven't left mine and they're so full of lust and sin, I think I could come just from looking in them.

"Guess you better keep going then sweetheart, give me a chance to work out what it is you're up to." He says, as I rise up just far enough that the head of his cock is resting just inside my pussy, as he finishes speaking I slam my body back down to meet his and he hisses out a breath between his teeth. Slowly I rise up and slam back down, again and again until his eyes actually roll into the back of his head, losing the ability to form words. I've never felt so sexy or sexual before. He brings out the best in me in every way, but to watch this strong man come undone because of me, it makes my head spin!

"Kami!" he says in a guttural voice I've never heard before and his movements become uncoordinated and messy.

"Come for me babe," I say, in a voice I've never heard before. It's rough and deep, almost smoky.

"You. First. Sweetheart." He grinds out, but he doesn't get his way this time.

I lean down, suck on his earlobe and whisper, "No baby, you come now." Then I move my body so that I can latch onto one nipple with my teeth and lightly pinch the other one with my fingers. I know he can't resist the sensations and that it will get him right where I want him to be, on the edge and ready to come!

"Fuck! Kami!" his eyes are clamped together so tightly, I'm worried he might cause himself some damage, but I know he's trying to keep his orgasm at bay.

"I am James, I am." I grasp his face in my hands, "James. James, look at me babe." I can see the effort it takes him to open his eyes a few seconds later, they're dark and stormy when he finally finds my eyes and I can feel my whole body tighten around him. "I need you to come babe, then I can come too. I need you to do it for me." his grip tightens on my hips and his body loses its last hold on control it was clinging to.. I'm bouncing up and down as he grits his teeth, "Come on babe, I'm so close but I need to watch you come first."

With those words, he throws his head back and roars through his orgasm. I watch as the pleasure plays across his face and that's all it takes for me to find my own. I sit up, my hands resting on his chest and with two more grinds of my hips, I'm calling out his name.

I fall down to lay on his chest, lightly kissing his throat, as we both catch our breaths.

"WOW!" Is all I can manage to say as I pull myself off his body and lay down beside him.

"You can say that again!" James says in a husky voice.

"WOW!" I say and let out a giggle.

"You're a fucking comedienne sweetheart!"

"I know I am, but you love me anyway!" I say without taking a second to think about my words. I've already rolled off my bed and started walking into the bathroom to, you know, clean up, when I realise what I've just said. Instead of acknowledging it, I close the bathroom door behind me and curse myself for being such an idiot!

JAMES

I know what Kami said was meant as a throwaway comment. A funny turn of phrase that is just said, but I saw in her face the minute she realised what she'd said and then she took off so fast I think I can smell the rubber she left behind on the carpet. If only she knew just how close to the mark, she hit with her comment.

I am so in love with her that I can't imagine my life without her, and I don't want to finish working at the bookstore because it means I won't get to see her as much. I want to tell her how I feel, but I still think it's too soon and I don't want to scare her. I feel like if I jump in full force right now, then it will be too much, and she'll run.

I can wait, I'm not going anywhere.

I watch as she walks out of the bathroom, looking at the floor so that she's not looking me in the eye. I hate that she's nervous around me once again.

"Hey sweetheart.." I wait until she finally meets my eyes, I need her to really look at me. "Sweetheart, your sense of humour is one the many reasons that I adore you. I can list at least a dozen more if you want me to?" She smiles but doesn't answer me, so I decide to have some fun with her.

I start by ticking my favourite things about her off on my fingers as I say them, "One, your humour. Two, you're sexy as fuck. Three, you're adorable. Four you've got a great arse. Five, you're smarter than me. Six, you're gorgeous. Seven, you decided to be with me. Eight, you've got great tits. Nine, you've got amazing legs that go for miles. Ten, well if I have to stop here I'm going to say you're amazing, you're mine and I adore you because you like me." By the time I've finished my ten favourite things about Kami, she's laughing and relaxed again. Which is exactly what I was hoping for when I started the whole list, not that that means my list isn't true because let me tell you, each and every one of those points is 100% accurate.

"You're an idiot Mr Harvey but it's one of the many reasons that I adore *you*." She says with a smile as bright as the sun shining in through the gap in her curtains. I grab her around the waist and pull her in close, drop my lips to hers and kiss her like it's going to be our last. I'm going to have to get going soon and I'm finding it hard to find my normal enthusiasm for my job. Just as I finish that wonderful thought, my phone rattles across the bedside table and makes an obnoxious noise alerting me to the fact that Joe is trying to either call or text me. Right now I can't remember which one that noise indicates because I'm too wrapped up in one of my favourite past times. Kissing Kami. "You better answer that." She murmurs against my lips and I sigh. I know she's right, but I don't want to. Kami takes the choice away from me by pulling back and getting off the bed again.

"Where are you going sweetheart?" I ask in a voice that sounds pathetic and whiny even to me!

"I'm going to have a shower, you're not the only one who has business to attend to today you know." She says with a smile as she walks away from me. I'm not sure if all women are taught at some point how to sway their hips to mesmerise men, but this woman sure does have that effect on me! My cocks hard again and I'm thinking about joining her in the shower, when my phone starts singing letting me know that Joe does, in fact, want to talk to me!

Deciding I'm just better off answering him now before he can get too pissed at me, I pick up my phone and say, "Good morning Joe, what can I help you with on this wonderful sunny morning?"

"What's so fucking wonderful about it? What's got you so chirpy at this hour of the day?" before I can offer him an answer he continues, "No, on second thoughts, don't answer that one, I think I can take a guess and I don't want to hear the details. Look I hate to burst your happiness bubble, but you've got an out-of-town appointment today, or did you forget?"

Shit! I did forget and I'm going to be away for a couple of days too. It's just not worth coming back for the night only to head straight back there the next day. "Thanks for reminding me because yeah I did forget!"

"This contract is a big deal for you James, how the fuck could you forget something like this?" Joe almost shouts down the phone at me.

"Fuck you Joe. I don't need you to tell me what this contract means to *MY* business." Sometimes I think he forgets that little fact, it's not his business but mine. I'm the one who put in all the hard work, blood, sweat and tears to get it up and running. To get repeat customers and new ones as well. "I think you forget some days that it is actually my business, man. I have the appointment in my calendar OK, so I would have been hitting the road soon anyway, even without your not so gentle reminder. You're my accountant, not my business partner Joe." Now it's my turn to get pissy with him! Anyone would think he's a jealous bastard, maybe he is, I'm not spending as much time with him lately and I guess I should make that effort. It's been the two of us against the world for so long, I forget his family life isn't great either.

"I know it's your business James, believe me, I know. Whether you want to believe it or not though, I have a stake in you succeeding too and it's not because of the business ties or lack of them. I want to see *you* succeed, you've worked too hard to let things start to slide now. That's all I'm trying to say." He says with a deep sigh.

"Start to slide now, what do you want to say, Joe? Spit it out." I ask, even though I know what the fuck he's going to say. He's going to blame Kami for me forgetting an appointment. An appointment I don't have to get to until this afternoon because even back when I set it up, I knew I wouldn't get there any earlier.

"You know what I mean, man." He says on a sigh.

"No, why don't you spell it out for me, *man?*" I ask, my voice is pretty tight now, but I just want to hear him say it.

"Since you started seeing Kami, you've let things slide and you know you have James. You haven't got anywhere near as many smaller projects because you did her shop. Something you usually don't do, *and* you've barely stepped foot in your workshop."

He's right about all of it but that doesn't mean that there's anything wrong with the choices I've made recently. "You're right Joe, about all of it, but I've got Kami. You know how long I've wanted her, and I've finally got the chance to have her." I take a deep breath, Joe has been my best friend and only supporter for years. He helped me build this business and while I know it's my name on the stationery, I'm not sure how much of it I could have done without his help, but he doesn't get the last say on any of my projects and he sure as fuck doesn't have a say in who I do or don't date. "Look I understand your concerns Joe, but it's all good. Being with Kami makes me happy, she makes me feel human, almost normal and I need her Joe. I won't let anything happen to the business, it's my blood, sweat and tears man and it's definitely taken my soul to get it to where it is, but it's not everything anymore Joe, it can't be."

"I can't believe you of all people just said that James, but we don't have the time to talk about that right now. You need to get moving and get on the road."

I move the phone from my ear to look at the time, he's right, I do have to get into gear before I'm late, well later than I want to be that's for sure. "I will talk to you later Joe." He grunts a goodbye into my ear and hangs up. Fuck he's a grumpy bastard in the mornings, who am I kidding he's a grumpy bastard all the fucking time.

"Hey babe, what did Joe want so early in the morning?" Kami asks as she walks out of the bathroom with a towel wrapped around her gorgeous body.

"He just wanted to make sure I remembered an appointment I have."

"I didn't realise that he had that much input on how you run your business. I thought he was your accountant, not your business partner."

It's an innocent question, at least I hope so and a pretty reasonable one too. How do I explain the situation to Kami? Without Joe, I wouldn't have a business and not just because he keeps my finances in order either.

<u>KAMI</u>

His uneasiness and hesitation to answer me makes me nervous. I don't want to pry into his business, how it all runs is his business, not mine. I just didn't realise that Joe had such an in-depth knowledge of the day to day running of Harvey Carpentry that he knows what appointments James has every day. I know they're close but that seems really close, even to me. I wait for his answer and the longer he takes, the more uncomfortable and ill at ease I feel.

"Joe helped me a lot when I first started out." James starts, "he didn't just do the books back then, he was my jack of all trades. Well, everything except actually lifting up a tool and doing any physical labour, anyway." He chuckles like he's remembering a particular time where Joe refused to pick up a hammer or something. He shakes his head to clear it and continues, "I guess, his role hasn't changed over the years. He's always been a mother hen and likes to organise people and things. Personally, I just want to get out there and get the job done, I've never liked answering the phone or doing the paperwork. At first, he did all the paperwork because he was my accountant and it just made sense for him to do it all. It's not like he wasn't paid for his work, he was, but he was a great support in every way back when I started out. He still is."

"It must be nice to have a friend like that. One that has your back no matter what." I say with a smile.

"Yeah, it is. You must understand it though Kami, I mean you've got Katy. You've known each other for years and I have no doubt that she supports you with the bookshop and anything else that you do, right?"

I nod and say, "Yeah she does, without a doubt." But inside, I can't help thinking that our friendship isn't anything like James and Joe's. We support each other, without a doubt but it's never in a controlling or manipulative way. I mean, Katy was a little concerned about James and I getting together, in whatever capacity it happened in, *but* she supported my choice to be with him and I know, if it goes south, then she'll be there to pick up the pieces. Joe, on the other hand, has tried to keep us apart in so many different ways from when we were all in high school, that I can't help but think that his protective streak is a little weird. He wants to keep us apart, not support his friend's decisions.

"Hey, do you mind if I have a quick shower before I head out?" James asks and when I look over at him to answer him, I almost swallow my tongue! He's standing naked, next to the bed and stretching like a cat! Every muscle and inch of skin on display, and I can't find my words! So instead, I nod my head and move my hand in a flourish towards the bathroom, hoping he takes that's as an invitation to go ahead. As he moves past me, I can't help but watch him in all his naked glory. He is the sexiest man I have ever met, and I'll never get tired of watching him move around, naked or not. Naked is awesome though. I watch him disappear into the bathroom and let out a sigh. Suddenly, his head pops around the doorframe and with a huge grin on his face he says, "Did you enjoy watching me walk away sweetheart? Cause I can tell you, I enjoyed watching you walk away and come back to me earlier. Best. Show. Ever."

I nod but then he's gone again, and I hear the shower turn on. Cheeky bugger! I laugh as I realise he's rendered me speechless, something not too many people have achieved in my lifetime! I may not always talk a *lot,* but I've been told more often than not, that I'm a chatterbox when you get to know me. The man has magic powers and apparently, they're not relegated to the bedroom.

I get myself dressed and walk out to the kitchen to get some coffee started. I wonder if James will have time to have one with me? I walk back into my room to ask him to find him fully dressed already. He wasn't joking when he said a quick shower! He looks up from tying up his boots and smiles at me. My heart melts just a little bit more for the boy that he was, but even more for the man he's become. He's so much more than I expected, and not just physically either, he's so charismatic and tempting.

"Hey, you, do you have time for a coffee, or do you have to head out right away?" I ask with a smile. I don't want him to leave but I know he has to go. He's got work and so do I.

He stands up as he answers me and steals my breath again with just how handsome he is. "I can have a quick one. I need to tell you something before I leave, anyway."

I don't like the sound of that and seeing that he's already had a conversation with Joe this morning, I have a sinking feeling in the pit of my stomach. I plaster a smile on my face and walk back out to the kitchen and pour our coffee. "So what is it you need to tell me, James?"

He coughs and waits for me to hand his drink before he starts to speak, not looking up from his cup when he starts, "Joe called to remind me of an appointment I have today."

"So you said. What kind of appointment? Are you OK?" I ask, suddenly worried that it's actually something to do with his health and not business.

"No. I mean I'm OK Kami. He reminded me that I have to leave town for a couple of days." He looks up at me, I'm guessing to gauge my thoughts.

"For business?" He nods at me, "OK so you're going to be away for a couple of days, why do you look so worried about that?" I ask, feeling just a little confused. If he has business, then he has business. Unless.

"It's not with a woman Kami, well I'm sure there will be females involved in the process, but I'm not meeting up with anyone and it wasn't something I'd planned to do before we got together either." It's my turn to nod, "It's just that, what Joe doesn't know is that the deal is done. We actually signed off on the work just before I started work on the bookshop."

"So, I was the fill-in job. Is that what you're saying?" I ask I don't know whether to be happy or little annoyed.

"No, well yes, but no, not in the way you mean," he stutters out. "We had other jobs Kami, I took your bookshop on because I wanted to. I wanted to get to know you, the adult you and I wanted to spend time with you. I had no idea that spending time with you would turn into us being together. I'm not going to say I didn't *hope* that's what would happen, but honestly, I wanted to build a new adult friendship with you." He places his cup on the table, reaches his hand out to me and I take it, allowing him to pull me in close to him. "This job isn't a small one sweetheart, and it means I'm going to be away for a couple of weeks. I took it before I had a reason to stay home, but at this stage, I couldn't cancel it even if that's what I wanted to do. I have to be honest Kami, I don't want to pull out the job. I've been looking forward to doing this job for months, it's exactly the kind of work I want to do."

"I wouldn't ask you to pull out of a job James, I hope you understand that?" I look directly into his eyes, "You need to do this and any other job that you want. Me being in your life, us being together, it doesn't change anything in our business life. We both run our own businesses James, we should be able to understand and support each other better than anyone."

"I know, I was worried you were going to be annoyed with me for leaving for so long when we've just gotten together." He coughs and lets out a low chuckle, "Joe was worried that I'd completely forgotten about the job and was going to blow it off."

"Because you're with me? Really? I thought you said he was your best friend and knew you better than anyone? Even I know that you wouldn't pull out of a contract even if there weren't legal ramifications involved." How the hell can a friend believe that kind of nonsense?

"He just worries about me. I haven't always made the best decisions sweetheart, and he's always looked out for me."

I nod, I understand that, but the guy is a jerk! "OK so how long are you going to be away and when exactly do you have to leave?"

"I have to leave soon, like within the next half an hour. I'm hoping I can get this done in two weeks, but I should definitely have it done within three. I'm taking a few of the guys with me and we're staying there because it's just too far to warrant driving back and forth every day or even every week, really."

I nod, taking the information in and coming to terms with going from seeing him all day every day to not seeing him for potentially the next three weeks. "Well, that takes us from everything to nothing really quickly doesn't it?" I say with a nervous laugh.

"It won't be nothing Kami, we have all this wonderful stuff we call phones and internet these days. We can even video chat with each other, in real time, so it's almost like we're sitting together."

"Very funny jerk," I say with a laugh and smacking his shoulder at the same time. "I guess I just got used to having you around and now you're leaving."

"I'm coming back Kami, I promise. Now that I've got you, I'm not letting you go, and we can talk every day." He pulls me in closer to him, so that we're chest to chest, pelvis to pelvis and drops his lips to mine. "Now give me a kiss I can remember for the next few weeks while I'm away from you."

We kiss like it's the last one we're ever going to have and then he has to go. I walk him to the door and say goodbye. Anyone would think we were never going to see or talk to one another ever again! I refuse to cry though, mainly because that's ridiculous. He's going away for work, not to war and he's coming back. He's coming back to *me.*

"See you soon sweetheart."

"Message me when you get there so I know you've made it in one piece, please?" I ask because I need to know he's safe.

"Sure sweetheart. Just remember that's going to be a few hours away OK?" I nod as he climbs into his car and then I watch him drive away until I can't see his car anymore. Then I sigh and tell myself to get my head together and get to work. I've got a business to run too and I need to go open up.

Chapter Nineteen

JAMES

If anyone was to ask me what the hardest thing I'd ever done in my life before this morning was, I would have said getting my carpentry business up off the ground. After this morning, I would have to say that leaving Kami's house and packing to leave her for the next few weeks, and driving out of town, would definitely rival my business for the top position.

Looking in the review mirror of my truck, I can no longer see home behind me, and I feel the loss. Not of the town even though I've lived there my entire life. No, I'm feeling the distance between Kami, the woman who has my heart and my car driving away. When I took this job, I was more than happy to get out of town for a few weeks. Get away from the prying eyes, the gossips and people who think they know me, they don't but you can't change what some people believe.

I'd planned on using it for a kind of holiday as well a job opportunity. I haven't had more than a week's break since I started the business years ago and I've been happy with that. It's my business and I'm willing to put in the time and effort to make it successful.

Now I have a brilliant crew that works for me, a great couple of foremen who I can send on jobs with crews of their own and know that the job will get done to my standards. Sure I check in on the other sites on a pretty regular basis, but I try not to micromanage anyone.

This out-of-town job is supposed to create new opportunities for us, for the crews and myself, but now that I'm driving away from town and I know I won't be back for a few weeks, I'm feeling a little less excited about those prospects, and more like I want to work closer to home.

Closer to Kami Parker.

I flick on the radio and tune into the music and shut those thoughts down. I agreed to do this job and I need to get it done. The sooner I can get it done, the sooner I can get home.

Music is pumping through my speakers and I'm singing away to myself, feeling better than I did when I set out on this drive. My phone beeps letting me know I have a message. It's time to make a pit stop anyway, so as soon as I see the next rest stop, I pull in. I fuel up the truck for the rest of the trip, head to the bathroom, grab a coffee and jump back in the driver's seat to keep going. My phone vibrates to remind me that I have an unread message.

Joe: *hey saw Kami just now she said you got away reasonably early are you there yet?*

I want to tell him to get fucked. I want to ask why he went to see Kami. I want to ask him why he feels the need to check on either one of us. I want to tell him to mind his own fucking business. I want to tell him to concentrate on his own fucking job, but I don't do any of those things. Instead, I answer him with a few simple words;

James: *almost there*

I hope he gets the chills from those two words, just as I intended. He must, because he doesn't answer me and I'm happy about that.

KAMI

I can only assume that running into Joe at the café this morning when I went to grab Ed and myself a coffee, is his way of checking up on James and whether he left my house this morning to head out of town. I've *never* run into Joe anywhere in town before in all our years of living here. The more that I think about it that's pretty strange, actually. It's not like this is a huge town, it's not a small town either but it does seem rather unusual for us to have *never* crossed paths before in all these years. We're both in business in this town, you would think that with just that in common it would have happened at least a few times since high school.

I know I've never run into him in the café before. Maybe it's just a case of never being in the same place at the same time, I don't know but I do know that I would remember running into the kid who made my life miserable while we were at school. The funny thing is, Joe wasn't from the wrong family or area, but he chose to be the rebel and hang out with James.

Even though it was well known that his parents didn't like their friendship, he didn't care. He didn't seem to care about anyone except himself, James and Sammi. He always seemed to hold his decision against everyone else, whether we had done anything wrong or not, and he really hated me.

He made my life downright uncomfortable some days and the only thing that stopped his assaults was James. James telling him it was enough and to shut up.

These days it would seem that we've managed to avoid each other as much as we possibly could. I don't use him as my accountant for the bookshop, I found someone else to look after my books. Even though Joe was recommended by almost everyone I know, there was no chance I was going to give him my business. I had so many people telling me to let it go, that people change, he's grown up since then, we all have, they would say, but I just couldn't stand the thought of giving him money. Paying *him* after the torment he caused. I'm pretty sure he wouldn't have taken my business anyway, so the feelings are mutual.

Just after I've grabbed some lunch off Josie at the café, I get a text message off James;

James: *hey sweetheart, I just got into town and checked into my hotel. I'll call you later tonight and you can tell me all about your day*

I can feel the smile spread across my face. Knowing that James got there in one piece makes me happy, but knowing I'm going to be hearing his voice later tonight makes me even happier. I take lunch back to my office to get some paperwork done and try not to watch the clock, counting the minutes until I can get out of here and talk to James.

I do a great job of distracting myself with paperwork after lunch because before I know it Ed is leaning against the doorframe to my office. "Hey Ed, what can I do for you?"

"I just wanted to let you know I've locked up and Mel and I are about to head out. Do you need me to do anything before I leave?"

"Shoot! Really the day is over already?" I ask, not totally believing that I've managed to spend all afternoon in here.

"Sure is boss, you've been in here since lunch and we haven't heard a noise from in here except the shuffling of papers." He stops there, but I can see he wants to say something else.

"What's on your mind, Ed?"

"It's none of my business, so..."

"So? Just spit it out Ed, I think we've known each other long enough that you can speak freely. We're friends as well as boss and employee, aren't we?" I ask, not really sure what he wants to say or where we stand with each other anymore.

"I like to think that we're friends as well Kami, but maybe sometimes I should keep my mouth shut and mind my own business. At least that's what Mel tells me anyway," he says with a shrug of his shoulder and a small grin.

"You can ask me anything Ed, if I don't want to answer you, I won't. Same goes for you I hope, we've both got the option of telling the other one to mind their own business."

"I just ... I wanted to ask if everything was OK? You know, with you and James. I know," he pauses as he holds his hand up to stop me from speaking. "I know I was concerned at the start Kami, but you've just been so happy with him around and now, today he's not here. I mean I know that the job finished here, but you've spent the day really quiet and it feels like you were hiding in here. It's just you don't normally spend this time much in your office and I was a little worried, that's all."

"Oh. Well I know I don't normally spend a lot of time in my office during open hours, mainly because I enjoy being in the shop, around books and helping customers. The truth is though, I either stayed late or took it home with me, but I hate doing paperwork. I caught up on so much while James and the guys were here, and I really don't want to fall behind again, if I can help it. That and I know I can trust you and Mel out on the floor, if you need me you know where I am." I smile gratefully at Ed, hoping that he understands just how much I value his work here and his friendship. I'm also hoping he doesn't pick up the fact that I sat in my office doing paperwork while the guys were here because I didn't want to be out there ogling James while he worked. There wouldn't have been much work getting done, by anyone if I'd done that. "As for James and myself, well that's going OK. He had to leave town for a job this morning and he's going to be away for a few weeks, I guess I just threw myself into work so that I would forget that I won't see him tonight."

Ed grins and says, "As long as you're happy Kami, that's all I want."

"I am Ed." I smile, "What time is it, anyway?"

"It's just after 6, why?"

"Why are you guys here so late? And I have to go, I've got a date with James."

"We had a couple of customers that hung around and I didn't want to rush them out, so we just stayed until they were done. We have dinner plans later, so it saved us from filling in time." He replies with another shrug of his shoulder. "Hang on, didn't you say James was out of town? How can you have a date with the guy if he's not even here?"

I gather up the last of my paperwork, then decide it can wait until to-morrow and drop it back onto the desk. As Ed watches me drop the pa-pers down I say, "There's this little thing we like to call technology Ed, you might have heard of it? The internet and video chats aren't that new you know. Not to mention we can just talk on the phone if the video chatting fails us." I let out a laugh at the shocked look on his face. "What's so sur-prising Ed? That I can use technology or that I know about it?"

He lets out a loud laugh of his own as we walk towards the counter where Mel looks up in surprise.

"What's so funny?" Mel asks.

"Your boyfriend here thinks I'm stuck in the dark ages, that's what's so funny!" I place my hand on my forehead in dramatic fashion and say, "Oh gosh whatever shall I do? How can I use the technology to keep in contact with my boyfriend for a few weeks? Oh I know, maybe I can call him on the telephone or video chat with him!" I say with both my hands on my cheeks, mouth agape in shock and slightly hunched over.

Ed and Mel crack up laughing at my antics and I join in. I can't help it. I'm happy because it's almost time for me to see James' gorgeous face and catch up with what he's done today.

"So, I take it James is out of town for a few days then?" Mel asks.

"Yeah. He booked a job out of town a few months ago and it started today. So, we agreed to evening video chats and if the internet lets us down, then we can chat on the phone." I look at the clock on the wall above the counter. "On that note, I'm going to push you guys out the door, with a thanks for a job well done today and every other day we work together, then I'm going to lock up and get home. I have a date with a sexy carpenter tonight!"

Ed groans and shuffles Mel out the door as she sighs dreamily, "You have a real live date with *me*, Mel, let's go to dinner."

I laugh again as I watch them walk away, waving to me and play shoving each other, as they disappear into the distance. I'm happy to see everyone happy and I can't wait to 'see' James either, so I jump in my car and head home to get comfy.

<u>JAMES</u>

I can't wait to get back to the hotel that will be my home for the next couple of weeks and put my fucking feet up.

When I pulled into town earlier today, I called the client, and everything was all set and ready to go. I said I was just going to check in to the hotel then drive over to check out the work site. When I got there, the client was waiting, and he had a list of fucking issues I hadn't even known were issues yet. After going through each and every one of his perceived fucking issues, I told him I would take his list and do my usual walk through of site, but until I did that walk through, on my own, I wouldn't have any answers for him.

I had numerous calls with this company while we were going through the process of my application for the job. They seemed normal, easy going and seemed to know what they wanted and what they were talking about. If I had seen a glimpse, even a smaller glimmer, that they'd become a pain in my arse once I *got* the fucking contract, I would have never signed on to the job. This guy isn't my original contact, but everything had already been signed off.

The last five hours have been the longest and most frustrating of my entire life! That's coming from the guy who had to fight his father's reputation to build a business that people can rely on! I can't wait to just sit back on the bed in my room, eat some takeout and relax.

The guys are coming in first thing in the morning and hopefully, we can get all the shit sorted by the end of the day. I rest my head on the wall behind the bed, and I let out a long drawn-out groan when I feel my phone vibrate. If this guy is calling me again, I think I might just lose my shit. I pick up my phone to look at the screen, debating the entire time whether

I'll tell him that I'm off the clock and it can wait until morning, or whether I'll answer and put up with it. I decide that I'm going to put my foot down now, stand my ground early on and hopefully we can draw the line in the sand, before we get too deep into the project and I can't change bad habits.

All that debating with myself is null and void though, because it's not Simon, my contact for what I've already started calling 'Project Hell', it's the very gorgeous and heavenly Miss Kami Parker!

"Good evening you gorgeous and heavenly creature! How is my favourite girl on the planet doing tonight?" I can feel the smile spread across my face.

"Good evening Mr Harvey, I'm doing better now that I can hear your voice. How was your day?" Ohhhh that voice! I can't believe how much I miss her, and it hasn't even been 24 hours since I last saw her.

"It feels fantastic to hear your voice, sweetheart. Tell me all about your day because I've had enough of my day, and I don't want to relive it."

"Well, that sounds like you've had a great day. Isn't your new project working out very well?"

"There are always some issues to begin with, which is why I came up the day before the guys, but this one is in a group all of its own. The contact here is a real piece of work, I've only spoken to him once before and he seemed so relaxed and easygoing. Now that I'm here he wants answers before I've even looked at anything. I hadn't even stepped onto the work site before he was bombarding me with problems and demanding solutions. I've been putting out fires everywhere all damn day." I take a breath and realise I've been rattling on about work for way too long, even after I said I didn't want to talk about it. "I'm sorry sweetheart, I said I didn't want to talk about it and then I rambled on without taking a breath! Now tell me about your day, please."

"You sound like you need to get it off your chest more than I do, babe. My day was just like every other day around here, actually." She says on a sigh and I wonder what she means by that. "After you left my house this morning, I had some breakfast, then headed to the bookshop. I worked out on the shop floor until late morning when Ed came in for his shift, then I headed over to the café and grabbed some lunch. Josie says hi, by the way. I took lunch back to the shop and sat in the office doing paperwork until Ed came in and told me he had closed up and was heading out with Mel. That's when I realised I could come home, get comfy and call you."

"This is by far the highlight of my day. Well except for that parting kiss from you this morning because *that* was a definite highlight for me." I say, and I get laughter in response from Kami. "Was it not the highlight of *your* day sweetheart. Be careful how you answer that, I'm in a pretty fragile state tonight you know."

"Oh yes you're so very fragile and precious tonight aren't you babe?" she laughs again, and it instantly makes me feel better, lighter and takes away the stresses of my day. "I have to agree though, that parting kiss was the highlight of my day too." She says in a soft, husky, almost shy voice.

"Have you eaten dinner yet?" I ask suddenly. I know I've changed the mood, but I have an idea.

"Umm no not yet, why?" she asks confused.

"Can we eat dinner together tonight, please?"

"How are we going to do that James?" I can her the confusion on her voice.

"If you give me ten minutes to have a quick shower and order in some dinner, we can set up a video chat and eat together. What do you say, sweetheart?" I ask, hopefully.

I can hear the smile in her voice when she replies, "Ok James. You go have your shower and I'll order in some dinner as well. Call me when you're done, and we'll eat together."

"See you soon, sweetheart," I say before I hang up and head to the shower, happier than I was ten minutes ago.

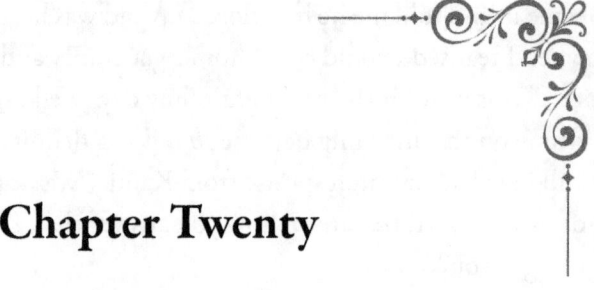

Chapter Twenty

Ten minutes.

Ten minutes, that's all the time I have to get myself ready. But ready for what? That's the question isn't it? I mean what do I want to happen tonight? Do we eat, drink and Netflix together? Or do we get together without being in the same room? If you get my meaning? If I can't say it in my head or out loud, should I even be contemplating *doing* it?

There's a lot of questions hanging in the air there and I'm not sure which one to start with.

First thing first, I have to order myself some dinner, because I'm starving, and I can't think about anything else until I know I'm going to be getting food. Decision made, I call up and place my order. Delivery in half an hour, so they say, let's hope they're right.

Next is, what? Do I change into something more 'comfortable', something to make James wish he was here and peeling it off my body, or do I play it cool and just stay the way I am? I decide to do both. These are my rules and I can do whatever I want, making them up as I go along is part of the fun. Just as I finish tidying myself up, my phone starts ringing. I let out a giggle as I answer the video call.

"What's so funny, sweetheart? A man doesn't really want to hear his woman laughing before he's even done anything to her." Then he gets this thoughtful look on his face and says, "Then again, if a man is doing *things* to his woman, he doesn't want to hear her laughing then either." He frowns, causing me to giggle some more. "So, now you have to tell me, what's so funny sweetheart? You're bruising my ego."

He's frowning, but the corner of his mouth is tilting up with the start of a smirk. Dang if I'm not a little in love with that smirk of his. Who am I kidding? I'm completely in love with everything about him.

"Holy crap on a cracker!" I'm actually in love with James.

"Holy crap on a cracker what?" James' deep voice asks me through the screen, and I realise I've said it out loud. I'm really hoping my shock and surprise doesn't register on my face, but by the look on his, it's showing completely.

I laugh, trying to relax my face and my rapidly beating heart at the same time, and say, "Nothing important babe, I just forgot that I have to call Katy tonight."

"Are you cutting our video chat short sweetheart? We've barely started and I'm really looking forward to our screen date." His face is warm, and his eyes are full of mischief.

"No. No, I'm not going anywhere, I've been looking forward to our digital date all day and I'm not giving it up. Just let me send a quick message to Katy and then you'll have my full and undivided attention." I smile at screen James and hope that I've managed to cover myself for once.

"Well, in that case, you send your message because it sounds like my dinner has arrived. I'll be back in a second." With a grin, he's gone from my screen and quickly send Katy a text.

Kami: *do you have time to meet me for a cuppa tomorrow morning?*

I swap screens and James isn't back yet, but I can hear his deep voice, speaking to the person delivering his food in the background. It makes me miss him even more. I can hear him, but I can't touch him. Just as my thoughts go to touching James, my phone vibrates in my hand and when I look down Katy as replied to my text.

Katy: *Who is this? The number used to belong to my best friend, but she's been AWOL for a few weeks*

I let out a long and loud sigh. I know she's right, but I've been busy, even so, I shouldn't have ignored my oldest friend for a guy, even when that guy is the love of my life. I'm about to send her an apology when my phone vibrates with another message.

Katy: *I'm joking Kami, and yes I can and will most definitely meet you for a cuppa in the morning. 10am at the café sound good?*

Kami: *Perfect and I'm sorry Katy, I've been a bad friend*

Katy: *Meh no you haven't, you've been busy, and I can understand why*

I smile at my phone and wonder what on earth I did to get such an amazing friend. Then I notice another text come through and I shake my head.

Katy: *I hope you're getting busy on top as well as under him*

Then I remember why we're such good friends. She's crazy, but she's got a heart of gold and she's never held any of my weirdness against me, just embraced it and me and called us friends. I don't answer her though because when I swap screens to see if he's back, I'm looking at his handsome face and suddenly all I can think about is my need to touch him.

"Don't look at me like that sweetheart, not when I can't reach out and touch you like I'm itching to." Then he lets out a soft groan and I melt all over. "You're killing me woman. Look what you do to me and with no relief in sight either." He angles the camera down his body, and I can't help the gasp that escapes me. He's hard. For me. There's a definite tent in his pants and I'm at a loss for words.

He moves the screen back up to his face and I blink, looking into his eyes that are now a dark blue and stormy. I can't stop looking at him and wishing with everything I have that he was actually here, in the flesh, so that I can touch him.

He growls at me again but before either one of us can speak, my doorbell rings, calling me to the door and hopefully my dinner. The dinner I'd completely forgotten about as soon as I saw the *hard* evidence of how much James misses me.

"I'll be right back," my voice is breathy and husky. I get up from the couch and move towards the door, I cough to clear my throat and then open the door with a smile.

"Evening Kami, I have your order," Ben, the delivery driver from the local Chinese shop says, looking past me into the kitchen. "No, Katy tonight?"

"No Ben, just me tonight. I paid over the phone, so I'm good to go right?" I ask, hoping with everything in me that he takes the hint and leaves before James decides to speak up from my phone.

"Oh yeah, I'm sorry Kami. You're right you did, have a great night." He waves at me and smiles as he turns to leave.

I lock the door and make my way back to the couch, I can't wait to see James. When I get there, he's scowling at the screen, with a forkful of food halfway to his mouth, but before I can ask him what's wrong he says, "Does Ben deliver to you every time you order?"

"Yeah, he does when I order Chinese. Normally Katy's here and we're having a girl's night in. You know drinks and a movie or two, maybe even no movie, who knows."

"So he was looking into your house looking for Katy? Not checking out to see if you were alone or anything?" He asks, looking pretty concerned.

"He has a thing for Katy, but she's told him she wants to be friends."

"Does Ben understand that? Because honestly sweetheart, he was behaving a little creepy and I'm worried about you now, especially if he now knows you're home alone."

"James, thank you for worrying about me, but I'm OK. The door is locked, dead-bolted in fact and all the windows have locks too. As bad as I'm about to sound, it's not me he wants babe, but I promise to be extra careful, OK?"

"I'm not saying we should set him up with Katy, but he was a little too interested in whether you were alone or not for my liking."

"Let's not talk about Ben or Katy for that matter. I'll tell her to keep her eye out for him when I see her in the morning." We set about finding a movie to watch together while we eat dinner. Together. But a few hours away from each other.

JAMES

We settle in and watch an action movie that's all explosions, car chases and banter between the lead characters. It's easy to watch and we can still have a conversation in between mouthfuls of food. It's the weirdest feeling, being this far away from Kami and yet still watching the same movie and sharing a meal. It's also the best part of my day.

Talking to Kami on the phone was relaxing but being able to see her face as we talk, that makes something in my gut and my chest feel right, settled. I'm loving technology tonight.

"So, how are Ed and Mel doing? Are they still seeing each other?" I ask because I want to show an interest in what's happening around her and I want to hear her voice. When she laughs, I smile because it's the best sound in the world. "What's so funny?" I ask her.

"James, you've only been gone for a day, not even, it's not like all that much has changed around here since you left you." She tells me with a huge smile spreading across her beautiful face, making her eyes sparkle.

"I know how long I've been gone woman, I was just asking how they were going you know, to make conversation. A lot can happen in 24 hours, and I was just curious." I say with a shrug of my shoulders.

"Well, I'm sure they'll be happy to know you're concerned about them, but they're going well and still together. It's OK, Ed isn't going to try jumping my bones now that you're out of town." She says with a cheeky grin and a quiet chuckle.

"I wasn't even concerned about that Miss Parker, do I need to be worried about you jumping Ed's bones now that I'm away? Maybe I should give Mel a call and warn her about your intentions towards her man. Hmmmmm?" I raise my right eyebrow in question and twist my lips up like I'm thinking about it.

The damn woman cracks up laughing at me. Rolling around on her couch, clutching at her stomach, tears rolling down her cheek's kind of hysterical laughing, too. I'd be offended if she didn't look so adorable, scratch that sexy as fuck, because as she tries to right herself into a sitting position again, I realise just what she's been wearing this entire time. She's got one of my shirts on and the tiniest pyjama shorts I've ever fucking seen. I'm pretty sure she doesn't have a bra on either.

Sexy. As. Fuck.

There's not much between her being clothed and me seeing everything I'm missing tonight.

I cough at that thought then ask, "Kami." She's trying to catch her breath after her laughing fit. "Kami." I put more command in my voice and that makes her stop wiping at her eyes and looking me in the eye down the camera of her phone.

"Yes, James?" Her voice is husky from laughing and trying to catch her breath.

"Did you answer the door to Ben looking like that?" My eyes look at what I can see of her body up and down, full of heat and want.

"Like what?" she asks and looks down at her own body like she forgot what she was wearing, or not wearing as the case seems to be. "Oh. You mean in my pj's?" she says with an almost shy smile.

"That's your pj's sweetheart? Seriously?" I ask, and I hear the way my voice cracks when I do. I don't know whether I'm pissed or turned on.

"Well, yeah. While you're away, this is what I'm sleeping in." She says, "But in answer to your question, no. No, I didn't open the door to Ben looking like this. I had a bra and pants on when my dinner was delivered, but I knew it was going to be just us after that and well, I didn't think you'd mind too much." She says with a small shrug of her own. "You kind of left a shirt here in your rush to get going this morning and I took the liberty of deciding that while my man is away, I'm going to wear his shirt to bed. It still smells like you and it makes me feel closer to you, like you're still here."

I don't know what to say. I've never had anyone miss me when I've gone away before. There's never been a woman waiting for me to get back to her and wanting a way of being close to me. Well, other than in a creepy, clingy kind of way anyway.

I notice that Kami's phone is moving, and she's focused it completely on her face, "You're not mad are you?"

"Mad? About what sweetheart?" I manage to choke out.

"That I'm wearing your shirt? I can take it off if you want?"

With my dinner forgotten completely, I say in a voice I barely recognise as mine, "Undo every button. Slowly, sweetheart."

Kami looks surprised for a second but then the phone moves again as she places it down on the table and starts undoing all those tiny fucking buttons. Never have I been more annoyed with buttons in my life, if I was there with her, I would have ripped the fucker apart.

"Fair is fair Mr Harvey, start taking your shirt off too." Her voice is as husky and filled lust that mine is. I don't hesitate, I grab the back of my shirt at the neck and rip it up and off my body. If Kami wants to see my naked chest, she gets to see my naked chest. I don't take my eyes off Kami and her fingers dancing along those buttons. When she gets to the bottom she stops, the shirt is only slightly open, showing just the smallest sliver of skin, teasing me.

"Fair is fair Miss Parker. You wanted my chest naked, you got your wish. Now it's my turn to get my wish, open up that shirt and show me those gorgeous breasts sweetheart."

She flashes me the sweetest, yet somehow hottest smile I've ever fucking seen, as the last button slides through the hole in the fabric. She moves her back slightly and then, my breath catches in my lungs. The shirt opens and slides down the sides of her body, revealing her stomach and full, round breasts. My mouth can't decide if it's dry or salivating at the sight.

Her hands slide up her stomach and start to knead her breasts, it's all I can do to keep my eyes open. When she pinches both of her nipples between her finger and thumb, she lets out a small moan, I can't stop myself from groaning out loud myself. Fuck she's the hottest thing I have ever seen. That is until her left-hand travels back down her stomach towards the scrap of purple lace covering her pussy.

"Holy fuck Kami," is all I manage to say my voice sounding like I'm struggling, even to me.

"What do you want me to do James?" she asks. Does she really expect me to be able to speak while I watch her pleasure herself?

"Take 'em off sweetheart," I growl.

"Take what off babe?"

Ohhh she thinks she's smart does she? "Take 'em off and I'll show you how hard you've made me."

She lets out a loud moan and raises her hips up, her hands removing the purple scrap of lace that's in the way of me looking at her pussy. "Is that what you want babe?"

"Fuck yes!" I ground out between clenched teeth.

"Now you have to show me how hard you are, you promised, and I need to see your cock."

I move my phone to sit on the table next to the sofa and make sure it's pointing up towards my body, between my spread legs. I know she can see the outline of my cock in jeans, so I take my time opening the button and dragging the zip down. I can hear her breathing getting uneven. She's not the only one struggling to keep her breathing under control.

When my jeans are completely opened my cock springs out of his confines, relieved to have some space to stretch out. Without thinking about what I'm doing, my hand reaches down and starts to pump my cock. I look down to the screen on my phone and it's full of Kami's face, she's drawn her bottom lip between her teeth and is moaning so loudly I'm sure the room next door can hear her.

"Lean back sweetheart, I need to see you." I manage as my hand drags up and over the head of my cock, making my stomach clench and my balls pull up slightly.

Kami lies back, and I realise she's got a finger on her clit, rubbing herself while watching me slide my fist up and down my cock. While her other hand teases and plays with her breasts, before I can say anything or take a full breath, she's pushed in a second finger to join the first one.

"Oh. Fuck. James. I'm gonna. Come." Kami pants out.

I'm hard, hot and ready to fucking explode.

"Play with your clit for me Kami but keep those fingers pumping in and out of your pussy sweetheart." She let's go of her breast and I watch as her breasts bounce slightly in her rush to get to her clit. She stretches her neck out, eyes rolling into the back of her head as she drops her head back to the armrest and her back arches. It's the sexiest fucking thing I've seen in my entire life. Something that I didn't even know I was missing until right now.

"I'm gonna come James. I'm com...."

"Come for me, sweetheart. Now!" I can't hold out for much longer, but I want to watch her fall apart first.

"Jamessssss." Her voice is breathless and hoarse, her body is slick with sweat and blushing all over. "Yes. Oh. My. God. YES!" Her body goes slack, and she lets out a huge sigh.

"Fuck Kami. You're the sexiest woman I've ever seen. I wish I was there to touch you and hold you." My voice is barely above a whisper and I don't even know if she heard me.

My body gives in and I rest my head on the back of the sofa, still pumping my cock and then I hear Kami's sweet, husky voice say, "Show me James. Show me what I do to you. Come for me."

That's all I need to bring myself the edge and then I fall over. My balls pull up closer to the base of my cock, my breathing falters, and my whole body starts to shake. I rub my thumb over the slit in the head of my cock and spread the liquid leaking out down the length of cock and back up, to do it all again. Once, twice and then I'm coming all over my stomach with a loud groan. "Arghh fuck, Kami!" I almost tell her I love her, but I'm not going there when I'm too far away to touch her. I rest my hand at the base of my cock and try to bring my breathing back to something resembling normal.

"Holy. Fucking. Shit. James. That was the hottest thing I've ever seen. I mean ever." Kami says in a breathy voice. A smile spreads across my face, but I'm just not ready to move yet. I know I have to clean myself up, but I can't bring myself to care too much. I look down at my phone and Kami is looking back at me, my shirt barely hanging onto her shoulders, but otherwise naked. I can't help thinking, I'd rather be there with her than here or anywhere else, any day of the week.

I wish I was my damn shirt.

KAMI

Watching James come like that, was the sexiest and hottest thing I think I've ever seen. We've been together for a while now, but I've never watched him pleasure himself. Sure he's given himself a few priming pumps to relieve a little bit of pressure before he rolls on a condom and enters my body, but nothing like what I just witnessed.

While James gets himself back together, I go to the bathroom and you know, pee and clean up. When I get back to the couch, James has disappeared. I clean up the dinner that I only ate half of and then take my phone into my bedroom. I do up most of the buttons on James' shirt and get myself comfy in my bed and rest my phone on the pillow next to me.

"Hey sweetheart, are you going to sleep on me now?" I hear James ask and I open my eyes to look at him. Damn, I wish there wasn't a screen and a couple of hours' distance between us. "You and me both sweetheart. I wish I was holding you in my arms right now and we were falling asleep together."

"Oh shit, I didn't realise I said that out loud." I'm going to have to be more careful about thinking out loud. I have no intention of telling this man that I've fallen in love with him while he's so far away and we can only talk through a screen. "No, I was just resting my eyes until you got back, that's all," I say with a nervous giggle. Nervous because I hope didn't say that I love him out loud, but he seems to not have heard that, so I'm safe.

"You should get some sleep Kami. It's late and you've got work tomorrow," he says. Maybe I did speak out loud again and now he's trying to let me down easy.

"You've got an early start too James, not just me. Why don't you get some sleep too, babe?" I say with a smile.

"You're right, we both need to get up for work in the morning. The guys will be here early and hopefully that means we can get this shit show started. The sooner we get started, the sooner I can be finished, and home, with you." He says with a slow smirk.

He's between the covers of his bed himself now too, it's only a matter of time before we're both asleep now.

"Good night James. Can we talk again tomorrow night?" I ask half asleep already.

"We can do this every damned night while I'm here, sweetheart." He says with a sleepy, sexy growl. "Dream dirty dreams about me sweetheart."

I chuckle and say, "Good night babe, sleep well and dream sexy about us." As the screen goes black, and I put the phone on the side table, I whisper, "I love you James Harvey." My dreams are filled with a sexy carpenter, with blue eyes that are full of mischief and love.

Chapter Twenty-One

KAMI

The next morning, I wake up with a smile on my face, but it disappears when I realise that James isn't lying in bed next to me but in a bed alone a couple of hours away.

I roll onto my back and stare at the ceiling, wondering how missing and wanting him next to me all the time happened so damned fast. I understand that I've felt this connection to James since we were teenagers, but we didn't have a relationship back then, not even a friendship, so how have I managed to become so attached to him in a few short weeks?

I sigh and drag my sorry self out of bed and into the shower. When I close my eyes to wash the shampoo out of my hair, I can't help seeing the image of James coming all over his stomach and it makes me feel hot all over. I keep my eyes closed, hoping that the image won't fade away as I run my hands over my body, spreading soap suds all over. I hear James growl out my name as he comes again, my hand make its way down my stomach and when my finger touches my clit, I almost jump in shock. Not shock that my hand is there, although that's part of it, but because my clit is sensitive. I slide two fingers into my already wet pussy, and I groan. I can't open my eyes because I'll lose the video looping in my brain of James stroking himself to orgasm and growling out my name. When the loop runs again, and I hear and see him come, I'm done. I'm crying out his name on a moan of my own.

I rest my forehead on the tiled wall, bring my hands up to rest next to my head and just lean there, catching my breath, while the warm water rains down on my back.

Well, that was one way to start the morning. If James can't be here to give me that kind of start in person, I guess I'll just have to imagine the feel of his skin next to mine and that will have to do for now. I wonder if he's doing the same thing in his shower this morning?

I turn the shower off, step out, wrap myself in a towel, walk to my bedroom and get dressed for the day. When I sit on the side of the bed to put on my shoes, I notice that my phone is blinking, telling me that I have a message waiting for me.

A smile spreads across my face as I read the text;

James: *Good morning sweetheart hope you slept well? Miss you James x*

Kami: *Good morning handsome I did sleep well hope you did too? Miss you Kami x*

I finish putting on my shoes and walk to the kitchen to grab myself some breakfast and a coffee before getting in my car and heading to the shop. My mind can't stop thinking and analysing that message. He misses me but what does that mean? What does the 'x' at the end of his message mean? I get that it's the way of giving a kiss in a message, I'm not stupid, but what did *he* mean? Do guys actually sign off messages, emails and the like with kisses in the form of an 'x'? Us girls do it without even thinking about it with each other, that much I do know, but I doubt men have the same kind of sign off with each other or other people. Or do they? I guess if they're affectionate people they might, and James is definitely affectionate, to me anyway.

I have to stop or I'm going to drive myself insane. I'll ask Ed what he thinks when he gets here, I don't have the time to worry about it now. I have to get the shop open and books sorted.

I have a busy morning with customers coming to pick up orders and looking for something new to read. This is the part of having a bookstore that I love, talking to people and working out what kinds of books they're interested in and getting a selection of them in. Some I would have never thought of getting for a smaller town, but we get people from nearby towns as well.

Before I know it, Ed comes in for his shift and I'm running out the door to meet Katy at the café. When I walk in the door, Josie looks up from the order she's taking and smiles at me. She actually smiles at me, wonders will never cease. I honestly never thought I'd see the day where Josie might be happy to see me, especially without James around as well, but here we are.

I look around and find Katy already seated, drinking a coffee with a second one sitting there waiting for me. "You're the best friend a girl could have, you know that right?" I say with a smile as I sit down and sip my coffee.

"Yes I do know but it's nice to hear it every now and then," she says a grin twitching the corners of her mouth up. "I also know that Ed starts at 10am and that you'd rush over to have a coffee with me even though I would wait the extra 10 minutes for you to just take your sweet time to get here. Hence the coffee sitting here waiting for you because I also know you haven't had one since just after you got to the shop." The grin has now spread across her face and she's arched an eyebrow up at me.

"Anyone would think you know me a little too well by all that," I laugh, a grin spreading across my face. I missed this girl, and it's about time she knew it. "I'm sorry I ditched you Katy, I've missed you, you know that right?"

"I've missed you too but let's face it, you didn't ditch me hun. We've been in communication. I kind of fell off the planet for a while too. Trust me, I get you wanting to spend time with a certain carpenter, it's not like you haven't been dreaming of such things for, oh I don't know, almost as long as I've known you." She says with an even bigger grin.

"You know what, you're right. I have been dreaming about James for a long time and I have to say, he was worth the wait. More than worth it. Oh. My. God. So worth it. Even if we had managed to connect somehow when we were at school or not long after, I don't think it would have been anywhere near what we could possibly have now." I take a deep breath and sigh, "He's something else Katy, truly. I know it's only been a few weeks, but I can't get enough of him and we took some time to get to know each other as adults as well before we fell into bed together." I know I have a stupid grin on my face, I'm the happiest I think I've been since I managed to get the shop up and running.

"I can see how happy you are Kami. You're radiating happiness." She sighs and continues with, "I just want you to be careful, OK?." When I go to speak, she holds up her hand to stop me and says, "Look, I know. You're a grown woman, who has her own business and is more than capable of kicking arse. I know and I'm so very proud of you, especially after all the crap you've been through, *but* I don't want to see you get hurt. I don't think he'd do it on purpose, but I *know* he has the potential to hurt you in a big way if things go wrong."

"He wouldn't hurt me on purpose Katy, but I understand what you mean. I promise to be careful and not get in too deep, too soon."

Katy laughs, "I think that ship has sailed hun. You're already in deep, I just hope that he feels the same way about you."

"What makes you think he doesn't?"

A weird look crosses her face, but it's gone in a second and I'm not even sure that I saw it. "It's not that I think he doesn't care about you Kam, I actually have no doubt that he does in fact care about you. I just don't know if you're on the same page about relationships, that's all."

That makes me angry, I thought Katy of all people wouldn't judge James by his past or his father. "He's not his father you know Katy, and it's unfair of you to put him in that box. It's not like you to judge someone, especially for someone else's actions."

"I know he's not Kam, but he has his own reputation too you know, and I think you should remember that."

"I know he does Katy. I also know how rumours start and how false they can be." I sigh. "let's not talk about it anymore and enjoy our coffee."

Katy nods, just as Josie comes to ask us if we want something to eat. After our conversation, I decide I need some chocolate, so I order a muffin and another coffee. When I look over to Katy, she's got a sad smile on her face as she tells Josie that she'll have the same thing. It's then that I realise I'm not the only one who has been absent the last few weeks, in fact, Katy kind of disappeared herself a few weeks before I started all this with James.

"So, what have you been doing the past few weeks then? You kind of went quiet yourself before James started work at the bookshop." She shifts uncomfortably in her chair and I wonder what she hasn't told me. We don't normally hide stuff from each other and I'm worried that something serious is going on. "Are you OK? Have you been to your check-up?" I can help feeling worried.

"No, no I'm fine. Well, yes, I did go back for my check-up and everything is fine Kami, there's nothing to worry about I'm in the clear." She says in a rush and my heart starts beating like a normal person's again.

Katy was diagnosed with endometriosis when we were teenagers and as a result was told there was a possibility that having kids could prove difficult. Children may not even happen for her at all, not naturally anyway. She's had a procedure where they use lasers to remove the excess tissue causing her pain a few times over the years, but there is no 'cure' or guarantees. I know it affects her relationships, she feels like she can't give guys everything they want. Why she can't find the guy who knows that she's enough, with or without kids, is beyond me. Maybe she can't let herself find him?

"Don't give me that look Kam, I'm fine." She shakes her head at me, then thanks Josie when she delivers our chocolate muffins and coffee. "I was seeing someone for a few weeks and ummmm," she can't look me in the eyes when she says, "then he started seeing someone else and that was the end of that."

I'm trying to *not* to jump to conclusions, but her remarks earlier about James not being who I think he is and then her not being able to meet my eyes while telling me about this guy she was seeing, I can't help but wonder if they're connected. "Were you with James, Katy?" My voice is a whispered kind of squeak. If they were seeing each other just weeks or days before we started seeing each other, I don't even know what I'll do. I can't think, I feel like I'm going to be sick. I feel a hand grab hold of mine and I look up to see the concern in her eyes. Crap, they were seeing each other, weren't they? I'm going to have to break up with him, I can't do that Katy and I won't let him do it to me.

"Kami. Kami, hun, I wasn't seeing James. Look at me Kami, I wasn't seeing James, OK?" She waits until I'm looking at her before she continues. "It wasn't him, but I guess I can see why you would jump to that conclusion after what I said before." She sighs, "I guess I was projecting my feelings about certain men onto James and your relationship with him. I know James isn't the same kind of man his father was, even when he was having a bit of fun with women."

"Then who were you seeing Katy? I can see that you really liked him, and he hurt you. You forget that I've known you a long time too, hun." I say with a sad smile. "Do I need to go punch some guy in the balls for you? Cause you know I can do that now after all those self-defence classes we took together." That gets a huge laugh out of her, just like I hoped it would.

"Yeah, you've got the moves hun, you're a regular Bruce Lee," she lets out another laugh. "Do you use those moves on James?"

"No, I don't need to. He comes to me of his own free will and I love that about him. I love how he makes me feel Katy. Like I'm sexy and special. Like I mean something to him. I've never felt anything like it before, ever." I can feel the blush creep up my neck and across my cheeks. I can't help it though, because when I think about James, I get all hot and bothered, and it shows on my face. She knows it and so do I.

"That's a good thing Kami. No. It's amazing, I'm glad you've found someone who makes you feel like that. I thought I had for a while too, but it would appear I'm still waiting." She says on a sigh.

I reach my hand over to cover hers this time, offering comfort, "You'll find him one day Katy and you'll just know it's him." She smiles at me.

"I hope you're right Kami."

"I know I'm right Katy. He's around somewhere, just waiting for you." I say with a smile.

"I hope so, because I thought I'd found him. I honestly thought I'd found him, but it didn't work out."

I don't know who this guy is or was, but Katy really liked him. I'll get her over for dinner this week, we'll have a few wines and then maybe she'll spill some of these secrets of hers.

We finish our coffee and muffin while talking about everything and nothing. There is no more mention of men, feelings for them or warnings. Just good old-fashioned girl talk about anything that isn't man related. By the time we leave to head back to our jobs and the real world, we're hugging and laughing again. Just like always.

JAMES

Joe calls to check in with me and I tell him everything's fine. I'm fine, the jobs fine, it's all fucking fine. Of course, when I say it's all fucking fine, he laughs and says, "Yeah sure I can tell it's all fucking just fine, Harvey. Now tell me how it's really going out there?"

So, I do. I tell him all about the area we're building on being changed, how the guy who I'm dealing with is a douche, how the guys who came up this morning are bitching about the extra work we now have to do, how the orders weren't right and to top it all off deliveries were a complete fucking joke.

Now that I've finished yelling at him about everything that's fucked about the job, I start to tell him everything that's gone well. Which is fucking nothing.

"I hate this fucking place Joe. Why the fuck did I ever agree to do this job? Nothing can get here on time, the guy is driving me nuts changing shit all day, every day and the guys are ready to drop tools and run. They haven't even put in a full day yet!"

"So, you're doing well then?" he laughs, he actually laughs at me. If he was standing in front of me, he'd have a bloody nose.

"Yeah Joe, a real barrel of laughs going on here."

"If I remember correctly, you took the job because it was a good opportunity to expand your business and get your name out there. You took the job because you didn't want to work in just this town for the rest of your life." Joe says with a sigh, like he's disappointed in me for some reason. "You took this job because you didn't want to be doing shop fittings, house renovations and the like, for the rest of your life."

"Well, maybe I've changed my mind. I like my little corner of the world and I think I might just stay there." I snort and continue, "You've got no idea what this guy is like, man. He's a fuckstick, I mean we signed a contract and at every damned turn he's changing shit."

"Why did I need to call you to find out that he's changing the contract? I'm your goddamn accountant and I know that contract inside and out. I'm coming there to sort this shit out. You should have told me sooner James."

"Don't talk to me like I'm a fucking child Joe, sometimes you're a tool too. You're right, you're my accountant, not my fucking lawyer. You didn't write up the contract, I did, and Fred Cooke made it legal. What are you coming here for? What are you going to do about it?"

"Well then, call Fred and get.."

"I'm getting Fred down here, no one else needs to come here. I'm dealing with it in my own way and hopefully, I still have my crew with me when I'm done. I better only be here for the week and a bit or I'm going to go insane."

"It is the job or someone else?"

"What is it you're trying to ask Joe?" I ask, in my mood I could be about to lose a friend I've had for as long as I can remember.

"I'm just asking if your mind is on the job or is it someplace else? With someone else?"

"If you're asking if I'm missing Kami, then the answer is hell yes. Of course I miss her, we just got together and I'm away for two weeks, but we've made a deal to talk to each other every night, have a meal together. We may not be in the same place, but we can still share a meal."

"Right. Yeah sounds like you're completely on top of the job." Joe scoffs. I can't believe his attitude.

"What about the woman you've been seeing? What will she say if you just come on down here for a day or two? Hmmmmm?"

I hear his sudden intake of breath and laugh at his quiet stuttering over what to say next, "Well, she won't care it's nothing serious. In fact, it's nothing at all, we're over." He splutters out and I don't know if I believe him. I know he thinks he kept it secret, but I know that he's been talking about the same woman for weeks now and he's been trying to hide it. "So, she won't care a bit if I come to the site."

"You don't need to come here, I've got it under control. I just needed to get it off my chest is all and well, you asked."

"You're right I did, so I guess it was my own fault that you unloaded all that shit on me. I should have let you vent to Kami."

"Shut up Joe, you're a nasty bastard sometimes you know that? I'm in love with Kami, so you better start showing her some respect or things are going to get tough between you and me, OK?"

"Wow! Have you told *her* you love her? I didn't realise you were that serious about her." He sounds shocked, but he shouldn't be, it's always been leading to this.

"Yes Joseph, I'm deadly serious about her. Kami is it for me, I'm done. No more hooking up or one night stands. Kami and I are in a relationship. I haven't told her I love her yet and if you even hint at it to her before I have the chance to, I guarantee you'll have a fat lip my friend.

"How did you know?" he asks quietly. I'm not sure what he's talking about until he says, "that I was seeing someone. How did you know?"

I sigh, does he really have to ask me? "I've known you for a long time Joe. Even though you haven't said her name, I know you were seeing the same woman because you were happy. Consistently happy. You had regular dates, not a date here and a date there. You were messaging on your phone and smiling, no business message could ever cause that kind of smile. You were happy and now you're a grumpy jerk again, so I'm guessing something happened and you guys broke up."

I'm right, I know I'm right, but the stubborn bastard probably won't admit it.

"You're right, I was seeing someone, but I stuffed up and now she won't talk to me." Joe actually sounds like he misses this woman.

"What did you do? Surely you guys can talk it through, and work it out?"

"No, I ummm. No, it doesn't matter, it's over. Done. She can't forgive me so, we're done."

Well, OK then, that sounds like the Joe I know. Stubborn bastard that he is.

"I'm getting myself back to work so that the guys and I can finish up and get some rest for tomorrow." We say our goodbyes and then I head back to work.

When the guys and I are done for the day, we head back to the hotel to take hot showers and relax. Some of the guys have families that they want to call when they get back to their rooms before they all fall asleep. The others go and have a few drinks, but I want to hear Kami's voice. After the crappy day and weird conversation with Joe, I just want to hear her voice.

I'm lying in my bed when Kami calls. I didn't make it any further than that after my shower. We talk for a while, I tell her about my day and then she starts telling me about the weird conversation she had with Katy. I tell her about my weird conversation with Joe too and we decide, it must be something in the air with our friends this week.

When I yawn for what feels like the millionth time in a minute, Kami tells me to get some sleep, but I want to talk to her for longer.

"I was hoping for a repeat of last night's performance sweetheart," I say, but even I can hear the sleepiness in my voice.

"I'm not sure you could stay awake for it James." She laughs letting out a yawn of her own.

"I'll teach you a thing or two when I get home about staying awake, Miss Parker," I say, just as another yawn takes control of my body.

"I look forward to those lessons Mr Harvey, but for now I think you need to get some sleep." She lets out this soft chuckle and I want to tell her that I love her.

"I miss you Kami," I say. I'm almost asleep while we speak.

"I miss you too, James. Now get some sleep." She says in a whisper. "Goodnight James."

"Goodnight, Kami." That's the last thing I remember before falling asleep.

KAMI

Poor James. He sounded exhausted on the phone tonight, I wanted to be there to give him a massage, a hot meal and put him to bed.

I'm in so deep with this man. I actually want to feed him and look after him. Katy's right, James has the ability to absolutely break me and right now, I don't care one bit. She's right about something else too, I've been a little in love with him since high school, but I'm glad nothing ever happened back then. I like adult James a whole lot more than teenager James.

I send Katy a text;

Kami: *I think I'm in love with him Katy*

Almost immediately I get a text back;

Katy: *ahh no shit woman I know you're in love with him*

Katy: *It's not a bad thing Kami just be careful*

I get the second one straight after the first one before I could even think about responding. So I send her back the only thing I can that would make us both feel slightly better.

Kami: *I love you Katy*

I get the same text back from her and I relax into my covers.

I go to sleep with a smile on my face. I don't like arguing with Katy, and telling each other that we love each other, even when we argue, it's our way of making peace with the disagreements. I can sleep easier knowing that we were OK again.

When I wake up the next morning, I'm on autopilot getting ready for work. My alarm goes off and it's one of those mornings where I just have a shower, get my coffee, some breakfast, and get in the car and head to the shop, without me even realising that I've done it.

My mind is too busy thinking about my conversations with James and Katy last night.

There's something niggling at the back of my mind that the two conversations are linked somehow. That the guy Katy was seeing for a while and the fact that Joe just broke up with a 'lady friend'. I shake my head to get rid of this uneasy feeling I have and put it all down to a bizarre coincidence. I laugh at myself when a thought hits my brain. Maybe Katy and Joe were seeing each other? I can't imagine it, Katy has never liked Joe, and Joe's been very vocal about his dislike for the both of us. That would be really weird.

I push the thought to the back of my mind as the bell over the door jingles and the first customer of the day enters the shop.

Chapter Twenty-Two

JAMES

As the new day looms in front of me, I want to stay in bed and think about Kami. I wish she was here, curled into my body all warm and soft. When I start to imagine all the ways I could wake her up, my cock stands to attention wishing any of those ideas would actually come to life in front of him, but they're not going to.

I drag my body out of the bed and have a quick shower. I push thoughts of Kami out of my mind to concentrate on the job at hand, and not my hand on my cock. Not that I'm really in the mood once the face of Simon the douchebag comes to mind, anyway.

Kami had one thing right last night, I wasn't in the mood for the same fun we'd had the night before. I was exhausted mentally and physically from this dickhead changing his mind all the fucking time. My guys aren't the only ones pissed off with his behaviour. If he starts down the same road again today, he'll be getting a piece of mind that he probably won't enjoy. I'll be blowing my chances on this job and any others that have a chance from coming from it, but sometimes your sanity and the sanity of the guys working for you, are worth more than any one job or any potential jobs.

The guys are away from their families and I'm away from Kami. None of us are willing to take on too much bullshit to be away from the ones we love even if the pay check is a good one.

Now I'm in a grumpy mood already and I need coffee. I walk out of my room, heading towards my car, the coffee I made in my hand, and see the guys leaning against my car.

"Morning boss."

"Morning Jeffery, guys. What's up?" I ask, even though I'm pretty sure I know what I'm going to hear from the lead guy on the crew. I nod at the other two guys, Billy and Leo, who both nod in return.

"James, I think you know what I'm going to say, but I'm still going to say it. We've worked together for a long time, but this job boss, it's.." I don't let him finish, he's about to say exactly what I was expecting him to.

"Yeah, I know Jeff, I've got a meeting with the charming Simon this morning and I am going to get the final plans off him. He is going to sign off on them and then he's going to let us do our job. If he doesn't, then we don't have a job here anymore." I sigh and continue, "I'm sorry guys. When I first met up with this group, they had their ideas set in stone and plans in place. Simon isn't the person I signed the contracts with, and I have no idea what happened to that original contact, but I haven't seen or heard from her."

"This isn't your fault James, you couldn't know this jerk was going to keep changing his mind and the plans." Billy says.

"He's right boss." Leo chimes in.

"Thanks guys but it's my job to deal with these kinds of details guys and I'm supposed to make sure that the job goes as smoothly as it can. This guy is busting my balls and I've been here for a couple of days." I growl out and then I realise I have to pull myself back, these are my employees, not a group of mates standing around having a chat. "Why don't you guys go inside, sit down and have breakfast and coffee, I'll go have my meeting with Simon and then we can get back to work."

"Thanks boss. We'll see you when we're done, we won't be long though." Jeff says as he pushes the other two guys into the hotel dining room. I get into my truck and head over to the building site for my meeting with Simon. I'm not looking forward to it, but there have to be some answers this morning. One way or another.

KAMI

The next day is like the ones before James and I got together.

I get my butt out of bed and ready for work. Open the shop, get into the dreaded paperwork once Ed comes in and then go to grab lunch at the café. The biggest difference to my days these days, is missing James. I've gotten so used to him being around and having lunch together, that dining alone is boring and lonely. At least Josie is nice to me these days when I head in there now, she doesn't just take my order and then bring it over. She actually talks to me and asks how I am. I guess she's over her infatuation with James. He told me, when I asked him about it, that she was also possessive of him, even in school but he couldn't ever understand why, nothing ever happened between them and he never gave her any indication that it would.

With all the time I've spent in my office while James and his crew were working on the renovations, I've caught up on all my paperwork and I get to spend more time in the shop. Which is exactly what I do after I get back from lunch.

"Why don't you take the afternoon off boss?" Ed asks after he's had his lunch.

"Why would I take the afternoon off?" I ask, looking at him in confusion. I'm always here, the shop is what I do.

"Ahhhh cause you can? I've got everything under control, you don't have any paperwork. When was the last time you took some time for yourself?"

I look at him, completely confused and thinking about his question. He's right, I have no clue when the last time was that I wasn't here, doing something. "I don't know Ed, I can't remember. The last few years have been all about getting the shop open and keeping it running."

"Exactly my point. Maybe you should take some time away while you can."

"But what am I going to do?" I ask, honestly not sure what I should do with 'spare' time. If James was in town, I would see him. Maybe even put some time in to cook him a meal.

"Well, geez Kami, maybe you could take a bath? Read one of the many books you purchase 'for the shop', cook yourself something nice, relax a little?" Ed says on a sigh and I get the feeling he's slightly annoyed with me. I'm just not used to having much down time. "Maybe you can catch up with Katy, it's been a while, hasn't it?"

"You might be onto something there Ed. I'll call Katy and see if she can come over for dinner and a few drinks tonight." He smiles at me and he's got me thinking. It's been too long since Katy and I had a catch up. We were meant to go out a few weeks ago and well, we all know how that ended up.

"Off ya go then. Get out of here before I change my mind, or we get busy."

"Ohhh what if you get busy and I'm not here? No you're right, I think I should stay."

"*Get out of here Kami.*" He gives me a stern look and points to the door. Pushy bastard, sometimes I think he forgets who the boss is around here.

"OK I'll go but only if you promise to call me if you need me to come back for anything," he nods his agreement and I continue, "OK, I'll grab my bag and get the out of here then."

I walk out the back door after yelling out my goodbye to Ed, and as I'm getting into my car, I call Katy.

"Hey gorgeous, what can I do for you on this lovely day?" she answers.

"Wow, you're in a better mood today hun."

"Yes, I am. Nothing can keep this chick down," she replies, and I can hear the smile in her voice. Which makes me happy, because the last time we spoke, she didn't have that lightness in her voice. "Why are you calling me in the middle of the afternoon hun? Is everything OK?"

"Yeah of course everything's fine. It's not like I never call you anymore Katy." I say feeling a little offended. I may not have called her for a while, but she hasn't called me either. "The phone works both ways you know Katy," I say with a bit more snark than I actually mean to.

"I know Kami, I honestly didn't mean anything by it. I know I haven't called you either, let's just agree that we've both been a little, distracted OK?" Her voice is quiet, and I know without a doubt, that we both feel bad about the situation.

"I'm sorry Katy, I know we've both been busy," I say quietly. I'm still wondering who the guy was she was seeing, and why she didn't tell me about him. "Come over for dinner tonight? Ed kicked me out of the shop early and told me do something for myself that didn't include the shop. We haven't caught up for ages and I really want to hear what you've been up to. I'll feed you and we can have a few glasses of wine and talk."

"That sounds," she hesitates for a few seconds and I think she's going to say no, instead she says, "perfect. Actually, that sounds like the perfect night. You cook, and I'll bring the wine, just let me finish up a few things and I'll try to get out of the office a little early."

"I'm really looking forward to it Katy, I've missed you, you know. I know we've messaged, but it's not the same thing."

"Yeah I know Kami, I'm looking forward to catching up. Now get off the phone and let me finish up some work that way I can come over sooner rather than later."

"Alright, get off the phone then." I say with a laugh, and Katy laughs too.

"Well, you hang up then." Katy says, laughing loudly.

I laugh because she's started one of the things we've done since we were kids. We always picked on those teen couples that couldn't stand to be the first one to hang up the phone.

"You hang up."

"No *you* hang up."

"No, no *you* hang up dork." I'm laughing so hard, I can barely get the words out now.

"Dork you say? Well, *nerd* I'm hanging up now, that means I get the last laugh." The last thing I hear is her crazy laugh as she hangs up the phone. I've missed having that crazy girl around and I'm looking forward to our get together tonight. It's been way too long.

JAMES

I leave the crew at the hotel eating their hot breakfast, something that I really would have enjoyed myself this morning. It certainly feels like a better place to be than sitting across from Simon the douche, at my makeshift workbench at the work site, trying to get him to nail down the plans once and for all. I need him to make these decisions and to get his signature on them before the guys get here. Before I lose it at this guy and tell him where to shove his job because I can't stand the changes anymore. Dozens of fucking changes every fucking day, he's driving me crazy, and despite what I said to Joe, I do actually want to finish this job. I'm hoping it will give me the opportunity to do more jobs like it, only with less douche like behaviours.

Simon's talking to me, but I've spaced out thinking about how much of a douche he is, and I have no idea what he just said to me. Instead of asking him to repeat himself, I ask him the question I've been wanting to for the last of couple of days.

"Simon, is there a reason you keep changing the plans? Is there something I don't know about the requirements for the building? Because when I first met up with your predecessor, we had designs and plans all signed off," I start.

Simon interrupts me, "Yes but I'm not …"

"No, you're right," I cut in. "You're not the person I spoke to originally and you obviously have different views of the project, but the thing is, you're making my job very difficult. I had plans signed off and supplies ordered. Now, I've been here a couple of days and the supplies I ordered aren't needed, the suppliers are pissed at me for changing my mind, even though it's your mind that's making changes and asking for returns and then placing new orders with them." I take a breath and hold up my hand to stop him from talking, "No let me finish, please. My crew aren't getting any work done, there is no progress at all, because every time we get something started, you change your mind." I take another deep breath and much to my surprise Simon doesn't try to speak, "Look, if you've changed your mind and don't want my company here or you're not happy with our work, then speak up. No harm, no foul, but I can't deal with the dozen or more changes you're making every day anymore. It's not fair to me, my crew or you. This job is never going to be completed if we continue on like this."

"No. No I want you and your crew to see this project through to the end." He pauses but I don't speak, I've got nothing else to say, the rest is all his choice now. I'm not *happy* as such to walk away from this project, but I am willing to do it. "It's just that.. as you're aware, I took over this project at short notice, and I've only known about its existence for about a couple of weeks. Julia left suddenly, and I was handed the project and told to 'get it done'. Now, I'm left with a project that has someone else's ideas ingrained into it, but the responsibility of success or failure of it. I'm trying to change the things I don't like but I've hit the ground running and now, we're all paying for it." He takes another breath and I nod at him to keep going and he sighs. "You're right though, that approach really isn't working. How about, we let your guys continue on with the changes we made yesterday, and you and I sit down with the current plans and see if some of the things I'm thinking about can be accommodated? Then we can finalise the plans and sign off on them."

Simon's looking at me and I'm taking my time answering him. I don't really want to make him uncomfortable, but I do want him to realise that he can't fuck me or my crew around anymore. He shifts slightly on his feet, I probably wouldn't have noticed except that we're standing on gravel and they shuffled as he moved.

"Simon." I say, then I hesitate. I'm not sure what I want to say to be honest. "*If* we can sit down this morning and come to final agreements, then my crew and I will stay to finish the job, but if we can't come to an agreement today, we're done." I don't want to walk away from this project, it's a huge deal for my business and I want more like it, but I don't want this guy to think I'm a pushover and I don't want future clients to think so either.

I know, by the look on Simon's face that he doesn't think I'm serious, but I don't back down, looking him dead in the eyes, completely serious. After a few minutes, his attitude changes and he reaches out his hand, "You've got a deal James. Why don't we grab a coffee and sit down now? Get the ball rolling." I nod and just as we sit down with our coffee's, my phone rings.

"Excuse me Simon, I'll only be a minute." When I look at it and see it's Jeff, I can only assume he's checking in to see if we still have a job to do. "Hey Jeff, how was breakfast?" I ask, answering the phone.

"Yeah, good boss. What's going on? Just thought we'd check in before we came out to the site, just in case you managed to lose us the contract." I can't help the half laugh that comes out of my mouth, he was hoping I'd talked us out of this contract, he sounds pretty hopeful.

"You guys need to get up here to get moving on what we were working on late yesterday. The rest I'm discussing with Simon this morning, if we can't come to an agreement, then we may be going home early."

"OK boss, we're in the car and on the way." I don't know if I'd say that Jeff sounds happy about it, but he's still got a job to do and he'll get it done, that's why he's the foreman on this crew. It's also why I give him some young guys on his crew, he can mentor them and teach them that a hard day's work is worth the effort and he doesn't put up with their shit.

"See you soon Jeff," I say and hang up.

When I walk back over to where Simon is sitting going over the plans that I've seen more of in the last few days than I did even when I drew the fuckers up. I can understand that he doesn't like some of the decisions that Julia made, but the fucker has changed one detail in almost every step so far. There's material he doesn't like, or a colour that doesn't match. Everyone has different tastes, but this isn't his fucking home, he doesn't have to live in it, so I don't get why he's being so picky.

"I'm guessing that was your crew checking to see if they still had a job to come to?" he asks as I take my seat again.

"Yeah it was, so let's get this meeting going so that I can give them an answer, one way or the other." I know I sound annoyed, but fuck it, I am annoyed, and I want this meeting over and done with so that we can get on with the job.

Two and a bit hours later, we've agreed, disagreed, argued and made changes that we can both live with. I'm glad that I spoke to Simon this morning and we've finally got this shit sorted. Now the crew and I can get on to getting the project done and get the fuck out of here. Simon still isn't my favourite person, but I think we can manage to deal with each other for the next couple of weeks.

I stand up and shake his hand, "Glad we could sort this out Simon. I'll get the new plans drawn up today and once you've signed off on them, I'll order the new materials and the crew can get moving."

He shakes my hand and nods, "Thank you for your patience James, I know I've been difficult, and I appreciate you coming to me to talk it out. Let me know when you've redone the plans I'll come over right away to sign off on them so you can keep moving forward."

"I hope you know that these changes are going to create a few delays. I may not be able to get the materials here as early as we'd like, after all it's in the hands of the suppliers and I may not be their favourite person this week."

At least he has the decency to look slightly embarrassed as he replies, "I can understand that and again, I apologise for stuffing you around. If you need me for anything else, just call and I'll see what I can do."

With that he's gone, and I breathe a sigh of relief. Thank fuck that shit is all done, and I can sit down and redraw these plans. Honestly, I managed to talk him out of the bigger changes that he wanted to do, the ones he agreed to, are simple enough. It's getting the materials I need here in time to get it all done. I can only hope that the suppliers aren't too pissed off with me with all the changes I've already made two orders this week. I've only been here for a couple of days and I've already had to make too many phone calls to them.

Just as my butt hits my chair, Jeff knocks and walks in the door. "Hey bossman. Just saw the douchebag leave in his car, are we all sorted or are we out of here?"

I can't fault him for asking, I was pretty pissed off when I left the hotel this morning, and he knows how much shit I'm willing to take. Not much if I'm being honest.

"Hey Jeff, yeah we're staying. Simon and myself just spent the last couple of hours going through everything he was thinking about changing and I managed to talk him out any major changes, but there are a few things I need to do. I'm going to sit in here and draw up the plan again, once I'm done he's coming back to sign off on them. Then I'll call around and hopefully get the supplies. You can continue on what you're doing for now, by the time you're done I should be ready with everything else."

Jeff nods and says, "No worries boss. Just thought I'd check in and see where we were at before we kept going. Don't want to be doing something if it's about to be someone else's job."

"Yeah, I get that. Now get back to it so I can get these plans done." He smiles and ducks back out of my makeshift on-site office and I get stuck into drawing up the new plans.

Chapter Twenty-Three

KAMI

After I've set up my music to play through my speakers, I decide to run a bath and relax for a while before I start dinner for Katy and myself. After all, Ed did tell me to take off early for some me time. I don't get a lot of that, so why not take advantage of it?

I pile my hair up in a messy bun on top of my head, strip off my clothes and sink in to the hot water. I sink below the bubbles that smell like berries and vanilla, take a deep breath and feel every muscle relax. It's been a while since I took the time to soak in the bathtub and I realise I've missed it. It's not something I can fit in in the mornings and then by the time I'm home, I just want to have dinner, finish off paperwork and then head to bed. Then it just starts all over again. Rinse and repeat.

Not today. Thanks to Ed, I'm taking the day to chill and catch up with my best friend. I'm grateful that Ed made me leave early today, I know he's more than capable of holding down the fort at the shop, but it's my business and it's really hard letting someone help out, but I wouldn't have hired Ed if I didn't think I could trust him.

I don't know how long I've been stretched out in the bathtub and I don't care. I didn't even bring my phone into the bathroom, I thought about reading while in here but decided against it. I know myself well enough to know that I'd get distracted and start doing stuff for work on there. I can't help myself and if I didn't go searching for work, I know I'd have been all over social media and the point was to relax.

I've got my eyes closed, reclined back against the side of the tub and I can hear my music playing faintly in the background. Then there's this jingling noise interrupting the music and my relaxed vibe. It takes me until it starts up again to realise it's my damned phone ringing. I guess my soaking time is over, the waters starting to get chilly anyway, so I pull the plug and rinse myself off. I love having a soak in the tub, but I still feel like I need a shower afterwards for some ridiculous reason.

I step out, wrap my body and hair in towels trying to keep a little warm and walk out to the lounge room to grab my phone. Just as I reach for it, it starts ringing, again. The only thing running through my head is that something's happened at the shop and I need to get there, but when I look at the screen before I answer, it's James calling. Surely he hasn't blown up my phone for a chat?

"Hi James, is everything OK?" I ask when I answer.

"Hey beautiful. Everything's fine, even better now that I can hear your voice." He says in that deep baritone voice of his that I love listening to.

"So what was so urgent that you felt the need to blow up my phone babe?" I ask, still wondering why he needed to call me so often in a few minutes.

"Sorry I didn't mean to, it's just that I only have a few minutes spare and I wanted to hear your voice."

"Oh." Is all I can manage, because honestly I don't know whether to be happy or offended.

"I'm sorry, were you busy with a customer?" he asks, sounding genuinely concerned that he interrupted me.

"No. Actually, Ed told me to take off early and do something relaxing for a change. So the only thing you interrupted was me soaking in a bubble bath."

"Oh Kami, that's one mental image I didn't need right now," he groans, sending a shiver down my spine.

"Oh well, you asked me what I was doing, and the bath is what I was doing when you called. I guess you'd rather not know that I'm wearing just a towel right now either then, huh?" I ask with a smile, flirting over the phone with James is fun.

"Fucking hell woman are you trying to kill me right now?" I can hear his breathing get heavy, and I laugh at him. "Damn it! I knew I should have called you from my office or later tonight from the hotel. You're killing me sweetheart. You have no idea how much I want to be there with you and knowing that you're warm, damp and smell extra amazing is making me miss you even more."

"If it's any consolation, I didn't 'flick the bean' and I wish you were here too, but you're not so I guess we both have to just deal with it."

"Flick the bean, is that what we're calling self pleasure these days? Personally, I call it what it is, masturbation. Simple and to the point. The point being I'm now trying to hide my hard-on while walking around a fucking building site, because the mental images that you just conjured up like a magician are driving me fucking crazy."

This brings more growls out of him. I like the growls, growly James is sexy.

"Surely there's enough wood lying around that you don't need to add anymore James." I say, still laughing, because I can. I'm not walking around with a hard-on at work.

"Easy for you to laugh, you don't have three guys looking at you like you've lost the plot." He grumbles.

"I guess you want me to say I'm sorry, but I'm not," I laugh again. "So, what is it you wanted to talk to me about or were you just calling because you had a minute?"

"Cheeky woman, this is not a laughing matter, it's quite a serious situation you know. I'm supposed to be the adult here, the boss. Not some schmuck walking around with a woody while talking to his girlfriend." He sounds serious for a second, but then he chuckles, "I was calling for two reasons actually, I have a few minutes to call and I have something to tell you." He takes a deep breath before speaking again, "Unfortunately, this job is going to take a little longer than I first expected. My contact here has made so many changes to the original plans that it's going to take us some time to catch up and get them all finished."

He sounds so miserable at the prospect of staying there longer than expected, but it's his job and he has to do what he has to do. "Oh well, I'm sorry you have to stay there longer than you were hoping, but you've got a job to finish, so finish it."

"Yeah I know, I just wish this idiot hadn't screwed with my timelines. I mean I've got more than this job to think about." I hadn't even thought about how running over on this job would push back start times on other jobs he'd already have lined up. "But, I managed to get this guy to sign off on new plans this morning which I am over the moon about because anymore changes now, and I swear to god the guys and I will walk. He's lucky I hadn't really lined up another job the week after his, but I did have plans that will now have to be changed."

"Well, at least they were plans that you can rearrange easily."

"No, they were plans I had for you. I don't want to rearrange them, but because of Simon, I have to now. I'm sorry Kami. To make matters worse, I'm going to be so busy the next few days organising suppliers and materials that I won't have time to call you either. They're going to be long days out here, just so I can get back to some sort of decent deadline and I can come home."

"That's OK James, how about we stay radio silent for the rest of the week? If we manage to get some time on the weekend, we can catch up? I'd rather you concentrate on your job and getting things moving than worrying about me back here. I'm a big girl you know, I know you're working, not partying in Hawaii with beach babes in bikinis. Even if you were, I'm not sure I have any rights to say that you can't, but you're not you're working. Maybe, if you get things sorted out, I can even come visit for the weekend?"

"You'd have every right to have something to say about that Hawaii scenario and I wouldn't do that to you anyway." I hear a mumbled voice in the background and then James says, "Yeah ok give me a second and I'll be there." To me he says, "I'm sorry sweetheart, but I have to go, Jeff needs my help with something so that we can finish up for the day. I can't call you tonight because I'm eating with the guys and then having one final meeting with Simon. I'll let you know if a visit would be worth the trip for you, OK?"

"That's OK babe. I've got Katy coming over tonight and I've promised her dinner and a movie. We can catch up in a couple of days."

"OK sweetheart tell Katy I said hi and I'll talk to you in a few days when I get all this shit settled." James hesitates for just a second and then says, "Bye sweetheart."

"Talk soon James, take care." I say and then he's gone, and my heart is in my throat. I was so dang close to saying I loved him. There's no way I'm saying it to him for the first time over the phone though, especially when he's half a day's drive away.

My body temperature has really chilled since I've been talking to James, so I head into my bedroom to get dressed. Jeans and a t-shirt are my outfit of choice, I don't even slip socks or shoes on my feet. When I'm lounging around the house, I hate having shoes on. Unless it's cold, I won't even put some socks on my feet. Katy doesn't expect anything fancy though, and that means my clothes or dinner. She'll just be happy to eat something she hasn't ordered in or cooked herself.

I turn up the music and shake my butt while I get dinner prepared and ready to cook. A roast chicken, roast vegetables, with some homemade gravy, is just what the comfort food doctor ordered. Once that's all sorted I move onto dessert. No girl's night in, would be complete without a little something sweet and I decide that brownies fit in with the comfort food doctor's orders. I've got some vanilla ice cream sitting in the freezer just waiting to be smothered over some oozy, chocolatey goodness. My mouth waters just thinking about it.

Twenty minutes later, I'm pulling the brownies out of the oven when I hear the front door open and close. Katy's here. Well, I hope it's Katy otherwise I'm in trouble.

"Oh. My. God. Kami. It smells delicious in here!" Katy squeals and I let out the breath I didn't even know I was holding.

"I hope you're hungry Katy, cause I have plenty of food." I say with a laugh.

"You know me Kami honey, I'm always ready for a decent feed and your meals are always top of my list to eat too much of." We both laugh at the truth of that statement and then both seem to realise at the same time, just how long it's been since we ate a meal together, never less me actually cook one for us to eat together.

"I'm sorry Katy, I know it's been a while since we shared a meal, whether it's one I've cooked or one we've ordered in."

"Don't apologise Kami, because even though you're right and it's been a while, no-one is at fault. We're busy women, you own your own business and I'm killing in the office right now. The point is, we're here now, and that's what matters." She walks over, places the wine bag on the kitchen bench and wraps me up in a hug that doesn't last long enough.

"You're right, I know you are, but that doesn't make it feel any less strange that we haven't done this in what feels like forever. You were busy with work and that guy you were seeing and now I'm busy with work and James." She steps away from me to grab some glasses, "What happened with that guy, anyway? I never even got the chance to meet him before you guys were over." As she opens and then pours the wine, I get the feeling she's keeping busy so that she doesn't have to look me in the eye. Which is unusual for Katy, she's a very straight forward kind of girl. It's one of the main reasons I love her so fiercely.

"Well, the fact is Kam, I wasn't sure it could work out from the very beginning. Actually, that's a half truth. I was *really* hoping that we could make it work from the beginning but some things, ohhh honey, some things just can't be overlooked. Whether he's right or wrong for me doesn't really matter in the end, the timing wasn't right, and we agreed to leave it while we could still call ourselves friends. Sort of." She looks at me as she hands me over the glass of wine, and she's got a sad, yet accepting smile on her face. It makes me wonder what really went on and I hope like hell this butthead didn't flake out on my best friend because of her medical issues.

"Ohhhhh Katy, that doesn't sound like you at all. You don't put the time in to a guy if you can't see something that makes you want to move forward with him." She's not picky per se, but she's had a couple of jerks run her around when they find out that their future could look different than what they were expecting.

"Oh Kam, there was a future there, it was just a little hard to work out some of the finer details. He didn't do anything wrong, neither did I. It just wasn't going to work out and we decided to save ourselves the heartache down the track and move on now." I can see it in her face, this guy meant, *still* means, something to her, and she's had to walk away for whatever reason.

"I'm sorry it didn't work out for you guys honey, I can see that it hurts. You must have really liked this one." She nods sadly, and I can feel her pain just standing next to her, "Did he have reservations because of your health, or was it something else? Whatever it was, I can see that he hurt you and if you tell me who he is, I can go and hit him in the nose. Or I can send James to do it for me?" I say with a smile, hoping to lighten up the mood but it only seems to make her sadder.

"Actually, no he was fine with the whole idea that I may not be able to have kids, and not because he didn't want them but because he wanted me." I can see the tears building in her eyes and I reach out to hold her. "No Kam, please don't. The truth is there were too many other things that we couldn't change, it wouldn't have worked. Honestly it's for the best and I'd rather not keep talking about him, OK?"

"Yeah OK hun, I'm really sorry it didn't work out for you. It sounds like he was perfect." I say sadly and walk over to the oven to check on the chicken and to hide the couple of tears I let slide down my own face. My best friend deserves to be happy and I'm upset that she's so sad but tonight we'll have a great night of fun and laughter. Hopefully I can cheer her up and even when James gets home, I promise myself that I'll make the effort to catch up with Katy more often than I have been. I jump as the timer rings out through the house, scaring the life out of both of us.

"Holy shit honey, do you really need a timer that's so loud it wakes up the dead? That thing just scared the crap out of me!" Katy squeals and I start to laugh.

"How do you think I feel? I was standing next to it when it went off." When I see her shocked face, my laughter becomes uncontrollable. We're both bent over, tears streaming down our faces and struggling to catch our breath, sucking in air, for I don't even know how long. All I do know is that I managed to turn off the oven before we started laughing uncontrollably, so hopefully dinner isn't ruined.

"Arghhh crap Kami, I needed that." Katy says as she catches her breath first and wipes her eyes.

"Me too. I haven't laughed like that for a long dang time and I've missed it." I smile, while wiping the tears off my cheeks. I turn and take the chicken out of the oven, along with the vegetables and check them all out. "Perfect! Now if you get some plates, I can dish up some dinner. I think we deserve some food after that workout."

"I can agree with that. Not that I'd ever say no to your cooking honey, you know that and if the price I have to pay is grabbing the implements that help us to eat it, it's a price I'm more than willing to pay."

I laugh while I dish up our dinner and we sit at the table with our wine and just talk. Catching up on everything that's happened since the last time we saw each other. Skirting around the few months were she was seeing the guy that sounds about as close to perfection for my best friend than she's likely to find again. If only I knew who he was, I could have a talk to him and maybe work out a way for them to be together. I know she's not going to tell me anything more about him though, I can see the pain on her face every time she thinks about him and thinks I'm not looking.

When we finish dinner, I slice off some big chunks of brownie, warm them up a bit in the microwave and the scoop out some ice cream to plunk on top. Then we take our bowls into the lounge room, settle down onto the couch, pulling throw blankets up over our legs and putting cushions behind our backs. I go to pick up the remote to search Netflix and Katy grabs it before I can get to it.

"My choice tonight. You'll pick some action packed, car chasing, explosion filled, adrenaline junkie performance driven blockbuster and while normally I'm all for that, mainly because they've also got some sexy brooding bad boy in them, not tonight. Tonight I'm making you watch a soppy romance, so we can have all the feels for a different kind of sexy man. One that has his shit together and knows he wants the girl and chases her, keeps her forever. That's what I want to watch tonight."

She looks over at me when her rant is finished, and I can't do anything except nod in agreement. My best friend is hurting and the least I can do is let her watch a soppy, romance filled movie. "Sure it's Katy's choice tonight. So what are we watching then and which sexy man is in it?"

We've both finished dessert and I'm totally enthralled in the movie she's picked. It's full of all the feels and I can see why she wanted to watch it. By the end, I've got tears rolling down my face but when I speak to Katy and she doesn't answer me, I'm not sure if she's dealing with the emotions quietly or not, so I look over and realise she's asleep. Dang it! I watched that soppy thing all on my own. I don't know how I didn't notice she was asleep earlier, she's managed to go from a sitting position into almost laying down next to me. I don't have the heart to wake her up and send her home, so instead I place my blanket over her. I pick up all our dishes and deposit them in the kitchen, they can wait until the morning. When I reach over to take her phone out of her hand, I notice a message has just come through, I don't catch the name as it flashes up on the screen, but I do manage to read at least some of the message, *babe, I miss you*, before her screen goes black again and my heart breaks just a little bit more for my best friend.

She shifts on the couch, making herself more comfortable and I turn off the tv and all the lights, then head to my bedroom. I get into my pyjamas and go to turn off the lights when I notice a message on my phone too.

James: *Goodnight sweetheart, I miss you x*

Kami: Goodnight babe, I miss you too x

My hearts does this little flutter as I reply to his message and I realise just how lucky I am to have reconnected with James and we were able to make this relationship work for us.

Chapter Twenty-Four

JAMES

S tupid fucking work sites.

Stupid fucking phones.

Stupid fucking me!

Thank fuck Joe came out to check on shit today, cause I need him to go get me a new phone. Why do I need a new phone? Cause I dropped the mother fucking thing on stones, there's grass all around me and I drop it on the stones, and it shattered. Yeah it didn't just crack, it *shattered* to pieces! Kami's calling me tonight, so I need a new phone. We haven't spoken all week like we agreed and I'm dying to hear her voice tonight. I don't care what phone it is, I just need to be able to answer her call, and I can't get away from the site today to go buy one myself.

I feel bad asking him to run around for me, but I really have no time to do it. I've gotten suppliers back on side and I need to be here when they deliver, otherwise I'm going to have a bunch of businesses pissed at me again. I agreed to personally sign off on every delivery, otherwise they wouldn't deliver out here. I can't say I blame them, but it pissed me off, anyway. Then I dropped my phone and let's just say the guys are giving me a wide berth because my mood can only be described as fucking dark.

Joe sets off into town and says he'll bring lunch back for all of us as well. One less thing for me to worry about I guess. I don't even notice how long he's been gone, I've taken deliveries, helped out the guys and then taken more deliveries.

The guys take a break when Joe gets back with lunch but I'm still accepting deliveries.

"James, come on man come and eat something." Joe says as he wanders over while I sign off on the latest delivery.

"Yeah, give me a couple of minutes and I'll come over."

"I got your favourite," he says.

"What's that Joe? Food?" I say with a laugh, but I still don't look over to him

"Come on man, you have to eat. You can't exist on air and love alone you know." Now I know he's trying to get my attention with the love jab, but all I can think about is Kami. I want to be having lunch with Kami and telling her I love her. There is nothing I want more, not even finishing this stupid, pain in the arse job would make me happier.

"You know what Joe? I know I can't live on air and love alone, but love will keep me moving on this project, if for no reason other than to get back home to Kami." He has my attention now and I can see the shock on his face, before he closes down again. "You come back to me when you've found a woman to love and who loves you, then tell me how she motivates you to get your work done so that you can get home to her." I turn and walk over to my crew who are halfway through eating their lunch.

"Hey boss, I saved you some, Billy was trying to eat it for you." Jeff says. I look over at Billy and he can't look me in the eyes.

"Was he just? Let me give you a word of advice Billy, it's never a good idea to eat the boss' food. Just remember he's the one who signs your pay-checks, keep him happy and he'll at least try to keep you happy."

"Yes, boss." Billy nods, he looks so serious and nervous that I can't help laughing at him.

"It's a joke Billy. Sort of anyway, the general rule is, don't eat anyone's lunch and you'll be happy and safe on a job site." He nods again, "Don't look so serious, I have food in the office, anyway." I can see his shoulders visibly relax.

When we're finished with lunch, the guys get back to work and Joe and I go into my office.

"So, what's the real reason you came all the way out here Joe? I thought you were too busy with your own job to worry about mine. I mean don't get me wrong, the timing was perfect, for me but there has to be a reason you're here." I ask. I think I know why he's checking up on me and if I'm right, we are in for an argument he's not counting on.

"I could hear you were stressing out up here, so I thought I'd drive up and check out the situation for myself. It doesn't look as bad as you made it sound you know? You look like you've got everything under control now." He sounds surprised and I'm not sure I want to know why he's so surprised.

"This isn't my first rodeo you know Joe. I think you forget sometimes that I've grown this business from the ground up, by myself. I know you've helped me along the way with the financial side of things and maybe a few contacts for jobs and the like, but this is *my* business Joe. I've worked hard to make happen."

"I know all that James. Remember I was there when you started up Harvey Carpentry. I know how hard you've worked, and I know what this project means for the company as well. That's why I came down to see how you were going, you sounded unusually stressed out and pissed off about this project taking longer than originally planned. That's not something that gets under your skin normally, you understand that things change, and delays are normal, that sometimes they just can't be helped."

"You're right, but I had this job organised and signed off with Julia and then I wasn't notified until I got here that she wasn't the project manager anymore and I had to deal with Simon." I sigh and take a breath to calm down because I know I'm getting worked up ...again. "To top it off, he didn't even know the project existed until a week before I was due here and he's got different ideas to what Julia had, which meant changes. Every. Damn. Day. He changes things, until I finally sat him down and told him to tell me every change he was thinking about so that I didn't have to deal with that shit every day. I've also had ..."

"I get it, but I can't help but think that the real reason you're feeling frustrated is because of Kami. You're never this restless or aggravated James, I'm sure even the guys have noticed."

"Well, I do miss Kami and I don't really want to be away from her for this long at one stretch again, but this job was already in motion before we got together, and the fact is she's been great about me being away. The guys on the crew are missing their families too, I think Jeff was hoping I'd tell Simon to shove the job and we could head home."

"I understand Jeff wanting to get home, he's got a wife and kids waiting for him, but you and Kami barely know each other." There's something else going on here, I'm not sure what, but I don't think it's totally because I'm with Kami now. "I'm worried that you might start neglecting the business you've worked so hard to build because you can't see past being with this woman."

"First off Joe, *this woman* has a name. Secondly, *KAMI* means the world to me and if I want to take jobs that have me closer to home then that's my business, in every way." I shake my head, I don't want to argue with my closest friend. The one that has stuck by me from childhood through to being a functioning adult with our own businesses, but damn it I will.

"You've worked hard to get these bigger contracts James, I don't want you to sacrifice all your hard work for a woman, any woman not just Kami. I know I haven't always had good things to say about Kami, but this isn't about her specifically, I would feel the same way about any woman you decided to put before your work." Joe says, I guess he's trying to justify his words, but I know how he really feels about Kami, I just don't understand why he feels the way he does.

"I wouldn't sacrifice my work for anything, or just 'any' woman either Joe. I think you know as well as I do that Kami isn't just 'any' woman, and just so you know, I don't feel like I'm sacrificing anything at all. This job will be complete, and Kami wasn't a factor in the whether we walked away from the job either. It was all about how Simon was behaving and me not wanting word to get out that my crew and I could be treated with disrespect."

"OK James, as long as you've got everything sorted with Simon, I just wanted to come up and check on you because you sounded pissed off and frustrated." The look on his face tells me he doesn't believe me about Kami not being a reason for me wanting to go home from this project early, he forgets how long we've known each other, but I don't give two shits what he thinks.

"At least it wasn't a wasted trip, you did get me a new phone, right?" I ask him.

"Yeah, I got you your phone, it's not the latest and greatest and I'm sure you'll get a new one when you get back home, but it'll work for you while you're here." He takes the phone out of his pocket and hands it over. "There is a problem though,' I nod, "Unfortunately, we couldn't transfer most of the numbers and contacts over. The ones you've added while you've been here weren't an issue, and I'm really hoping that you've got a contacts list lying around somewhere, either on the computer or in written form. Otherwise, you've lost a lot of contacts my man."

"I should be OK, I've got everything backed up on the laptop that I bought with me."

"That's good news then. Obviously, I already added my number in there and some of the crew and other contacts that I know that we both had, but if you need any numbers that you think I'd have let me know." I nod my thanks and finish my last bite of lunch. "Hey, is it OK with you if I sit down in here and get some work done? I thought we could have some dinner tonight and catch up."

"Yeah that sounds great, but that'll make for a late night trip back home, or do you plan on heading back tomorrow?"

"I'll see how late we are from dinner and decide from there but I'm planning on going home in the morning. I don't have any appointments until after lunch, so I have time."

"Well isn't that lovely for you? I'm going to get back to work now, if that's alright with you? Ya lazy bastard." I chuckle and walk away, leaving him to do whatever the fuck it is he needs to do while I get back to doing to real work.

AFTER A BUSY AFTERNOON of deliveries and working with the guys, I send them all back to the hotel for food and sleep.

"Aren't you coming now too boss?" Billy asks.

"I won't be far behind, I just have to get some paperwork from the office and lock it up."

"Don't take too long James, you're allowed to get some rest too you know." Jeff says to me, with a knowing look on his face.

I laugh and reply, "I know Jeffrey and I won't be too far behind you guys, I've got a date with a special woman tonight." Jeff nods and gives me a knowing look.

"That's good to know boss, I'm glad you've found happiness and life is about more than the business." He leads the boys to his car, and I watch as they drive away.

I didn't think that I lived and breathed work before Kami, but maybe Jeff and Ed, who says we're *both* distracted, are right. She may be distracting me from business, but I think it's a good thing if I've been so focused on building Harvey Carpentry that I've lost sight of having some fun.

I'm still thinking about what Jeff said when I walk into my office and a movement in there startles me. "Holy shit Joe, I forgot you were in here. You scared the crap out of me."

He jumps as if I've startled him too, "Fuck I didn't realise the time, sorry James I didn't mean to use your office for so long."

He looks nervous, but I don't know what reason he could possibly have to be nervous. "Joe, I told you to sit in here and get some work done. You've got nothing to apologise for, but it's knock off time and I've had it for the day. Let's get out of here and grab some dinner." I reach over to grab my laptop, only to realise that it's open and turned on. That's unusual, I normally make sure I've logged out of it or turned it off completely before I walk out of the office. "Did you use my computer for something Joe?"

"Oh.. umm.. yeah.. actually.. yeah.. I did. Sorry I meant to close it after I loaded all your contacts onto your phone for you. Must have gotten distracted by my own work before I could." Joe stutters and stammers.

"Did I give you my password?" I don't remember giving it to him but I'm sure I must have at some point.

"James, you haven't changed it since I helped you set up the damn thing, so no you didn't tell me, I already knew it." He laughs, but it doesn't sound like his normal laugh. I'm too tired to give a shit about what might be his issue tonight.

"I'm hungry, let's go get some food." I say while packing up the computer and a few other things as Joe packs up all the papers and crap he was using for his work today.

"Are there any good places to eat in this town?" he asks me as I lock up the office and make sure everything is secure. The last thing I need on this job site, is someone coming in and stealing our crap, least of all because I made it easy for them.

"You're such a food snob Joe, it's a small town, but it's not completely in the middle of nowhere, enjoy the simple things in life. Like a good meal that'll stick to your ribs and keep you full for hours to come."

"Yeah and makes you feel like a slug and you don't want to get up the next morning." He mumbles, and I laugh, while slapping him on the shoulder.

"Just follow me idiot and I'll show you where we can get a decent meal in this little town."

When Joe pulls up next me in the parking lot of where we're eating tonight, I look over to see his face. I just want to see his initial reaction and it's fucking worth it. I knew he wouldn't be impressed with an old country pub, but the food is amazing. Comfort food at its finest and even some of the best fine dining for my best friend who is the biggest food snob I know.

I jump out of the car and walk to the entrance. "This is the best place in town? I stayed here for a pub meal, seriously?"

"Come on, cut it out and I never asked you stay, you chose to stay and wanted dinner. This is where we've been eating if we don't eat at the hotel. The food is delicious, and the owners are amazing. Get your snobby self inside."

I open the door and wave him ahead of me, earning me a dirty look and a roll of his eyes. I love the guy like a brother, but he's so easy to wind up. This place is the best example of not judging a book by its cover that I have ever found. That theory is completely backed up within about two seconds when I hear Joe gasp in shock as he sees the interior.

"Holy shit!"

"I told you, but no you've got to be a food snob and tell me I know nothing about eating food."

"You didn't tell me anything. You said it was the best place to eat in town, you didn't tell me it was going to be this good."

"You haven't even sat down Joe, maybe we should do that first and then you can order. Once you've had some of the food, I'll take your opinion and probably still shove it where the sun doesn't shine." I laugh at the shocked look on his face.

Once his shock wears off and he manages to order some food, we just sit back and talk shit. I feel like I haven't seen him for a while and I can't help asking him what happened with the woman he was seeing not so long ago, but he doesn't want to talk about her because, 'it's over and there's no point reliving the situation', even if it means explaining it to me. Fair enough too I guess.

"Well, James, I can admit when I'm wrong and tonight was just the occasion. I can't say I've learnt my lesson, because you and I both know I'll keep judging a book by its cover when it comes to food, but this place is definitely the exception to my rule."

"No wonder you can't keep a woman dude, you keep judging everyone before you can even get to know them." I regret it as soon as I've said it, "I'm sorry Joe, that was uncalled for." I see the flash of pain across his face before he recovers, shrugging his shoulders.

"You're right though. She left me because I couldn't accept a few things in her life, and I couldn't ask her to give them up for me. She shouldn't have to and wouldn't have even if I had asked. Which is her right, obviously? There were also things that she just couldn't see passed with me either and even though we tried to work through all of it, in the end, it just didn't work. I wouldn't give in and I couldn't ask her to, so we walked away."

"That's harsh man. I'm really sorry, I wish it could have worked out differently for you. It seems like you really care about this woman Joe." He looks so damned sad when he nods his agreement. "Are you sure you can't sort out these issues? If you love each other, surely it's worth the effort to work everything out and be together?"

"We tried. Sometimes things just aren't meant to be James, it hurts like hell trust me, but I can't make her change her mind and if I could, then it wouldn't make me happy, anyway. She'd be miserable, and I wouldn't want to see her like that, that's not how I want her to live her life."

"So you gave her up so that she could be happy?" I ask, and he nods miserably. "How's that working out for the two of you? Cause if she looks anything like you, I don't think you've done each other any favours my friend. Maybe you should call her and see how she's doing, the right woman can make your life a thousand times better Joe."

"Would you be giving me that same advice if you hadn't gotten together with Kami? Cause I recall in the not so recent past that you would have just taken me out to get drunk and find someone to get over her with."

"You're right and you would have done the same for me, but I can see how miserable you are and you're right, maybe before Kami and I had found each other again, I would have given you some different advice, but that doesn't mean I'm wrong Joe."

"I'm hearing you James, but sometimes it's just better for everyone to walk away." He sighs and pulls out some cash to pay for his share of dinner, so I do the same and we walk outside. "I booked a room at the hotel for the night, I'm not feeling up to driving home tonight. Lead the way your highness, seeing as you know this crappy town like the back of your hand."

When we get back to the hotel, we say goodnight. I don't think Joe wants to talk anymore tonight and I have a phone call to answer. "Night Joe."

"Night James."

I wait until I can't wait any more for a call from Kami that never comes. I can't call her to make sure that everything is OK, because I don't have her number in my phone anymore. I tried to set up a video call to her on my laptop too, but I couldn't find her details on there either. I fall asleep, fully clothed and with my phone in my hand and the laptop sitting next to me. All ready and waiting, but she never calls.

Chapter Twenty-Five

KAMI

"Hey boss, are you OK? You're kind of staring off into space a lot this afternoon." Ed asks.

"Hmmmmm? Oh yes, I'm fine Ed, just thinking that's all." I smile in response,

"Anything I can help you with, Kami?"

"No, not really Ed. I just got a strange message on my phone and I don't know whether to reply and tell them they got the wrong number, or to just leave it alone."

"You don't have the number in your phone?" Ed asks me, and I shake my head no, "Do you mind if I read it? Never know, I might be able to shed some light on it. Stranger things have happened you know."

I smile and grab my phone off the counter, open the message and then pass it over to Ed.

Ed silently reads the message a couple of times and then reads it aloud, "Getting out of town and putting some distance between us, will make breaking it off a little easier." He takes a minute before he keeps going, "Well, whoever sent it seems to mean business. I really hope whoever 'she' is, isn't hurt too much by receiving that message. I can't help you with the number either, so I guess it was a simple case of a wrong number being entered."

"I guess you're right, but I can't help this weird feeling that this simple wrong number message, isn't as innocent as it seems. I just can't work out the who or what will be affected."

Business is slow today for some reason, so when Mel comes in to see Ed in the early afternoon, I send him out the door. It's a beautiful day, the sun is shining, the sky is blue, and the grass seems really green. It seems like a waste of a beautiful day if we all have to be inside. Ed tried to protest, but I just opened the door and shoved him out, when it looked like he was going to come back in, I locked it. Mel stood there laughing and eventually managed to drag him away.

I'm happy to give him an afternoon off, just like he gave me one not so long ago. We all need a break from the humdrum of living and enjoying time with friends and lovers.

I tried calling James last night, but the call didn't connect. I put it down to him working out in the middle of nowhere but between that weird message and his phone not connecting, I've got a really weird feeling in my chest.

The rest of the afternoon goes by slowly and it gives me plenty of time to think. Which also gives my stupid brain time to make up theories and explanations on what's going on with James.

Maybe he's sick of me.

Maybe, he found someone else.

Maybe I meant nothing to him.

Maybe, this is his easy way out.

Maybe Joe was right from the very beginning.

Holy crap I can't believe I'm letting Joe of all people, get into my head. James and I have talked about where we stand, and we're together. No one else matters and I shouldn't let one weird text get to me. Ed's right, it's just a wrong number.

As I'm locking up the book shop I hear a cough from behind me. Without looking around I say, "I'm sorry but we're closed for the day, come back tomorrow and I'll help you anyway I can."

"I'm not here for a book Kami." A deep voice says as I turn to smile at who I thought was a potential customer but is, in actual fact, my worst nightmare.

I try to keep the smile on my face, to prove to him and me that he doesn't bother me, but I can't, instead I frown as I ask, "So why are you here then Joe? We both know you don't want to be here."

He clears his throat again before he speaks, "I'm here because James asked me to come by and let you know that he broke his phone yesterday. I was there checking up on how things were going, so I went into town to grab him a new one. Unfortunately, he's lost most of the contacts because he had them saved wrong." He looks away from me before continuing, "Anyway, he wanted me to give you his new number, so you can call him, and he can save your number again, so here it is." He hands me a piece of paper with a number written on it. I know he doesn't want to be here, and he sure doesn't want to be James' errand boy for this.

"Thank you Joe." I look him in the eyes, but he can't seem to meet my eye.

I start to walk away from him when he speaks again, "He's also going to be away for longer than he originally planned. Things aren't going to well on this one."

"I know, he told me that the new project manager was being a pain in the butt. He also told me that he might be there longer than he originally thought." I turn and look back at him, "You're not telling me anything I didn't already know Joe. We have spoken since he's been gone you know." I can't help the snark that enters my voice. I don't normally talk to people like this, but he just rubs me the wrong way. I guess that's what happens when someone has shown you how much they hate you year upon year.

"I just want you to understand." He looks down at his feet, then looks me dead in the eyes for the first time since he got my attention. "He's worked really hard to get where he is Kami. He's pulled himself up out of the mess that his father made of the family name and made a business and a life for himself. He was dragged down and made to feel less than, all because his father was a drunk and couldn't keep it in his pants. He has respect now, a business that is successful and even if people still associate him with Kevin Harvey, they can see that he's nothing like the guy who let everyone down."

"I know that Joe. I know how hard it is to get a business started and to keep it running." I take a breath and one step closer to him, because I want him to hear me, loud and clear. "I don't know why you hate me so much Joe, I have no idea what you have against me, but I don't care anymore either. I know how hard James has worked to get out from under his father's reputation. You think that I'm going to somehow ruin him and his business, I can see it written all over your face Joe, but I have no intention of doing that. Ever."

"I never said it was your intention Kami, I just think that -" but I don't let him finish.

"No Joe don't finish that sentence. We could break each other's hearts Joe, but that's still none of your business. You're telling me not to ruin him, but maybe you should think about being a good friend and supporting him in his decisions?"

I turn and walk to my car and I hear him curse behind me. I can't talk to him anymore, we'll both say things that can't be taken back, and I don't know if I could fix that with him or James for that matter. I wait until I can't see him or the book shop anymore before I let the tears fall. I won't let Joe see me cry, he saw that enough in high school. I won't let him know that he's planted the seeds of doubt in my mind.

When I get home I wipe my eyes, sit down on the couch and pull out the piece of paper Joe gave me. The numbers look oddly familiar, but they can't be because Joe said he just got the number for James. I start to enter the number into my phone contacts and that's when I realise where I've seen it before. That message. The one that seemed like a wrong number, it came from James' new number.

How could I be so stupid!? He said this job wasn't a way of putting some distance between us, that we would talk every day when he could, but we haven't. He was tired and then he 'replaced' his phone, and then with Joe coming by the shop just now, was he trying to tell me that James is done?

The tears fall down my face as I realise just how stupid I've been. Maybe this was their plan from beginning, one last joke to pull on Kamo Kami. Make her think James like her and then Joe gets to be the one who cuts me back down.

Oh god! I almost told him I loved him! They must be laughing their heads off at me right now. I can't believe how easily I got sucked into their game. I can't believe James used me.

JAMES

I messaged Joe earlier to ask if he'd spoken to Kami yet and given her my new number, but he hasn't gotten back to me yet. I'm barely keeping my eyes open waiting for him to message me back. I want to call him, but I also don't want to let on just how much I need to talk to her. He's my best friend, but he can be a jerk sometimes, and for whatever reason, Kami isn't his favourite person.

I've lost count of how many times my eyes have closed sitting here waiting. I'm so fucking tired, we're busting our arses every day trying to catch up on the days we lost so that we don't have to be here any longer than necessary. Eventually, I give up and get in to bed, I won't be talking to her tonight even if he *has* seen her and passed on my new number.

My phone vibrates across the bedside table just as I'm drifting off to sleep and I jump, hoping it's Kami, but it's Joe.

Joe: *yeah I passed on the new number but dude she didn't really look very happy*

I read the message a few times before I understand it, and even then, I don't understand why she wouldn't be happy. Except for the fact that Joe was the messenger.

Me: *what do you mean she wasn't happy?*

His reply comes through almost immediately, like he was waiting for me to respond.

Joe: *as in she didn't seem to believe me, but she took the paper*

Joe: *hasn't she called yet? She said she would*

She took the number and said she'd call, but she hasn't yet.

Me: *nah she probably got busy at the shop*

Joe: *she was closing up and going home when I gave it to her dude. I'm sorry*

I throw my phone down on the bed, I know I should reply to Joe, but I don't want to. If Kami has my number why hasn't she called me? I can't call her, because I don't have her number anymore. I pick up my phone and send him another message.

Me: *did you get her number off her?*

Joe: *no .... do you really think she'd give it to me dude?*

Me: *no ... thanks*

I throw the phone back down onto the covers and throw my arm over my eyes. I can't contact her if she doesn't call me, I can't get her number. She doesn't have a home phone because she doesn't need it and I don't know if she's got one at the shop. Oh my god, she'd have to have a phone at the shop right?

I jump out of bed, grab my laptop and fire it up. I search for her shop and when I find it, it has a contact number and email address. I can't call her at the shop until tomorrow, so I send her an email asking for her number or for her to call me. Then I add the shop number to my contacts on my phone and I can breathe again. After I get some sleep, I can speak to her and explain what happened, I should have known she wouldn't take Joe at his word, they don't exactly get along.

I go back to bed feeling a shitload better about the situation. I'm kicking myself for not thinking about contacting her at the shop today when I actually had no phone. I could have emailed her earlier and gotten the whole thing sorted out in seconds.

When I wake up early the next morning, after not even close to enough sleep, I rush out to my laptop to see if Kami has emailed me back, only to find the fucking thing flat. How much of a fucking idiot can I be? I left it on all night, and it went into sleep mode, but it still chewed through the battery. I left the charger in the office, so now I'm going to have wait until I get out to the site and meet Simon early again, to plug it in. I get myself dressed, gather up all my crap and head out to the car so that I can get into the on-site office and get this laptop plugged in.

Pulling into the parking lot, I breathe out a sigh of relief when I see I'm the only one here. I wasn't expecting any of my guys to be here just yet, but I'm relieved to see that Simon hasn't arrived yet either. It gives me some time to plug this fucker in and get it fired up. I need to check my emails, and I want to do it before my meeting with Simon.

I'm sitting at my desk waiting for there to be enough charge on the damned thing to start it up and tapping away on the desk with a pen. It's too early to call the shop, Kami won't even be there yet, but hopefully she's checked her emails. Finally, the fucking thing fires up and I've got this lead weight in my stomach as I load up my email.

There it is, a reply from the Kami's book shop and I breathe out a huge sigh of relief. She saw my email, and she replied. My relief is short-lived, because when I open it, I realise it's just a standard auto-reply stating their business hours and telling me that someone will get back to me when the store opens. Just when I think it's over, I still have to wait. I look at the clock and wonder if she would be there already, I mean I know she doesn't show up just in time to open the doors. I pick up the phone to call her and that's when Simon decides to show up. As if I needed another reason to dislike the guy, he handed me one anyway.

"Good morning James, how are you today? Everything looks like it's going well here, everything's on time now?" he asks, after the sort of compliment he gave me.

I grunt in reply and then think better of it and decide to be professional, I can't let what's going on with Kami affect my business, otherwise Joe won't let me forget it. "Good morning Simon, how are you? Everything is on track for the *new* timeline, yes. The crew are busting their butts to get it all done in time."

"I know they are James, and I'm very grateful that they agreed to stay on the job." At least he has the decency to look a little embarrassed by his admission.

"Me too. Let's get down to business then." I say, probably with a little more hostility that I should or that I mean.

KAMI

I saw the notification come through on my phone. I get all the emails from the shops email address on my phone because I like to be able to answer them if they're easy enough, at any time. But when I saw the name on the sender's email address, I couldn't bring myself to even look at it. I don't know why he's emailing me, but I really don't want to read it, I mean it can't be good news, can it? So, I don't read it.

Ed gives me a strange look when he comes in for his shift, but he doesn't say anything. I know I'm being quiet, but I can't explain it to him just yet. I need to get over my hurt and anger before I listen to his. He's going to want to kill James, and I want to be able to tell him not to do it. Even though that's how I'm feeling myself right now. I could wrap my hands around his throat and look into those gorgeous light blue eyes of his that change and go dark and stormy when he gets turned on ..... no. No, I have to not think of him that way. I have to stop because if I don't I'm going to forgive him, and I don't want to forgive him. He told me, promised me that this was real, and that Joe would get over whatever his problem is. As it turns out, it was all just a bit of fun. I should have trusted my instincts and believed his reputation. That's what annoys me the most, I knew, and I still went into this and now I'm devastated. Even after all of it, even if I'd known how it would all end, I think I would have still gone into it with him.

"Kami." I hear Ed, but it's not until he touches me that I react to him, "Kami. Sweetheart ..." I don't let him finish.

"Don't."

"Don't what?" he looks confused and I have no doubt he is.

"Don't call me that, he calls me that and I don't want to hear it ever again."

"OK darlin', I know it's a stupid question, but is everything OK Kami?"

"No, but it will be Ed. I'm going into my office, if you need me, call me." I say and walk away.

Ed calls out as I get to the door of my office, "I'm sure whatever he did, you can forgive him for it darlin', I've seen the way you two look at each other. You can work it out."

If only he knew the truth, he'd be singing a very different tune. In order to not think about Mr Harvey, I throw myself into ordering some new books and customer requests.

It's working well until Ed taps softly on the doorframe and says, "James is on the phone for you, do you want me to ...."

He doesn't get to finish, "Tell him I'm not here and you don't know when I'll be back."

"Kami, I already told him you were in your office, I don't feel right lying to him."

"Why? You didn't like him not so long ago Ed, and now you're his best friend?" Honestly, I don't understand the male of the species, he wasn't good enough for me a few weeks ago and now Ed's looking at me like I killed his favourite pet. "What? I said I'm not here, tell him I left, and you didn't realise. Tell him I just walked out the door, and you couldn't catch me, I don't care Ed, I'm not talking to him." Then I look down at the papers in front of me, not seeing anything except a blur of black and white. I will not cry over him, at least not here, not in my sanctuary.

As I try to gather myself I hear Ed speaking. "Yeah sorry James, she managed to slip out the door while I was busy with a customer." There's a pause and then he says, "Yeah you're right, she does normally yell out to let me know she's heading out, but today wasn't one of those days." Another pause and then, "She must have been distracted about something, you know how she can get when she gets an idea in her head." He gives me a look of disapproval as he listens to James again. "No, I didn't hear about an email, but I'll check that we got it. You definitely sent it to the right address." Another glare is sent my way and then I hear him say, "Yeah, I'll definitely check it out and then get the boss to read it. It explains everything, hey? OK I'll make sure she reads it, bye, James."

He hangs up as I reach for my bag and start to stand up to leave. "Where do you think you're going Kami?"

"I'm leaving so you don't feel so bad about lying to your new best friend. If I go now, it won't be too much of a lie, will it?" I feel guilty for asking him to do that, but I just can't talk to James right now. No matter what his explanation is, I don't think I can forgive him. My heart is too broken.

"He sounds distraught Kami. I don't know what happened between you two, but he sounds like all he wants to do is talk to you darlin'."

"I can't Ed." I shake my head, "let's just leave it there for now OK?"

"But.." he starts but I'm saved from further explanation by the bell over the front door, indicating that a customer has entered the shop. He gives me what I think he wants to be a deadly stare that means this conversation isn't over, but he doesn't scare me. I'm not feeling too much of anything right now and that look doesn't even touch me.

"You've got a customer Ed, and I'm going out for a while. If you need me, call but assume I'm out for the day." I say and walk towards the back door. I don't want to run into customers, I don't want to have to pretend to smile and be interested when in fact I just want out of here. For the first time since I decided to open the store, I don't want to be here.

As I reach out to grab hold of the door handle to the storeroom, Ed speaks behind me. "I'm sorry boss, maybe I'm stepping over some invisible line you've drawn today, but I just read James' email and I really think you should read it yourself."

"Thanks for the advice Ed, but I don't want to deal with any of that today OK? In fact, consider me gone for the day. I'm going home, and I don't want to be interrupted, by anyone for anything. Don't call me, don't call James and for the love of all that's holy, don't call Katy and tell her anything.

I want some time to myself to digest everything. James and I are done Ed, don't pass messages on to me from him, I don't want to hear them."

"Oh darlin', but I don't think you guys are over. At least James doesn't seem to think so, and I think there's been some kind of communication break down and I just don't want you to regret anything." He's speaking fast, but quietly for him.

"The only thing I'm regretting right now is not listening to the advice you and Katy gave me from the beginning. I knew what I was getting into and he's still managed to hurt me, and I don't know if I can forgive myself for that Ed. I need today, OK? Just let me have today." I smile, and I know it doesn't reach my eyes, because I don't feel happy.

"OK darlin', go home and do whatever you need to do. I can open tomorrow if you need more time." He says with a sad smile.

"I'll be back and ready to roll tomorrow Ed. Just give me today, please?"

I walk out the back door of the shop, my dream, drive home and lock the house down tight. No-one is getting in here unless I let them in and I'm over letting people in. Hopefully no one even knows I'm here and they don't try.

When I wake up on the couch the next morning, I send Ed a message and ask him to run the shop for the next few days and when the phone rings a few minutes later I answer it, "Good morning Ed."

"Morning boss. I can run the shop for as long as you need, but I needed to know that you were good before I agreed."

"I'm good Ed, but I'm thinking of heading out of town for a few days. If something comes up and you can't open for whatever reason, don't."

"We always open the shop Kami." He sounds shocked, but I don't want to pressure him to open every day, not when I've just dumped it in his lap like this without any notice at all.

"Well, things change Ed and I've just dumped this all on you. So if you've got plans that can't be changed, then close the store for however long you need to. Customers will understand, or they won't, so be it." I close my eyes and take a deep breath, I can't believe I'm walking away from the bookshop so easily, but it has memories and I can't be here for a few days. "I'm sorry Ed and thank you for everything." I don't wait for his answer, I hang up, then turn my phone off. I don't want him to message me or call me back.

I look around my house and realise what I said to Ed was right, I need to get out of here for a while. I shower, pack a few things into an overnight bag and get in my car. Then I just drive. To where? I don't have a clue, I just know it's in the opposite direction that I know James headed in for his 'out of town project'.

JAMES

Kami hasn't called me, and my mood is getting worse and worse.

When I finally got around to calling the shop, Ed answered and told me she was there. I heard them talking but I couldn't make out anything they said, but I know she was there. Even when he lied to me and said she'd just left the shop without letting him know. She always fucking tells him when she's leaving that fucking shop. It used to drive me insane, because I thought it meant she was answering to him, but I realised it was just her. She didn't want him to go looking for her and not know where she was in case something went wrong.

She didn't read my email either. She must have seen it, I know she checks them every morning. Does she think I'm an idiot? That I haven't noticed all the things she does, every little fucking detail of her life?

It's been a few days since I broke my phone, and everything went to shit. I've called the bookshop every day and Ed tells me the same fucking thing. She's still not back. I didn't believe him when he said she'd taken off and not given him a day when she'd be back. Even when I blew up at him and told him to put her on the fucking phone, his only answer was an apology. I asked for her phone number, he knew I'd have it in a second if I was at home, it's on all the paperwork from the job at the shop, but still he wouldn't give it to me.

The angrier I get with him, the sadder his voice became. When I asked him why, he couldn't answer me, and I could tell it wasn't because he didn't want to, but simply because he didn't know why.

I even called Katy, but she couldn't tell me anything more than what Ed could. She hadn't even known that Kami had left town until I called her to ask if she knew why or where she might go. She promised she'd call Kami and make sure she was OK and get back to me. She got back to me alright, but only to tell me that Kami wasn't answering her phone. Not just not answering, but it wasn't even turned on.

I guess I can take a little bit of comfort in the fact that it's not just me she doesn't want to talk to. I just wish I knew why, what the fuck went so wrong that she's not at the shop and even went to the extreme of leaving town without telling a soul where she's going? Not even Ed or Katy.

My crew are walking around on eggshells, but we're getting this job knocked out pretty fast. There's no joking, slacking off or mucking about. Just work, work and more hard work. I'm working even after I send them back to the hotel for the night. I can't sleep, so I might as well get this fucking job done.

Simon has come to talk to me a few times, but even he's noticed the difference in my already gruff demeanour and left me mostly alone to get the job done. I'm not trying to be an arsehole, but the sooner I can get this project fucking complete, the sooner I can get back home and sort this out with Kami.

So, instead of blowing up everyone else's phones, I work until I can't work anymore and then when I finally get back to the hotel, I fall into bed and pass out. Then, the next day plays out the same way, until we're so far ahead of their scheduled timeline, that I'm almost back on track with the original completion date.

I will sort it out. I'm not letting her walk away from me, from us, this easily. I'm in love with her and I know she feels the same way about me. I won't let her walk away from me. Not without a fight anyway. Not without hearing her tell me why.

She can explain it to my face that way I can see the lies written all over *her* face.

Chapter Twenty-Six

KAMI

After driving for a few hours, I found this gorgeous little B&B in the middle of nowhere, run by the sweetest older lady that reminds me of my long gone grandmother. She asked me that first night if I was OK and even though we both knew I was lying when I said yes, she left it alone. Now after being here for a few days, with nothing but the country and Mrs Clarke for company, I feel like I'm leaving a much loved friend behind.

"I don't like to see such a beautiful young lady so sad, but you do seem to be feeling a bit better today." She pats my cheek as we stand next to my car.

"Thank you Mrs Clarke. I feel much stronger than when I first arrived, it must be from the company and the comfort food." I smile warmly at her and this time, unlike when I first arrived, I can actually feel the smile in my heart. Oh, it's still broken, but it's starting to mend now. Kind of. Enough for me to head back home and to the bookshop anyway. I'm not sure how it will hold up the first time I lay eyes on Mr Harvey, but I'll deal with that when I have to.

"It's been an absolute pleasure to have you here Kami. You come back any time and I will make sure I have a room for you, sweetie."

"Thank you Mrs Clarke, I might hold you to that sooner than you think." I hug her tight and when I release her, she looks way too deeply into my eyes.

"Hopefully you can sort out the issues with your young man and you can bring him here and introduce him to me?" she asks hopefully, and I can't stand to disappoint her, so I smile and nod.

"Maybe," is all I say. She doesn't know any details, I'm not even sure if I told her that I was upset over a man, but I guess there aren't too many reasons a lone girl walks into a B&B in the middle of nowhere and cried herself to sleep for a couple of nights.

I'm rewarded with another warm hand patting my cheek. "Now get along so that you can beat the traffic and get home before it gets dark." She smiles, making me miss my grandmother more than ever, "I worry about you driving in the dark and late at night Kami."

I hold her hand to my cheek for just a few more seconds and say, "I promise to call and let you know that I'm home safely." Before I can think about it anymore, I get in the car because otherwise I might not leave at all and that wouldn't be fair on Ed.

I drive out of the small driveway, waving until Mrs Clarke is no longer in my rearview mirror.

The couple of hours it takes me to get home gives me a chance to think and steal myself for the conversations I'm going to have to have. I know Katy's going to be mad at me for disappearing, not telling her where I was, but she's also going to be angry that I didn't let her know that I was OK. I can't help but wonder if she'll forgive me for that one. At least Ed knew I was leaving, he just didn't know for how long, but then neither did I in all honestly.

I pull up the driveway of my house and breathe out a sigh of relief. I'm not sure why, but I was half expecting to see a car or two in my driveway waiting for me. Katy's, James' or who knows, maybe even the police? I laugh at my own dramatics, of course no one would have called the police, Ed knew I was leaving town. I don't know whether I'm relieved or upset that no one is here.

I know I need to talk to Katy and explain myself. I can tell you that's one conversation I'm not looking forward to.

I also know that eventually I'm going to run into James. That's going to be awkward without a doubt, but I'm sure he's moved on by now and we can go back to not running in the same circles just like we have for most of our existence. The town is small, but not so small that we can't manage to avoid each other. Joe's proof of that.

I laugh to myself as I grab my bag and the packaged dinner from the passenger seat. Mrs Clarke didn't want me to have think about making myself something to eat when I got back home so late. The funny thing is, it's still daylight and will be for an hour, or so.

I throw my bag on my bed and put dinner in the fridge. I turn my phone back on and it goes insane with missed calls and messages. Most of them are from Katy, there are a few from Joe, yes I have his number saved in there, so I know if it's him on the other end. There's even a few from Ed. None from James, I guess he didn't work too hard to find my number, if he even lost it to start with.

I delete the ones from Joe without even looking at them. There's nothing he could say to me that I have any interest in. I look through the messages from Ed, they're checking up on me and letting me know that the shop is doing well. So, I message him back and tell him I'll be back in there tomorrow. I get a message right back saying he'll see me there in the morning.

Then I make my way through the messages and voicemails left by my best friend. I can hear it in her voice, at first she's worried to death and then it sounds like she's planning my death. I can't put off the inevitable any longer, I take a deep breath and call her, she picks up on the first ring. No surprises there and answers with a simple, straight to the point, "And where the *fuck* have you been bitchface?"

"Hi to you too Katybear." I smile, using my childhood nickname for her, hoping to calm the anger I know she must be feeling with me.

"Don't you dare fucking Katybear me! Do you know how worried I've been about you? What the fuck Kami? You can't leave town without telling anyone, but you *especially* don't leave town without telling *me*!" she's yelling at me and I know it's just her way of telling me how worried she was, but I don't want her to yell.

"Please don't yell at me Katy. I told Ed I was leaving town, but I'm sorry I didn't let you know I was OK. Can we meet for lunch tomorrow and I'll tell you everything?" She's silent and this woman is never silent, that's when I realise just how much I've hurt her by not telling her I was going out of town and that I was OK. "Please?" I'm not above begging.

"OK. I'll meet you at the shop when I get a break. I assume you're going into the shop tomorrow?"

"Yes, I am. I'm meeting Ed there in the morning." I reply.

"Of course you are. I'll meet you there then." Without another word, she's gone. Yup, I'm in for a fun conversation tomorrow.

JAMES

I've worked until I've fallen over with exhaustion, but we're done. This fucking project is complete and only a couple of days later than the original completion date to boot.

The crew are stuffed, but happy to be heading home earlier than expected and even though it was my aim to get this shit done early, I can't say I'm feeling the same amount of exuberance to get back home. If Kami would answer my calls at the shop or even my emails, then I might actually have an idea of what I'm going home to, but she hasn't, and I still have no fucking idea what went wrong.

The rest of the guys have taken off, we did one last walk around the work site after we packed up and checked out of the hotel. Marking off all the last minute things on our lists. I still have to sit and wait for Simon to come so that we can do a last walk through too. I can't wait to sign off on this one and make it all his to deal with again.

I'm sitting in the office, I've packed everything of mine into my car and it's looking pretty empty now. Nothing like it was for the last couple of weeks.

I hear a cough and then my name and I look over to the door. Simon's standing there like he doesn't know if he should come in or not, it's his fucking office, he doesn't need my permission. Instead of showing the grumpy bastard side that I have been the last few days, I chuckle and says, "Good morning Simon, how are you?"

"I'm good. You're happy this morning, I guess you're happy this project is over finally?" he says with an embarrassed look. He's not wrong, but I'm not going to tell him the truth. The fact is, I'm glad this job is over for so many reasons, I can't even begin to explain them to him.

"I'm looking forward to heading home Simon. To sleeping in my own bed, being in my own space and catching up with my family." Well, two out of three isn't too bad, right? If I had a family to catch up with, maybe I wouldn't be feeling this lost. I do have Joe to catch up with that's a bonus but not really who I was looking forward to going home to a few days ago.

I shake my head to clear it as Simon says, "Well, let's get this walk through done so we can sign off on everything. I know it's just a formality at this point, but it still has to be done."

"Lead the way Simon. Let's get it done."

Close to two hours later, unbelievably, we're done. Here I was thinking we'd be an hour tops, but no, should have known better when it comes to Simon. The man can talk, I give him that, but by the time we're near the end of our walk through I think he can tell that I'm done. We're literally just nit-picking now and in reality, he's got a cleaning crew coming through before anyone else will see it, anyway.

"I think we're done James. I know we started off on the wrong foot and I've been a royal pain in your arse, but I have enjoyed working with you. No matter what I threw at you, you took it on board. You were honest with me if it couldn't work, and you were always quick with a solution. Even though I know it must have been costing you some sanity."

I smile and stretch out my hand, "Thanks Simon. I want to say it's been a pleasure but what I'll say instead is that it's been a real challenge." Then I take a second to think about the job and say, "It's been interesting to say the least and I'm glad we made it to the finish line."

Simon and I shake hands and I get ready to walk away, leave this job in the past.

"I, ummmm, I hope you and your girl can work it out James." He says and then coughs as I look back at him. "I heard the guys talking and figured out that you guys broke up. I hope me stuffing you around out here didn't contribute to the situation. If it did, I am really and truly sorry."

"Thanks Simon, but I don't think you or this job had anything to do with that particular situation." I shake my head. "To be honest, I have no damned clue what happened, but I'm going to find out, that's for certain." With that I get into my truck with the huge 'Harvey Carpentry' decal on both sides and start the drive home, towards uncertainty.

I will get answers though, she can't hide from me forever.

KAMI

I wake up the following morning and feel, refreshed. I probably shouldn't, because I've got a couple of uncomfortable conversations ahead of me today, but the few days break seem to have done me some good. I think Mrs Clarke's company, wisdom and perfect comfort food have given me the boost that I needed as well.

Sleeping in my own bed, in my own house hasn't done me any harm either. Being in my own space, even as comfortable as I felt with Mrs Clarke, is so much better than being somewhere else. I turn off the alarm that I set last night that hasn't even gone off yet, roll out of bed and head to the bathroom. I shower, get dressed, grab a coffee and something to eat. After that, I should be ready to face Ed at the bookshop and then, hopefully Katy at lunchtime. If she waits that long.

When I pull into the rear parking lot of the bookshop, I can see that Ed is here already. I wonder if he's waiting for me, or is something wrong and he's trying to fix it before I get in?

I unlock the door and head inside, as I walk through the door leading onto the shop floor from the storeroom, I yell out, "Hey Ed, I'm here. You're in early today, is everything OK?"

I don't get more than a few steps into the shop before I'm engulfed in strong arms, squeezing me so tight, I fear I might stop breathing if he doesn't let up soon. "Jesus Christ Kami. I swear to god if you *ever* pull a stunt like that again, I *will* kill you! I mean I'll be lining up for my turn, but I will get a turn and I will *kill* you." He lets me go long enough to hold me at arm's length and bend down slightly to look me in the eyes.

"Good morning to you too Ed." I laugh, trying but not actually succeeding in making light of the situation. I can tell by the look on his face and the way his eyes are searching mine, that he's been worried about me, but was he really worried that I wouldn't come back? "I was always coming back Ed, it was always going to be only a few days break, not forever. This is my business, I would never leave it behind, and I would never leave you behind either. You do know that, right?"

"I know nothing of the kind Kami Parker. You took off out of nowhere and when I found out that even Katy had no idea where you were, well actually she had no freaking idea you had *gone* anywhere to start with, I really started worrying about you. You weren't you the day before you left, and when you just took off, well let's just say I wasn't sure of your state of mind."

"Ohhh Ed, I'm so sorry I worried you, I didn't mean to, but I needed to get away for a couple of days to clear my head. I'm ok now though, everything is much clearer, and we can get back to business." I smile my biggest smile at one of my closest friends. He may have started out as an employee, but he truly feels more like family to be me now after the last few years of working together.

"Ohhhh no you don't darlin'. You don't get to just walk away without explaining what the hell happened. Tell me what he did. He's been calling here every day since the day before you left asking to talk to you. He didn't believe me when I told him you weren't here, or that you'd gone away. He said you'd never leave the shop for so long unless something was wrong. He's been emailing too, I didn't read them after the first one, because they were a little more personal than I think either of you want me to read. I don't know what he did, but he sure does miss you darlin'."

"You want me to explain?" he nods his agreement and so I tell him the story, the shortened version but the story, nonetheless. "That weird text message that we thought was so random? Yeah well it wasn't so random after all." I take a breath to steady myself and trudge along, I know this is the first, but not the last time I'll be telling this story today. "Joe met me here that night, after I sent you home early. He kind of scared the crap out of me as I was locking up, but that's beside the point, he wanted to give me a piece of paper. He took a trip out to see James, when he got there, he found out that James had broken his phone. So, he went into the closest town to buy him a new one. Anyway, that piece of paper Joe handed me had James' new number on it. For some reason James couldn't keep the old number and all his contacts were lost. I thanked Joe and left. When I got home, I opened my contacts to enter in the new details for James and guess what?" Ed shakes his head, but I can see he's waiting for the bomb to drop, "I'd already had contact with that particular number in the form of a text message."

Ed looks shocked, "Nooooooo. Not that weird message about getting out of town for a few weeks making breaking things off easier?" his mouth is hanging open in shock.

I nod in answer to his question because, quite frankly, it still hurts that he could even think that, never lone send a text saying it. To anyone. "Needless to say, I threw the paper in the bin and you know what happened next." I shrug my shoulders as if to say, what else can I say? "I needed to get away and so I went in the opposite direction to where I knew James was, so that there wasn't a chance in hell that I'd run into him."

"Look, I know what I said about him before you started seeing him, but honestly, I can't see him doing something like this, Kami. I can't imagine those words leaving his mouth or entering his brain for that matter. Not about you, not about anyone that he was seeing before you. And yes I use the term 'seeing' very loosely about the ladies before you darlin'."

"Well, he did say and think them Ed, so that's that." I say with a finality I don't really feel. "Now that you know the whole sorry tale, can we get back to work? Catch me up on everything that's been going on."

That's how the rest of the morning goes along. Ed fills me in on everything shop related that happened while I was away, including the daily visits from Katy to see if Ed was actually hiding me in here somewhere and not telling her. Crazy woman, but it's why I love her. The morning passes quickly and before I know it, it's almost lunchtime.

"Do you want to grab a quick lunch Ed? I don't think my lunch with Katy is going to be a short one, so this might be your only chance to get away."

"No you go ahead and catch up with Katy, I asked Mel to come in and cover me for a couple of hours again, like she did while you were away. I thought you might not be ready to jump back totally on your first day back." I smile, appreciating that he's thought of everything. "That and I figured you had to see Katy and well, I can't imagine that being a quick talk at all. Fair warning, she's madder at you than I was." He grimaces as he says it and now I'm really not looking forward to having lunch with her. Her bark can be pretty vicious, but her bite is generally gentle.

"All right then, thanks for the warning. If you're sure you're organised, I'm going to head out to my car to grab something and then I'll head out with Katy. See you after my lunch of reckoning." He laughs as I walk away but it doesn't really sound like he's really finding the joke in what I said.

She can't be that mad at me, can she? I know I didn't tell her I was taking off, but she'll understand once I explain why I did it.

The noise of the shop fades as I get closer to the back door which I can now see is slightly ajar. I'm about to turn around and have a go at Ed when I hear a voice, not just any voice, but Katy's voice. I sigh and figure she opened the door then got a call she had to take and didn't close it properly. Until I hear another, deeper rumbling voice join hers and realise they're arguing.

"What are you doing here? If she sees you she's going to work it out you idiot and then I'll lose my best friend." Katy says.

"I saw you drive passed, and I took a guess as to where you were going. She rarely uses this door, she won't see or hear us Katy." He sighs, this must be the guy she was seeing, but how could he know which door I use? "I needed to see you, I've had a shit few days. I did something Katy, something stupid. I screwed up." That's when I realise who it is.

"Joe, I don't have time for this shit. She called me last night, she wants to have lunch and talk. Seeing that she left town for a few days without notice, I really want to talk to her to find out what the hell is going, because the last time I spoke to her she was happy, so happy and I was freaking stoked for her. I know you're not happy about them being together Joe, but I am. He's good for her, they work together, and I won't have you ruining it for them."

"I miss you Katy. I miss you so fucking much, and I can accept them together, now. I just, I can't accept you not being in my arms. I love you more than—"

"No, Joe." She sighs. "Joe, I can't do this, it broke my heart to walk away from you, from us but you can't get over whatever you have against Kami and I won't lose my best friend."

"I can Katy, that's what I'm trying to tell you. I made a mistake, so many mistakes, James is miserable because she won't call him back, and it's all my fault. I can't keep blaming Kami for things that aren't her fault, I know that now."

"Oh Joe, what the hell did you do?"

I can't stand there hiding behind the door any longer, I have to know what this douchebag has done this time. I push the door open and they both jump, "Yeah Joe, what did you do to ruin my life this time? Hmmmmmm?"

"Fucking hell Kami, how long have you been standing behind the fucking door listening?" Katy yells.

"It's *my* fucking door *Katy*, in case you forgot?" I never curse, the only one who hears me let out any kind of expletive is the guy making me orgasm, neither of the two people in front of me know that though and Katy's face registers the shock of my cursing.

"I'm sorry Kami, you're right. If we wanted to have a private conversation, it shouldn't have been here." She says with a filthy look at Joe.

"Don't let me stand in the way of you two getting all cosy in my parking lot, not at all." Katy goes to speak but I hold up my hand to stop her, "I heard enough to understand a few things Katy, and one of them is that this man has never grown up and still likes to play with my emotions and interfere in my life. You've played with me for the last fucking time Joe French, I've had enough of your mind games to last me a lifetime and I'm not playing anymore." I take one step towards him with every word I speak, "What. The. Fuck. Did. You. Do. To. Fuck. With. Me. This. Time?"

"Now Kami, calm down and let him speak, I've never seen you like this before—" Katy stops mid-sentence when I turn my glare her way. How dare she try to defend this bastard, after all the years he spent tormenting me at school, now he's ruined my chance to be happy with James?

"You want *me* to give *him* a chance to speak and explain himself, after all these years and torture, *you* want *me* to take it easy on *him*. Thanks for your loyalty Katy, I really appreciate it."

"That's not what I meant Kami and you know it. I meant let him explain himself before you go ripping his head off. You look like you could kill him, hun."

"Depending on what he says next, I could." I snarl in response.

When I look back to Joe, he's actually shaking, and I can't help but take a little joy out of his fear.

"You're all going to hate me once you know." He barely whispers, I only hear it because I'm so close to him.

"Don't worry Joe, I already do so you're not losing anything with me."

"That's where you're wrong, I am losing everything because of you." He growls out.

"No, you're losing things because of your actions, not mine. What. Did. You. Do. Joe?"

"It wasn't James. That text you got from the unknown number that ended up being James' new number. He didn't send it, I did. He didn't lose any contacts when I got him the new phone either. I deleted a few, including yours, so that he couldn't call you. He needed to concentrate on the job he was on, it was a big deal for his company and his plans to expand—"

"YOU DID *WHAT*, Joseph?"

We all look up to see James' truck parked right next to mine, I don't know when he arrived, but we all know he's here now.

Chapter Twenty-Seven

JAMES

I have never felt so much rage towards another human being before in my entire life. Not even my father in all of his stupidity and most certainly never, ever towards the man I considered to be more of a brother than a friend.

He did this? He created whatever it was that made Kami leave me without explanation?

"I just, you know why James." He stutters, Joe never stutters about anything.

"No, I don't know why Joe. I know you've hated Kami for as long we've known each other, but you've never explained why. You're about to though."

"I'd rather not have that conversation out here James." He says, his bravado back in full force, he's in for a newsflash, he doesn't get to dictate what happens here today.

"I don't really care what you want Joe, not today." I growl, *"What* did you do? Tell me NOW, Joseph."

"Stop fucking calling me Joseph and I'll think about it." He grounds out, but when he looks at me he takes a deep swallow that I can track by watching his Adam's apple bob up and down. I hope that my face is spelling it all out to him. He shuffles his feet, but no-one else is moving. He clears his throat and then speaks, "I was worried about you and your business James, I want to make that very clear from the beginning." Still no-one makes any movements or noise, only Joe. He's got a captive audience whether he wants it or not. "Look, I didn't set out to do this, I just …. I took advantage of a situation I guess."

"Ohhh Joe, why?" I hear Katy murmur.

"When I came out to visit you, all I was honestly doing was checking in on you. I knew you were having some trouble out there with the new project manager, Simon. The last conversation we had, you made it sound like you were going to tell him to shove the job and walk away, but I know how hard you worked to get that contract. You worked your arse off to get it so that you could branch out and get bigger contracts."

"Instead of crappy little contracts like bookshops hey Joe?" Kami says, her voice full of disgust.

"No, well yes but not necessarily shops or yours in particular Kami," he looks from Kami back to me, "but you were working to move away from the smaller jobs and then you couldn't wait to get away from the first larger contract you had."

"Because the guy was being a douchebag, much like you have been lately. It wasn't because of the job, it was the person I was dealing with." I close my eyes and take a deep breath, because I'm not sure I want to know the answer to my next question, but I ask it anyway, "What did you do Joe? What was so bad that Kami didn't want to talk to me anymore, to not even listen to an explanation? Not that I had one because I *still* don't even what I'm supposed to have fucking done!" I look towards Kami for a second, I want to see her face, but I don't want to take my eyes off Joe for a second. He isn't getting away from me that easily.

"I, well I ummm – I deleted all her details from your phone." He mumbles, but I still managed to make out what he says.

"Okayyyy. That means I couldn't contact her, but Kami knew I was in a dodgy area, that wouldn't have made her so mad that she'd never wants to see me again. There has to be more, what else did you do Joe?"

"I also deleted her from the files on your laptop."

"Again, that meant that I couldn't contact Kami, nothing about that relates to *her* contacting *me*. That is unless you didn't give her my new number like I fucking asked you to. You *did* give her the new number when you got back into town, didn't you Joseph?"

"Oh yeah, he gave me your number James. How long had you had that one for?" Kami confirms that Joe did what I asked, so why is she still pissed at me? "I'd already received a text from that number earlier, that text is the reason I don't want to see you anymore. You could have just told me *before* you left town that we were through, you didn't need to break it off via a cryptic message." I'm so fucking confused, I have no response to Kami's accusation simply because I have no idea what she's talking about.

"James didn't have his new phone or number when you got that text Kami." Joe speaks up before I can tell her exactly that and that I have no clue what she's talking about.

"I sent a total of maybe four texts the day I got it and they were all to the arsehole standing over there." I point to Joe, but I'm looking at Kami.

"I'm sorry Kami, that text, it was one that I sent James about the woman I'd been seeing. I told him I needed out of town for even just a few hours because everywhere I turned she was all I could see. The message I sent you was an edited version of that."

Katy, who had been standing away from the rest of us and being unusually quiet suddenly speaks up, "Did you do this because of *me?* Because of *us?* Ohhh Joe."

"What?" I ask, completely stunned by the new revelation. "*Katy* is the woman you're all bent out of shape over? How many fucking secrets do you have Joe?"

"Oh yeah, they kept that one to themselves and deceived us for over six months, from what I've managed to piece together. Neither one of them told us even after we started seeing each other." Kami spits out. I've never heard that the kind of venom in her voice before. "No Katy. You know he's always hated me and as far as I can tell, it's been for no reason. I understand that you can't help who you fall for, trust me on this one, but really? Did you think I didn't love *you* enough to at least *try* to get over it? You didn't trust me, you didn't even give me a chance." She shakes her head, but her eyes are full of sadness, I want to take it away for her, or at least comfort her but I don't think she's ready for me to touch her yet. "As for you Joe, I don't care why you did it, I only care that you did. You've been doing this kind of shit to me since we were kids, humiliating me, embarrassing me, harassing me and just plain hating me. This is some new level to stoop to even for you, I can understand wanting to protect a friend, but this. This is just, I have no words."

Kami starts to walk away to get in her car to drive away from me. I didn't do anything, and I know she's still mad at me, but I can't explain anything to her if she doesn't let me.

"Your mother and my father, they were a couple when they were younger." Joe says, and this stops Kami in her tracks.

"What on earth does that have to do with us? How does that explain how you've treated me all these years? Whatever happened between them, was exactly that, between them." Kami says, she's turned around to face Joe who's moved closer to her.

"He was in love with her and then she left town. When she came back, she had a husband and you." He closes his eyes, breathes deeply and continues, "He was devastated."

"But that would mean he would have already married your mother and had you by then as well. So why was he so bent out of shape?" Kami asks.

"My mother was his second choice, yours was his first. He got on with his life when she left because she told him she would never give him what he wanted. A family. They would never get married and never have children. When she came back to town with all that she'd said she wouldn't give him, he got bitter. My mother suffered, and so did I. I wasn't *you*. He became the nastiest bastard I've ever met and made my life fucking miserable."

"So that was *my* fault? Great reasoning there Joe." Kami makes a move to leave again, until I finally speak.

"So, let me get this straight. You've made Kami's life a living hell all because your father couldn't deal with being dumped?" I ask in disbelief, you think you know someone. I knew his father was a giant prick, but I never knew why. "You've hurt Kami emotionally and sometimes physically, for years and kept me from asking her out, all because your father had his feelings hurt?" I still can't believe what I'm hearing. "Even since we got together however many months ago, you've been planting seeds of doubt in my head the entire time. Then you go and delete her details from my contacts, not just in my phone but in my laptop as well, while I'm away, knowing that I can't get away to come home and see her. Knowing full well that I wanted that contract and more like it, because I'm the fucking idiot that never thought to keep secrets. Then you send her a message that you know she's going to misconstrue to mean that I don't want to be with her anymore. No wonder you had that look on your face when I walked into the office that night. I thought you were caught off guard because you'd been concentrating on your work. Instead you'd been setting up this little plot of revenge on your father's behalf, the father that treated you like you didn't exist. So, instead of being loyal to the friend that has had your back for close to twenty years, you tried to gain daddy's approval by breaking Kami's heart and in turn, you broke mine. You can't break the heart of the woman I love without hurting me too Joe. I told you how I felt, and you still went through with it all."

"I'm sorry James. I didn't really think you were that invested and then, I couldn't stop it from happening. It just had a life of its own and _" He doesn't get the chance to finish what he's saying, he can keep his thoughts and apologies to himself. Although, I'm hoping he won't be speaking to anyone for a while after today.

"JAMES!!"

"JOE!!"

Kami and Katy yell in unison, but I can't see anything other than a red haze and the face of the man that used to be a brother to me. The only other thing I can see, is my fist hitting that arseholes face until he's bleeding.

"James, stop it!" Kami yells, pulling on my arm, trying to get me off the jerk.

I look up at her and say, "Kami, he's tried to destroy us from day one. He deserves this and more." I look into her eyes and realise she's crying, so I let go of the piece of shit and cradle her face in my hands, using my thumbs to wipe away her tears. "Don't cry sweetheart, he's never going to come between us again, we're done. Him and me, not us. I don't want us to be done." I'm not passed begging her for another chance right now, not that I did anything to break us apart, except have an arsehole for a friend.

"James, I think you broke his nose." She sniffs.

"Good, I hope I broke his jaw too." I say, my anger is nowhere near close to easing off just yet.

"You can't mean that James, he's been your friend, your brother for most of your life." Katy cries and it takes everything in me to look her in the eye, because she betrayed Kami as well.

"I can, and I do Katy. You can choose to be with him, but I'm done. He's screwed Kami over for the last time. I thought we were brothers, but his loyalty has been to the father he's always hated. All these years I thought we were looking out for each other, but that's just not true. You hear me arsehole? We're done. I'll be moving all my business elsewhere and when you get that call, you'll hand it all over, no questions asked. You understand me?" he nods, I can see the regret in his eyes. "and you stay away from Kami – and me."

I hear Katy gasp and Joe groan, but I couldn't give a fuck about them right now. My only concern is to get Kami out of here and away from Joe's bullshit so that we can talk things through. I reach for Kami's hand, but she pulls away, at least I think she does until I hear her cry out and then I think maybe she's hurt, "What's wrong, sweetheart?" I reach up to touch her cheek and that's when I see the blood coming out of my split knuckles. Kami pushes me around to the passenger side of her car and opens the door, pushing me in. "What are you doing Kami?"

"I'm taking you to see Doc Roberts, get in the car James. Please?"

<u>KAMI</u>

I didn't realise how damaged James' hand was until he went to touch my face. I know he hit Joe pretty hard, but it didn't seem like it was hard enough to split skin.

"I don't need a doctor sweetheart, I'm OK." He says, the idiot.

"No James, you're not OK. You've split the skin on your knuckles open and you need to see a damned doctor you idiot." I half yell, half screech at him. "Just get your butt in the car." I look into the backseat and notice a scarf I've got stashed there, I grab it and start to wrap it around his hand.

"No sweetheart, don't ruin your scarf by getting blood all over it, I'm fine."

"I'm wrapping up your hand, so you don't get blood all over my car, ya dumb arse, so shut the hell up." I yell at him as I slam the door shut. I walk around the front of the car to my door and see Joe sitting up now and resting in Katy's arms. "You best get him to the hospital Katy, I think his nose is broken."

"Thanks Kami, I will. I'll call you later and check in with you." Katy replies with a hesitant smile.

"Just text me what's wrong with him, I don't really want to talk to you right now." I reply a little more brusquely than I intended to.

"Sure, can you let me know how James' hand is, please?" she asks, quietly with a dejected look on her face. I nod and jump in the car, just as the back door to the shop swings open and Ed comes flying out.

"What the hell is happening out here? Are you OK Kami? We could hear yelling in the shop, I just got the last customer out the door so that I could lock up and come out here to check on you." He yells out all in one breath, and then he surveys where everyone is.

"Everything is just fine Ed, my best friend was seeing the one guy who hates me, that guy hates me so much that he faked text messages to break James and I up and then James hit him. Now, they both need a doctor. One needs stitches, and the other needs a nose reset." I take a breath, "anything else you need to know before I take James to see Doc Roberts?"

"Are you OK Kami? Can I do anything?" Poor Ed, he looks completely confused.

"Just look after the shop, please? I'll let you know what happened soon, OK? Thanks Ed." I don't really give him a chance to answer me as I jump in my car, start it up and drive away.

"Kami," James says, quietly, "Sweetheart, I'm sorry."

"For what? For the behaviour of my best friend or yours? For the lies, the absolute bald-faced lies?" I ask, getting angrier with every word I speak.

"No, not for any of that. They've made their own choices and they have to live with them. I'm talking about not trying harder to get in touch with you. For not suspecting that Joe was up to something. I don't know why he doesn't like you Kami, he's never explained it to me. I heard more about it just now than I have in all the years we've known each other." He leans his head back on the seat and closes his eyes.

I don't answer him, there's not a lot to say. I'm still confused about what just happened, and what role everyone plays in this little drama we've managed to get into. All that I do know is, Katy has some explaining to do and so does James for that matter, I'm not interested in what Joe has to say, but it can all wait for now.

"Come on James, we're here, let's get you cleaned up and sewn up." When he doesn't answer me, I look over to find him asleep. Head back, mouth slightly ajar, eyes closed tight with his wrapped hand resting in his lap. I didn't even stop to think about what time he started to drive home today, or how long he's been driving for. I realise now that he drove straight to the shop, straight to see me and he didn't even know if I was there.

I can't let him sleep, because he needs to get that damned hand fixed. "James. Come on James wake up." I push his shoulder gently. "Come on James, you need to wake up so that we can get you cleaned up." I shove on his shoulder even harder. I'm about to shove him harder again, when I notice the smirk on his face as his undamaged hand grabs hold of mine before I can move it away.

"Kami, sweetheart, thank you." He pulls my hand up to his lips and kisses my knuckles. My heart melts just a little bit towards him. Not that he did anything wrong, but I can't forget everything that I was feeling just because Joe confessed his mistakes.

"What are you thanking me for James?" I ask, completely confused.

"For looking after me and giving me the chance to explain." He says with a huge grin.

"No-one said anything about letting you talk Mr Harvey, but you are getting that hand looked at and fixed. Come on, move your butt." I pull my hand from his grasp and get out of the car. James gets out of the car before I can help him, and we walk into Doc Roberts clinic together.

"Good afternoon Kami, I didn't see your name in the appointments, what can we do for you today?" The receptionist greets me with a smile.

"Good afternoon Susie, I'm not here for me. James busted his knuckles open – working. He needs to see Doc Roberts to clean them up, please." I say, I know if I tell Susie Mahoney the real reason James' knuckles are split open, it'll be all over town before we leave the clinic. I've known the woman all my life, and she's the biggest gossip in town, but Doc Roberts keeps her on because she's great at her job.

Chapter Twenty-Eight

JAMES

Susie leads us back to a treatment room, "You two sit tight in here for a few minutes and I'll send Doc Roberts in as soon as he's finished with his current patient."

"Thanks, Susie, how long do you think he'll be?" Kami asks.

"Not long at all. We need to get those knuckles stitched up." She smiles at me and touches my arm. "If you need me for anything, just yell out." Her hand trails down my arm and I flinch at her touch, she thinks it's because I'm in pain by the sympathetic look on her face, in reality, it's because the woman is way too touchy-feely and she's flirting with me. I'm here with Kami and Susie's flirting with me. I don't want Kami to have another reason to not trust me.

"Thanks, Susie, but Kami can take it from here," I reply.

"OK, if you're sure handsome?" she smiles and bats her eyelashes. What the hell is she thinking?

"Yeah, I'm pretty sure my girlfriend knows how to look after me better than anyone else, with the exception of Doc Roberts of course." I smile back at her, hoping to god I've made myself very clear.

"Oh, yeah, sure handsome." She looks Kami up and down, then leaves the room.

"Wow!" Kami says quietly, and I can't help but chuckle.

"Yeah I know, she's been trying for years to get me to take her out, but I can't believe she'd be so bold about it while you're standing right there, next to me," I say.

"She's been trying for years. To what? Hump you like a sex-starved lion? She looked like she was ready to devour you and me being here made no damned difference James Harvey. It's not like we look like we're together, it looks like I'm just bringing you in to see the Doc. For all she knew, you *are* still fair game. I mean obviously, I'm no competition." I can't tell if she's mad or astounded by the other woman's brazenness. I can't imagine Kami even being that uncaring about another person's feeling, ever.

"Sweetheart, I don't care what she thinks, but you're right about one thing," I reach over and take her hand in the hand that isn't bleeding everywhere and say, "You're right, you're no competition," I feel her entire body stiffen and I smirk at her, which makes her angry. "You've got no competition Kami because you've got me, I don't even look at other women and trust me Susie has never been on my radar, ever. I've got you now and I'm not letting you get away that easily. I'm yours, sweetheart, no-one can change that for me." Her body relaxes, but she still wears a look that lets me know that she's pretty sceptical about the whole situation, but before I can say anything else to reassure her, Doc Roberts walks in the door. Great timing Doc, thanks.

"Good afternoon James, what have you done to yourself today? Susie tells me you've done yourself some damage." He says as he enters the room, looking at some notes on a clipboard in his hand. When he looks up waiting for my answer, he notices Kami standing there too. "Good afternoon Kami, how are you today?"

"I'm good thanks Doc Roberts, I bought James in for you to have a look at his hand. He had an accident at work and appears to have to split his knuckles open."

"Alrighty then let's have a look then shall we?" he unwraps Kami's scarf that she'll never wear again, there's just no way she can get all the blood out of it, she'd need a miracle. "Are you sure you did this at work James? It looks more like you hit something or someone with that fist." He gives me a stern look and then swings it around to Kami. I can't let her take the heat for me, so I speak up.

"You're right Doc, I hit something."

He looks at Kami like he's checking her over for injuries and it pisses me off. I may be many things, but I would never hit a woman, but more specifically I would never, ever hurt Kami like that.

"He didn't hit me Doc, don't worry about that. Trust me you'd be treating more than his hand if he laid his hands on me like that."

"Good girl." He smiles in approval at Kami. He's got stars in his eyes when he looks at her and I can't even be pissed at him for it, he's old enough to be her father. "Now, what really happened here?" He sees the hesitation in both our faces and quietens his voice, "I hope you both know that whatever is said in this room stays in this room. I can assure you that no one will find out the truth from me."

"That's not what we're worried about." I hear Kami mumble and before I can say anything the Doc's already answering in his quiet, reassuring voice.

"No-one in my office will tell a soul Kami, I made sure that they're all very busy and can't be anywhere but where they should and that's nowhere near this room."

"I hit Joe," I state plainly.

"Joe French? What on earth did he do?" Doc Roberts looks baffled.

"So many things Doc, but all I really need right now is for you to clean me up and let me get out of here with my girl so that I can explain a few things to her. If you don't mind?"

KAMI

"Let me go grab a suture kit and I'll be right back." He's back in the room before either of us can look at each other. Mind you, I don't really want to look at James right now. For one, I can't stand looking at his injured hand knowing that I was in some way responsible for it. Two, I don't want to have any kind of discussion here in the clinic and three, I'm still trying to make sense of what he meant when he said he was mine. That's insane, I don't know how to feel because until about half an hour ago, I was convinced that we were over. It's just not that easy to turn those kinds of emotions off.

"Hey, are you doing OK over there, sweetheart?"

"Hmmmm? Yeah, I'm fine, you're the one getting stitched up, not me." I say. Guess I'm staring off into space when really I should be concentrating on James' treatment. "Sorry, what do you need me to do?"

"I don't need you to do anything sweetheart, but I wouldn't mind you coming over here and holding the hand that isn't damaged. Doc's going to hurt me, and I wouldn't mind some of your sweet comforting." He gives me his cheeky smirk and I can't help it, it melts away at some of my confusion.

That doesn't stop me from rolling my eyes at him though, even as I walk over to him and reach out to take his hand in mine. "Don't be using that as an excuse Mr Harvey, you're the strongest man I know, I think you can deal with a needle and a few stitches."

"A needle? No-one said anything about a fucking needle." His face pales and suddenly he looks like he's going to pass out.

"Language James, and yes, of course, a needle you idiot. Doc has to numb the area, so he can stitch you up."

"Anything but a needle. Please Kami, if you have any love in your heart for me, no needles." I'm looking in his eyes to see if he's joking with me, but I really think he's terrified.

I go to speak, but we both notice that Doc has finished preparing the needle, "Ahhh yes young James here is deathly afraid of needles. Has been since he was a child, I can see the irony of it isn't lost on you either, Kami." Doc chuckles as he moves towards James' hand with the needle, "which is why we make sure he's lying down. I'd say relax but you're going to be out in three, two, one and there he goes."

Just like that, his eyes close, his hand goes limp in mine and his entire body relaxes. "Well, that makes it easy to stitch him up then Doc. Do you even use anaesthetic with him at all?"

Doc Roberts chuckles and shakes his head, "Nope, I haven't had to use anaesthetic on him in years, the needle has saline in it, and I've discovered if I work fast enough, a little bit of numbing gel on the area and he never even knows." He says, followed by more laughter as he cleans the wound and then stitches it up.

Doc moves fast and finishes just as James starts to come around. I didn't even know people passed out for that long, but he sure uses it to his advantage.

"There you go James, all cleaned up. You're ready to go home now, but you are going to need some help in the next few days because you can't get that wet." He looks my way and asks, "Will you be able to help him out Kami or should I send a nurse around to check on him every day?"

I take a few seconds to think because while I'm not sure I want to be around him all day every day for the next few days, I don't really like the idea of a nurse coming in to look after him either. Not unless said nurse is a big burly man, anyway. What can I say, I might still be a little annoyed with him, but I don't want anyone else doing it either.

"Please Kami?" James asks, fluttering his eyelashes and setting his pleading light blue eyes on mine. "I'm going to need some help to shower you know, and I don't know if I'm comfortable having another woman's hands running all over my body." His bottom lip drops out in a pout and his eyes are full of pathetic pleading.

"You know you don't need sponge baths or the like James, but he is right Kami, he's going to need helping washing himself for at least a few days," Doc says laughing.

"Come on Doc, give a man a helping hand. Tell her I need nursing and gentle hands."

"Sorry son, that's the best I can do, Kami can volunteer but I'm not going to a part of coercing her into being your nursemaid."

"You've got a couple of days Mr Harvey, but if you misbehave, I'm calling in a big burly male nurse to help you shower."

"Your place or mine, sweetheart?"

Doc Roberts cracks up laughing and says, "I'll let you two to sort out the details. Call me if you need anything or you're worried Kami. James, don't forget to sign out with Susie before you leave."

WE DECIDE TO STAY AT James' house, but first I want to go past my place to grab a few things, including clean clothes. When we get there, I make James come inside with me, mainly so I can keep an eye on him, because who knows what he would get up to if I left him alone. Knowing him, he'd start building me a new table or something.

I sit him on the edge of my bed while I grab my bag and start packing some clothes. James is talking to me the whole time about the job he just completed and how annoying Simon was to work with. I can understand now why he was thinking about walking away from the damned contract. Simon sounds like he'd test the patience of a saint.

"I'm going into the bathroom to grab a few things, we can pick the conversation up when I get back. I won't be able to understand you from the bathroom." I tell James as I watch him sit back against the headboard and bring up legs to the bed.

"Sure sweetheart, I'll be waiting right here for you." He replies sleepily.

"I'm only going into the next room James, I'm not going to be away for more than a few minutes," I laugh at him. Anyone would swear that Doc Roberts had injected him with drugs earlier.

"Mmm, kay." He says quietly.

When I get back into my bedroom a few minutes later, James is asleep. He's slipped down the headboard and his head is resting on my pillow. He's got his injured hand resting on his chest and the other one behind his head. I don't have the heart to wake him, he's had a very traumatic and long day, so I finish packing my bag quietly. I pull a spare blanket up over him and walk out to the kitchen. I think a cup of coffee is in order after the day I've had.

Maybe a stiff drink is more in order, but I still don't know what the rest of the day and night could bring, so a coffee is going to have to do for now.

JAMES

I wake with Kami's scent enveloping me and I don't want to open my eyes in case she's not here. I can't take it if I wake up without her near me another morning. I reach out across the bed and realise I'm alone. I open my eyes and it takes a few seconds for them to adjust and my brain to work out where I am.

I'm lying in Kami's bed, that explains why all my senses can think about is her. Yet, I'm alone. It's dark outside, but I'm not actually under the covers. I move to sit up and my hand hurts and I let out what I think is a low moan. That moan becomes an even louder growl when it suddenly hits me, everything that happened to today and in the last few weeks.

"Fucking Joe," I curse loudly, my best friend, my brother. Everything he's done comes rushing back and I can't help the anger building up in my chest.

"Ummmm, James. Are you OK? Does your hand hurt? I picked up some painkillers while you were sleeping if you need any?" she asks, standing at the door and not looking like she wants to come any closer. Guess it's time we talk things through, I don't want her to be uncomfortable around me. Ever.

I pat the bed next to me with my uninjured hand, "Come sit down sweetheart, I think I've got a few things to explain to you." She hesitates, it's only a few seconds, but I see it in her eyes and her body language. I'm not gonna lie, that hurts like a son of a bitch, but I can't say I blame her.

"I don't know what to say, James. I'm sorry Joe hurt you." She's always thinking of someone else and not herself, this is one of the many reasons I love her. Yeah, I love her.

"Joe didn't hurt just me Kami. He's been hurting you for years and I'm sorry I didn't put an end to it before now. I tried to, but he just couldn't get past whatever it is he's been holding against you. At least now we have some idea as to why, but I still don't understand him at all. The crap he pulled these past few days, just isn't acceptable Kami. I won't allow him to hurt you anymore, you mean too much to me to let him come between us for one more day." I take a breath before continuing, "I think there are some things that need to be said before anything else can happen between us, OK?" She nods and doesn't look away from me, so I continue. "Joe was right about one thing, while I was away the only thing I could think about was getting back home to you, but Simon was also a giant arsehole. That contract and design was signed off weeks ago, but when he took over, he wanted to make changes because it wasn't what he would have chosen to do. In fairness to him, he'd only been handed the project a week before our start date, but that's no excuse for the shit he put me through." I take another breath, I'm not sure where everything else fits into in the time I was away, so I decide to just tell her what I do know. "The morning that Joe showed up on the site, I dropped my phone on gravel, it smashed to pieces and I couldn't call you. It didn't just shatter the screen or a small part of it, it was unusable. I didn't know Joe had planned on coming out, but I was grateful that he showed up. I couldn't get away from the job that day to get into the closest town to get myself a new phone. I knew we had a phone date that night and I didn't want to miss it. When Joe showed up, I mistakenly thought I could trust him to get me a new phone. I can't believe how wrong I was sweetheart."

"What he did isn't your fault James. He made choices all of his own and we both ended up his victims." She says sadly, "but that explains how he got access to your phone, even though everything should have swapped over easily, he managed to explain it away. How did he get to your laptop?" Kami asks, and it's a fair question.

"When he got back and gave me the new phone, he asked if he could go into the on-site office and get some of his own work done. I didn't have a problem with him going in there because I trusted him. Let me assure you that's past tense after today. He took my new phone with him and said he'd see if he could get some of my contacts off my laptop and put them onto the phone." I shake my head and drop my chin to my chest. Tired, disappointed and if I'm being honest, embarrassed. "I can't believe I was so naïve Kami. He was more than a friend to me, he was like a brother, or at least I thought he was. I mean, I know he's always held *something* against you, but I've never known what it was, honestly. I was hoping that he'd grown out of all the stupidity. Especially after I told him to back off and leave you alone, that we were together, and he couldn't stop that from being the truth. Hell Kami, he asked me if I was serious about you before I left town and I told him I was in love with you. Yet, he still did this, he still pulled all this crap and I just, I hope you know how sorry I am about all his bullshit. His actions and feelings, they don't reflect mine at all." When I stop to look at her, trying to see if she believes me, I see shock written all over her face. What the hell have I said now?

"Did you mean that? What you said to Joe, is that true?" she asks, her voice is quieter than usual and unsure. Now I have to think about what I said because everything I just said was true, I'm trying to pick out which truth she means.

"Everything I just said was the truth sweetheart, but which thing specifically are you asking about?" I ask, but just as she starts to speak, I realise what I said and what she's asking.

"What you said to Joe when he asked if you were serious about me? Did you mean your answer?" her voice is still low, and she can't look me in the eyes.

I reach over with my good hand, place my fingers under her chin and force her to look me in the eyes. There is no way in this world I am confessing my feelings to the top of her head. I want to look into her beautiful gold-flecked, hazel eyes and watch her reaction as she understands exactly what she means to me.

"Look at me, sweetheart." I wait until she opens her eyes properly and looks directly into mine. "When Joe asked me if I was serious about you and our relationship, I told him that I was deadly serious, that you were the one for me. In answer to your question, yes, I told him I love you and I was yours for as long as you'd have me." I smile at her because I'm confident in my feelings and I want her to know that. Even though, inside I'm dying, dying to know if she feels the same way about me or if I'm about to get my stupid heartbroken. I've been guarding this heart of mine for so long, that if she doesn't love me, I feel like I'll shatter into a million pieces.

"Wow!" she says on a breath out, meanwhile, I'm holding my breath waiting for her response. "I didn't know you felt that way. I thought that, well I thought it was just me being romantic and stupid." Her hands have made their way to the wrist of my hand that has her chin resting in it. "I don't know what to say, James."

"You don't have to say a thing sweetheart. Especially if you don't feel the same way yet, it's OK, take your time. I was going to tell you when I got back from this work trip, not quite like this but I had plans." My hand makes its way to rest on the back of her neck, gently bringing her lips to mine, we're not so close that I can't see into her eyes though, not yet, when I say, "I love you, Kami Parker, with everything I have. I'm yours, for as long you'll have me." Then I pull her lips to mine and I kiss her. I kiss her until we're both gasping for breath and I'm hoping my kiss tells her just how much she means to me.

"Ohhh, James." She breathes out.

"Just kiss me Kami."

Chapter Twenty-Nine

<u>KAMI</u>

He loves me. James freaking Harvey *loves* me. He loves me. *ME*. I wanna tell him I love him because he thinks we're not on the same page, but we are. If only he'd stop kissing me long enough for me to speak or even breathe I'd be able to tell him that.

I need to calm down, I need to make my heartbeat slow down a little. I'm so happy I feel like I might explode. "James." I manage to mumble against his lips, "James, babe, stop for just a second, I need to catch my breath."

"Breathing's overrated sweetheart. Just keep panting and I'm sure you can still get enough breath into your lungs." He says, smiling against my lips. "I don't want to move away from your perfectly kissable lips. Lips that I've been dreaming of kissing the whole time I was out of town. These lips have fuelled some pretty fantastic dreams for me I'll have you know Miss Parker."

He pulls back just enough to look into my eyes, so I take my opportunity. I place my hands on his cheeks and hold his head still, looking directly into his eyes. "I love you, too." I see the shock and then the happiness register is his eyes. "James Harvey, I. Am. Yours. For as long as you want me to be, which I'm kind of hoping is forever." I start laying soft kisses all over his face.

"Really, Kami?" I nod and smile at him. "What the hell did I ever do to deserve a woman like you loving me?"

"You love me in return." I say as I slide my legs on either side of his hips, to sit in his lap and straddle him. "Yes, really. I love you with everything I have James."

"Fuck me Kami, I've never felt like this before." He groans as he pulls my lips back to his and starts devouring my mouth again.

Before his lips can distract me for too long I say, "I'd love to James, but I don't want to hurt your hand, so you're going to have to put up with just some kissing tonight." I laugh at the surprise on his face when he realises what I mean.

"You can't hurt me tonight, sweetheart." He says that, but I can see in his eyes that I can hurt him, and I don't mean his hand.

Looking into my eyes, he lays his hand on my thigh, it's pretty stiff and he can't seem to move it properly, but he doesn't look like he's in any pain. His hand isn't the only part of his body that I can feel that's stiff as he pushes his hips up towards me, so that his cock rubs along the seam of my jeans. I can't help the groan that falls from my lips as I grind down onto him, but my mind is fighting with my body. I don't want to hurt his hand, but I want him just as much as I can feel that he wants me. We just admitted that we love one another and the need to *show* the other one just how much, is overwhelming.

"Give in to us sweetheart," he whispers in my ear. "If my hand starts hurting, I swear we'll stop."

When I pull back to see his face, I see the mischief written all over his gorgeous face and the smirk tipping up the corner of his kissable lips. I know that he won't be telling me if I hurt him. I make to move off him and the bed, and his grip on my hip tightens, "James, babe, if you want me naked I need to get off the bed."

"Come back here, I want to help." James' voice is husky, full of desire. Dang, the desire in his voice is so sexy I squeeze my thighs together to relieve my own building need.

"No, you stay there and enjoy the show babe." I say, my own voice so raspy I can hardly believe it's mine. I send James what I hope is a sexy look and start slowly undoing the buttons of my shirt. As my shirt slowly starts to gape open, revealing my skin, I watch James' Adam's apple bob up and down as he swallows deeply. I can hear his breathing getting more erratic as I let the shirt fall to the floor and start working on the button and zip on my jeans. I turn my back to the bed and bend over slowly dragging my jeans down my legs and James growls out a "fuck Kami!" I can't help the smile that spreads across my face as I bend all the way to my feet and slide my jeans off completely. I turn back around to face him in just my underwear, and he motions with his good hand for me to come closer. I do, but not close enough for him to touch me. I'm not ready for him to touch me, this is my show, not his. "No touching yet." I say, shaking my head.

"But sweetheart–" he protests, and I shake my head again, "Nope." I say as I reach behind me and undo my bra, letting the straps slide down my shoulders. I put my hands on the cups of my bra, holding them to my boobs, dropping my head back, I moan as I start to massage them, running my fingers over my stiff, sensitive nipples. Then, without thinking about it, I let my bra fall to the floor leaving my boobs free for James to look at. That is until I start to take my underwear off, I slide them down my hips and then wiggle my butt until they fall down to my ankles, then I kick them to the side. "Sweetheart come here. Please?" James' voice is so deep and husky, it barely even sounds like him.

I walk over to the bed and say, "Lean forward babe." He pushes his back off the headboard and I slowly drag his t-shirt up his body, over his head and carefully over his injured hand, being careful not to knock it. Then I say, "Lift up babe." He leans back and rests on the headboard again so that he raises his hips up off the bed.

"You know I can do this myself, right sweetheart?" James asks, his voice still husky.

"I do, but isn't it much more fun this way?" I ask, my voice a raspy whisper. I grab the waistbands of both his sweatpants and his boxers, then pull them down off his hips, down his legs and add them to the pile of clothes on the floor. God, he looks edible, and that's exactly what I plan on doing.

Keeping my eyes on his, I climb onto the bed, and he spreads his legs so that I can move up his body. I rest my hands on his hips and get myself comfortably settled between his thighs. With my eyes never leaving his I lean down, and drag my tongue from his balls, all the way up his hard cock to the slit in the head, licking up the beads of pre-cum settling there. I don't wrap my lips around him, just run my tongue from his balls to the tip, I don't know how many times I do it, but I hold his eyes with mine the whole time, until he can stand it anymore and his eyes close. "Fuck Kami." He growls, but it's a whisper, like he's forcing his voice to work. "Fuck Kami, what are you __" he doesn't finish his sentence because I choose that moment to draw the head of his cock into my mouth and I suck. Hard. With one hand on the bed for balance, I wrap the other one around the base of his cock, squeezing and releasing as I draw my mouth up and down his hard cock and tonguing the head when I reach it. I can feel the muscles in his stomach and thighs tense and his hips are bouncing off the bed with the need for more. His good hand rests on the back of my head, there's no pressure in his touch, he's massaging my scalp and wrapping my hair around his fingers. "Kami, I'm gonna come if you keep that up sweetheart."

I take his cock in my mouth one more time, then I take my hand away and run my tongue from his balls to his tip once again. My hands trail up his thighs, hips, not touching his cock that I can see pulsing right in front of me, begging for attention. I feel up his stomach, to his chest, I pinch each nipple between my thumbs and forefingers. James hisses in a breath between his teeth while his hips jump off the bed again. He is by far the sexiest thing I have ever seen in my life. Letting me play with his body and the arousal his reactions create in me are undeniable. I'm so wet and my pussy is pulsing with the need to have his cock inside me, so I lean over his body and reach into my drawer for a condom. I'm watching James as I tear the foil open, grab the condom and toss the wrapper away. His chest is heaving, his eyes are half closed and there's a light sheen of sweat all over his body. I sit back between his thighs, my butt resting on my calves and I take his hard cock in my hand, stroking him a few more times before rolling the condom on. I move back up his body to straddle his hips and reach back to guide his cock into my pussy. With the head of his cock resting at my ready pussy, I lean down and kiss him softly, feathering along his jaw until I reach the lobe of his ear and give it a light nibble. The groan James lets out is animalistic and I can't help but lower myself down onto his cock a little more, then I whisper in his ear, "I need you James."

"Oh Kami you've got me, you've got me for as long as you'll have me sweetheart." He takes a deep shuddering breathe, "I need you Kami, fuck me, I need you too." Those blue eyes of his are staring right into mine and they're filled with love and longing.

"I plan on fucking you James, believe me." I lower my body down until my butt is on his thighs, and my pussy is taking him all in, down to the base of his cock. "Argghhh fuck, James, you feel so good."

He sits up, his bandaged hand resting on my back, his good hand resting on my hip, the movement pushing his cock a little further into my body and making me gasp. He kisses along my jaw, and whispers in my ear, "That's it sweetheart, fuck me hard." So, I do. I push my arms through his and wrap my hands up around his shoulders, holding on tightly to his body to steady me. I start moving my hips, making us both groan with pleasure. I've had a few partners, but nothing has ever felt as good as being with James. It's never been such a full body experience before. With my boobs pressed against his chest, my hips moving faster and faster and James whispering his dirty words in my ear, "fuck me Kami, make yourself come, harder, faster sweetheart, come on my cock." My body has taken over my movements and my hips are pounding into his. All I can hear is the slap of flesh against flesh, his dirty words and both of our groans filling the night air. There is nothing and no-one else on the planet. "Come for me Kami, I'm going to come any second and I need you to come now too sweetheart." He kisses me from my ear down to my neck and nibbles on just the right spot.

"Ohhhh Jamessssssssssssss." I scream out hoarsely. My entire body starts to convulse, I pull my arms from around his back and wrap them around his neck tangling my fingers in his hair, pulling lightly. "I love you James Harvey." I barely a whisper as I come.

"Fuck, I love you too Kami Parker." Then he roars out his release and falls back onto the bed, pulling me with him.

JAMES

She loves me! That's what she said, right?

We just had the most amazing sex of my life and now, I've got the sexiest woman I've ever known lying on top of me and we're both trying to catch our breath. I can feel her body starting to relax and as much as I want her to stay right where she is, I need to clean myself up. "Kami, sweetheart, you have to move." I kiss the top of her head.

"Mmmmhmmmm OK." She murmurs, and I chuckle.

"I need to go clean myself up Kami, so I kinda need you to move my love." I chuckle again.

"Ohh crap on a cracker I'm so sorry, I was lying right on top of you wasn't I? I'm too heavy aren't I? What about your hand, does it hurt? Did I hurt you?" She sits up in a panic and pushes her elbow into my stomach in the process. I grunt, and she apologises again. I can't help but love this woman. "Ohhh geeezzz I'm so sorry James."

I grab her hand, so she can't get any further away from me and say, "Sweetheart none of those things are the reason I need you to move. I just need to go clean myself up and then I want to come back to bed. So I can hold you and fall asleep with the woman I love in my arms." Her eyes warm and I see her body relax as she realises what I've said is true. "I'll be back in a couple of minutes, OK?" she nods as I release her hand and walk into the bathroom. It's only when I get there that I realise I've only got one hand to get the condom off my dick, something I've never had any practice with, but there's no way in hell I'm asking the beautiful woman who finally told me she loves me, for help with this. I laugh at my fumbling, but I finally manage to get myself cleaned up and walk back into Kami's bedroom. What I find there is all of my dreams come true.

Kami. Naked. Laying on her bed. Waiting for me to come back to her.

I realise this is what I want for the rest of my life, Kami. Us coming home to each other at the end of the day.

I reach the edge of the bed and I can feel my cock getting hard again as I look at the most delectable woman I've ever met, waiting for me. "Move in with me Kami?" I don't know who's more surprised, Kami or me, but as soon as the words are out of my mouth I know that's exactly what I want. I want to be in the same space as her, to share that space and to know she is my home.

"James." Is all she says, and I shake my head, as I climb back into bed with her and bring her back to my front. Pulling her in close to me, resting my lips on the base of her neck where it meets her shoulder.

"Don't answer me now, just think about it, OK?" I feel her nod, so I continue. "Just know that that's what I want. Whenever you're ready. Whether that's now, in a few weeks or a few months. I'll wait. I'll wait for you Kami Parker, because I love you."

"I'm not ready right now James, but soon, I promise." I kiss her shoulder and nod against her skin. "I love you too, James Harvey."

I smile against her skin, I hear her sigh and feel her body relax. Within minutes, she's asleep and laying there, with this extraordinary woman who loves me, wrapped up in my arms, promising that one day we'll have this every night. I couldn't be happier.

Then, I move my hand and remember that the man I once called brother won't be sharing in the happiness he tried so hard to destroy and it kills me, because he was once the person I would have run to with anything that was news. Good or bad. Not anymore though, he's destroyed that.

I sigh, not wanting to think of Joe fucking French, not when I'm this happy. Instead, I snuggle my body even tighter into Kami's and take comfort in everything that she is and fall asleep. Dreaming of us being together just like this. Forever.

Epilogue
6 months later

<u>KAMI</u>

It's been a long, difficult and uncomfortable 6 months since Joe dropped his unbelievable truth bombshell.

James can't find a way to forgive his 'traitorous best friend'. He can't reconcile his lifelong friend with the pain he's caused, not just in the past few months but the years beforehand as well. James believes that there is an underlying cause behind Joe's behaviour, he just isn't in the frame of mind to listen to what that might be just yet.

I want to forgive Joe and move forward, but I'm not sure how to. There's a lot of pain and anguish under that particular bridge, and while I think James is right, and there's something else behind his behaviour, until he's willing to share what that is, I don't know how to forgive him. I want to try though because Katy's in love with him. I don't think I can ever forget all he's done, but I want the peace of mind of forgiveness, not for him, but for me.

A few weeks after the bomb that Joe dropped, James asked me to move in with him again. My place, his place or a new place, he didn't care, as long as it was together. He said he was sick and tired of shuffling between the two houses and making that decision every day. He wasn't the only one but still I hesitated. I know that my hesitation hurt him, but my reasons weren't what he thought they were.

He said, "Move in with me Kami." Not a question, a statement.

"Why do you want to live together James?" I remember asking him.

"I want to live in the same house as you. I don't want to have to think about what house I'm going to, or where I'm heading to work from so that I know what time to set an alarm for."

"That's it? That's why you want to live together, because it's inconvenient not to?" I asked. I knew it wasn't what he meant, but damn it still hurt a little bit. "Maybe we're moving too fast James. We should take some time to think about this."

He nodded but didn't say a word. I knew that I'd hurt his feelings, but he kind of hurt mine too. I know he was tired, so was I. While I understood his reasons for wanting to live together, it still felt like it was for the wrong reasons.

A few days later, I walked into the lounge room at James' house, he was sitting on the couch watching some Friday night sports something or other on the TV. I'd been listening to the show from the bedroom and knew it was almost finished. So I walked over to him, straddled his lap in my short shorts and oversized t-shirt that was hanging off one naked shoulder. I leaned in and started kissing up his neck until I reached his ear and nibbled on his lobe. I felt a growl rumble in his chest through my hands that I had resting on his flexing pecs. Taking that as a hint to keep going, I started leaving small kisses and bites along his jawline until I reached the spot where his lips almost reach his cheek and I stopped moving. His hands settled on my hips, I'm not sure whether he wants to push me off or hold me in place. Either way, I'm still straddling his hips and I can feel his cock swelling beneath me.

"Fuck me sweetheart, what are you doing to me?" James says, his voice quiet and husky.

"That's exactly what I plan on doing James, and if you don't know that, then I must be doing something wrong." I go to move off his lap not really intending to stop, but his hands hold me still.

"Where do you think you're going, sweetheart?" He's pulled back just far enough that he can look into my eyes and I think I could stay here forever and drown in him.

"I'm not going anywhere James. Ever." I smile at him and wait for the penny to drop, but it doesn't. I can't really blame him, I'm being a little too cryptic. "I was thinking that if you still want to, I could move my stuff over here and.." I don't get to finish my thought.

"Are you saying what I *think* you're saying Kami?" he asks, and I can't hold back the smile or my laughter at the look on his face. "Are you sure? Don't fuck with me Kami Parker, you know how much I want this. Us together. I don't care if it's here, your place or somewhere the fuck else."

I take his face in my hands, look deep into his eyes and say, "There is nothing else I want more either James Harvey. My hesitation wasn't because I didn't want to, or that I didn't trust you and it wasn't because I didn't want to live here. I was scared James. Scared that we were moving too fast, moving our relationship to the next level because of everything that Joe tried to do to ruin it. I didn't want to do this for all the wrong reasons, but I've realised there isn't a wrong reason. I want to be with you every day and I'm tired of choosing which place to stay at too."

"It's not too fast sweetheart, we've known each other for years. I know it's never been as intimate as it is now, but I've always known you in some way." He rubs his hands up and down my back in what is supposed to be a soothing manner but is really just firing up all my senses. "You don't have to move in here either, we can go find a place that is ours."

"No. I want to live here, with you if that's OK? My house is too small to give you the space you need to run your business, and finding a new place seems ridiculous when you've got everything you need set up here like you want it. My business is at the shop, I can work from anywhere after the shop closes as long as I have a laptop and internet access."

"As long as you're sure sweetheart? I don't want you to do this because you think it'll make me happy and you'll be miserable. This is for both of us, not just me."

"I am," I kiss his lips, "doing exactly," I kiss him again, a little longer this time, "what I want," I give him another, deeper kiss, "James Harvey," I plant an even deeper kiss on him and nip his jaw as I pull away again, "I love you," I nip along his jaw, "and I want to," I nip some more, "live here," I've reached his ear so I nibble there a little, "and fuck you," I lick up the shell of his ear and then lean into it to whisper, "any damned time I want to."

"You don't have to live with me to do that sweetheart, but it sure will help with access to my body." He says, his breath is raspy, but deep rumble.

His hands are flexing on my hips and I can feel his cock straining to get out of his track pants. I know he's commando, because I watched his sexiness get dressed when he got out of the shower earlier. "Does that mean I get the same privileges with your gorgeous self?" his hands slide up my body and cup my boobs, his thumbs rubbing across my already standing to attention nipples.

"Oh god yes James. I wouldn't have it any other way." I moan as he pinches both nipples between his thumb and forefinger through my t-shirt. I don't have a bra on, so I can feel the pleasure along with the slight sting of pain, making my desire for this man of mine combust. "James, I need you. Please babe?"

Without another thought, he stands up from the couch with me in his arms and walks us to the bedroom. I guess I can call it *our* bedroom now? Without me even being aware of what he's doing, he drops me to my feet, holds me steady and strips me of my shorts and I lift my arms from around his shoulders so that he can pull my t-shirt off. Within seconds I'm naked and then I start on pulling his pants off his hips and he kicks them off his feet. He sits on the edge of the bed with my legs wrapped around his body again, and tugs his own t-shirt up and over his, it joins the rest of our clothes on the floor.

My hands are running around his body, touching as much skin as I possibly can. I can't get enough of him, of feeling his muscles ripple and jump as my fingers touch him. He kisses me from my shoulder, up the side of my neck and nibbles on my earlobe, where he whispers, "Hold on tight sweetheart."

"Mmmmhmmmm." Is all I manage before we're both moving sideways, and I squeal while gripping tighter onto his shoulders. "What the—?" He chuckles, and I realise he's leaning towards his bedside table to grab a condom. "you could have warned a girl you know." I huff out.

James laughs quietly again and says, "I thought I did when I told you to hang on sweetheart. What did you think I meant?"

"Well, I thought, well it doesn't matter what I thought now does it?" He starts kissing my shoulder again, moving those lips of his until they're at the sensitive spot where my shoulder meets my neck and I moan. Any previous thoughts are lost as he sends sparks through my body with just his lips. Then he lightly nips at my skin and I'm rubbing myself against his thigh and telling him to hurry the hell up. I hear the foil of the condom rip and feel the movement of his arm rolling it onto his cock. Then he lifts me until my pussy hovers above his cock, "You ready sweetheart?" Like he needs to asks.

"Always." With that one word he loosens his grip on my body, allowing my pussy to slide down the length of his cock until he can't go any deeper. Our lips are resting against each other. His exhale fills my lungs and my exhale fills his. We just sit there for a minute, a few seconds, hours, who the fuck knows and who cares? This is home, no matter where we are, this is where my home is. Wherever James is, then I'm home.

"I agree sweetheart, you're my home too," I didn't even know I'd spoken the words out loud, "but I really need you to start moving, otherwise I'm going to embarrass myself Kami." He sounds pained and I start moving, just like he asked me to because I feel it too. This urgent need to make him mine.

With my knees resting on the edge of the bed, I use them to start moving up and down. Up and down. Creating the friction we both need. "Oh fuck! James, I'm gonna come."

"That's it come for me, sweetheart." He has one hand resting at the back my neck, cradling my head, and the other one reaches down to press a thumb my clit. My movements get faster and more erratic as he holds me upright, pressing and then releasing my clit over and over again. His voice all husky and full of desire whispers in my ear, "come on my cock sweetheart." That's all I need to start screaming his name as my body shakes with my orgasm. "Yes, Kami." He growls into the crook of my neck as his orgasm shivers through his body.

We're both dragging air into our lungs and bringing ourselves back down to earth, when with his arms still wrapped tightly around me, he falls back onto the bed and I'm laying on top of his still heaving chest. I start to pull myself up and off his cock so that he can go clean up, but he won't let me go.

"Do you mean it Kami? Are we going to live together, here, in this house? Is this our bedroom now?" He opens his eyes to look at me. I can see how vulnerable and nervous he's feeling.

"James, if you'll have me, I want to live here in this house with you." I feel rather than see or hear his sigh of relief. "I've already asked Katy to help me start packing and moving my stuff over tomorrow. If that's ok with you? I was hoping that seeing it's the weekend you might have some time to help me with the bigger stuff?" I ask, suddenly feeling unsure and shy.

"Of course, I have all the time in the world to help you move into *our house* Kami." He makes me feel better with just a few words as I slip off his body to the mattress. I happily watch him as he walks off the bathroom to clean up. Within minutes the man is sauntering his sexy butt back towards the bed, back to me, and I'm enjoying the view. "See something you like sweetheart?" he says with a cocky grin.

"Nope. I see someone I love." He growls and suddenly I'm on my back with his hard-on pressed into my thigh. We're up for a second round and I'm going to enjoy every second of my man.

JAMES

The afternoon Kami straddled my hips and told me she wanted to move in with me was the single best day of my life so far. It had nothing to do with the amazing celebration sex, as she called it, we had either. Not that I'm complaining, not even for one fucking second. Not on your life. What made it even better though, was that she'd already started packing her stuff and arranged for Katy to help her with the rest of it. I'm grateful that she wanted to move in here, but what I told her when I first asked her to live with me was true. I would have lived anywhere as long as she was with me. Moving my workshop and business would have been a lot of work, but I would have done it in a heartbeat.

What I hadn't expected when I got to her place to pack my truck with what she wanted to bring, was to find Joseph there waiting to help with the heavy stuff. He looked at me and said, "I hope you don't mind, but when Katy told me she was helping Kami move in with you I figured you could use some help with any heavy lifting?"

He wasn't wrong, but I wasn't sure that it was *his* help that I needed. Instead of bitching about it I nodded my agreement and at the end of the day I shook his hand and thanked him for helping. We barely spoke while moving stuff unless it had to do with what we were carrying or moving at the time. Nothing extra, no joking or mucking around and definitely no unnecessary talking. It felt good to have him around again, but awkward and uncomfortable at the same time. I just don't know how to talk to him anymore.

After close to two decades of friendship, I was left feeling kind of sad. Which in turn made me fucking angry because *he did this*.

I didn't see or hear from him or about him until about a month after Kami moved in with me. She wanted to go out for dinner, and I guess I should have picked up that something was going on, but I was just enjoying being with her. When we walked into the restaurant and I saw Katy sitting at a table for four with Joe, I knew I'd been duped. I was royally pissed off until I looked at Kami's sweet face and saw the pleading in her eyes. So, instead we sat down and ordered our meals. I could see by the look on Joe's face that he'd been conned too, but that didn't make the evening any less uncomfortable. On the drive home, Kami apologised for lying by omission, I wasn't angry at her, I understood where she was coming from. Her best friend was seeing a guy, and she just wanted us to be able to get together now and then. I made her promise me though, no more surprise dinners, if we were meeting up with them, I wanted to know. Time to prepare myself for that was better than getting thrown into the deep end, but I also told her that if I didn't want to go, I wasn't going.

After that, Kami and Katy planned their time together as just that. Their time together, just the two of them or with only one of us guys there. I guess I wasn't the only one to have laid down some rules after that disaster of a dinner. I don't like surprises, especially when it feels like I've been manipulated into something. My old man did that for years and I won't put up with it anymore, from anyone. Even though I know I want my friend back, I'm not sure how to go about it. What I do know is that surprise dinners isn't the way. I know that Joe's waiting for me to reach out, I just can't bring myself to do it.

That's why when Kami told me that Katy wanted us to go over to her place for dinner, with her *and* Joe a couple of weeks ago, I took a few minutes, but eventually agreed to it. I guess it's the girls way of trying to get one of us (me) to take the chance. Kami smiled so broadly when I agreed to go that I thought her cheeks might split open. I just hoped that she would still be smiling after the dinner.

Plenty of alcoholic beverages were drunk that night at Katy's and just as we finished dessert, we were sitting there quietly. I guess each of us were contemplating what to do or say next. For most of the evening the girls had been talking comfortably between the two of them and dragging Joe and myself into the conversation occasionally. It wasn't as uncomfortable as that first time weeks ago, but it sure wasn't easy by any means. It wasn't made any easier when Joe cleared his throat and starting speaking either.

"I'm sorry James, about everything, but you have to know that I never meant to hurt anyone. Especially not you and whether you believe me or not, I didn't mean to hurt Kami either. I just never wanted to get to know her or let her get close to you."

"I get that Joseph, I really do man, but I still don't understand *why*. What the fuck did Kami ever do to you? I've never understood why you hated her so fucking much. She's the sweetest person on the planet and I love her, yet you couldn't even bring yourself to like her. It never even seemed like you tried to be honest."

"You're right, I didn't try to get to know Kami. Not even once and for that, I am truly sorry Kami." He takes a deep breath and Katy reached over to hold his hand, for comfort and encouragement I assume. I don't know what he could have to say that would need this kind of build-up, I'm just glad he's finally going to tell us what his problem has been. "Our parents were together in high school. Apparently, they were all starry eyes and going to be together forever. Children, marriage and white picket fences were spoken about every day and then one day, things changed."

"What are you talking about Joe?" Kami asked him, I had no clue what he was babbling on about.

"Your mother, Helen dumped Harry and then Harry met Felicity. It was a whirlwind romance, they got married and then, there I was, and everyone was happy. That was until Helen strolled back into town without taking Harry's feelings into consideration. Not only did she come back into town, but to add to his humiliation, she bought a husband and children with her. Everything she'd told Harry that she didn't want. All he saw was that she left him and everything he thought was in their future, then went and did it all with someone else and within in months of leaving town. Harry took the hit to his fragile ego and guess who paid the price? Yeah me and

Felicity. I wasn't good enough for him after you came to town. I wasn't female, I wasn't smart enough, I hung out with the wrong people, I said and did all the wrong things." He looks back over to me, "Sorry James, I never felt that way man, it's how Harry felt." I nod and Joe turns back to face Kami. "I know it's no excuse at all, but as a teenage boy, with hormones and rage running rampant, you were the only one I could take it out on. If I took it out on Harry, life at home just became unbearable, for all of us and that hurt Felicity as well. Being a teenage boy and not knowing how to deal with my emotions, I took it out on you."

"You haven't been a teenage boy for a long time though Joseph, so what happened months ago? Surely you should have outgrown the need to make Harry's issues your own or Kami's?" I ask him. I want his answer, because even though I can see where he's coming from, Harry was a fucking nasty bastard when we were kids, he's been out of that house for years. Even Felicity left the bastard a few years ago.

"I know. There's no excuse for my current behaviour. I think I just got so used to behaving a certain way towards you Kami that it became normal." I go to speak, but Joe holds his hand up to stop. "I know that's no excuse James, believe me I know. I assumed that Kami was like her mother and that she was using you. That you would end up hurt and miserable like Harry and I couldn't even think about it. I know now, after getting to know Kami through her friendship with Katy over the last few months, that she's nothing like Helen. I also understand that it's going to take you both time to forgive me, if you ever can. I don't like the idea, but I have to accept it."

"I'm trying Joe." I reply.

"It's all I'm asking for James. Honestly." He says, and I nod my head in his direction. He knows I mean it, we've known each other long enough to know that we don't say shit just to speak.

"I'm going to make some tea and coffee. Anyone else want anything?" Kami asks, and I shake my head.

I'm still finishing off my beer, to be honest I think I could do with another one after this one. Katy heads to the bathroom and Joe starts cleaning up the dessert dishes, when I make a move to help him, he shakes his head, "I've got it but thanks," he says. He seems pretty comfortable in Katy's house and I can't help but wonder how much time he's been spending here and how serious they really are. Joe's never really been serious about any girl. It's about time he found someone to settle down with. I shake my head, just like that I'm wishing for my friend to find happiness, and I don't know how to feel about it.

I've been left here at the table on my own for a while, and I start to wonder where everyone is. Katy comes back to the table just as I'm about to go into the kitchen to check in with Kami, and we start chatting. When Kami and Joe join us back at the table there seems to be more tension between them than there has been all night. I want to ask her what happened in there, but Kami speaks.

"You know, I'm feeling tired. I hope you don't mind if we call it a night Katy?" Kami asks her friend suddenly. I look over at Joe and he's looking down at his hands, Kami's looking anywhere but at me and Katy looks as confused as I feel. Tonight wasn't as easy as it could have been, but it was definitely more comfortable than the last few times we've all been together and 100% more comfortable than that god awful dinner months ago.

"Are you OK sweetheart?" I ask, when what I really want to know is if Joe hurt her in some way in the kitchen, but I don't want to start an argument tonight.

"Yeah, I just feel like heading home now, if that's OK?" Kami replies, quietly.

"Of course, if that's what you want sweetheart, let's get going," I tell her. "Thanks for dinner Katy, it was delicious." Katy and Joe walk us out to the car, and we head home.

We pull up in our driveway, Kami moves to get out of the car, but I hesitate. She turns to face me and asks, "Are you coming inside James?"

"Am I being unreasonable about not being able to forgive Joe? Am I holding a grudge too long and being unfair?" I ask, my voice almost a whisper.

"That's up to you James, not me. You're the only one who knows if you can forgive him. Or not, that decision is yours alone." Kami says, her voice still quiet.

"What did he say or do to you in the kitchen tonight Kami?" I ask, my voice full of concern and a fair amount of anger.

"He said some stuff about our parents, and it upset me a little. What he said also made me think about a few things that have happened in my family's history. There is nothing and I mean *nothing* for you to worry about, but he shared some thoughts with me, and I guess if he's right it might go further to explaining why Joe was so hell bent on making my life hell. I'm not saying I'm going to forget what he's done anytime soon, but I'm beginning to understand his reasons a little more."

"What the hell does that even mean Kami?" I ask frustrated and annoyed. Her cryptic words don't make me feel any better than I did before she spoke.

"Can you trust me James? Not Joe, not anyone else. Me. Just for a few more weeks, maybe less. We should have some answers to his questions by then." I can hear the desperate tone to her voice. She needs me to trust *her*, to show her that I love and believe in *her*.

"OK sweetheart," I close my eyes and nod my head slightly, "I'll give you a few weeks, but after that, regardless of whether you've got answers or not, I need you to tell me what the fuck is going on."

"That I can promise." she says with a smile, reaching over to rest her palm on my cheek, "I love you, James Harvey, with everything in me and I swear no matter if we get the answers or not, I will tell you everything in a few weeks' time, sooner if I can."

I take her hand in mine, lacing our fingers together and bringing her hand to my lips, kissing her knuckles. "I love you too Kami Parker and I'm going to trust you, please don't break me."

<u>KAMI</u>

I don't want to break James, but I don't want to *be* broken either.

I need some time to deal with what Joe told me. He seems to think that there's more to the story of our parents. Information that Harry and my mum haven't told anyone. We suspect they haven't told each other either. They're suspicions so far though, not facts and until we have facts, I'm not up to confessing anything to anyone. Not even James.

I haven't said a word about what Joe told me to Katy either. We met at the café near the bookshop for lunch the week after that dinner at her place. Once our food was put on the table in front of us, the conversation I knew was coming, but was absolutely dreading, started.

"How are you Kami? You weren't tired when you left my place the other night, were you?" Katy asks me. I don't know what to say so I just shrug my shoulders and have a drink of my coffee. "What's going on Kami? What did Joe say to you in the kitchen that night?" she holds up one hand, the other one has a fork in it and I'm just glad she isn't waving that in my face, and says, "Now before you say anything, I want you to think about your answer, and to know that when I asked Joe all he said was, 'we're sorting it out.' Sorting out *what* exactly Kami?"

I take my time just like she asked me to, to think about my answer. I take a bite of my lunch and another sip of my coffee. He's right, to a degree.

"He's right Katy, we *are* working a few things out." I take a deep breath. "He told me a few things. Things about our parents, Helen and Harry, that I didn't know and there's something that he suspects, but until we have answers, real irrefutable answers, to those questions, we don't want to open up another hornets nest. We've all got a lot to deal with as it is, we don't want to add any unnecessary stress to an already stressful situation."

She nods like she understands, but I know she doesn't. Just like James, she wants to trust us, but she wants answers as well. They both deserve the truth but without the stress. I also know that even though she looks relaxed, she's not going to let this go that easily.

"So you're saying that you and a guy you've hated forever and for all appearances he's hated you as well, are sorting though some shit, but neither of you want to share? Not with me, or with James?"

I reach my hand over and rest it on her hand that's lying flat on the table. "I know what it possibly sounds and looks like to you and to James, but the truth is it could change everything, Katy. Everything we've ever know could be turned upside down and we're both just trying to deal with it and not bring everyone else into the shitstorm just yet." I look into her eyes, pleadingly, "We just need some time and your trust."

"OK Kami. I don't like it, but OK." Katy nods her head. "You've got a couple of weeks, because that's what you've both asked for. After that I think James and I deserve to know what the fuck is going on. Deal?" she holds her hand out to me.

"Deal." I say shaking her hand to seal the deal.

We finished lunch talking about all kinds of stuff like we used to. We avoid talking about James or Joe, kind of like an unspoken agreement. When lunch is over, we hug outside the café before going opposite ways to get back to work.

The following weekend, James and I are sitting at home snuggled up on the couch after dinner and I'm trying to work up the courage to see if he would be OK with having Katy and Joe over for dinner the following weekend. I don't want to push the guys to get past their issues, but I can also see how much James is hurting without having his friend around. Not to mention, by then Joe should have the results that we need to have this shit settled one way or another.

"Spit it out sweetheart." James says quietly, my cheek is lying against his chest and I feel his voice rumble through me. "You've got something to say, I can feel you thinking about it. Why don't you say it so that we can go back to relaxing?"

"I'm not sure how to." I say in a whisper that even I can barely hear.

James touches his lips to the top of my head and says, "Kami, sweetheart, you can tell me anything."

Here goes nothing. "I was just wondering if you would be comfortable having Katy and Joe over for dinner next weekend?" I ask in what feels like one long word rather than a dozen or so separate ones.

"Is that all?" he laughs. "Am I that bad that you feel uncomfortable asking me if your friend can come over for dinner?"

"It's not just *my* friend that I want to come over James, she's bringing *your* friend too."

"Sure, you can have anyone you want over sweetheart, it's your house now too." He smiles down at me, but he doesn't move in any other way.

"Are you sure you're OK with Joe coming around?" I ask again just to make sure.

"Sure why not?" he says but his voice is sharp.

"I'm just making sure, we don't have to have them here."

"You seem to be OK with him coming into our home, the one he tried to destroy before we even made it. Even after all the years of torment he put you through before all of that." He doesn't look at me while he speaks, but I can't look away from him and I can see it written all over his face that he's upset because on the surface at least I *look* like I've forgiven Joe for all the trouble he caused over the years.

I sit up and pull away from him, "Is that what you think?" He answers me with a shrug of his shoulders, "It may appear that way to you and maybe even to Katy and Joe, but the truth is, I will never forget what he's done to me or to us for that matter. I will never trust him completely, but my best friend is in love with him and he is best friend's with the man I love." He gives me a look full of surprise, "Yes, he is still your best friend James and one day soon you *will* admit that. For me to move forward, with Joe and this other crap, I need to forgive him James. I have to say he sure does seem to regret his behaviour and not just because he lost you either. That means something to me babe. If he didn't regret his actions and the effect, it's had on those around him, I'd be telling you something different."

"So you do forgive him?" he asks me, surprised.

"I can forgive his actions James, he was a kid, and he didn't know how else to deal with the crappy hand he was dealt. Do I think as an adult he made wrong choices? Ahhh yeah, I do but he's trying to make up for them now James. I can't forget what he's done though and like I said, I'll never completely trust him."

"Let's set up this dinner then and see if we can sort all this crap out once and for all huh?" he says, reaching out and wrapping his arm around my shoulder to bring me back to snuggle into his side again.

"I love you James Harvey." I say.

"I love you too, Kami Parker." He says and kisses my top of my head, as I send Katy a text about coming over for dinner the following weekend. Her reply only takes a minute:

Katy: *we'll be there with bells on hun*

I sigh with relief, then I try to relax and enjoy the rest of the evening with James.

JAMES

A couple of weeks after the dinner at Katy's, Kami asks if I would be comfortable having Katy and Joe over for dinner. If I'm being honest, I'm still a little uncomfortable at the thought of being around him, but I *am* grateful for Kami's determination to see my fucked up friendship with Joe back on track. For making it her business and extending the olive brand to him on my behalf. I know it can't be easy for her to have him around either. I doubt I would have had the courage to do it on my own. My pride alone hasn't allowed to make first contact with him so far and I know he's waiting for me to make the next move.

Joe and I are OK after that dinner at Katy's, but we're nowhere near where we used to be. I didn't take my business away from his accountancy firm, but I don't deal directly with him anymore either. One of his colleagues took over my account and the same guy has helped Kami with renting her house out.

It's been two weeks since she asked me to trust her, and she still hasn't said anything. So either she doesn't realise her deadline is up or our dinner tonight with Katy and Joe isn't a coincidence. I'm enjoying the view as she manoeuvres about the house and the kitchen, getting ready for Katy and Joe to join us tonight.

"Hey babe, everything's ready for dinner tonight until Katy and Joe get here. Do you have time for a chat?" Kami asks me quietly, looking up at me through her eyelashes.

"Of course sweetheart, I always have time for my favourite girl." I reply, my heart thumping in my chest as we move to the living room and sit on the couch. "Did you get the information you were waiting for? You and Joe." I ask, and I know I sound more suspicious and distrustful, but I don't mean to. It's just that the situation with all its secrecy makes me feel jealous that they have something that the two of them share. I know it makes me a dick, she's my woman, my love and if she has secrets with anyone, it should be with me. Fuck! Now I know I'm a fucking idiot. I'm waiting for her to answer me, and she's looking at me like she doesn't know how to say what she needs to.

"Not yet, but I wanted to kind of forewarn you I guess. I don't want you blindsided by whatever may or may not be revealed at dinner tonight." Now she's making me nervous. So, like I suspected, dinner tonight wasn't a coincidence.

"You're making me nervous sweetheart." I say as she takes a deep breath and gets ready to speak. I reach over and take both of her hands in mine, "You can tell me anything sweetheart, anything at all." Doesn't mean I have to like it, but she can tell me anything.

"Joe and I, we got a DNA test done." She spills out it out in what feels like one word and takes me a few seconds to decipher. Why would they need DNA testing?

"What the fuck? Do you mean you think you guys are—?"

I don't get to finish my sentence because there's a knock at the door, as Kami says, "It's a real possibility James."

"Well fuck, that could explain things I guess." I mutter, more to myself than to anyone in particular.

Kami walks to the door and greets Katy and Joe, letting them into the house while I sit at the kitchen bench in shock.

"By the look on your face I'm guessing Kami told you about our suspicions?" Joe asks as he wanders in passed me. I look up at him and nod.

Looking past him I ask, "Do you know too Katy?"

"I found out just before we left to come here." Katy replies and that's when I notice that she's looking a little shell shocked herself. "But I don't know the results, he hasn't even opened the envelope himself yet."

"Why didn't you tell us sooner? Why wait until now to tell us?" I ask them both.

"We didn't tell either of you or anyone else for that matter, any earlier because we didn't want anyone freaking out." Kami says. "There was no point in making everyone anxious about the results. This way, the four of us can read the results together and deal with whatever the outcome is."

"I still wish you had told me Kami, you didn't need to go through it alone." I tell her, and I can't help the anger that is in my voice.

"She wasn't alone James," says Joe and I growl at him, but he just keeps talking, "but I understand what you mean, and I would be annoyed with Katy if the situations were reversed. We decided there wasn't any point getting everyone worked up over it if it was nothing."

"I wouldn't call it nothing, Joe."

"Look he's right, you're right we're all right OK?" Katy says, more on edge than I've ever heard her. She's normally the level headed one out of the four of us, always has been. Even the quiet and reserved Kami gets more worked up than I've ever seen Katy behave. "Can we just get the big reveal done and deal with it, please?"

That's when I finally notice the huge envelope Joe is holding. I guess all the answers are in that one white envelope.

"You open it Joe, I don't think I can." Kami says, wringing her hands nervously.

I feel terrible for being so annoyed when this news could literally change her life. It could change her whole existence and what she believes her life is, was. I reach out for her and pull her tight against me. Kami pulls Katy in close to her side and Katy rests one hand on Joe's bicep in support.

Joe rips open the envelope and then looks at the three of us, all staring at him waiting for him to read the truth. I'm not sure whether any of us are breathing or not, but as Joe reads the results and then looks at Kami. I know. I can read him like a fucking book.

She's his fucking sister!

KAMI

I don't think I could love James any more than I do right now. He trusted me with a secret, even after everything that's happened in the past few months. A secret that involves the man who created most those of troubles to begin with.

I realise that when the truth comes out, if the answer is what we both think it will be, there's going to be plenty of drama and decisions to be made. Decisions I'm going to want James' input on, because I'm going to need him more than ever to get my head around it all.

I don't get to finish telling James about Joe's crazy theory because the man in question and Katy arrive for dinner. Along with the largest, whitest envelope I've ever seen.

"You open it Joe, I don't think I can." I say, wringing my hands nervously. James pulls me into his side, I pull Katy into my side and Joe is standing close to Katy while he tears the envelope open. He hesitates for a few seconds, glancing up at us, before he pulls out the report and starts reading it.

I hear James' sudden intake of breathe and look up at his face to find his face full of shock. Joe clears his throat and I drag my eyes over to meet his. "Well, what does it say?" I ask.

"The test is," he swallows deeply and quickly glances at his feet. "The test is positive."

"Positive? What does that mean?" I hear myself say, in a squeaky voice that doesn't even sound like me.

"The probability of share paternity is 98.5%. Meaning, we share a father, Kami. You're not a Parker, you're a French."

That's the last thing I remember, before James picks me up and carries me over to the couch and sits me on his lap.

FUCK ME, WE'RE SIBLINGS! THE COCKSUCKING ARSEHOLE THAT IS JOE FRENCH IS MY FUCKING BROTHER!!

Other books by Chelle Pimblott:
<u>SNEAKY LOVE SERIES</u>
Sneaky – Book 1
Sneaking Around – Book 2
No More Sneaking Around – Book 3
<u>BUILT FOR LOVE</u>
Built to Last – Book .1.
Built for Trouble – Book .2.

OUT NOW .....
Barefoot and ... Dumped!

FIND CHELLE HERE
https://www.goodreads.com/author/show/17494691.Chelle_Pimblott[1]
http://facebook.com/chelle.pimblott

---

1. https://www.goodreads.com/author/show/17494691.Chelle_Pimblott?fbclid=IwAR0VSdPZ94bp-
1xF4PowBygaMMXmKDBFfuRNjLygTlgDGaKVwfC3-CIFTxc

Also by Chelle Pimblott

Built for Love
Built to Last
Built for Trouble

Drake Wines
Vineyard
Sandy Cove - A Drake Wines Novella
Winery
Lori's Memories - A Drake Wines Novella
Brewery
Sara's Forever

Sneaky Love
Sneaky
Sneaking Around
No More Sneaking Around

Standalone
Barefoot & Dumped!

www.ingramcontent.com/pod-product-compliance
Lightning Source LLC
Chambersburg PA
CBHW061921130726
47908CB00016B/578